SUGAR

SUGAR

An Ethnographic Novel

EDWARD NARAIN and **TARRYN PHILLIPS**

TC▷ TEACHING CULTURE

UNIVERSITY OF TORONTO PRESS
Toronto Buffalo London

Library and Archives Canada Cataloguing in Publication

Title: Sugar : an ethnographic novel / Edward Narain and Tarryn Phillips.
Names: Narain, Edward, author. | Phillips, Tarryn, author.
Series: Teaching culture.
Description: Series statement: Teaching culture: ethnographies
for the classroom | Includes bibliographical references.
Identifiers: Canadiana (print) 20230521371 | Canadiana (ebook) 20230521428 |
ISBN 9781487554972 (cloth) | ISBN 9781487554989 (paper) |
ISBN 9781487554996 (EPUB) | ISBN 9781487555009 (PDF)
Classification: LCC PR9619.4.N37 S84 2024 | DDC 823/.92 – dc23

ISBN 978-1-4875-5497-2 (cloth)   ISBN 978-1-4875-5499-6 (EPUB)
ISBN 978-1-4875-5498-9 (paper)   ISBN 978-1-4875-5500-9 (PDF)

Printed and bound by CPI Group (UK) Ltd, Croydon, CR0 4YY

Cover design: Heng Wee Tan
Cover images: iStock.com/mirabellart; iStock.com/Наталия Юдина;
iStock.com/Vect0r0vich

We wish to acknowledge the land on which the University of Toronto Press operates. This land is the traditional territory of the Wendat, the Anishnaabeg, the Haudenosaunee, the Métis, and the Mississaugas of the Credit First Nation.

University of Toronto Press acknowledges the financial support of the Government of Canada and the Ontario Arts Council, an agency of the Government of Ontario, for its publishing activities.

ONTARIO ARTS COUNCIL
CONSEIL DES ARTS DE L'ONTARIO
an Ontario government agency
un organisme du gouvernement de l'Ontario

Funded by the   Financé par le
Government   gouvernement   Canadä
of Canada   du Canada

Contents

Authors' Note

This story is a work of fiction, although it is based on ethnographic research and our lived experience as Fijian and Australian authors. A supplementary chapter is provided at the end of the book outlining the context, research, and social critique that lie behind the novel, along with a glossary of terms in Fijian and Fijian Hindi. Many readers will prefer to immerse themselves in the mystery before reading the supplementary chapter (which does contain plot spoilers). Others, however, may wish to read the supplementary chapter first or concurrently as a kind of running commentary. Either way, we hope the story finds its way into readers' hearts and minds and prompts them to reflect upon their place in the world in new ways.

Prologue

WHEN SHE is finally left alone on the fifth day of mourning, Rishika can breathe again. For a moment she stands completely still in the kitchen, listening to the distant sounds of a car door slamming and the last taxi retreating down her driveway. The sweet incense still lingers from this morning's prayer, clinging to her hair, her sari, the curtains. Even the dog smells faintly smoky. Only an hour ago the *pundit* was carrying the pot of glowing sticks with him as he shuffled into each room of the house, ribbons of smoke curling in his wake. His chanting offered Rishika little solace, partly because she found no comfort in his religious platitudes and partly because the priest seemed in a rush to get to his next engagement (a wedding in Nasinu). He hurried out to his car as soon as the last prayer was finished, arms stacked with ice cream containers full of Nadi Aunty's curry.

The aunties all cleared the plates before they left, scraping the puddles of dal and half-eaten roti into the rubbish bin. They washed the dishes in silence, then ushered their unusually quiet husbands into waiting cars and taxis. Rishika stood in the

doorway and thanked them for coming, a tired airhostess over-
seeing her passengers' exit. Nadi Aunty made her promise to
call if she needed anything. Sigatoka Aunty wept, again, on her
shoulder. Nausori Aunty smothered her to her ample bosom before releasing her a little too suddenly.

And now Rishika is sitting at the kitchen table, her pearl-white
sari crumpled beneath her. Solomon, her elderly black Doberman, lies on the floor beside her, his shoulders rising and falling,
sighing, as though he too is relieved the house is quiet again.
Vijay never liked him inside the house, but here he is, flopped
on the tiles.

She welcomes the heavy silence at first, broken only by the
clock in the loungeroom. It logs the passing of each second
with ruthless efficiency, seemingly unmoved by what it has witnessed. Minutes pass like this, perhaps hours. It is only when a
gecko behind the fridge begins its shrill clucking that her reverie
is disrupted.

"Why *do* cyclones have names, Solomon?" she says aloud. Ears
pricked at his name, the dog looks up, head cocked to one side.

The question seems pressing. Profound. Rishika feels pleased
with the sense of purpose it gives her. The cyclone that hit Fiji last
Friday was called Tropical Cyclone Dorothy, but everyone called
her Dorothy for short. Dorothy initially missed the islands but
then doubled back around, as though a vengeful afterthought,
raging and swirling, then lulling, then raging again. Rishika's
uncles say she was as bad as Winston, the storm that swept
destruction across Fiji's shores in 2016, propelling the country
onto the international stage. But there was something different
about Winston. Fijians felt a palpable sense of patriotism after
him; a collective mourning, a national pride in how resilient and
neighborly they all were in the face of a common enemy. That
was, of course, before the accusations started about where all

the aid money went. But in the immediate aftermath, Fiji was united and sentimental. When playing for their nation in the weeks that followed, Fijian rugby players looked at the cameras whenever they scored a try and crafted a W with their fingers, meaning "Stronger than Winston." Even the most stoic Fijians were brought to tears by that. That rugby team went on to win the Olympic gold medal that year.

The camaraderie hasn't been as strong after Dorothy. The branding hasn't been as effective. Part of the problem is that the name Dorothy evokes a frail little grandmother. "Stronger than Dorothy" doesn't sound particularly courageous.

Everyone is still talking about the storm, of course; they will for months. Her neighbor mentioned it this morning when she came over to talk to Rishika through the fence. This neighbor has barely talked to her over the years, but has suddenly become curious after seeing all the other neighbors visit with food and gifts, and presumably having seen the news, the police cars, and the endless flow of family members dressed in white. She too wanted the details of that night, little gems of gossip to unveil to her friends. And yet she danced around the topic, not wanting to seem improper, before she found her segue.

"Cyclones always used to hit the outer islands, *haana*? We all can't believe it!" The woman's head bobbed more animatedly than usual and Rishika felt like readjusting it to sit firmly on her shoulders. "You know what they say," her neighbor continued in her stilted English now, "it is the global warmings!" She peered up at Rishika, and then – getting no response – tried a different tack, circling ever closer to her point. "So … lots of visitors for you …?"

A clumsy attempt. Rishika couldn't bear it. "Yes," she replied, taking a deep breath, and then added, "it seems my husband has been murdered." She didn't get the tone right. She knew the phrasing sounded odd as soon as the words left her lips. She blinked twice, watching her neighbor's face in front of her quickly hide the initial horror. Uncharacteristically lost for words, the woman muttered something about deep sympathies and then scurried back into her house.

Rishika accidentally chuckles aloud now at the woman's discomfort. The sound reverberates throughout the kitchen, hollow and mirthless. At her feet, Solomon rests his nose on his two front paws and looks up at her in concern.

PART I

Wednesday

Two weeks earlier

THERE IS nothing like the smell of Suva at dusk. It's the scent of recent rain on bitumen with a hint of honey-vanilla from the frangipani trees. Hannah Wilson breathes it in and smiles with a familiar sense of anticipation. The sun has melted over the horizon now, leaving only the dusty glow of the streetlights on the deserted road ahead. Locals always tell her not to walk alone in the dark here, especially so close to the squatter settlement. "Those people are desperate," someone warned a few weeks back, with more contempt than compassion. But it couldn't be helped tonight. Her housemate, Jess, canceled at the last minute to FaceTime her boyfriend in Sydney. "No worries!" Hannah said lightly. "It's only a short walk!" Even still, she is pleased when she catches a glimpse of the busy main road ahead and slightly speeds up her pace.

Before she gets there, the slow crunch of gravel behind her makes her spin around. It's a taxi, its sign unlit, purring to a crawl alongside her. The driver leans over the gearshift and raises his eyebrows. She has learned now that a subtle lift of the brow can mean many things here. "Thank you," she says, stepping into the back seat. "O'Hannigan's, please."

She feels for a seatbelt but there isn't one. The driver speeds her through the back roads, one bony hand draped across the steering wheel while the other switches between radio channels. He eventually rests on an eighties love song that he obviously thinks she will like. A golden ornament of Ganesh, the Hindu elephant God, is stuck on the dashboard with Blu-Tack. Hannah has a vague recollection that it's supposed to bring luck or something. She hopes so, as she clutches the armrest.

The driver glances over his shoulder. "Where you from? Australia? New Zealand?" They always start with that.

"Australia," she smiles. "Perth." She doesn't feel like explaining the whereabouts of the small country town of Donnybrook in Western Australia.

"Ah, Perth. My cousin lives there. Lots of money in the mines, eh? If you do the fly-out-fly-in?"

Hannah smiles. "Yeah. That's Perth for you."

He seems pleased with this, settling in for a conversation. "Enjoying your holiday?"

"Actually, I'm here for work."

He glances at her through the rearview mirror with renewed interest. "Work, eh?"

She does not tell him, of course, that she only came here because of a series of accidents.

Fiji was not her first choice. It wasn't even her second. It was over a year ago and she was bored at work, scrolling through online advertisements for ethical jobs and not-for-profit work, wanting to do something meaningful with her life. To help people. Initially, she was searching for graduate positions in remote Aboriginal communities, toying with the idea of living up north for a stint. She felt it was time to do something tough but rewarding and find herself in the process. Inconveniently, however, they all specified the need for "experience." That was why, when the little advertisement popped up on her screen for a government program to send young graduate volunteers to developing countries, she filled in the online application. She ticked Mongolia as her preferred placement. She had read a few blogs written by past volunteers and imagined herself assisting rural communities on donkey-back and partying in Ulan Bator on weekends.

A few months later, she received the acceptance letter for the program and whooped around the loungeroom in front of her bemused flatmates. She read the whole letter out to them, stumbling over the sentence that said she had been assigned to Fiji. She was disappointed at first. So many middle-class Australian families went there for holidays; it felt more run-of-the-mill, like being assigned to Bali. But her reservations quickly faded after she purchased a Lonely Planet guide and skim-read the country's rich history. Cannibalism. British colonial rule. Military coups. Quite edgy, really.

The driver breaks suddenly, lurching Hannah forward and backward. The taxi stops in front of a zebra-lined pedestrian crossing, where two afroed Indigenous – iTaukei – men are midway across the road. They stare at the taxi, faces pale in the headlights, then turn away and keep crossing, perhaps deliberately slowly now. The driver glances at Hannah through the rearview mirror and shakes his head.

"Cheeky, eh? They should wait."

"Haha."

He adds, "They're not like us."

"Right," she says cautiously, turning to look out the window and affecting a look of concentration to deter him from a longer monologue.

As the streets of Suva whiz past, she wonders which of the other Australians will be at the bar tonight. Her volunteer friends hail from all around Australia – Melbourne, Sydney, Brisbane, Hobart. They met at the briefing sessions in Canberra, and then reconnected when they arrived in Suva. They got to know each other while finding houses to share, buying third-hand cars from outgoing volunteers, and discovering where to get a decent coffee that wasn't made with long-life milk.

In between the weekly house parties, they began their assignments; placements at non-government organizations, civil society groups, and public departments. Their brief here, as skilled graduates, is to "transfer skills, build capacity, and strengthen institutions." Interesting, important work. Some of them have been granted projects that would be considered well beyond their expertise in Australia. Michelle, for example, recently attended an international convention *on behalf of* Fiji. Pip is helping to design the country's first secondary school curriculum on some thing or another. The entire country's curriculum! They feel like big fish in a small pond. All of them profess to feeling uncomfortable about such responsibility – and unprepared – like apologetic imposters. But it is going to look *great* on their CVs.

The taxi hurtles down the hill toward the small city center with its handful of mid-rise buildings and a scattering of lights twinkling on the harbor. A lit-up billboard looms beside the road advertising the upcoming Fiji versus New Zealand rugby game. Handsome brown rugby players with their arms crossed look down at Hannah. "Island Cola: Taste the win," it says.

On the radio, a newsreader is giving an update on the tropical weather system that has been gathering momentum as it travels southeast from Vanuatu. It has now been upgraded to a category one cyclone, and Fijian meteorological authorities have assigned it the name Tropical Cyclone Dorothy, which is, Hannah thinks, a ridiculous name for a cyclone.

"Cyclone coming," the driver says.

"Yes, that's a bit scary," she says. The very concept of a cyclone seems dissonant and unlikely right now, given the stillness of the trees outside.

He shrugs. "It's Fiji. We're used to it, eh?"

Finally, he pulls the taxi in beside O'Hannigan's. She picks out the correct change from her wallet, marveling, as always, at how cheap the fare is. She has taken a pay cut to come here, but living in Suva is easy.

The driver inspects the coins. "*Set*," he says, followed by the oddly formal, "have a blessed evening."

Stepping out of the air-conditioned car onto the sidewalk, she is hit by a wall of oppressive heat. In front of her, the security guards flash a smile of recognition. One of them opens the heavy door for her, unleashing a roar of nostalgic nineties R&B.

Hannah gazes across the bar, easily finding her pale-faced friends at the back of the crowd. They're sitting on tall stools around a table cluttered with drinks, heads thrown back in laughter. They haven't seen her yet. Hannah stops by the bar, asking the young man behind it for a glass of white wine. He smiles and turns back to the shelf behind him. She glances back over at her friends' table while she waits. Beside the Aussie volunteers, Hannah can see some of the other young expats are here too. Rather than by surname, she knows the others by their nationalities or the workplaces they're posted at: there is Swiss Dave and World Bank Dave, German Jana and that Dutch medical intern guy, whose name they've all forgotten an embarrassing number of times, now affectionately referred to as "mate."

Hannah approaches the table carrying her warm white wine, beads of sweat already forming on the glass. Pip is pointing angrily at World Bank Dave, her frizzy mop of red hair flopping over her eyes, obviously in yet another argument. Pip is a gender studies major who holds Dave guilty by association for all the wrongs in the world. She is generally anti-privatization, anti-capitalism, anti-free trade. This is, of course, a losing battle globally, and it is all Dave's fault for being an economist at the World Bank. Most of the time Dave playfully – half-heartedly – defends free market economics, toeing his company line, for the first half hour at least. Then eventually, when Pip gets really riled, he throws his hands up in self-defense and says, "Give me a break! I just crunch the numbers!" Everyone knows Dave actually has a big crush on Pip, but no one can quite work out if Pip feels the same. It is possible that she genuinely hates him.

Hannah's arrival distracts Pip from her slurred monologue. "Han!" She rushes around the table to give her a hug, and Dave looks noticeably grateful for the interruption. Dutch-doctor-guy waves to Hannah across the table. "Oh, hey!" She smiles. "Good to see you, mate."

By the time Hannah is on her second glass of wine the friends are skipping through travel stories as badges of honor, little stepping stones of conversation. "Guess what happened to me today?" Michelle begins. She ran into a Swedish guy – "like, literally bumped into him" in the downtown supermarket – and he looked familiar to her. "Turns out we met at a restaurant years ago, a few hours outside Marrakech. Must have been 2014, 2015?"

Hannah raises her eyebrows in surprise. She is only half listening, rifling through her own repertoire for a travel anecdote that she will share next.

"I mean," Michelle continues, "this place was seriously remote. He was the only white guy I'd seen for days. We had couscous together, he flew out of the country the next day, and I never saw him again. And then he turns up in Suva. Of all places. It blew my mind."

"That's so random," remarks German Jana. She is looking at her beer bottle, picking at the label.

"What's he doing in Suva?" Pip asks.

"Just traveling, I think. He might join us tonight actually." Michelle checks her phone.

"Where did you say you met him?" Hannah asks.

"Near Marrakech."

Hannah nods while mentally scanning her incomplete map of the world.

Michelle recognizes her blank expression immediately. "Morrocco. North Africa." Hannah suppresses a flash of irritation.

Michelle has a Cambodian mother and Australian father, which resulted in olive skin and noble eyes. Her black hair is cut casually at shoulder length, with a straight fringe that frames her soft features. When Hannah first met her, her accent was hard to place – it seemed mostly posh English with something elusive on every fifth word or so. She apparently attended international schools in each of her father's diplomatic postings: Phnom Penh, Bangkok, Geneva. When she first arrived in Suva, Aaron teasingly called her a Diplobrat. She laughed good-naturedly at the time, but she has been telling stories of independence and humility ever since.

"So let me get this straight," Dave says. "You had 'couscous' with this guy." He performs suggestive quotation marks.

"We *did*!" Michelle lightly slaps Dave's shoulder.

"I bet you did."

She winks. "Best couscous I've ever had."

Michelle went volunteering in North Africa when she was nineteen, she explains, and helped to build a local primary school. "I have never cried as much or laughed as much as I did in those three weeks."

"Sounds pretty intense," Pip says.

Michelle affects a look of deep sincerity. "I will never forget the faces of those children."

German Jana transitions seamlessly into "that time" when she and her ex-boyfriend went road tripping through South America. Life was so simple, she says, her long neck emphasized by her short blond hair. They had no money – "seriously, *no* money" – and survived on rice and pinto beans for four months. "You could see my ribs by the end of that trip," Jana says. "Happiest I've ever been."

Hannah laughs.

"Seriously," Jana says, so Hannah stops laughing.

Hannah has no anecdotes that can compete. She always secretly covets the idea that she is the well-traveled, risk-taking one when compared to her family and circle of friends back home. But amongst the other volunteers in Suva, her travel experiences pale as unremarkable, almost *suburban*. She has been on a few tame overseas trips lasting no more than three weeks each, in which the worst that has happened was a misplaced passport that she nearly reported stolen in Thailand until it was found in a different pocket of her backpack. She is both impressed by and envious of her friends' daring exploits, and wonders if she will ever earn her own wings of proper adventure.

Aaron soon arrives, wearing his baseball cap as always, accompanied by a new guy that Hannah has never seen before. Aaron introduces him as John. The table smiles at John, sizing him up as a new addition to the relatively small pool of eligible male expats – tall and slim, his dark, wavy hair tied above his head in a bun, like a European soccer player. Aaron, meanwhile, is ranting about why the two of them are late. Apparently the cash machine only spat out hundred dollar notes. The taxi driver didn't have change for such big bills, so they went from corner store to corner store, trying to find a shopkeeper who would break the large

note. It is a familiar story; this has happened to Hannah countless times in Suva.

"Why do they even print hundred dollar notes if no one deals
in them here?" Aaron grumbles.

"Argh!" says Pip, "it's the bane of my life!"

There is a smattering of "I know!"s.

Ethan smirks. "Seriously? Listen to you all. 'Hundred dollar
bills.'" Ethan scans their bemused faces. "Talk about first-world
problems."

"Oh my God," Pip hiccups. "When did I become so bourgeois?"

Ethan delights in playing devil's advocate. He is from Merimbula on the east coast of New South Wales and has the ac-
companying unruly blond hair of a surfer, often on the verge of
dreadlocks. People are usually surprised to learn he is a graduate
lawyer volunteering at legal aid here.

The bar has filled up now and the bass is thumping heavily.
The new guy sits next to Hannah while Aaron goes to buy him
a beer.

"John, was it?" She smiles charmingly.

"No, it's Sean," he says, but she can't quite hear him above the
music.

She leans in. "Oh, sorry! Sean, did you say?"

He seems irritated now. "*Non, Jean*. With a soft 'j.'"

"Oh, Jean?"

"That is correct." He says it like "zat is correcter," in a strong
French accent.

"Right. Nice to meet you, Jean."

He nods, gazing past her toward the bar where Aaron is buying his drink.

Around them, colored polka dots of light swirl across the room,
landing on people and then quickly escaping. Three young Indo-
Fijian women have ventured onto the dance floor, hips joined

and giggling, sidling away from the drunken man dancing at them in a leering, pelvic way.

The expats love the tackiness of O'Hannigan's – they forgive it for its cheap wine and cheesy pop music – partly to be ironic, partly because the locals come here, and partly to avoid the pompous tourists at the Old Victoria Hotel.

She turns back to Jean. "And you're a friend of Aaron's?"

"Yes. I am."

Hannah nods and takes a sip of her wine. He seems preoccupied, or perhaps there is a language barrier. She takes a discreet, envious look at Pip's conversation with World Bank Dave and Michelle. They are huddled in close, amiably shouting at each other. She takes another sip, relieved to see Aaron returning to the table. But rather than joining the conversation, he passes a beer to Jean and swiftly leaves to join Ethan for a game of pool.

After another gulp of wine, feeling a shudder of recklessness, she tries again. "So … *just* Jean?" she says. "Not Jean-*Pierre*, Jean-*Luc*, Jean-*Paul*?" She accidentally hams up her French accent. He looks at her and she briefly worries she has been inappropriate, until a very faint glimmer of amusement flashes across his eyes. Perhaps this situation is salvageable.

"*Non.* Just Jean."

"And how long have you been in Suva, Just Jean?"

"This is my third year."

"Oh." Hannah is actually impressed. He has trumped her. She is surprised they haven't met before.

"So, what do you do here?"

"I am a French teacher. At *Alliance Francaise.*"

Of course. She knows about the *Alliance Francaise* in Suva. They offer French lessons, which are mostly frequented by older expat women who have accompanied their diplomatic husbands to Suva on spousal visas. Not permitted to work, many of these women put their time into French and tennis lessons and aggressively organize charity events. They drink champagne most lunchtimes and give well-intentioned but borderline-racist compliments to the waitstaff.

"Oh right," Hannah says. She adds, *"Tres bien!"* for want of anything better to say, and then immediately regrets it.

Jean's eyebrows manage to display both boredom and mild surprise. *"Tu parles Francais?"*

"Nope, I don't. I mean, I learned it in high school. I went on a school trip to Paris in year nine. But I've forgotten everything."

"I do not believe you," he says as he takes a sip of his beer.

"I did! We climbed the Eiffel Tower and everything."

"Non. I do not believe that you have forgotten."

"Oh. Well, I have, pretty much."

"Non. Languages do not disappear. The French you learned is – how do you say it? *Latente.* Sleeping in your brain."

She scoffs, tipsily. "I think you overestimate my brain."

He looks at her blankly.

Tough crowd. She takes a gulp of her wine, and then another.

Over at the pool table, Ethan is staring down his cue in careful concentration. He and Aaron are playing against a pair of familiar iTaukei guys who are often here on Wednesday nights. (Hannah can't remember their names.) It is a running joke that Ethan loves playing pool, but he is terrible at it.

Hannah turns back to Jean. "Actually, I do remember how to say *je m'appelle Hannah."*

"Voilà. Enchanté, Hannah." He pronounces her name with no "H" – Anna. She feels like she is one of his students, seeking his approval.

"Oh! And," she's on a roll, "I can say, *je suis un poisson."*

"Un poisson? You can say, 'I am a fish'?"

"Yep."

"There is absolutely no context in which that will be useful."

"Yeah, well. That memory should probably have stayed – how did you say it? – 'sleeping in my brain'?"

He smiles, finally. The dimple on his left cheek is deeper than the one on his right. Hannah has fought hard for that smile, and she is slightly disarmed by its asymmetry.

A burst of laughter erupts from the pool table. Ethan, it seems, has just sunk the white ball. "Faaaark," he laughs as he holds out the cue to his opponent. "You've got two shots, mate."

ON THE other side of Suva, Isikeli Tiko's ankle is itchy. He tries to ignore it, focusing instead on the houses on Chamberlain Street below. He can feel Seru getting restless beside him in the darkness. Earlier in the evening, they'd heard faint gospel singing, which seemed to be floating over from the Pentecostal Church where he used to go to Sunday school. Isikeli tried to sing along in his head, but he always seemed to stumble over the lyrics of the second verse. The night has fallen quiet now, except for the faint hum of traffic and their own smacking as they chew gum. Aunty and Uncle will be walking home from the sermon, looking splendid in their matching floral *kalavata*.

Periodically, an ambulance wails past and all the neighborhood dogs howl in protest. Three of these dogs belong to the small block of apartments on the street below. They are a motley crew of Fijian mongrels; one looks more beagle, another more sausage dog, another mostly German shepherd. Their territory is impenetrable, girdled by a two meter high fence with sharp medieval prongs at the top.

But Isikeli and Seru cannot see any dogs at the compound on the opposite side of the road down there. What they have seen are two silhouettes – slight figures, most likely *Kai Idia* – sitting together on the second floor balcony. About an hour ago, the silhouettes went back inside the house; first the man, then the woman about ten minutes later. The woman locked the security grill with a padlock and flicked off the main light. All of the curtains have been drawn except one; it seems to have been forgotten.

Isikeli's knees start to ache, but he knows he must wait.

Minutes pass. Seru suddenly flicks his ear, startling him, and he topples backwards.

"*Magaitinamu!*" Isikeli hisses, hoisting himself back up to a squat.

Seru stifles a giggle and Isikeli rubs his ear, a reluctant smile tugging at the corners of his mouth.

It is after midnight before Isikeli and Seru hear another ambulance approaching and can finally make their move. This time the dogs are not barking at the ambulance but rather at the barefooted teenagers running down the alleyway. No one will hear the difference. Tall, broad-shouldered Isikeli is almost a foot taller than lithe, athletic Seru, yet it is Isikeli who scales the fence with impressive agility, gathering together the three strands of barbed wire at the top, tip-toeing between the barbs, and quietly thudding onto the lawn below. On the street side, Seru passes over to him a broom handle with a little wire hook at the end and a long piece of PVC pipe before slinking back into the shadows to wait on guard. Isikeli collects the poles under his arm and makes his way hastily toward the concrete steps.

He is suddenly – strangely – reminded of Bu holding a similar length pole underneath a mango tree. *Where was this?* The memory begins to take shape. Much younger then, she was on her tiptoes and reaching the rod into the tallest branches, showing him how to bump the ripe mangoes on their bottoms. Each fruit she struck did a little jump – as if startled – and then fell, self-plucking from its stem and nosediving until it was caught – or sometimes dropped – by the hands of little Isikeli. Afterwards, they chewed off the tops of the mangoes and drank their flesh, sitting side by side.

No time to think about that now. His feet pad up the steps, careful not to catch the poles on anything, artfully silent. When he reaches the top storey, he sidles up to the window – slightly ajar, as he suspected. He's grateful to find the room dimly lit by a hallway light. He scans what he can see inside, focusing on a bookshelf above the television, a smartphone sitting on a glass-topped coffee table, and a leather sofa with a backpack lying on it. This is almost too easy. *Don't get cocky. Don't lose concentration.* He will hook out the backpack, but the phone will have to wait. He bends down and works quickly in the darkness to connect the poles, making a long rod.

Suddenly, the harsh overhead light flashes on and the *Kai Idia* man appears in the hallway inside. Butterflies ricochet off Isikeli's ribcage. He ducks away from the window. The temptation is to drop the pole and sprint down the steps at this point. But he resists the urge and instead places the tool on the ground quietly. He creeps down the stairs, listening in case he is being pursued. No noise so far. He continues quickly; only twenty more meters until escape.

Just as he turns at the bottom of the steps, he is suddenly confronted by a large drooling Doberman, growling quietly, just louder than a purr. His thoughts scream, *how did we not see this dog?!* He considers pelting toward the fence, but a past experience – and the half moon–shaped scar on his thigh – tells him this will make the dog lunge angrily.

He knows he must crouch down to the dog's eye level in submission and, if possible, offer it something. *But what?*

Hands trembling, Isikeli crouches down. He slowly removes the chewing gum from his mouth and lays it at the dog's front paws. The dog lowers its head – still growling – and sniffs the gum. Nothing happens. Isikeli waits breathlessly. The dog suddenly slurps up the gum and begins to chew, at first experimentally, then with conviction, eventually sitting down on its hind legs contentedly and smelling faintly minty. Isikeli gives the dog a wide berth and backs away toward the fence.

He scales the fence again and lands on the sidewalk. A sharp cry from the balcony rings out: *"Butako!"* in a *Kai Idia* accent. The boys sprint back through the alleyway, up the hill and down the other side to the creek. Isikeli's heart is thumping against his chest rhythmically now, like the drumming of a *lali*.

Finally safe, they slow to a stop under a coconut palm, the edges of each leaf lined by pale moonlight. A nearby rustling startles them, but it is only a mongoose rippling away, its tail hovering in its wake. They give in to giggles of adrenaline.

Later, just before the break of dawn, Isikeli and Seru part ways with a tired sliding handshake, their fingertips locking before snapping away. He carries his share of the rewards for the evening: one children's scooter retrieved from a double-storey house on the street where all the *Kai Valagi* expats live, and $5.60 in coins, reached for through a kitchen window left ajar. With aching feet, he walks back along the creek toward home.

Thursday

THIS IS not the first time that Rishika and Vijay have experienced a break-in. Once a fold-up chair was stolen from the balcony; another time a bunch of almost-ripe bananas was torn from the tree at the back of their compound. Rishika has always assumed it's just some young kids. They probably needed a chair! They were probably hungry! But Vijay is always enraged about it. He seems mostly annoyed that he has been outwitted. All that money he's spent on gates and barbed wire and security grills, all that time and mental energy he's spent on his militaristic lock-up routine each night, and they have still gotten in. "And Solomon!" he always mutters. "Where the hell was the stupid dog?"

Rishika goes to the balcony now and watches her husband reverse the little hatchback up the driveway. She gives him a small wave, but he doesn't meet her eyes, concentrating instead on the rearview mirror. The three dogs across the road race to the fence, yelping and snarling as the car disappears around the corner. At her feet, Solomon responds defensively with two half-hearted barks before flopping down, the old dog wheezing from the effort.

It isn't just the break-in; Vijay is in a mood. He has been for months. It hangs on him heavily like a sodden woolen coat, dragging his shoulders down and slowing his gait. Vijay's mother, Samriti, was concerned about him when she visited last. She stayed for a whole month, and brought with her a never-ending trail of visiting aunties. Samriti and her sisters cross-examined Rishika while they manually washed the dishes, not trusting the dishwasher. Does Rishika make roti everyday? Has Rishika stopped ironing his handkerchiefs? Does she nag him too much?

It was only Nadi Aunty who thought to ask Rishika how she was doing. They were standing in an aisle of Modi's Bazaar, inspecting a display of large saucepans.

"You okay, *beti*?" Aunty asked suddenly, watching her closely.

It caught Rishika off guard. "*Haan*," she replied too quickly, and then compensated with, "definitely!"

Nadi Aunty gave her a narrowed look but soon let the subject go, piling Rishika's arms with crockery and leading the way toward the counter, the folds of her skin wobbling out from under her sari top. Rishika liked Nadi Aunty. She wishes now that she had seized that moment, confided in her.

She has tried hard to understand. Every day, Vijay drives his little car to the depot, gets into a sleek four-wheel drive with its blue government plates and tinted, bullet-proof windows, and waits and drives and waits and drives. For eight years, he has been a driver for the Federal People's Party, driving politicians to and from parliament and to special events. He works long hours, depending on the political calendar. One of his frequent passengers is the leader of the party, an iTaukei man named Ratu Apenisa Lewanivanua. In April last year, Lewanivanua was elected prime minister of Fiji. At first, Vijay seemed jubilant, hope shimmering off him about his country's future. He would hum when he got dressed for work.

It didn't last long. He soon became dark and broody, as though drowning in increased responsibility. He said once that he was concerned that the roads were filling up with erratic young taxi drivers who hadn't learned to drive properly. That was one of the rare occasions in which he actually mentioned his work to her. He is always the picture of discretion, never revealing anything about his celebrity passengers. Even on Friday nights when he drinks kava and watches English Premier League with his cousins and uncles and they playfully prod him for political tidbits, he always remains unflinching.

Rishika is proud of Vijay's prestigious position. She admires his unfailing loyalty, his stony dedication. But sometimes, just sometimes, when they turn out the bedside lamp, she craves a snippet of gossip; a delicious little secret with which he will trust no one but her.

Samriti sees Vijay's job as the best thing that has ever happened to her. Vijay is her favorite son, something she announces regularly at family gatherings with no irony as far as Rishika can tell. A few years back, when Lewanivanua was still opposition leader and they were driving back after a campaign meeting on the western side, Vijay took a detour and invited him into Samriti's village for tea. According to Samriti, the *Ratu* was very humble; a lovely man. More importantly, he declared Samriti's *halwa* to be the best he'd ever tasted – a story her neighbors now know by heart. Of course, it is possible that it was the only *halwa* he'd ever tasted. But Samriti was smitten. She still defends any of the prime minister's unpopular political decisions amongst her friends. "We must remember he has a very fine sense of quality," she reminds them.

That seems so long ago now, when Vijay used to have an easy smile, a spring in his step. Rishika has tried to lift him out of his dark spirits; she cooks his favorite duck curry, she brings home weekly (pirated) blockbuster films. Last Friday night, she even let her hand trail down to his bellybutton, but he waved her away. He was too tired, he said. He really *was* in a mood.

Now Rishika kneels on the tiled floor over her mortar and pestle, crushing the chilies into the garlic and ginger for tonight's curry. She pounds and pounds, even after it has become a paste. Oddly, she finds herself thinking, *what would Wendy do?*

It is silly, really, that Wendy made such an impression on her. She only knew her for a short time. Rishika vividly remembers the day Julia Morris, Wendy's daughter, stood with pale knees at the front of class 4B of Mahatma Ghandi Memorial Primary School. Rishika and her friends were stunned – a *gora*! Usually a white girl would go to the International School with all the other bank managers' and diplomats' children. Rishika found out later that Wendy was an ethnomusicologist doing her PhD at a Queensland university. Something about Indian songs and how they changed with Indian migration. She was doing her fieldwork in Fiji, and she and Julia's father wanted their daughter to learn Hindi and meet local friends.

On that first day of school, Master Maharaj put Julia in the seat next to Rishika. At lunch, Rishika said in her stilted English, "You sit with me and Lakshmi?" and Julia said yes. The next day, Julia lined up next to Rishika outside the classroom. The day after that, they were best friends.

When Rishika and Lakshmi were invited to Julia's house, they sat in Julia's loungeroom, watching her flickering television. Fiji didn't have broadcast television then, so instead they watched videotapes of entire evenings of Australian television – ads and all. They watched, bemused, as the Morrises fell over themselves in laughter when Red Simons gonged hopeful performers on *Hey Hey It's Saturday*.

Julia's parents insisted Rishika and Lakshmi use their first names, although mostly they couldn't help it and called them

Aunty and Uncle. For dinner, they ate strange things – "spaghetti bolognese," "tuna salad," "cauliflower cheese." When she ate at the Morrises, the food was bland – no chili or spices – and some of it was bordering on inedible; Wendy wasn't a very good cook. But Rishika loved her visits to the Morris house. They all ate at the same time, talking at the table. They laughed with Rishika and Lakshmi as they learned how to use a knife and fork. Wendy called them sweetheart, and sometimes she asked the girls how to say particular words in Hindi, hanging off their every sound.

Julia's father asked Rishika what she wanted to be when she grew up – a flattering, unfamiliar question. She hadn't really thought about it. At the time, she answered, "an ethno-music-ist like Aunty," and Wendy placed her fork down on the table. "You would make a wonderful one, sweetheart."

Rishika pleaded with her mother to be able to have a sleepover at Julia's house, and her mother eventually, reluctantly, agreed. Her mother told her father that Rishika was going to go to Nausori Aunty's for the evening. It was one of those rare moments in which her mother had done something defiant – in which she had stood up to her husband – and Rishika had cherished that feeling almost as much as the sleepover itself.

After Wendy's fieldwork finished, the Morrises moved back to Brisbane. Rishika and Julia wrote to each other once or twice and then they stopped. But Rishika still thinks of Wendy sometimes, and wonders what she would do in this situation.

If she were Wendy, she would probably shake her husband and say, "Talk to me! Where have you gone?"

༚

ISIKELI LIFTS his heavy eyelids, eyes adjusting to the mid-morning light. Eta is sitting a meter away, staring at him.

"*Oilei*," he says, rubbing his eyes.

The four-year-old raises her eyebrows and takes a swig from a bottle of flat, raspberry cola, the bottle almost as big as her. He leans over and places his hand affectionately on his niece's head. "Got a present for you."

Her eyes widen.

He rolls over and begins to sit up, wincing at his aching arm muscles. When he arrived home this morning at dawn, Aunty and Uncle were asleep on the old mattress, now rolled up in the corner. They must have already gone to the market.

Isikeli's grandmother sits on the mat in the main room with Isikeli's sister, Mere, who is half smiling at something on her phone. A purple *sulu* covers the old lady's lap, the material falling away where her left leg used to be.

She looks up when she notices him. "You slept in again," she says.

"Morning, Bu." He ignores the implied question and bows his head and shoulders in respect as he walks in front of her, "*tulou, tulou, tulou.*"

He walks behind the small television where he has hidden the scooter.

"*Qori*," he reveals it to Eta. Mere looks up from her phone. In the light of day, Isikeli now sees the scooter is blue, with pictures of a skull and crossbones and the words *Speed Demon!* on it. The little girl's eyes light up. She steps on it with one foot and manages one wonky glide across the mat before stumbling off.

Mere admonishes her daughter. "Eta, say thank you to *Momo* Keli." But to her brother, she shoots a narrowed, suspicious look. Isikeli pretends not to know what she means. She annoys him these days; her righteous, meaningful glances. She has slid into the role of his mother far too easily.

The irony is that their mother – Na – is never like that. Na is fun-loving and cheeky, a quick temper followed by warm forgiveness. She works as a maid for the Tribe Resort on a little island off the other side of the mainland. The resort's website gives itself a generous three and a half stars and advertises photos of beautiful tanned backpackers at moonlit beach parties. In reality, the tourists aren't that tanned or beautiful and the resort is known for bed bugs. Na spends six days a week collecting damp bath towels and smoothing bedsheets, her nights spent drinking *yaqona* with the other maids, the cooks, the porters, and the pool boys.

When they were younger, Isikeli and Mere used to visit Na on school holidays. They stayed in the staff quarters, watching pay television in the empty rooms and sometimes being smuggled in to eat leftovers from the buffet breakfast. When the management changed at the resort they weren't allowed to visit anymore.

Last year, Na was granted a week of leave, and she caught the ferry and two buses to surprise Isikeli for his birthday. They ordered buckets of fried chicken and a massive chocolate cake that said "Happy Birthday Keli!" in orange icing.

But she hasn't been back since Christmas. She wires half of her weekly pay back to Bu for groceries.

"Time for these, Bu." Isikeli kneels next to his grandmother with a small crumpled ziplock bag full of tablets.

She raises her eyebrows. "*Sega.*"

"Come on, Bu, what did the nurse say?"

"She said don't take the pills."

Isikeli smiles in exasperation. "Bu, you have to take the medication, eh?"

"I don't need it. *Vuniwai* said the spirits were gone."

The exchange continues until Isikeli shakes his head and gives up.

Eta shadows him as he puts the bag of pills away, grabs a towel, and walks outside, setting off down the narrow alleyway to the communal outdoor shower block. Gray clouds hang heavily in the sky, pregnant with afternoon rain. The little sounds of the settlement are amplified in the still, muggy air: the creaking of tin against tin; Mrs Karawalevu pegging her *sulus* on the makeshift clothesline; Eta dragging her scooter along the bumpy path of trodden dirt behind him.

He creaks open the door, leaving Eta on her scooter outside. Last week, the water stopped running for several days. This began while Isikeli was mid-shower, standing under the showerhead, naked, soapy, and waiting. This time, though, Isikeli feels the relief of a dribble and then a weak burst of cold water on his back. He contemplates how he will narrate the story of the dog last night to his friends.

He returns from the shower and hangs his wet towel on the back of a chair. Returning an unwilling Eta to her mother, he leaves the house and winds his way through the muddy paths of the settlement he grew up in. He walks around the *vaya vaya* tree, still fiery red with its Christmas blooms, the elbows of its branches stretching around the tin houses as though to hug them. The shacks themselves lean out as though escaping down the hill on their stilts, coming to a sudden halt before the road.

He reaches in his pocket and feels a slight thrill at the clinking of coins from last night. He stops in at the concrete corner store. The Chinese shopkeeper peers through the security grill. Isikeli points to a long white loaf of bread and a tin of minced mutton. He lays out his coins for the shopkeeper – he is ten cents short. After a brief standoff, the shopkeeper eventually grabs the coins and thrusts the items at him, muttering angrily in Chinese.

It is on the next street corner that Isikeli's friends are waiting.

Seru is swiveling on a broken office chair, cutting shavings off the top of a green coconut with a machete. "Keli! *Vacava tiko?*"

"*Set tiko,*" he says.

Jone looks up from where he is constructing a pyramid of coconuts just beside the curb. "Heeeey, brother." They give each other a handshake, Jone's chubby fingers sliding and snapping away from Isikeli's.

Epeli and Save are seated on an old wooden milk crate.

"*Set, Tavale*?" Isikeli greets Epeli, but his cousin-brother seems sullen and doesn't respond.

Isikeli sits cross-legged on the tarpaulin and rips open the loaf of bread, gutting it like a fish. His friends watch him closely. He peels back the lid of the can and fills the loaf with glistening mutton with his finger to make a long sub sandwich. He breaks off generous portions and hands them to each of his friends. For the second time that day, he enjoys the powerful feeling of being the bearer of gifts.

Epeli, however, snatches his sandwich in annoyance. His anger makes him look flushed and child-like, like he used to when they were kids. Epeli is from the same village as Isikeli's father, on the northeastern island of Mataqai. It is one of Isikeli's favorite things to do in the world, to tease Epeli. Epeli used to throw moody tantrums when Isikeli wrestled him too roughly in the shallow water near his house, or when his team lost to Isikeli's on the village rugby pitch. One memorable time, Epeli's father took the two boys hunting for turtle in the little rusted dinghy. The boat had a heyday in the nineties when Epeli's dad used to take tourists snorkelling on the reef, until the *Princess Margaret* cruise ship changed its route and the tourists stopped coming. That day, Isikeli and Epeli were giddy with excitement at the idea of turtle fishing for the first time, desperate to be the best at it, to discover some innate talent for the skills of their ancestors. They scanned the sapphire water below like Uncle showed them. *Please let me see one first, please let me see one first*. Out of the corner of his eye, Isikeli saw a brown shape careering in the deep. "There's one!" he shouted.

"Good boy," Uncle said, and Epeli looked flushed and annoyed, just like he does now. Uncle steered the dinghy, following the turtle as it desperately sought to swim away from the ominous shadow of the boat. When the animal was finally too tired to swim anymore, Uncle plopped into the water, leaving the boys peering over the side. The ripples in the water widened until the sea around them flattened, with Uncle nowhere to be seen. The boys heard only the sound of small waves lapping against the tin, waiting, waiting, waiting. Finally, Uncle reappeared on the other side, holding the big brown creature with flurried, flapping flippers, and the boys laughed in lightheaded relief, Epeli's annoyance forgotten. Afterwards – friends again – they helped place the food prepared by their aunties on the hot stones of the *lovo* in preparation for the visiting chief. Breadfruit wrapped in banana leaves, plucked beheaded chickens roasting in aluminum foil, and Isikeli's favorite *palusami* – corned beef with taro leaves and coconut milk cooked in old tuna cans.

Now, the young men eat their mutton sandwiches in silence. A fly slowly buzzes its way from one coconut to another. The occasional person walks past, averting their eyes from the boys at the coconut stand. Some days you can make okay money selling coconut drinks, but only if the weather is good, if the right people come by, and if there aren't too many other guys selling coconuts up the street. Today is not one of those days.

When Epeli finishes eating, he wipes his hands on his shorts.

"You guys should get the coconuts today," he spits.

"What?" Jone says.

"You haven't gotten the coconuts for weeks. It's always Save and me."

Save looks uncomfortable. "Don't worry about it, bro!" he whispers.

Epeli continues, unstoppable now. "You just sit here doing the easy shit. I'm sick of it. No respect."

It's true that Epeli and Save are the ones who usually get the coconuts. As a group, they rely on finding coconuts in easily accessible areas, growing on trees in abandoned lots, beside the sea, or on the verge beyond people's fences. Climbing the skinny trunks can be perilous; one of the boys in Mataqai has a permanently injured neck from an unfortunate misstep. But Epeli has a special knack for climbing; he always has. His feet seem adhesive as he shimmies up the tree trunks, throwing down the green coconuts to his friends below. That's one skill that Epeli will always have over Isikeli.

"It's because you're the best, Epi," Isikeli admits.

"*Io*," says Jone.

Seru adds, "No one wants to see Jone's fat arse up a coconut tree. It'd snap!"

Even Jone laughs at this.

Epeli is not so easily placated. The fly buzzes around his face now, and he waves it away in irritation.

The boys are interrupted by a girl walking hurriedly past them, talking on her phone. She's wearing a fitted gray business skirt, which hugs her hips.

"Coconut, *lewa*?" Seru asks, charmingly, his gold tooth glinting. The girl looks at him distractedly, still talking on her phone, continuing down the sidewalk followed by the clip, clip, clip of her high heels.

Seru gives a low whistle when she is out of earshot. "I like *her* coconuts."

Jone squeals with laughter. Even Epeli has a smile at the corner of his lips, to Isikeli's relief. He never likes his cousin-brother staying mad for too long.

Later, in the quiet moments when the sidewalk is empty, Isikeli and Seru recount last night's adventures to their friends. In the retelling, the fences are slightly higher, the dogs more vicious, and the escapes much narrower.

※

A FAINT call to prayer floats on a breeze through the window shutters of Hannah's bedroom. Her temple is pounding slightly, a gentle throbbing pain, yet she feels strangely invigorated. All these late nights and drunken philosophical arguments with people from all around the world. Even the hangover feels delightfully bohemian.

After the awkward beginning with Jean last night, he and Hannah had a long conversation, somehow winding their way onto the topic of healthcare. At least, he spent a lot of time explaining Castro's healthcare system after his recent trip to Cuba. She listened attentively, never quite finding the right moment to explain she has a degree in public health. Instead, she asked incisive, thoughtful questions and liked the way he said "good question" before explaining his answer. At the end of the evening, he said it was a *"pleasir"* and hoped to see her again some time.

She accidentally finds herself imagining what he would be like as a boyfriend. Her friends back home would all be impressed if she brought home a suave European man. *"We met in Suva ..."* She wonders what her ex-boyfriend's reaction would be. Behind his hipster beard, only she would recognize the envy that would flash across his face, and the ostentatious affection he would show his new girlfriend for the rest of the evening.

Oh, for God's sake. She feels disappointed in herself for being so predictable. She is a carefree traveler, embarking on a rich and interesting career in international development. She doesn't need a man!

And yet. Back in Perth, her university friends have begun to pair off in solid, long-term relationships. They have all started using the term "partner," the smug, grown-up term for boyfriend. They all met in traditional ways – locking eyes across a bar, competing against each other in a corporate touch rugby competition, or meeting at a friend's fancy-dress party. They are consequently "fascinated" by Hannah's hilarious stories of online dating. They relish her anecdotes about failed Tinder dates, which she dutifully curates for them. She always embellishes the stories for their benefit, parodying herself and stylizing the embarrassing moments. She leaves out the moments where she returns home and cries until her face is blotchy.

When she first arrived in Suva, Hannah fell dizzyingly in love with her new circle of volunteer friends. They spent most weeknights and weekends together: dinners out, house parties, trips to outer islands. Whenever family or partners visit from overseas, they always seem taken aback by how intimate the volunteers are. They laugh uncomfortably at the in-jokes they don't understand. And of course, in those first few weeks, the parties dripped with ticklish tension. Simply the amount of time they were spending together seemed like innuendo. Even grocery shopping seems sexy when you are doing it with other young singles on a balmy tropical evening after two gin and tonics.

Inevitably, some of the volunteers have slept with each other – including Aaron and Michelle at one point; Swiss Dave and German Jana at another. Hannah always seems to find out about a fling after the fact; she seems to miss the precise moments of flirtation and footsies under the table that precipitate it, instead only noticing when it's all over and her two friends are awkwardly avoiding eye contact. "Wait, what?!" she says, and they blush and wave her interest away.

Over time, though, the volunteers have settled into a more relaxed intimacy. The innuendo lingers, but it's more rehearsed now. They have gotten to know each other's annoying traits. Pip gets irritable when she is hungry. Ethan's humor has a mean edge when he's tired.

So it's nice to have another person on the scene to shake the dynamic up a little.

And yet, a mean little soundbite begins to reverberate in her head. It is a throwaway comment made by someone she met on Tinder not long before she came here – "you look different from your profile picture." It is true that her Tinder profile contains a flattering picture of her, taken from a slimming angle with nice lighting, on a rare day when her shoulder-length hair was elegantly voluminous. An optical illusion.

Remembering the comment now makes her redden with insecurity. He was probably right. The idea that Jean – or anyone – could find her attractive suddenly seems less likely. She vows to do more exercise, to go for disciplinary jogs. She can't now, of course, because she has to get ready for work. She is finding it enough of an effort to just get out of bed.

When she is finally up, she sees her housemate, Jess, wandering around the house in her underwear, searching for her missing work pants. Hannah gets herself a bowl of muesli and calmly suggests a few potential hiding spots, trying to refrain from the always annoying, *where did you last see them?*

Jess finally finds the pants at the bottom of the washing basket. "Thank God Ili is coming today," she grumbles. Ili cleans their house three days a week. Hannah and Jess initially thought that having a cleaner was preposterously spoiled and extravagant. But according to the previous expat tenants, Ili "came with the house" and Hannah and Jess would put her out of a job if they didn't continue the arrangement. And it turns out it is really nice to have your clothes washed and folded at the foot of your bed, or to know that you can have a last-minute party for which you won't have to clean up afterwards. (There was that time when World Bank Dave vomited in their bathroom before passing out on the couch, and Ili had come and cleaned it up before any of them had even woken.)

Hannah is relieved that she won't be home today when Ili comes. She hates it when she has to step through a patch of floor that Ili has just finished mopping, or if Ili has nearly finished washing the dishes and Hannah places an extra coffee cup in the sink. It feels so symbolic or something. "Sorry, Ili!" She always cringes. She tries to make it a meaningful sorry, as if to say, "sorry about colonization!" Ili always laughs and says, "It's okay, Hannah," which does make Hannah feel better about it all.

On their ten-minute walk to work, the girls walk almost as fast as the slowly moving line of traffic. They can feel the gaze of each taxi driver rolling past them, windows open, elbows resting irreverently over their car doors. Hannah always feels so visible in Fiji, as though she is *interesting* to passersby in a way she simply isn't back home.

Jess chatters away about her conversation with her boyfriend, Brad, last night, her long black hair tied in a loose bun on top of her head. Jess grew up in the western suburbs of Sydney, has some Lebanese in her ancestry, and has a funny tendency to be blunt. She is gorgeous and curvy and endearingly unselfconscious about it. Brad visited Suva at Christmas, and Hannah took a road trip with them up to Rakiraki. She finds Brad's broad handsome face and slightly receding hairline grating in ways that she finds hard to articulate. Even when he is being charmingly self-deprecating, Brad has the assured confidence of someone who has gone to an elite private school. He says things like, "you're amazing at that, I'm hopeless," or, when he sees some of the poorer villages, "puts it all into perspective, doesn't it?" To Hannah, Brad's likeable humility seems like another extra-curricular activity he has mastered, like piano or tennis or chess. *But that's unfair*, Hannah reprimands herself. He is actually very generous, and he is smitten with Jess, always laughing uproari-ously at her refreshing honesty. Admittedly, Hannah is probably a little bit jealous.

They reach the block of offices where they both work. Jess walks into the GoGirl office on the ground floor, where she is working on a project about empowering poor women through microfinance opportunities. Unlike the other volunteers, Jess feels underutilized and frustrated in her placement. "They've got me doing grant applications and shit," she complained to the group last week. "Why can't they let me do the real work? I want to do outreach in the villages. I didn't get a development studies degree and come all this way to do bloody spreadsheets." Every-one listened supportively and suggested that she should have a candid conversation with her boss. Everyone except for Ethan, who said, "Maybe development is more about spreadsheets than you think," somewhat unhelpfully.

Hannah walks up the poky stairs to the third floor. It always strikes her how different this daily passage is compared to that of her last workplace on St George's Terrace. There she used to walk through a shiny revolving door and take a smooth, fast el-evator to the fourteenth floor. She was working for a marketing organization that exclusively worked on health promotion pro-jects, mostly about aging. She worked with designers and crea-tive teams to produce brochures full of bossy health messages. "Start discussing aged care options with your parents early" and "Recognize the signs of dementia." Most of her work involved browsing through stock images of happy-looking white-haired folks being hugged by supportive-looking middle-aged people.

In Suva, she is working in the tired old offices of FijiHealth on the problem of diabetes. It is a crisis here, and Hannah quite likes the idea of helping with a crisis. This island nation with less than a million people has one of the highest rates of diabetes in the world. Fijians have all the risk factors, like too much sugar, salt, and fat in their diets, not doing enough exercise, drinking too much alcohol, and smoking. It causes blindness and kidney problems and amputations. Even early death.

So Hannah spends most of her days in Suva thinking about sugar: how too much of it contributes to type two diabetes; how diabetic bodies can't process sugar properly; how to educate Fijians about sugar; and – when she gets hungry – how yummy it is on cinnamon buns. *Sugar, sugar, sugar, sugar, sugar.* It is one of those words that sounds weird when you say it too many times.

Now she plonks her bag on her desk and walks into the tiny staff kitchen that doubles as the boardroom. Her colleagues are already gathered for the meeting. The aqua-colored paint job in the small kitchenette is the kind that can't be scrubbed clean, parts of it peeling off to reveal an earlier layer of red. A laminated poster of a dove with a peace branch in its beak is sticky taped to the wall near the microwave, just above the handwritten sign: "Pliz wash your own dishes ☺."

Her colleagues are mostly women, who have a playful relationship with each other in the office. When it is someone's birthday, they bring in cakes – enormous creamy sponge cakes with frosted messages. On one or two occasions they have all gone out for drinks together on a Friday night. "Everyone's so lovely," Hannah told her mum during a phone call when she first arrived. Gradually, however, she has started to see fault lines appear that were once invisible to her. Her Indo-Fijian colleagues always sit on one side of the table speaking mostly in Hindi, and the iTaukei sit on the other speaking mostly in Fijian. Now that she has noticed, she sees it everywhere in Suva – in the food court, in the cinema, on the sidewalk, in the taxi last night. Not in a sinister way, just in a that's-how-it's-always-been kind of way. She does see the odd mixed couple, or mixed group of friends, but those moments are always rare enough to be interesting.

Today when she walks in, her colleagues stop their conversations to say warm hellos to her. In English now, for her benefit, everyone talks about the impending cyclone. They shrug at her concerned questions with a kind of amused fatalism, having lived through many before. Their conversation stops when Hannah's boss, Dr Sireli, walks in holding a manila folder. He says quietly, *"Bula vinaka, ladies, we'll get started, eh?"*

A softly spoken man with an immense, rugby-player physique, Dr Sireli practiced endocrinology for ten years in London before entering public health and coming back to Fiji. Apparently he used to be a brilliant doctor: one of the women in the office said he won some kind of international award. He also likes to insert a bible passage at the end of every official report his team produces. In one report, just under the table of statistics about diabetes prevalence by gender and age in Fiji, he inserted:

1 Corinthians 6:19 – Do you not know that your bodies are temples of the Holy Spirit, who is in you, whom you have received from God? You are not your own.

When Hannah recounted this to her friends at O'Hannigan's one night ("It was in purple, and in Comic Sans!") everyone was very amused. It sparked a long drunken conversation about Christianity in Fiji. They talked about historical missionaries, contemporary earnest Mormans, charismatic prayer groups, and a particularly avid group of Zionists that sometimes hand out brochures on the street corner. "Have they even met an Israeli?"

Aaron asked. Ethan said there was a Fijian contingent of UN peacekeepers on the Syrian-Israeli border. "They come back and spread The Word, I guess."

Pip, a zealous atheist, gave an impassioned speech about the importance of secular states. "The poor need education and good healthcare, not some kind of imaginary sky daddy!" she cried. German Jana, who volunteered at a local primary school, was shocked by the presence of Christianity in every single textbook. "In maths, they're like, 'If Jesus had twelve disciples over for dinner, but three went to church, how many disciples did he have left?' and I'm like, are you fucking *serious*?"

That night, Hannah laughed until her stomach hurt at the observations of her new, funny friends.

And yet, over time, Hannah has become more ambivalent about Dr Sireli's faith. It is kind of admirable how he takes every case of diabetes in Fiji personally. Hannah saw him in tears once, when he sat on a woven mat with a man whose father had recently died of kidney failure. He always works long hours but is generous and playful with his staff. He lets them play the radio while they work. Once, when everyone was working late on a report due to the minister the next day, one staff member phoned *Bula!FM* and requested a song for "Dr Sireli at FijiHealth." It was Harry Belafonte's "Jamaica Farewell" and they all sang along from their desks. Hannah's iTaukei colleagues immediately fell into layered gospel harmonies. Even Dr Sireli joined in, and Hannah shed a little tear. It's actually possible that Dr Sireli is the best boss she has ever had.

The first item on the agenda this morning is the Soft Drink Bill. Hannah's team has been talking about this ever since she arrived. It is a proposed law that all sugary drinks are going to be plain-packaged by the next financial year. Similar to what occurred with cigarette packets a while ago, all colors, corporate logos, and trademarks are going to be removed from soft drink bottles and other sugary drinks. The idea is based on research that people (especially young people) are very responsive to branding and the coolness of a product – logos make people's brains go *ping!* with recognition and they start salivating. With this bill, the name of each drink is going to be printed in whatever small, boring font is mandated. Because who wants an Island Cola when it's advertised in barely visible, 12 point, Times New Roman?

No country has done this yet, so little Fiji is about to do something quite big. Dr Sireli has been on the working group, and the new prime minister has shown support for the bill. Finally it looks like it is going to get through parliament, so Hannah's team is starting to brainstorm health promotion campaigns to accompany the new change.

"Rethink the drink," someone says.

"Quiz the fizz!" says someone else.

Hannah wants to contribute something witty, but her humor does not always translate well here. She has seen her colleagues in tears of laughter at each other's jokes in their own languages, but her attempts at humor do not get the same reaction. In a recent meeting, for example, one of the women raised the problem of junior staff being undertrained.

A colleague agreed. "It's as though we've hired cats and we're asking them to fetch, *haana*?"

Everyone around the table nodded.

Another colleague spoke up. "Maybe we're hiring all wrong. If it's about fetching, we need dogs, you know? Revisit our recruitment process."

Hannah spoke up. "Yeah, we'd be like, why are we hiring cats and dogs? How did they get through the interview process? Haha!"

The table looked at her blankly.

Her colleague explained patiently, "We don't actually hire cats or dogs."

"Right. I just … yep. Sure."

So Hannah stays silent this time.

The team soon begins talking about the second item on the agenda, the community diabetes research, the project Hannah has been assigned to. They are focusing on the areas that have the worst health outcomes – the informal settlements that sprawl across suburbs and scatter the main road leading out of Suva. Dr. Sireli wants to understand what makes this community especially vulnerable. Hannah has seen these squatter settlements on the way from the airport. Jumbly derelict shacks crowded together, jostling for space. Many of the tenants have migrated from rural areas searching for a better life in the city, only to find Suva brimming to capacity. They build makeshift houses on hills and riverbanks. Some of them are illegally using the space, and some of them have borrowed it through complex cultural arrangements.

Hannah has suggested interviewing them, which was something she had learned about in one of her university courses. Finally, last week, she received approval from the university ethics committee: the go-ahead to get started. She's never done interviews before (unless you count the three fellow students she interviewed for an undergraduate essay once). She will be attending the settlements tomorrow with an outreach nurse, so that Hannah can sit and interview the household while the nurse treats any patients who require it. They are going to start at the biggest informal settlement, the one that sprawls across three suburbs. It's called Paradise Estate, the irony long since worn away.

Hannah goes over her interview schedule, tweaking the questions she is going to ask. The team reminds her to take copies of the consent forms and ensure that she has fully charged batteries in her voice recorder. They warn her to be careful. It's a "red zone"; a high crime area.

Hannah can't wait to get started. She's excited to be helping proper poor people with proper poor people problems. She is – she realizes in a moment of self-reflection – imagining her day as a series of gritty urban photos that would look cool on Instagram.

After the meeting, Hannah and a colleague are tasked with taking photos of the new exercise area on the waterfront, which will be added to a report for the sponsors. They wait until some youth come by and the teenagers happily pose for the camera, doing chin-ups on the equipment and making peace signs above each other's heads. In each photo, Hannah is careful to foreground the sign with the sponsor's logo – they'll like that. *PacFone Exercise Area*, it says. *Answer the Call to a Healthier You!*

At the end of the day, as part of her fitness resolution, she walks home from work the long way, past the winding streets that circle the valley. The afternoon is still oppressively humid, aching for the relief of the daily afternoon downpour. She relishes the lush green of the tropical foliage on the side of the road. The greens of Suva are always so luxurious compared to the drought-ridden paddocks and dusty teal of the gum trees back home.

Taxi drivers slow down as they pass Hannah and give a short sharp toot, raising their eyebrows. She waves them all on, at first apologetically, and then with annoyance.

A tall, striking iTaukei teenager walking slightly ahead of her catches her eye. He is bearded and wearing a black floppy hat, which, she notes with interest when he turns his head, is embroidered with the words *Wagga Wagga Magpies*. Probably a sporting team. Lots of people wear second-hand Australian clothes here.

Suddenly, she realizes the young man is looking back at her.

"*Bula*," he calls.

"Oh, *bula!*" she says.

"Where're you from?" He waits for her to catch up to him.

"Australia. Perth." They walk in tandem now.

"Perth, eh? My cousin-brother lives in Perth."

"Oh, does he?" This is not a surprise to Hannah. Everyone's cousin seems to live in Perth. "Whereabouts?" she asks as a courtesy.

"*Isa* ... in the city ... near the airport?"

A big purple bus with open windows drives past, bursting with a pop song that has been remixed with an islander reggae beat. Brown passengers jerk forward and backward in unison with the bus's clunky gear changes. Several of them smile down at Hannah and the teenager as the bus passes.

"And where are you from?" Hannah turns back to the boy.

"Mataqai Island. Near Vanua Levu. You know the other island?"

"I know Mataqai. It's a nice place." Hannah visited the island by ferry with some of the volunteers a few months ago. It was a haunting place that smelled like fish and looked like a Wild West outpost. Its architecture was stuck in the time of the town's boom in the 1800s when it was an American trading station, full of missionaries and vagrants and shady businessmen. (To be honest, though, there weren't many good restaurants and the hotel pool was closed for renovations, so it was Hannah's least favorite mini-break so far).

"What brings you to Suva?" she asks him.

"I live here now," he says. "You know Paradise Estate?"

She stares at him. "Wait, you live in Paradise Estate?"

"*Io.*"

"No way! I'm going there tomorrow!" she blurts.

He looks disbelieving. "True? To Paradise?"

"Yep. I work for FijiHealth."

"Ohhhh. FijiHealth."

"Yep."

They continue to walk in silence.

"FijiHealth, eh?" He repeats.

"Yes. We want to know about people's experiences with '*nah-mah-tay-nee-soo-kah*.'" She is proud of herself for practising the Fijian word, literally meaning "the sugar sickness."

He doesn't respond, so she says it louder now.

"You know, *NAH-MAH-TAY-NEE-SOO-KAH*?"

"Ohhhh, *na mate ni suka*? Diabetes?"

"Yes! Diabetes. A nurse and I are going to come and talk to people about diabetes."

They walk again in silence.

"My *bubu*?" he says eventually. "My grandmother? She has diabetes."

"Oh, does she? I'm sorry to hear that."

"*Io*. You come and see her tomorrow, eh?"

"Um … I guess we could try to see her. It's kind of up to the nurse where –"

"*Io*, you come see her tomorrow," he says forcefully. He describes a corner of the settlement near his house where she should meet him. "You know the roundabout near Supa Valu supermarket?" he asks. "We meet there." Apparently, he doesn't have a phone, but if she sends him a friend request on Facebook, they can communicate that way – he will use his friend's phone, he says. They agree to meet at ten o'clock in the morning.

"So ten o'clock, at that … corner?" she confirms uncertainly.

"*Io. Set*," he says, and starts crossing the road.

"Wait!" she calls when he is halfway across. "I didn't catch your name? To friend you, on Facebook? I'm Hannah Wilson."

"Isikeli," he calls. "Isikeli Tiko."

Later, after everything that happens, Hannah Wilson will relive this moment over and over, pinpointing it as ground zero,

the starting point of the events that will spin her world upside
down. But on this particular Thursday, she marvels at the seren-
dipity of meeting someone from Paradise Estate. Perfect timing.

A COLONY of bats screeches across the sky, smothering the remaining sunlight. Beside Rishika on the balcony, Solomon sits
alert on his haunches, staring distrustfully at the little drag-
on-like beasts.

Vijay just sent a message to say he is going to be home late; he's
driving one of the ministers to some last-minute event. He didn't
say where it was or when he will be home. In the kitchen, she
wraps the warm roti with a tea towel and puts the pot of lamb
curry aside, amber-colored oil already beginning to congeal at
the top.

She flicks on the balcony light and sits down on the outdoor
seat, opening her little blue book. She re-reads the first sentence
of her writing.

> *Just after he married his childhood sweetheart in Royapuram, Madras,*
> *in 1879, Arjun Naidu accidentally caught a big ship to the other side of*
> *the world and never came back.*

There is a delicious feel to writing again, the infinite possibilities of a blank page waiting to be filled. When Rishika finished
high school, she desperately wanted to go to university. Her
mother protested: "A degree will not help you get married! Your
husband can't eat textbooks!" Her father forbade it at first. Yet
Rishika worked on them, chipping away at their reasons. Her
older brother even helped to convince them. Eventually, they
came to an agreement: she could study, but she would have to

quit when they arranged a husband for her. It was a compromise, but it bought her time.

There was, sadly, no ethnomusicology degree at the University of the South Pacific. The closest she could find was history. She loved it right from the very first class. She listened to the banter of her rowdy classmates, the warm breeze entering through the open shutters. She learned about the bloody history of the South Pacific; the quest for power in the English monarchy; the Russian Revolution; and the great muddy battles of the First World War. She loved the dusty smell of books in the library and the feeling of rifling through yellow Dewey cards, searching for books and archival material by call number. More than the big macho struggles over power, Rishika relished the more intimate stories about unlikely friendships over time. She was intrigued by the bizarre connection between the mysterious Rasputin and the beautiful tsarina. She was fascinated by the soccer games played by the warring soldiers during the 1914 Christmas truce on the Western Front. She got lost in the private love story between the young Queen Victoria and the progressive Prince Albert.

Midway through her third year, her parents organized an afternoon tea with a boy called Vijay and his parents, for reasons that were not spoken aloud but were obvious to everyone. She wasn't ready to marry! She wanted to travel, to do a PhD, to *be a historian*. Unable to stop the steam train of her parents' commitment to tradition, she resentfully attended the awkward gathering. She resolved to be as unattractive as possible: to snort unappealingly when she laughed and to talk about her terrible cooking skills.

Yet to her surprise, Vijay seemed just as uncomfortable and sullen as her. And later, when their parents unsubtly left them alone, Vijay said he had been determined to dislike her, and had deliberately refrained from wearing deodorant that morning. He made her laugh so unexpectedly that she actually *had* snorted accidentally.

It was also an undeniable fact that Vijay was very good looking, with his square jaw and chocolate-brown skin. When her cousin Lakshmi first met him, she elbowed Rishika in the ribs and whispered, "*Bahut* sexy, *haana*?"

Rishika plaintively requested for the wedding to be in late November after her final exams, but everyone shushed her, and the three-day event was set for October. It was easy to get swept up in the excited twitter of her aunties, the careful selection of silky saris, the mesmerizing *mehendi* spiraling on her hand.

In the end, she deferred the final three subjects of her degree; she could always finish them later.

The wedding came and went. The couple moved into a small flat and money was tight. They decided to focus on having a baby.

She never did finish that degree. She never did have those children either. So many *unfinished* things.

Yet even though Rishika has earned only fifteen-eighteenths of a history degree, she still likes the past. Sometimes she scrolls through the pages of the six volumes of the *Encyclopedia Britannica* – 1988 edition – which are kept in the display cabinet above the television. It is a pompous set of books, really. The bits about "peoples of the world" are always outdated and a little bit racist. Many of the facts have been debunked now: Pluto is no longer a planet, stomach ulcers are no longer caused by stress. These days, of course, it is so seductive to simply type search words into Google. But she still pulls the books down sometimes because she misses the tangible, *sensual* experience of scrolling her forefinger down a page to find something by alphabetical order.

Recently, Rishika set herself a personal history assignment. It began a few months ago, when she was looking through an old chest of belongings she inherited from her grandmother. In amongst old photos and a well-read *Baghavad Gita*, she found a stapled booklet of stained, crumbly paper. The words were written in messy Hindi script in old biro ink – the hallmark of her grandmother's writing. Rishika ran her finger across every word and tried to piece the sentences together. It was a short oral history of Arjun, her grandmother's grandfather, who had been brought to Fiji as a laborer. Rishika was instantly intrigued. She began to hungrily hoard information about him. Any archives, websites, or books she could find. Although most of her research reveals only cold, hard, chronological facts – the pure numbers of Indian laborers brought to Fiji, the Indian cities they left, the ports they landed in, the languages they spoke – Rishika likes to mentally embroider the history with little details about how it might have smelled, or tasted, or how people like her forefather might have *heard* the new world around him.

Sometimes when Vijay gets home from work, she babbles about the bits of history she has discovered that day. The other day she announced to him that she was going to write a biography about Arjun. Not a big, sweeping volume, but a heartfelt, personal, little history. She made a conscious decision to write it in English, consulting her dictionary or thesaurus when she needed. English always seemed rather playful, all those onomatopoeic words that sound like what they describe: *sizzle, boom, crunch*. She told Vijay that she wanted to submit her work to the *Fiji Herald* and maybe they would print it as a personal interest segment. He was engrossed in an installation manual at the time for a new toy he had purchased – a dashcam to place in his work car in order to capture any road incidents. He offered her glib, distracted words of encouragement and then tried to show her the features of the camera. Rishika pushed away her disappointment and feigned interest, surprised and pleased he was engaging in her at all.

She returns now to her little blue book and starts reading over her words so far, crossing out the ones she doesn't like and adding phrases in the margins.

Arjun lived with his mother and wife, Vashti, in rural Royapuram, which thundered every few hours with the clickety-clack of passing steam trains. He eked out a living as a coolie, carrying luggage for railway passengers who arrived and departed on the trains. At nights, Arjun and Vashti would stay up late playing board games to the flickering light of a kerosene lantern, rolling cowrie shells to make their moves on the cotton cloth. Arjun had long, skinny legs, and he would make his wife laugh with his funny slapstick impressions of the railway passengers. The family struggled to make ends meet; they ate dal and rice most nights and could rarely afford to make roti, let alone eat meat. Arjun's forty-year-old mother fell ill, and the medicine man said her spirit was depleted from poor nutrition.

One day on the railway platform, Arjun was approached by a man in a bowler hat. He asked if Arjun wanted some work, for which he would be paid handsomely. Intrigued and hopeful, Arjun followed him to a depot, a smoke-filled room full of men playing cards. There they proposed an agreement: Arjun could go to an island full of opportunity – Arjun imagined it to be nearby; perhaps only days away. He could work on the farms – Arjun imagined a wholesome agricultural existence unlike the barren fields that surrounded him. After five years, he could pay his own way home again and still have saved a small fortune to raise a family. If he worked for ten years, said the agent, the British administration would pay his return trip.

The men at the depot encouraged Arjun to press his thumbprint into the ink, to sign the agreement and get on the ship right now! But Arjun insisted that he must talk with his dear little Vashti and mother.

The women wept as Arjun left with a small duffle bag of belongings. They wept as he walked into the dark of dawn, toward a sacrifice for a brighter, happier future. Five years was not much in the broader scheme of things. Arjun had arranged with his neighbor to take care of the women in his absence.

Arjun felt nauseous as soon as he stepped on board the Hereford, *the ship rocking on the waves. As they set sail, the berthdeck was a chittery chattery hub of Indian brothers. Caste and religion no longer mattered so much. Brahmin and untouchables: they all bathed in the same lukewarm water and slept beside each other in hammocks. They all ate the same weevil-riddled meals. Hindus had no choice but to eat beef, and their Muslim friends gave up asking if the food was halal.*

After a couple of days on the sailing ship, Arjun began to realize they were traveling further than he had been led to believe. The ship was smuggling him halfway around the world to the new British colony of Fiji.

After the shock subsided, there was still a sense of adventure, of excitement and possibility. Together, speakers of Telengu, Hindi, Bhojpuri, and Urdu carved out a way to communicate with each other. Initially they learned necessary words like "food," "water," "wake up," "play cards?" and "no cheating!" Then, gradually, they developed a more complicated dialect that in time would become Fijian Hindi, a mishmash of Indian languages and "bastardized" English.

After arriving on the humid, tropical island of Nukulau, Arjun and his newfound friends were lined up in front of white businessmen, who bid for the strongest, healthiest-looking laborers. Arjun was chosen by the Australian Colonial Sugar Refining Company and taken to the bustling agricultural center of Nausori, where he was put to work on the sugarcane plantations. He worked under the watchful eye of Raymond, the rarely sober "overseer" from the colony of New South Wales.

From six in the morning until four in the afternoon, year after year, Arjun planted row upon back-breaking row of seed. He hacked at sugarcane stems and stacked them in bundles to load onto wagons and then onto little trains – almost toy-like compared to the billowing steam trains at home. At night, he smoked and played cards. The thought of Vashti would always help him fall asleep.

Raymond chose Harjit, a pointy-featured Punjabi, to be his sardar, his middle man. Harjit took to the job enthusiastically, committed and ruthless, regularly beating his fellow laborers for minor misdemeanors or disrespectful glances.

The agreement had said that Arjun would earn one shilling, sixpence per day. It had failed to mention that money would be deducted from his weekly pay for his food rations and that he would be required to slip a shilling a week into Harjit's pocket, lest he be beaten.

After five years, he had not saved anything, let alone enough to afford the trip home.

Seven years into his trip – three years before Raymond would, he said, honor the agreement and pay for his ticket home – Arjun met a man he knew from his hometown Royapuram – literally bumping into him in Nausori town. Breathless with excitement, he grabbed the man by the shoulders: what was the news of Vashti and his mother?

Arjun's face soon collapsed with grief. His mother had died shortly after Arjun had left, cholera clutching at her spirit. Vashti, his dear little Vashti, had given birth to a baby girl. He felt deeply moved: the birth of a daughter to balance the death of his mother. Yet he soon calculated the hurtful truth: the child was born three years after Arjun had left. Vashti had moved in with the neighbor, the one who had been entrusted with her. The man did not know where they had moved to.

Arjun Naidu never did return to Royapuram. Fiji was his only home now.

Rishika snaps the book shut. A lump is lodged in her throat, refusing to be swallowed. There are hundreds of stories like Arjun's – thousands. When Fiji was "given" to the British in 1874, the nation's first governor-general, with the very Englishy name Arthur Charles Hamilton-Gordon, wanted to grow sugarcane.

He needed labor, but a massive measles epidemic wiped out nearly a third of the Indigenous people in 1875 and, besides, he wanted them to stay in their villages. So Indians like Arjun were summoned to help build the new colony, like they had in other colonies – Trinidad, Guyana, South Africa.

Indenture is a funny word, meaning a "legally binding contract." Arjun wasn't – technically – a slave, because he gave his consent by placing his thumb in ink and pressing it onto a *girmit* – a singsong Indian mispronunciation of the word "agreement." It is this word, especially, that Rishika finds a little bit heartbreaking. It is not a coincidence that this system was invented just five years after slavery was abolished. *Girmitiya*. Slave. They were more similar than the history books would have us believe.

Rishika ruffles the fur on Solomon's head and locks the security grill behind her. She heats up a small portion of the lamb curry in the microwave and eats it in silence in front of the television, letting the garish colors of a Hindustani talent show wash over her.

And what about all the Vashtis left behind, scared, alone, and waiting?

अर्

HANNAH KNOWS she should not be hungover for her first day of research tomorrow, but she accidentally said yes to a quick drink. Pip texted:

Hibiscus Inn? Half an hour?

She messaged back immediately:

There with bells on x

The Hibiscus Inn is where the volunteers go for a relaxing drink rather than a Big Night Out. When Jess and Hannah arrive, their friends are seated on plastic chairs beside the hotel's infinity pool, its shiny reflection seemingly dropping away to reveal the Suva harbor. A band of elderly iTaukei musicians is playing jazz standards under the thatched pergola, a light *bossa nova* beat wafting along with the warm breeze.

They are surrounded by tables of people melting into their chairs, relaxed by alcohol and laughing loudly. Hannah can hear Australian accents everywhere, although there is a French table by the bar and the ones on the far right sound American. The demographic of the Hibiscus Inn is mainly middle-aged people here on diplomatic missions, business, or research. The shorts and sandals, the casual atmosphere, and the pizza menu belie the price of the rooms, which are paid on corporate credit cards. Ethan once quipped, "This is what we're going to be when we grow up, kids!"

Most of the Australians are here again tonight, and Hannah is happy to see that Pasepa has joined them too. They all just *love* Pasepa. Born in Suva, she went to the university in Canberra and now lectures in economics at the University of the South Pacific. She grows her fuzzy hair out like a 1970s disco filmclip and wears hipster jeans and expensive, tribal-themed necklaces. It always gives Hannah a little glimmer of pride to have Pasepa at their table. They really are becoming immersed in the culture.

Periodically, the waitress assigned to Hannah's table comes past, a frangipani slipped behind her ear. "Can I get you any more drinks?" she asks. At the start of the evening, they all learn her name from her name badge (it is Sema) and their table has a jokey, almost flirtatious relationship with her.

"Which white wine can you recommend, Sema?" the volunteers ask, then order her suggestion.

When she sets down their drinks, they gain meaningful eye contact and say, *"Vinaka vakalevu* – thank you very much, Sema!"

When Pip accidentally spills the last half of her beer, World Bank Dave shouts out, *"Mateni!"* – the Fijian word for "drunk." He has been taking classes.

"Io!" Sema giggles.

"Join us for a drink, Sema!" they implore, although they know she can't, of course.

French Jean is sitting on the other side of the table from Hannah. He acknowledged her with a half-smile when she arrived but has been talking to Michelle for most of the evening. Michelle's olive cheeks look rouged and particularly vibrant tonight.

On Hannah's side of the table, Aaron is chatting about his day at a workshop on cyclone preparedness. "There are constant workshops in my line of work," he announces. "I go to one every week. Sometimes two. They literally stop me from getting my work done."

"Me too. I was at a workshop on Tuesday," Pasepa says. "Climate change resilience."

World Bank Dave nods. "I nearly went to that one too, but I had a clash. Mine was called 'Removing Tariffs: Creating Global Competition.'"

"Of course it was," Pip rolls her eyes at him.

"Why *are* there so many workshops in development?" Jess asks no one in particular.

"It's to do with the structure of funding," Ethan says. "The NGOs have money left over that they have to spend quickly. And workshops are, you know, a quick way to meet KPIs. Your brief is to build capacity? No worries! Bring in a few experts from overseas, invite the local civil servants and get them brainstorming stuff. And then produce a glossy report. You always have to produce a report."

"Right," Jess says, as a pina colada is placed in front of her, pierced with a slice of pineapple. "*Vinaka vakalevu*, Sema!"

Out of the corner of Hannah's eye, she sees Michelle slap Jean on the shoulder playfully and say, "You *didn't*! That is hil*arious*!"

Ethan is still talking about workshops. His sandy blond hair is, as always, in a state of unruliness. "Everyone's tripping over their heels to be politically correct. Australia can't be seen to be walking in and telling Fiji how shit's gonna get done. At least not anymore. You've gotta lead from *behind*. You've gotta be *consultative*, mate. They still get their way, but it looks better."

"Gotcha," says Jess. "Hence all the workshops."

"Exactly."

Hannah is pretty sure that Ethan is being ironically obnoxious, but she is never quite sure. He is always so cynical about everything, while also participating cheerfully in everything that he is cynical about. Hannah has never been able to work out whether he is a pragmatic social critic with a dry sense of humor, or if he is an observant, happy-go-lucky arsehole. Once, for example, he and Hannah were shopping in one of the big, freezingly air-conditioned department stores – the ones that sell Gucci, Lego, and proper-fitting bras. "Watch this," he said, as they walked together through the fragrant perfume section toward the exit. He pulled the hood of his light jumper over his head, placed his hands in his pockets and deliberately looked over his shoulders shiftily.

The security guards smiled at him and opened the door – "*Vinaka*, have a blessed day," they said distractedly – before continuing their conversation in Fijian.

Ethan and Hannah left through the sliding doors and stood on the pavement as a throng of brown faces moved around them.

"See?" Ethan announced loudly, his gray eyes shining. "I could have walked out with a television-shaped lump under my jumper, and they *still* wouldn't have looked twice. It's amazing being white here."

"Sssssssshhhhh!" Hannah gasped. "You can't *say* that!"

Across the table, Aaron has started talking about his workshop. Aaron is a short fellow, loud and charming, from New South Wales. He has shaved his head, owning his early baldness, but wears a baseball cap most of the time. He works in the field of water and sanitation, so the focus of his meeting was on the water-borne and mosquito-borne diseases that often lurk in the pools of stagnant water left over from cyclone flooding.

"Oh, and it's important to remove dead bodies as soon as possible," he adds. "We learned how to do that in a weird little animated clip they showed us. And then we role-played it afterwards."

"Ew!" says Pip. "That's a bit dramatic."

"Just sayin'."

"But Cyclone Dorothy is only a category one, right?" Jess asks. "So there won't be any 'dead bodies,' surely."

"I think it's been upgraded to category two now. That's still pretty tame, but yeah … I guess after Winston, no one wants to be underprepared."

Everyone takes a sip of their drinks, contemplatively.

They are interrupted by the loud barking of "Excuse me! Excuse *me*!" from a man with an ocker Australian accent at a nearby table. His fluorescent orange, high-visibility vest hangs open; clearly one of the tradespeople brought in by the roadwork contractors.

"Oh, gawd," Pip whispers to her table.

"Cashed. Up. Bogan," Jess whispers.

"You can't escape them," whispers World Bank Dave to Pasepa. "Even here."

The man is trying to flag down Sema, who calmly sashays over to him. "I'm sorry, sir, what can I get for you?" He takes his time looking over the menu and loudly states his order at her.

As the waitress walks back past the volunteers' table, World Bank Dave gains eye contact with Sema and leans toward her.

"Dickhead!" he whispers in solidarity. Sema chuckles politely.

They relax back into their conversations and Ethan asks Hannah about her research, which he knows she is starting tomorrow. Several of his legal aid clients have come from Paradise Estate, so he wants to know more about the place. She says she doesn't know much yet and deflects a question back to him, keeping one eye on Jean and Michelle's conversation.

Ethan has a big day tomorrow, he tells Hannah. He is helping senior council in the High Court.

"I can't reveal much," he says. "Confidentiality and all that." But the alcohol has loosened him up and he proceeds to tell her everything he knows about the case. They are defending a small shopkeeper who has recently been arrested for breach of copyright. Ethan thinks the case is a farce. "Hundreds of people in this country sell pirated DVDs at the markets, right? You know the ones in little plastic sleeves? They've done it for decades. But they're just suddenly cracking down on it. The poor guy's just a scapegoat. They just want to test out these new laws."

"Have you had a case in the High Court before?" Hannah asks.

"Nope!" Ethan's eyes shine. "Totally out of my depth. I can barely *spell* copyright." He winks. "Can't be too hard though, right?"

Hannah can't tell if he is being falsely humble or grossly negligent.

At ten o'clock, Jean stands up. "I am going home now," he announces, seemingly catching Hannah's eye.

"I should probably leave, too," Michelle says quickly. "I've got an early start tomorrow. Where do you live, Jean? We could share a taxi."

"Tamavua," Jean answers.

"Great," says Michelle. "The taxi can drop you first and me next."

When they are out of earshot, Pip slaps the table. "Ha! That is one serious detour she's taking. She lives in the complete opposite direction!"

"Oooooo," Jess sings.

After another half an hour with her friends, Hannah decides to take a taxi home with Jess and Ethan. The taxi that slows down for them has a tube of flashing neon lights that traces the seats, and a boomy subwoofer reverberating with British-Punjabi dance music.

"Party bus?" Ethan asks the driver, who nods solemnly. Jess stifles a giggle.

The taxi pulls in to Jess and Hannah's place. They step out of the car and unlock the two padlocks on their gate.

Ethan calls from the window as he retreats, "Good luck tomorrow with your research, Han!"

"Thanks!" Hannah calls back, the tail lights disappearing around the corner. "You, too, with the High Court thingy!"

But she is thinking about something else. A little thing. It is tiny. Probably nothing. It's just that, when Jean was leaving tonight, he walked past her side of the table, placed his hand lightly on her lower back, and intoned, "goodnight, *poisson*."

※

ISIKELI LEANS his back against the wall on Seru's uncle's verandah, listening to the faint, tinny reggae music clipping the speakers on Seru's phone. Sitting beside him, Seru is kneading the teatowel full of *yaqona* into the bucket of water for the fifth time this evening. When he finishes swirling the mix, he uses the half coconut shell to scoop the drink, handing a bowlful to each of the men in the circle, one by one: Seru's uncle, his cousins and friends. Aunty sits outside of the circle leaning against the doorway, eyes closed, fanning her sleeping grandson with an old newspaper.

The house faces onto the main dirt road of Paradise Estate. Neighbors and relatives pass by on the sidewalk. "*Bula*, brother!" Seru's uncle calls. "*Iko lako i vei?*" After they tell him (home, or to midnight mass, or to get more *yaqona*), Seru's uncle says, "*Mai*, join us!" They always politely decline and go on their way.

Isikeli receives the coconut shell from Seru with two hands. "*Bula*," he says, making eye contact with Uncle. He gulps the earthy drink down and the rest of the men clap three times. At least, that is custom, but it is the end of the night and five buckets in. Most of them are beginning to sit with their eyes closed, or are lying on their stomachs and scrolling through their phones. He hands the bowl back to Seru and slumps further against the wall. A familiar sense of serenity washes over him, the sedative, numbing effect of the *yaqona* percolating into his bones.

Uncle scrolls through his phone, squinting at the shattered screen. He looks up and says something about the prime minister, who is, apparently, in Canberra for trade talks. Uncle is always talking about Lewanivanua. He's signed up to some kind of news app. He loves the guy, and – according to Seru – shed tears of joy when he got elected.

Jone speaks up. "Better watch his back while he's gone."

Uncle shoots Jone a glance.

Enjoying the attention, Jone says loftily, "There are rumors floating around."

Concern flashes across Uncle's face before he quickly replaces it with a look of skepticism. "What rumors?"

Aunty opens her eyes.

"You don't know what you're talking about," Uncle continues.

Jone raises his eyebrows. "Let's just say ... where there's smoke, there's fire, eh?"

He is probably just stirring. Uncle looks about to say something and then closes his mouth, choosing not to push the point.

An old silver sedan rattles past, its dented boot unable to close properly. The car slows down in front of the house, and the men on the mat sit up, alert. The passenger in the front seat winds the window down, and a muffled Fijian pop song bursts forth.

The driver peers out behind the passenger.

"*Bula*, Uncle, *bula*, Aunty!" he calls.

It is a man they all know from Mataqai.

After a brief rundown of the island's news and a promise to visit later, the car drives off, a loud backfire popping in its wake.

Seru gives the final coconut shell of *yaqona* to his uncle, claps definitively, and then pushes the empty bucket aside. He sits down next to Isikeli and Epeli and the boys break off into a slurred, whispered conversation.

Isikeli wants to go back to the Chamberlain Street house, he says, where the *Kai Idia* live. He wants to do a more thorough job this time. Seru isn't convinced. Isikeli outlines his reasoning: they know there's expensive stuff to grab; they've seen it. They know the dog is *lamu*, a scaredy-cat. They know what time the *Kai Idia* couple go to bed. And they know how to jump the fence.

Epeli tut-tuts loudly. He never joins them on their night adventures, instead preferring pious disapproval. The boys ignore him and discuss how they can jack open the grill, unscrew it from the window, and enter the house this time. They will need a proper crowbar and pliers. It's bold, but they know they are ready for things to go to the next level.

Epeli shakes his head. "You're gonna get in trouble one day."

"*Oooo*, are they your *Mosi* and *Mosa*?" Seru teases him with the Hindi words for aunty and uncle.

Isikeli chuckles; it's been a while since anyone has made a reference to Epeli's questionable parentage. He has a pointier nose than the rest of them, and straighter hair. The kids on the island all used to tease him relentlessly about being "half-half." There was a rumor that Epeli's real father was a *Kai Idia* driver, the one who worked for the family where his mother was a housegirl. They used to taunt him – *Lialia Kai Idia!* – until Epeli would launch at them, rugby tackling them to the ground. Nothing gets a rise out of Epeli more than hinting about an Indian father.

Tonight, however, Epeli remains coolly restrained. He shrugs. "Don't come to me when you get caught."

Isikeli ignores him and says to the others that they should do it next Tuesday. This will leave enough time for the couple's sense of cautiousness after the first break-in to begin to wear off.

"*Io*," says Seru. "That's smart."

They sit in meditative silence.

"But Keli?" Seru frowns.

"*Io*."

"Fiji plays the All Blacks on Tuesday."

Isikeli falls silent for a moment.

"We'll do it on Wednesday, eh?"

Friday

RISHIKA LOVES the haggle and heckle of the early morning market. She steps out of the taxi to find a cacophony of friendly banter – iTaukei, Hindi, Chinese, and English. Outside the official market shed, rugs are laid out on the sidewalk, laden with little heaps of mangoes in various shades of ripeness. The vendors sit cross-legged on the concrete, chuckling, flirting, competing with one another. She walks around two iTaukei men lying in their wheelbarrows, hands behind their heads as if in hammocks. One of them has his high-visibility vest – a safety requirement by the council – draped across his eyes as a shield from the glare, trying to sleep. She smiles; she will pay them later to carry her shopping.

To Rishika, the market is a vestige of humanness. It has spirit, deliberately escaping order, despite the very best efforts of the council to contain it, to stop it from spilling out onto the streets, to make it *taxable*.

As always, she avoids the stinky area where the fish market is situated (Rishika is allergic to fish). She does a round of the stalls, examining the quality of the vegetables and comparing the prices.

"*Aap kaise*?" she asks the elderly Indo-Fijian man, as she inspects a shiny eggplant.

"Right, *hai*. How are you?"

"Right, *hai*," she smiles.

"*Bula*," she says to the young iTaukei woman sitting on a wooden crate behind her stall.

Rishika sniffs one of her pineapples and picks a spiky green leaf, which gives way immediately. "Mmm, nice. *Vica*?"

"Five dollar bundle, Aunty."

This performance is redundant, really, because she knows what she is going to buy from whom before she arrives. She comes to the market every third day with a plan of what she is going to cook for that day's lunch and dinner, tomorrow's, and the next day's. It is the same people here every week, with the produce changing predictably from season to season. She does this little perusal because she has always done it, and because her mother used to do it when Rishika held her hand as a little girl. Rishika still remembers the feeling of awe as she walked with her mother amongst the tables of vivid color; the makeshift wooden shelves filled with orange pumpkin halves, pyramids of green-topped tomatoes, trays of knobbly brown ginger.

For the bulk of Rishika's childhood, her mother seemed tractable, without personality. She always blindly followed traditions and acquiesced to the demands of the men in her life; her father, her husband, her son. Her only real trait, it seemed to Rishika, was constant whingeing to her daughter about aches and pains, many of which were biologically dubious ("my hair hurts," she said on more than one occasion). And yet, whenever her mother stepped into the market, she transformed into someone confident and decisive. She always scrutinized, smelled, and squeezed each vegetable to ensure it was exactly the level of ripeness and quality she required. The same could be said of her mother in the kitchen – there, she knew how to flavor and sauté and pickle and cure. She bossily shooed her husband away whenever he tried to taste it before it was ready. Everyone knew that food was her mother's kingdom.

Now Rishika is the one who buys the vegetables, who says "No, that's too many, only half that" and hands over the money confidently. She still gets a feeling sometimes of *"look at me, being all grown up!"*

When Rishika has bought what she needs, she begins to make her way out of the market through the narrow, dirt-encrusted aisles. A breeze drifts past her, carrying a seaweedy whiff of fish. She feels nausea building up inside and she dry retches. She quickly makes her way onto the street, placing the shopping down at her feet and gulping in the fresh air.

If she is honest with herself, Rishika isn't actually allergic to fish. It is just that she holds them responsible for her fifth miscarriage – the last one, the most hurtful one – and her body reminds her of this in a visceral, *vomity* way.

It was several years ago, just after her thirty-fifth birthday, long after they had given up trying. She was over two weeks late, and she was never late. She hadn't told Vijay. She hadn't even gone to the chemist and done the test yet; she didn't want to jinx it in any way. She was at a pre-election staff party – one of the rare ones Vijay was invited into rather than waiting in the car park. She was wearing her favorite sari, in beautiful twilight purple with spirals of embroidered silver.

Ratu Lewanivanua, opposition leader at the time, shook her hand and said, *"Bula vinaka*, Rishika. You look beautiful." She was chuffed that he remembered her name. "Thank you, Uncle," she said.

Vijay smiled through gritted teeth, "We call him *Ratu*, Rishika."

That evening she felt extra hungry, which she knew was a *symptom* and she treasured this realization like a lovely little secret. And it was a good night to be hungry. There were trays of "Pacific fusion" finger food: slices of wagyu steak on taro chips; mini chicken tacos with pawpaw salsa; and Japanese soup spoons filled with *kakoda*, Rishika's favorite, thinly chopped snapper in salty, lemony, coconut cream. She kept stopping the waiters for spoon after spoon of the fish. Then she sat down on one of the wicker chairs feeling full and happy. An older iTaukei woman, the wife of one of the shadow ministers, sat down next to her and they chatted away happily; their husbands both lost in the crowd. They giggled together about the good-looking waiter and shared notes on what was in that pawpaw salsa. When the woman asked her the inevitable, "And how many children do you have, dear?" Rishika couldn't help herself. Finally she had an acceptable answer to the question that had been taunting her for years.

"I'm pregnant!" she shared with the complete stranger. The woman cooed and said that was wonderful and then told her she thought Rishika was going to have a little boy. This was a good sign, Rishika thought; iTaukei *bubu* tend to know these things.

But that evening, in the car on the way home, Rishika started to feel a strong pain in her lower back. Upon arrival, with a sense of dread, she rushed to the washroom. And there, sure enough, was a spot of blood, soon followed by a bloody clot in the toilet. She sat down against the toilet door and wept in silence, her pretty purple sari crumpling around her. Then she wiped her eyes, adjusted her facial expression, and went back into the bedroom. Vijay was undressing for bed. She didn't want to tell him – she didn't want to see his face fall, or find out if he felt betrayed that she hadn't even told him she was pregnant. He had probably stopped caring. He never talked about it anymore.

And for some reason, Rishika's body blamed the fish. She can never stomach the smell now, let alone eat *kokoda*.

"Want me to carry those for you, *marama*?" The wheelbarrow guy interrupts her thoughts, pointing to the plastic bags at her feet.

"Oh! Yes," she says gratefully, "just to the taxi stand, please."

Rishika hears the intercom buzz and pushes open the gate to her cousin Lakshmi's house. She walks across the concrete front yard lined with potted plants, stepping over an action figurine with its arm missing. At the door, she takes a deep breath and fixes a smile on her face.

The door swings open by itself before she even has a chance to knock. "Aunty!" beams Arveen, pointing a fluorescent orange gun at her head. "*Piew piew piew!*"

Rishika clutches at her heart before kneeling gingerly on the doormat and dying a careful, lady-like death against the doorframe.

The little boy shrieks with laughter. "I'm a trickster, Aunty! I got you!"

She gets to her feet, and he leads her down the immaculate tiles of the hallway.

Her cousin appears at the doorway of the kitchen, baby Karishma perched on her hip. "*Kaise?*"

Rishika holds her hands out to grab the baby. "*Thik hai*. What a big girl now," she cooes.

"That's because you haven't seen her in so long," Lakshmi reprimands, handing her over as she goes to put the kettle on. "We haven't seen you since Diwali!"

The Hindu festival of lights is one of Rishika's favorite days of the year. It is a national holiday and Indo-Fijians proudly share their festival with their compatriots. Rishika loves lining her house with flickering candles and twirling the balcony balustrade with fairy lights in the week preceding it. On the day, if Vijay isn't working, they drive to his cousin's village on the outskirts of Suva, where Vijay always plays in the annual "married versus singles" soccer game, inevitably limping off the pitch at some point when they are losing to the fit, young singles side. As the night grows dark, the fireworks from neighboring houses whir and crack and fizzle until midnight, cascading in the sky into millions of shooting stars. Everyone eats themselves silly with brightly colored *barfi*, sweet, milky *laddoo*, and syrupy *gulab jaamun*. Local kids come to the gate and call, "Uuuuuncle! Aaaaaunty!" until they are sent away with handfuls of sweets. And every year, poor old Solomon hides under the bench on the balcony, whining at the fireworks, until Rishika can convince Vijay to let him come inside the house.

Last year on Diwali, Rishika and Vijay accepted an invitation to a dinner party that Lakshmi and her husband, Sachin, were hosting. Always the businessman, Sachin invited several of his work associates, including an Australian client and his wife, who he introduced as Mr and Mrs Basinger. All the women fussed around the table, unwrapping the cling wrap from the curries, checking the rice cooker, preparing juice from packets of tangy powdered cordial. Mrs Basinger gushed over how wonderful the food smelled and tugged self-consciously at her peach-colored sari, not used to revealing her midriff. The women asked her where she'd bought her sari from, and then shook their heads gravely over how much she'd paid for it. "You could have gotten it for half that price at Modi's Bazaar!" Lakshmi tut-tutted. "I'll take you next time, *acha?*"

Rishika caught snatches of the men's conversation in the loungeroom. They were drinking whiskey and talking, predictably, about politics and real estate. She heard one of them say that Le-wanivanua's government was taxing businesses too heavily, which was scaring away investors. One of them was considering buying land on the Coral Coast but lamented that there wasn't enough freehold land for sale. Another said that the squatters on the city's outskirts were ruining the economy and that "*jaati-log* needed to quit complaining and pull themselves up by the bootstraps." Sachin jokingly suggested that Vijay should mention some of these things to the prime minister, "talk some sense into him," then he laughed. "But you're just the driver." Sachin was sharing his most expensive whiskey, presumably for the benefit of the Australian man.

The story of Sachin's financial success is one that Rishika has heard like a broken record: never from Sachin himself, but from Lakshmi, from Vijay, from a local newspaper write-up about him. Sachin began his career as a graduate accountant in Jogia Holdings Group, a company run by the well-known family of the same name. They are seemingly involved in everything – clothing, packaging, distribution of food and beverages, tourism. Mr Jogia saw "potential" in Sachin and hand-picked him to be senior auditor at the age of thirty-one. Now at forty-seven, he is the youngest chief financial officer ever in the company. He is billed to take it over in a couple of years (because, it is rumored, Jogia Junior has a bit of a gambling problem).

Lakshmi always used to tell Vijay and Rishika about Sachin's latest purchases: the house in Domain, a Mercedes-Benz, the first of its model to be imported into Fiji. Rishika once quipped to Vijay that Lakshmi was desperately trying to "keep up with the Jo-gias," which – back then – made Vijay splutter his tea in laughter.

Sachin's success didn't affect his friendship with Vijay. They would often hang out and watch soccer over a glass of whiskey – they probably saw each other more often than Rishika saw her

cousin. And Sachin always invited them to his parties, even as
the other guests rose in profile. Rishika never particularly enjoyed
these events, but she came because she adored Sachin and Lakshmi's children with a complicated, painful love. On Diwali, their
littlest two were being looked after by the nanny, who was under strict instructions to keep them in the playroom. At one point,
Arveen escaped her clutches and ran around the adults' table with
no pants on while the nanny ran after him in uncomfortable pur-
suit. The older two boys, Naveen and Raveen, now eleven and sixteen, got bored by the adult conversation at the dinner table and
took their plates to eat in their bedrooms. Rishika marveled at how
old they seemed – Raveen had a deep voice and said, "No thank
you, Aunty," when she offered him sweets. "Raveen!" she said to
Vijay on the drive home. "The little boy who used to play with
Solomon as a puppy!" Vijay grunted half-heartedly. His mood was
settling in at that point, gradually encloaking him.

"I'm sorry I haven't come over lately," Rishika says now to
Lakshmi, carrying the baby on her hip. "I've actually been quite
busy."

Baby Karishma starts to whimper and begins to slip off Rishika's hip. The whimper soon becomes a cry and the girl holds out
her hands to Lakshmi, who swoops the baby away from Rishika.
The girl looks instantly comfortable on Lakshmi's ample, moth-
erly hips.

"Busy with what?"

"Well, I've been researching the story of my ancestor, my
great-great-grandfather."

"Why?"

Rishika was confused by the question. "Why *not*? He was so
interesting. He was a *girmitiya*."

"*Haan, acha*," Lakshmi says, as though unsure why this makes
it interesting. Every Fijian knows the basics of the *girmitiya* story.

Lakshmi herself has a *girmitiya* past. Sachin, however, like the Jogias, is decended from the entrepreneurial Indians who migrated from Gujerat for economic opportunities in the 1930s.

"I mean," Rishika goes on, "the history of the *girmitiyas* is obviously very sad, but it's also really beautiful in some ways."

Lakshmi turns around. "Arveen! Do you need to do a weewee? *Nahi*? Are you sure?" She turns back to Rishika, her face peering out from behind the beaming baby on her lap.

Rishika tries to continue. "Most of the laborers couldn't go back to India. But they did make friends here. Profound, lifelong friendships. They put down roots."

"*Acha*," says Lakshmi, and then she seems to remember something. "I made *lakri* this morning." She jumps up. "Do you want *lakri*?"

"That's okay," Rishika says, but Lakshmi has already bustled to the kitchen, Karishma on her hip. When she returns, she places a small bowl of the sugary sticks on the table.

"*Khao*."

Rishika declines politely. Lakshmi helps herself and bites into one of the crunchy sticks. "What were you saying?"

Rishika gives up. "It doesn't matter," she says. Finding common ground, she asks how Raveen is doing at school. Lakshmi's children go to the International School with the mostly expat children and the Australian aligned curriculum.

Lakshmi's eyes shine as she tells her cousin each of Raveen's marks in his recent exams. "He wants to be a doctor."

Rishika stares at her. "But he always wanted to be a vet!" She is aware of a higher pitched tone creeping into her voice.

Lakshmi shrugs. "He decided to be a doctor now. More jobs."

Rishika gives her cousin a thin smile.

The two continue talking, Lakshmi recounting and Rishika affirming.

Later when Rishika gets up to leave, Lakshmi asks her a favor. "Can you come and stay with me on Wednesday?"

Rishika looks at her cousin blankly.

"Because Sachin is going to some work event with his boss. And the nanny can't come." Her cousin looks doe-eyed, imploring. "I will get scared at home alone with the kids. The cyclone is coming."

Rishika cannot think of a reason to decline. "Sure," she says. *It's not like Vijay will notice I'm gone, anyway.*

At that moment, Rishika sees a quick movement in her peripheral vision and she screams, taking a step back. It's just Arveen, jumping out from behind the couch in a Spider-Man mask. Heart pounding and embarrassed, she takes a long slow breath. She is so on edge these days.

※

HANNAH AND RUCI, the outreach nurse, are still waiting at half past ten.

"He's not coming," Ruci says. She is dressed in a crisp, white uniform with blue epaulettes and a white nurse's cap. There is something elegantly 1950s about it, except for the imitation Prada handbag she carries her medical gear in.

"He definitely said he'd meet me here at ten." Hannah looks around to get her bearings. They are outside the SupaValu supermarket, and the roundabout is just over there.

The nurse rolls her eyes at Hannah. "Fiji Time, eh?"

Hannah first learned about this concept of Fiji Time in the compulsory "Fijian Culture for Australian Development Volunteers" workshop in Canberra before she came. It was right after the catered lunch, in the same session as learning about the importance of taking your shoes off before you enter Fijian houses. Fiji Time is the idea that iTaukei have a sort of loose concept of time and punctuality. It means that emails don't get responded to, and meetings are often delayed, sometimes never happening. People use the term in different ways. Some of her Fijian colleagues use it to casually mock themselves when they have a lazy day. Once, when Hannah arrived sweaty and panting because she was late for a staff meeting, her colleagues all looked at her in amusement, as though her rushing around was novel and quaint. Ethan talks about Fiji Time with a kind of cynical admiration – it is permanent permission for everyone to be a bit late all the time, which he thinks is liberating. But Hannah regularly hears other people talk about Fiji Time in a bitter, jaded kind of way ("How can the country get ahead if the people don't have any *professionalism?*").

"He seemed really keen for us to see his grandma," Hannah says disappointedly. She looks down at her clipboard where she has written his name down. *Isikeli Tiko.* She checks her phone to see if he has accepted her friend request, but he hasn't.

Ruci shrugs. "He's a squatter, eh? Too much *yaqona*. They get lazy."

"What a shame," Hannah says.

They begin to walk the route for today, to several of Ruci's regular home-visit patients in the southeastern corner of Paradise Estate.

Hannah tries to make small talk. Ruci is largely unresponsive and checks her phone. Until this morning, Hannah has only spoken to Ruci twice. The nurse has always been perfectly civil, but Hannah has the distinct impression that Ruci resents her. She doesn't know why.

As the two women walk along the narrow, winding dirt paths, Hannah marvels at the closeness of the small houses. Perched on top of some are pay television dishes, which surprises her (*is it really poverty if you have pay TV?*). Several people sit on rickety verandahs and smile in greeting: *"Bula*, Sister!" they say to the nurse. Two Indo-Fijian children peer out at them from the dark interior of one of the houses. Hannah gives them a little wave and they smile coyly before retreating back into the shadows.

"This is the first house," Ruci suddenly stops. "Two families live here." The shack is cobbled together out of mismatched tin and iron sheets, a colorful, rusted patchwork. Some of the metal patches are old signs. Hannah can make out faded, outdated logos for Shell Petroleum and an old red STOP sign. She wonders whether this is out of resourceful necessity or a house-proud, creative touch.

She follows Ruci's lead and slips off her shoes at the door (*is it okay if my socks smell?*). Grateful for the advice from her colleagues, she retrieves the *sulu* she packed in her bag – a touristy sarong with a floral pattern – and wraps it around her waist in modest respect. Like Ruci, she bows her head as she enters.

Inside the house is a small room, with an even smaller room off to the side. Quiet, canned laughter from a Filipino sitcom emanates from an old television in the corner. Two men sit on the mat and are introduced to Hannah. One looks to be in his early seventies while the other is younger, perhaps in his late fifties – obviously brothers. They smile warmly and say, *"Bula vinaka."* A large, grandmotherly woman – their sister – is feeding a little baby with a bottle on the sofa. The woman shuffles herself and the child over to make space for the visitors. Hannah politely declines the seat and chooses instead to sit on the mat with the men. She wants to immerse herself in the experience.

Ruci begins talking to them in Fijian. In the middle of her monologue, she starts pointing at Hannah. She can hear *FijiHealth*, and *na mate ni suka*. The men look at Hannah, smile, and say, *"Vinaka, vinaka."* Ruci continues talking for a while, and then stops.

Everyone is looking at Hannah.

"Do I …?" She looks at Ruci. "Should I start?"

Ruci looks at her unsmilingly. "Yes, you ask your questions, I do their check-up, eh?" Ruci pulls out a small blood sugar machine and attaches a clasp to one of the older man's fingers.

"Okay, so …" Hannah opens her clipboard. "Like Ruci says, we are doing some research so that we can understand your perspective on diabetes and your experiences with it. We want to know how we can provide better health services and information on this issue."

The older man blinks. The younger man responds, "*Io*. The health, eh?"

Hannah nods and smiles. "Here's an information sheet that explains what it's all about." She hands two sheets to the men and reaches one of the sheets over to the woman on the sofa. The woman smiles and directs her head toward her brothers, as if to say, *not me! Them*. Hannah smiles back. "You sure? Okay, no worries." She slips the sheet back into the plastic sleeve of her folder.

The men peruse the white paper in front of them. From her ethics training, Hannah knows she needs to explain it all in plain language. She puts the folder aside and begins. "So … um … you don't have to participate in this research if you don't want to. You can pull out at any time and I won't ask any more questions. We're going to use what you say as part of our research, and maybe some publications. Um, what else? We won't tell anyone that you participated, and your name won't be attached to anything. So you can be as honest as you like!" She beams at them. "You can tell us exactly what you think. Do you have any questions?"

The men look at her and then look back at the sheet.

"No?" She fills the silence.

The men raise their eyebrows.

"Um … great! So, if you could just sign a consent form to say you are willing to participate?" She reveals more forms. "And do you mind if I record our interview? You just have to check the box there …"

The men stare at the sheet blankly. Hannah crawls over to their side of the mat to show exactly where to sign and check the box. They sign it, and Hannah feels a little glimmer of relief. The older man hands the forms back, and asks the nurse something in Fijian.

Hannah asks, "Is everything okay?"

"*Io,*" the nurse says. "He was just asking what 'participate' means."

Right, thinks Hannah. *This is going well.* She lays the digital voice recorder in front of them and turns it on, its little red light piercing the darkened room.

Hannah proceeds to ask the men general questions. The younger man answers for them both in stilted English. He explains that fourteen people live in this house. Seven are adults, three finished high school, two have paid work. They moved to Paradise Estate ten years ago from an outer island after the two brothers had a fight with the chief in their village, and they feared retribution.

Hannah writes notes in her spiral-bound notepad, in case of any technical failures with the recorder. *This is so fascinating!* she thinks. *Chiefs and fights!*

"Okay, good." She smiles, and then looks up. She feels she is already starting to have a nice rapport with them. "Now I would like to ask you about *na mate ni suka*. Is diabetes a big problem here, in this community, in Paradise Estate?"

The younger man raises his eyebrows.

"Sorry …" said Hannah. "By that do you mean, it *is* a problem?"

The younger man raises his eyebrows again. The older man just blinks.

"Right." She hovers over her notepad and eventually writes [*No? Unclear*].

It occurs to Hannah that the older man may not understand what she is saying. She addresses Ruci. "Could you please translate this? *What causes diabetes?*"

Ruci speaks to the men in Fijian. This time, the older man's eyes light up with understanding. He launches into a long and animated story. At one point, he puts both hands up and wiggles all of his fingers, as though miming "rain," and then, for some reason, he mimes looking over his shoulder in fear. At the end of his monologue, he laughs infectiously, revealing that all four of his top front teeth are missing. Hannah can't help but laugh too.

She looks at Ruci for the translation.

"He said diabetes is caused by too much sugar."

Hannah's smile drops. "Is that what he said? Is that *all* he said?"

"*Io,*" Ruci says.

With the help of Ruci's curt translation, Hannah asks the men about their diets, what they think are healthy and unhealthy foods, and what they eat on a normal day. The men talk about fruits and green vegetables. They say you should avoid sweet biscuits and white bread and soft drinks. They say they have tea (no sugar in it) and root vegetables like *dalo* for breakfast. They talk about exercise and not getting fat.

Eventually, Hannah wraps up the interview, thanks them, and gives them each a five-dollar SupaValu voucher for their time. Ruci unclasps the machine from the woman's finger and has a look at a small sore on her leg. She takes out a ziplock bag with medication in it and gives it to the woman, speaking sharply at her with matronly instructions.

After they leave the house, Hannah – exhausted – tries to make sense of the encounter. "So … it sounds like they have a relatively healthy diet, at least."

Ruci looks at her. "She's going to lose that leg soon, eh?"

"Pardon?"

"The woman? Her leg has an infection. From diabetes, eh?"

"She has diabetes?!" exclaims Hannah.

"*Io*, she and the old man. Those two have diabetes."

"I thought they said it wasn't a problem for them."

Ruci raises her eyebrows. Hannah is perplexed. She processes this new information.

"Will she go to the hospital, then, for her leg?"

"*Sega*, she doesn't want to."

"Oh," says Hannah.

Ruci sighs. "She's been treating the wound with pawpaw leaves. Some of the old people think that helps. Traditional medicine, eh? Then when they get to hospital, the leg gets amputated."

"Oh. Right."

"She needs antibiotics. We don't have any in stock. But it's too late anyway, eh? I could smell the flesh. It's starting to rot. I just gave her paracetamol. For the pain."

The thought of rotting flesh makes Hannah queasy. She has read about diabetes infections in science journals, of course, but it feels different when she's faced with it. She keeps walking in silence, watching her step on the rocky path.

The nurse has become surprisingly chatty. "Their blood sugar was dangerous, eh? Very high. That man had a reading of twenty."

"That's bad?" queries Hannah.

"That's bad."

"But they *said* all the right things," Hannah says. "They talked about green vegetables and taro for breakfast, and, like, exercise."

Ruci laughs – the first laugh where she looks genuinely amused. "They don't want to tell you the truth," she says. "Did you see the biscuit packet in the bin? And the cigarette butts? They don't care."

"Oh," says Hannah again.

She tags along with Ruci to five more households, two of them with Indo-Fijian families and iTaukei families in the other three. Each of her visits are the same. People are friendly enough, but they tell her what they think she wants to hear – health messages recited like rote-learned jingles. *Eat well, don't eat sugar, quit smoking, do exercise!* And then, when Hannah and Ruci leave each house, Ruci tells her that this woman has diabetes; that boy's grandfather just died from kidney failure; this man has high blood sugar; and so on and so on.

In the taxi on the way back to the office, Hannah's back is aching from sitting cross-legged on mats for so long. They are driving through an industrial area, past warehouses and yards of recycled wood. She thinks about the people she just met and blushes, imagining they are all laughing at her now. Ruci certainly is.

The Indo-Fijian taxi driver is staring at her through the rear-view mirror. A little figurine – a plastic Hawaiian girl with a grass skirt and flower behind her ear – is bobbing on the dashboard, dancing with the movement of the car.

"You shouldn't go to Paradise alone, *janta*. It's not safe for a girl like you."

Hannah knocks softly on the door of Dr Sireli's office.

He looks up from his computer, peering worriedly over crooked reading glasses. His face relaxes into a smile when he sees her.

"*Io*, Hannah. How was your day in the field?"

"It was good," she says out of habit, and then decides to be honest. "Actually, it was a bit … overwhelming."

"*Isa*," he says. "Sit down."

She sits down on the old office chair. A dusty framed picture of Jesus sits on his desk – shafts of light illuminating his thorny crown. She wants to tell her boss about her tensions with Ruci, but decides against it. It is hard to explain, and it might seem a bit ungrateful of her, or even a bit culturally insensitive. Instead, she tells him all about her experiences with the participants, the way people are friendly but wary. As a result, she feels like she hasn't gotten particularly useful data.

"*Io*." Dr Sireli nods. He looks at her thoughtfully. "They're ashamed, eh? They think you're going to get angry with them." He apologizes for not having discussed this with her earlier. In his softly spoken way, he helps Hannah to understand. He talks about how in both iTaukei and Indo-Fijian cultures, people are very respectful – even fearful – of authority, which includes doctors and nurses and, by extension, public health researchers. He says that shame plays a big part in the village, and people will go to great lengths to save face. She will need to develop strategies to gain her participants' trust to have them share their experiences honestly with her. He gives her some suggestions: for example, developing a rapport with a "key informant" from inside the Paradise community to assist with the research, who isn't associated with the nurse.

That boy Isikeli would have been helpful, Hannah thinks regretfully.

Dr Sireli takes off his glasses and rubs his eyes, before putting them back on and turning back to his computer. He moves his mouse around – click, click – and squints at the screen. Suddenly the old printer near the window begins to whir and hammer, feeding out pages at an achingly slow pace.

He gets up and walks toward the printer. "Read these, eh?" He staples and hands over two academic articles. The toner is nearly depleted, so the text is a barely legible light gray. "Not now – just when you get a chance. We'll talk about them early next week, before you go into the field again."

"Thanks, Dr Sireli," Hannah says, and slips them into her bag.

"And no worries, eh? These are lessons we all learn when we start research."

She feels a little bit better. Some of the despondency she felt earlier has dissipated with his kind words. She gets up to go, wishing him a good weekend.

"*Vinaka*, Hannah, you too. God bless." He smiles and looks back at his computer.

"May God also bless you as well!" she adds, bowing for some reason. She closes the door softly behind her, leaning against it. *May God also bless you as well*?! *You idiot, Hannah Wilson.*

ISIKELI IS dreaming of his father. They are walking in a shopping mall past jewelery shops, chemists, and hairdressers. It looks like the shopping mall in downtown Suva, yet Isikeli can feel it rocking back and forth, so he knows it is a ship floating on water. His father pulls him into a sports store. Isikeli tries on a pair of green studded rugby boots, and they fit perfectly. The shop attendant, who suddenly seems to be Isikeli's grade eight rugby coach, insists that he tries on an enormous boot that is three sizes too big. "You need some room to grow into them," the coach is saying, but Isikeli isn't listening because an owl is flying around the room. The wide-eyed bird seems to be staring at him from every angle, swooping viciously close to his head. Isikeli tries to tell his father, but his father just grabs his shoulder, shaking it roughly and slapping his cheek. "Keli. Keli. *Keli*!"

It isn't his dad's voice. He knows it from somewhere. *Who is it?*
"ISIKELI!"

His eyes flick open and adjust to the light. His sister Mere's face comes into focus, staring at him angrily. "Get up. Come home." She begins walking away.

A lightning bolt of fear strikes his stomach. *Something's happened to Bu.*

"*Na cava?*" He asks urgently, stumbling after her, head spinning. But nothing is wrong. Mere has been looking for him for an hour, until Jone told her he was at Uncle's house.

Mere needs Isikeli to look after Eta today. She has been offered a two-day job as a housegirl for an Indo-Fijian family that is hosting a party and needs extra help cleaning and preparing. Her friend is their regular housegirl and recommended Mere to the family.

When they arrive back at Bu's house, Eta is perched on her scooter on the front step, sucking on a lollipop. She raises her eyebrows as Isikeli approaches.

"*Yadra*, cheeky girl," he says, and ruffles her hair.

He walks inside the house, bowing as he sees his grandmother. She is sitting on the mat massaging the stump of her leg with coconut oil. "*Yadra*, Bu, you okay?" He flops down cross-legged on the mat beside her.

"*Yadra*, Isikeli," she says in a wary voice. "Where were you last night?"

He is pleased to have an answer she would like. "You know Seru's uncle?"

Bu raises her eyebrows. "Mm-mm."

"His house. We were drinking *yaqona* with them."

Her face softens. "*Isa*. How's the wife?"

"She's good, Bu."

"*Vinaka*." Bu smiles.

Mere flusters around to each of the neighbor's houses, trying to borrow an iron to press her only blouse. Finally dressed, she hurries out the door giving Eta a sniff on her forehead and telling Isikeli not to do anything stupid. A mist of sickly-sweet deodorant lingers behind her as she runs for the bus.

Isikeli tries again – unsuccessfully – to convince Bu to take her medication. But no luck. He throws a towel over his shoulder and begins walking to the shower block. Behind him, Eta keeps falling off her scooter on the uneven ground. Isikeli stops on the path. "Put the scooter inside the house, eh?" he calls, *someone will steal it if we leave it out front.* She does so obediently as he waits patiently for her to return. She then pads along barefooted behind him.

As he often does, Isikeli wonders when Eta's father – Etuate – is coming back. Etuate was studying at Fiji National University and living on campus when he kissed Mere on the dance floor at Uptown nightclub. After that he visited Mere's house in Paradise two or three times. He was nice enough to Isikeli and dutifully respectful toward Bu. Mere seemed so proud and happy with him – she was even nice to Isikeli in those days. When Mere fell pregnant four months later, Etuate talked about finishing his university degree, taking her back to his village, and marrying her. He was going to start a *yaqona* business, he said, because that was what everyone was talking about these days. They say it's a good return on investment because there is so much demand for it, even overseas.

But then Etuate was told he could earn money picking fruit in Australia. They told him he could earn twice as much there as he could doing any professional job here. He was doing it for Mere and the baby, he said. It was only temporary. It was for their future.

He left one month before Eta was born. Mere wept for days. Bu said that's why Eta came out early and purple, screaming into the world in the hallway of the Colonial War Memorial Hospital. Over Skype, Etuate shed tears of joy for his "little princess." Isikeli knew this because he held the phone up for his sister at the time, so that she could hold baby Eta up for her daddy to see. Etuate wired Mere some money for a pram, but he was not earning as much as he expected. He didn't get paid by the hour, but by bucket of grapes. They hadn't told him how long it would take to fill up a bucket.

Etuate's calls to Mere became less and less frequent and eventually stopped. Last Isikeli heard, he had overstayed his visa and is now hiding out in a caravan park somewhere in regional Victoria. Whenever Mere's phone pings, Isikeli sees the look of hope that lights up momentarily in her eyes.

Now, under the dribble of cold water, Isikeli thinks to himself, *when Etuate does come back, I'm going to beat his fucking face until it's unrecognizable.*

Isikeli uses a fork to scrape out a can of watery tuna onto three plates, sharing what is left of yesterday's white bread. As the kettle begins to whistle, he takes the plates to the mat; one for Bu, one for Eta, and one for himself. He grabs a cup from the shelf, flips in a tea bag and some powdered milk. He shovels in one teaspoon of sugar, then two, then three – just like Bu likes it. He knows she is supposed to be having less sugar. Mere and his aunties are constantly trying to limit her intake. No one has ever told him *why* sugar is bad for her, or what it will actually do to her body. It can't be *that* bad, surely. Or it can't get that much worse than it already is. Besides, Isikeli knows that sugar in her tea is the one thing that brings her comfort, a small reminder of the quality of life she once had.

He slops in hot water, carefully placing the cup beside Bu.

"*Masu mada,*" she says, and Isikeli sits beside her with eyes closed solemnly. He loves listening to Bu's powerful voice in prayer, the words rolling off her tongue as if *Turaga Jisu* is just a few feet away; as if she knows exactly what needs to be said. She thanks Him for the food on the table and the hands who have prepared it. She asks Him to protect Mere at her work, and to forever guard Na, Isikeli and Eta.

"*Emeni*," she finishes.

"*Emeni*," Isikeli echoes.

Bu leans over and gives Eta a light slap on her arm. "Your eyes were open again."

The little girl's eyes widen.

Isikeli grins at his grandmother. "How do you know her eyes were open, Bu?"

Bu gives a low chuckle, now slapping Isikeli's leg. Eta looks between them and her face relaxes in relief.

Isikeli looks at the two favorite women in his life, eating their tuna sandwiches. He is surprised by a sudden wrench of fear. *Turaga Jisu*, he prays, *please don't let anything happen to Bu.*

His mind suddenly recalls the Australian girl. What is her name? Anna? *Hannah.* She said she works for FijiHealth. He has seen so many do-gooders come through the settlement. He has even taken part in "interviews" and "focus groups" with them before; starry eyed *Kai Valagi* from UN Habitat, World Bank, and universities in Auckland, Tokyo, Canberra. They are all research-ing "housing security" or "water and sanitation." They all trip over themselves to be culturally sensitive and seem fascinated by his answers. They usually give him a supermarket voucher or mobile phone credit for his time. And then they just disappear. He never finds out what happens to his stories.

This girl is different though; she's a medical person. She is probably a doctor. She might actually help Bu. Maybe she has a new treatment for Bu, or maybe she can move Bu up the waiting list. Or maybe she will just be able to give them money. He needs to friend her on Facebook. He needs a phone.

Seru told him once that it is good to know Australians. A friend of Seru's uncle – a shoe-shine boy – befriended an elderly

Australian couple back in the eighties when the couple strayed from the day trips organized by their cruise ship. He met the tourists on the street, inviting them back to his house in the settlement where his wife fed them her famous beef *sui*. He said the Australian man wore very short shorts, and his legs were as white as coconut flesh. The couple – so the story goes – were so "shocked by the poverty," so "impressed by his and his wife's generosity," and so "grateful for the authentic experience" that they remained in touch. In fact, they wired money back to him every month for the next ten years. Isikeli knew of other examples of this kind of *sponsorship*. So whenever he sees a *Kai Valagi*, in the back of his mind he thinks: potential. "And remember," Seru said, "they like authentic, eh?"

Isikeli remembers there was a vague arrangement to meet the girl on the corner at some point. *Did she say a time?* Because that was another thing about *Kai Valagi*. They really love the time. They slice it up into little pieces and then get very particular about which piece is for what.

He realizes Bu is looking at him. She has just taken the first sip of her tea. "How many sugars in here?" she asks accusingly.

"Three," he says, taking a bite of his bread.

Bu takes another sip of her tea, and squints at him distrustfully. He will have to think about the *Kai Valagi* girl later.

RISHIKA PLACES a bowlful of stale roti and dog food at Solomon's feet, and the dog scoffs it down with a vigor that belies his age. Vijay says he will be home late from work again. Rishika hardly sees him these days. He leaves early in the morning and she is often asleep before he gets home. She is becoming resigned to the solitude. He isn't much company when he is home anyway.

Immersing herself in the history of Arjun helps pass the time. She sits on the balcony bench and clicks her pen a couple of times.

Sugar changed Arjun Naidu.

On the Royapuram railway, Arjun was a happy-go-lucky young man, full of energy, zest, and hope. This faded after the bitter news that he had lost his mother, his childhood sweetheart, and his beloved India.

By day, he continued the drudgery of harvesting sugar under the watchful eye of Harjit; sowing, hacking, bundling, stacking. Sowing, hacking, bundling, stacking. By night, he surrendered to the sweet relief of locally brewed rum. Fights began to break out amongst the Indian laborers over cards and money and women, the vastly outnumbered female laborers on this wild frontier. The newfound camaraderie between the girmitiyas *was strong, but not unbreakable.*

At times, Arjun and his fellow workers were denied food by Raymond the overseer, who gambled away their rations. Their ribs began to show until they were literally starving. They looked longingly at the smoke curling up from the nearby iTaukei village when a feast was taking place. Sometimes, when Harjit and Raymond weren't in sight, women from the village crossed the creek to smuggle food wrapped in banana leaves to the famished laborers. It must have looked a funny sight – tall, broad-shouldered iTaukei women making offerings to skinny little Indian men, who bowed their heads in hungry gratitude.

The always-obliging Harjit, tripping over himself to please Raymond, placed one of the young and pretty Indian girls, Ram Raji, so that she was working close to Raymond's estate. Every few days, Raymond would stray over to her and suggest through whiskey-laden breath that she come and help him inside the house. Arjun dared not stare, but out of the corner of his eye he saw the look of fear in the girl as she dutifully followed the overseer, and the look on her face when she emerged again, adjusting her sari, unable to lift her eyes.

After months of this display, Arjun couldn't take it anymore. He hitched a ride on a horse and cart to visit a European called Darcy on a nearby plantation who had a reputation for being fair. He knew it was risky – many men before him had tried to bring claims against their overseers and sardars, *but these were rarely successful, and would often result in the claimants being beaten badly or given the worst jobs. But in Arjun's broken English and mime (including some undignified pelvic thrusting) he communicated the story to Darcy.*

Harjit received a lashing for his role in the affair, and Arjun never saw him again. Raymond was redeployed to another plantation, but not before he had delivered one final blow to Arjun's stomach, leaving him doubled over next to the bundles of cane, while his friends averted their eyes in paralyzed horror.

And so it was that Arjun took Ram Raji as his wife, cobbling together a small wedding ceremony out of the little they had. At the end of their ten-year contracts the couple had saved enough to start a small vegetable farm, and they sold their produce at the markets for a small but steadily growing profit.

Arjun and Ram Raji went on to have six children who were fed and clothed and schooled. In fact, the oldest boy started a little corner store and eventually built a successful supermarket. Of my parent's genera-tion – the great-grandchildren of Arjun and Ram Raji – only a few have remained in Fiji while most have migrated to Australia, Canada, New Zealand, and the United States.

She looks up from her book, her eyes turning to the palm trees, motionless in the stifling air. Solomon is looking at the trees, too, on guard and alert. He has probably seen his nemesis, the bat.

In some ways, Arjun "made it." He and his Indian brothers did find the better economic opportunities they sailed halfway around the world for. Out of the barren countryside of Royapu-ram to the Fijian suburbs, via the cane fields. But that, Rishika feels, is more a credit to the human spirit than to the trickery and deception that was thinly veiled as a *girmit*.

She wishes she could write that Arjun found love again with Ram Raji, and that it was a happy marriage.

It wasn't.

This was never explicitly said to Rishika – no one really talked about these things. She has pieced it together from little snippets of conversation she overheard from her grandmother as a child. She knew that Ram Raji would often retrieve Arjun from a friend's house or a bar early in the morning. He would sometimes be wobbly and funny and affectionate, sometimes cantankerous, sometimes passed out. She also knew that Ram Raji often had bruises that she would cover up by bunching and hanging her sari in particular ways; big purply-yellow reminders that dinner should be on the table at the right time or that she shouldn't laugh at Arjun in front of his friends. Arjun's children had permanent scars on their backs from lashings with the belt – for being rude, or late, or bringing shame on their father by doing badly on exams. In turn, this violence was passed down to their children like a family heirloom and shared amongst new partners and their children. It had softened by the time it got to Rishika and her brothers, but it was still there – a permanent kinetic energy between them and their parents. These moments are laughed about flippantly at family gatherings (*we used to get into such trouble! Haha! You kids don't know how easy you've got it these days!*) but they hover in the shadows, ever present. Rishika wonders whether she too might have it in her – this tendency to lash out, this tendency toward violence. She has never been tested, but – under the right conditions – might she also snap?

Arjun was just doing to his family what had been done to him: by the British Raj, by Harjit, by Raymond. It was just a predictable cycle of violence and survival.

She goes to the English dictionary, leading her finger down the
Ts until she finds the word she is looking for:

Trauma /'trɔːmə/ (*n*)
　　1. a deeply distressing or disturbing experience
　　2. (*Medicine*) physical injury.

It makes sense. Arjun and his compatriots were traumatized.
Rishika begins to look up all the synonyms of trauma, a detective following lexical clues. Injury, damage, hurt, wound, cut,
rupture, abrasion. *Abrasion* is the process of scraping or wearing
something away. Abrasion is what happened to Arjun's personality – his peacefulness and hope just *eroded* over time. Ram Raji
herself was traumatized. It's hard to think how their marriage
would have been anything but dysfunctional.

The effects of trauma, Rishika reads, can be long-lasting. They
can be *intergenerational*.

The *girmitiyas* forged a unique identity for themselves when
they came to Fiji. They did away with India's traditional caste
system, creating a new form of equality and a new common language. But they always remained self-conscious about not being
considered "proper Indians." Even today, Indo-Fijian schools
teach official *Shud* Hindi from the motherland, as if students
should mend their "broken" Fijian Hindi, as if their language has
experienced trauma just like its speakers.

And yet, the *girmitiyas* lives were not only made of wounds
and erosions and ruptures. There is beauty in Arjun's story as
well. Rishika tries to capture some of this in the final paragraphs.

Arjun never forgot what the iTaukei village had done for him when he
was starving. He remained in contact and formed an unusual friend-
ship with Ratu, the chief. When Arjun's market garden was doing well,

he would deliver a wooden milk crate of vegetables to the headman. He would visit with Ratu, and the men would drink kava together and talk in their broken English. Arjun would always make the iTaukei men laugh with his slapstick impressions of the British administrators.

Sugar – or, more specifically, rum – killed Arjun Naidu, the boy from Royapuram. He died in 1903 from cirrhosis of the liver at the age of forty-seven. At his funeral service, the makeshift Hindu temple near his house was overflowing with iTaukei from the village, who wailed and sang for their funny Indian friend.

And that is the end of her first draft. Rishika looks up, thinking about that profound, unlikely friendship between Arjun and the chief.

Indians and iTaukei. Two fundamentally different people thrust together, eventually muddling their way out the other side of colonialism to build a country together.

She casts her eyes down the now-darkened street. She can't see any headlights coming; Vijay is a while away yet. "Come on, Solomon," she says. The old dog looks up at the sound of his name. "Let's go inside now."

THE SIGN on the lift says "No working. Use Stares." In other circumstances, Hannah would be amused and send a photo to Jess, but tonight she just sighs and begins to trudge up the five flights of stairs in front of her.

When she finally reaches the top, an iTaukei girl dressed in a kimono greets her with a bow.

"Phew! I'm a bit unfit," Hannah puffs, smiling at the waitress. But she is actually feeling the prickle of heat rash, sweaty and irritated. *Why doesn't anything work here?*

The girl laughs politely. "Table for one, ma'am?"

"No, I'm with …" She looks around the Japanese restaurant. Her eyes rest on Pip, Jess, and Ethan already seated on cushions at the low table near the window. She can't help but smile. After a day of feeling lost in translation and out of place, it is really nice to see her Australian friends. "I'm with those guys."

"Hi, Han," Pip says when Hannah crouches down next to her.

"Han! How was your field trip?" Ethan asks. He pours her a little porcelain cup of thick, clear liquid.

Hannah grins. "We're onto the sake already?"

"Oh, yes. Pip needs it," Ethan says. "She's had a bad day."

"Oh, no." Hannah looks at Pip. "You too?"

"Yep." Pip smiles ruefully. "But tell us about yours first."

Hannah tells them about her strange day in Paradise. The poverty, the friendliness, the unhelpful responses. Ethan and Pip listen attentively and say all the right things like "whoa" and "how fascinating" and "that's so annoying" and "at least your boss is really supportive."

They are intrigued by Ruci's behavior.

"It just seems like she hates me," Hannah says. "I felt like I annoyed her, before she even met me."

"You don't deserve that," Jess says loyally. "She sounds like a biatch."

"Maybe," Ethan says. "Or you could be, like, the billionth Australian volunteer she's had to show around."

Hannah feels stung at first. Then her shoulders deflate. "God. You're probably right."

One by one, their other friends join them at the table, still dressed in their work clothes, red-faced and puffing slightly. Swiss Dave, World Bank Dave, ADB Aaron.

World Bank Dave's glasses are slightly misty from condensation as he sits down on the other side of Pip. Pasepa arrives looking graceful as always, barely having broken a sweat. The nice Dutch-doctor-guy arrives next, and waves, "Hello everybody!"

"Mate! Glad you could join us," says Ethan, his words slurring slightly already.

The waitress helps them join two tables together. Ethan orders another bottle of sake.

When Jean and Michelle appear at the same time, Jess elbows Hannah in the ribs at the scandal of it. Hannah waves her away in irritation. She tries to make meaningful eye contact with Jean, but he sits down and gets caught up in a conversation in French with Swiss Dave.

"So tell us, Pip, why have you had a bad day?" Hannah asks.

"Okay, so remember I was telling you about Buna? Our 'house-girl'? I hate that word, but anyway."

"Oh, yes! That whole story. Tell us," says Jess. Everyone leans in, captivated to hear the next episode in the long-running saga. Pip rents an old colonial house with German Jana, and Buna is the woman in her forties who comes to clean their house four days a week. A few Fridays ago, Pip explained to the volunteers that Buna was diligent and hardworking for the most part but had recently been acting strangely. She had started asking for advances on her pay – fifty dollars here, fifty dollars there. "I mean it's *fine*, right, she always has her reasons," Pip explained. "She needs another school uniform for her daughter, the electricity bill is due, and her husband's been out of work, blah-di-blah-blah." But a month or so ago, she didn't come to work for three days. She called in to cancel on the first day, but then simply didn't arrive on the second and third. When she returned, she explained to Pip that her husband's grandmother's sister had passed away. Pip workshopped this with the volunteers at the time. "She's been helping prepare for the funeral," Pip said. "Apparently they need to prepare all this food for the feast or whatever – like *literally* buy and slaughter the cow and pig – and she's gotta meet the relatives coming in from the airport, and weave the mats and – I don't know, decorate the gravesite or something." At the time, Michelle had nodded. "It's the same thing in Africa, their funerals are massive." And Aaron had said, "Look, I love the whole funeral thing as much as the next guy, but I think there needs to be some limits. I can understand them taking a few days off work for their grandmother's funeral, but this is – what? – the great aunt-*in-law*. Isn't she a bit distant?"

"So *this* week," Pip is saying now, "Buna didn't come to work again yesterday and most of today."

"Here we go," says Aaron.

"Exactly. She didn't call at all. Then she comes in this afternoon, and I was like, what happened? And she said, sorry, it was her turn to host this church meeting or something. Apparently she had to bake for this fundraiser. All day. Both days. And that's fine, *sure*. I would have been happy to give her some leave. I'm a reasonable person! I believe in workers' rights. But the thing is, she didn't let me know in advance."

"Yeah, that's not cool," says World Bank Dave.

"I mean, she said she didn't have credit on her phone, but she could have figured something out." Pip takes another sip of her sake. "And I get it, right?" She glances sidelong at Pasepa. "I do get the whole cultural thing. Church, family obligations, all that stuff, but …"

"Yeah, but there's also Being an Employee," says World Bank Dave. "I mean, she's got a good gig."

Ethan raises his eyebrows. "At five dollars an hour?"

"No, but that's good for Fiji," Pasepa reassures Pip, who looks relieved at her approval.

Dave says, "Yeah. Nah, she's taking the piss."

"Well, exactly," says Pip, gratefully. "That's how I've been feeling. As though she's taking me for a bit of a ride. And I gave her a warning last time, and today, I just thought, I gave her a chance, and she blew it. So, I had to let her go."

"You had to let her go?" Hannah questions.

"Had to let her go," Pip confirms.

"So how did you do it? I mean, what did you say?" Hannah asks.

"Well, I just said she had abused my goodwill and I couldn't rely on her anymore."

"That's totally fair. And?" says World Bank Dave.

"She ... she cried."

Everyone winces.

"Ouch," Jess says.

"*Isa*," says Pasepa.

"And then she left. I actually feel really horrible. You know? She probably needed the job."

"Oh, d'you think?" says Ethan. Hannah shoots him a pointed look.

"It was the hardest thing I've ever done," Pip says.

"Mmm, you poor thing," Jess says, rubbing her arm. "It's so fraught isn't it?"

"It's not fraught!" Michelle says. "It's simple." She puts her hand on Pip's arm. "Hon, she was being unprofessional."

Pip looks at her gratefully. "Thanks, yeah."

"You did the right thing," World Bank Dave assures.

The waitress takes advantage of the pause in the conversation to edge in and ask if they are ready to order. Everyone's attention turns back to the menus. Ethan points at Hannah. "Don't forget our pact." They made a deal a few months back that they would always share dishes for more variety when they eat out. Tonight, they agree on tuna sashimi (the specials board says it was just caught this morning), ebi mayo prawns, and teriyaki chicken. Hannah hopes it comes quickly. She is starting to feel light-headed from the sake.

Pip's story is a gloomy overture that sets a bleak tone for the evening. As the sake flows, they all share stories about the dark side of Suva – its dirty, stifling corners.

Swiss Dave says that his neighbors have been burning rubbish again. "And I'm not talking about green rubbish. It's old tires and plastic fans. I smell this acrid smoke and I have to run around closing all the windows."

"Oh, God, I know!" Jess says. "Our neighbors do it too. It stinks out your clothes on the line."

Swiss Dave nods. "It drives me insane. Don't they know that shit is toxic?"

Jean segues into a story about his recent experience at his workplace, where the cleaner slipped and broke his collarbone. "It is absolutely ridiculous," he says. "In France, there are strict regulations about occupational health and safety. *Non!* Not here! The tiles outside our office are, are so ... *glissant* when it has been raining. Slippery."

Aaron shakes his head. "I've been saying this for ages. It's because they use indoor tiles outdoors."

"I told the management months ago that it was an accident that waits to happen. *Et voila* – on Wednesday, Manasa fell over and broke his collarbone. They tell me it has happened before. In France, we would stop work and take to the streets and protest. But not here, *non!* They just accept it. It is *stupide.*"

Everyone remembers similar hazards they have seen – pools without fences, jutting bits of concrete in sidewalks, potholes in the roads, the list goes on.

The waitress brings their food, and the table fills up with sizzling hot pots, plates of tender, raw fish and fresh, crunchy vegetables. Ethan laughs at Hannah's terrible chopstick technique.

As they begin to eat, Aaron follows up with his pet peeve: he hates queues in Suva. Everyone points at him drunkenly. "Yes! So true! People don't know how to queue here!" Aaron was recently queuing to get phone credit. "It was a really long queue. I'd been waiting for half an hour, right, and then I'm just at the front of the queue, and this guy walks straight in the door and goes directly to the counter. And the clerk starts serving him! So, I'm like, what's the point of a queue? And then! You wouldn't believe it, it happened again. This old woman walks straight to the front of the queue and gets served immediately. And I didn't want to seem like a white asshole. So I just stood there, like a chump. And I was late to work."

"Yup! Us white people love a good queue," Ethan says cheerfully.

Aaron laughs cautiously.

"Keeps the locals in line, doesn't it?" Ethan adds.

Aaron's eyes widen. "Whoa! That's not what I meant."

"You're drunk, Ethan." Pip rolls her eyes and changes the subject.

On the other side of the table from Hannah, Michelle and Jean's elbows are touching at the small, overcrowded table. Hannah feels an unpleasant twinge of jealousy.

Ethan interrupts her thoughts. "Do you want the last prawn, Han?"

She looks back at him, irritated. "No, I'm stuffed. You go for it."

Soon afterwards the waitress begins to clear away the plates.

"This place is doing my head in," Aaron says. "We need to get out of Suva for a while."

They all agree. They should go away for the weekend, perhaps to one of the resorts in Pacific Harbour. They begin to plan, until someone remembers that Cyclone Dorothy is anticipated next weekend.

"Why don't we just go to the Hibiscus Inn for a few nights when the cyclone hits?" Swiss Dave says. Everyone loves the idea. It will be fun to all stay together, like school camp. They have heard that the hotels are the safest, most comfortable place to be during a cyclone, and they have generators that will kick in when the city's power inevitably gets cut off.

Happy at the idea of their imminent getaway, they all give generous tips to the waitstaff and stumble laughing down the stairs, feeling a bit better.

"Let's go to O'Hannigan's!" Jess says as they open the doors, hitting a wall of muggy air. Sweat patches quickly appear through their shirts and World Bank Dave's glasses mist up again.

"No, let's go *clubbing*!" says Swiss Dave.

"Yay!" Everyone choruses.

Hannah feels unpleasantly drunk and it makes her melancholy. She walks halfway down the street with them and then stops. "I'm going to bail, guys," she says.

"Nooooo!" says Jess.

"Come on, Han! It'll be fun!" says Pip.

"I'm just feeling a bit tired."

Jean gives Hannah a mock pout. "You are not coming?"

"Nah," she says, but she likes his attention and feels the spark of a second wind. *If he tries to convince me again, I'll change my mind.*

Jean shrugs. "Okay Hannah, no problem." He begins walking down the street with Swiss Dave and Michelle.

Pip and Jess give her a kiss on the cheek and stumble off with everyone else. Everyone except Ethan, who stays back with Hannah to escort her to a taxi. As she steps into the car, he says, "Text me when you get –"

"Thanks," she cuts him off and shuts the door. *You'll probably be passed out by that point*, she thinks grumpily. He wanders off down the street to catch up with the others. As her taxi pulls out into the street, Hannah feels like crying, and she is not sure why.

Saturday

THE ROAR of rain pelting on the roof wrenches Hannah into consciousness. She lies back on her pillow heavily and stares at the cracks in the ceiling plaster. She vaguely recalls hearing Jess clumsily unlock the door and clod down the hallway some time in the early hours.

Unable to will herself back to sleep, she rolls over and picks up her phone from the bedside table and begins scrolling through Facebook. The first thing on her feed is a selfie posted by one of her iTaukei colleages with her two sons. The caption is in the quaint Fijian Facebook language that Hannah is now accustomed to, a mixture of Fijian English and texting shorthand:

Saturday vibez. i tank da Lord for dis tym wid my boyz. U all hav a blessed day, family n frenz! #fijigal

Hannah smiles, and "likes" the photo, along with the thirty-nine others that have aleady done so. She scrolls further and clicks on a link to a *New York Times* article about Yemen, which a university friend has shared. She sighs about the plight of the refugees. The article is very long, and she gets the gist after a couple of paragraphs, so she returns to her Facebook feed and places a crying-face emoji under the link.

She comes across last night's post from Pip. A few blurry photos from the volunteers' clubbing expedition: shots of Ethan and Swiss Dave mid-dance move with bottles of Fiji Gold in their hand; Jess and Michelle mock pole dancing while a crowd of mostly iTaukei club goers look on in amusement; a selfie of Pip and Pasepa pouting alluringly. Hannah feels an immediate pang of jealousy, wishing she had gone. She can't see Jean anywhere in the photos, which makes her feel a bit better. Maybe he went home early, disappointed that she hadn't joined them. *You're being ridiculous.*

Over the din of the rain, Hannah hears a ping, and a notification at the top of the screen alerts her to a message. She looks closely and is surprised to see it is the iTaukei guy from Paradise Estate, Isikeli, accepting her friend request. It is quickly followed by another ping, a message that says:

bula

Interesting. She swipes the screen and types out her reply:

Bula Isikeli! Nice to hear from you.

She stares at the screen waiting for his reply. But it remains blank for one minute, and then two. Eventually, Hannah adds,

We were sorry to miss you yesterday. Perhaps we were waiting in the wrong spot? ☺

She's intrigued to see what he will say. At the top of the app, she reads, *Isikeli is typing ...*

A bubble pops onto the screen.

okkkkkkkkkk

Hannah narrows her eyes at the screen. *What does that even mean?* She begins to respond, but she hears the ping of another message.

pliz you cum n c bu

Hannah cocks her head in bemusement. She types:

Yes, we would like to.

The reply pings through quickly.

vnaka

She stares at the screen, not quite sure what to do next. Hannah adds,

We had planned to go to Paradise Estate again on Wednesday. Would that suit you?

lo dats gud

Okay, great. Is there a good place to meet you?

da corna nea supavalu

Right, thinks Hannah. *That worked well last time.* Before she can reply, another message comes through.

R U in da rotary

She squints at the screen. *That's a weird question.* Is it a good thing to be a member of the Rotary?!

No, I'm not, sorry.

Okkkkkkkk

There is a long silence, and she doesn't know if this has been resolved. So, she continues with:

So we'll see you at the corner of Graham and Matai Streets, this Wednesday (January 24th) at 10am? Does that sound okay?

io

Excellent. Thanks for getting in touch ☺ I'll look forward to meeting your grandma then!

Hannah knows she should not hold out much hope, but it would be great to befriend Isikeli as an informant, an insider for the research. She hears the ping of a reply again.

set

Albeit not a very talkative informant.

She gets up from bed and putters around in the kitchen, slicing a banana into a bowl of muesli and plunging coffee. The rain continues to roar around the house, the downpour adding an opaque, silvery gleam to the world outside the window. For the first time in a long time, Hannah feels slightly cold. She puts on a light jumper, which still smells of Australia, where she last wore it. A hint of eucalyptus, perhaps, although she might be imagining that. Probably just different washing powder.

Jess is still asleep. With little else to do, Hannah retrieves the articles that Dr Sireli gave her and begins to read them. They contain words like *ethnographic methodology* and *cultural translators*. She sighs and accidentally thinks, *boring!*, briefly considering returning to Facebook. But then she reprimands herself, unclicks the lid from her highlighter, and draws a little wavy line on the top of the paper to test if it still has ink.

As she begins to read, she surprises herself. She actually reads the whole way through both articles, highlighting sentences and scribbling notes in the margins, such as *"interesting re: Paradise Estate"* and *"!!!"* She jots some notes on her laptop for her meeting with Dr Sireli. She is looking forward to showing him how engaged she is.

Suddenly, Jess flops onto the sofa beside her. "Hey, Han." Last night's mascara is spread around her eyes, her voice croaky. "It's a bit wet out there," she chuckles.

"Good morning," Hannah smiles. "Actually, good afternoon; it's just after twelve."

"Whoa. I slept in."

"How was last night?"

"It was good! I think. What I remember of it."

"I saw Pip put some photos on Facebook. There was some pole dancing I think?"

"Oh gawd! The pole dancing!" Jess cringes, and then laughs huskily. "What were we *thinking*?"

"Ha, it looked fun."

Jess lays her head back on the sofa and closes her eyes with a smile on her face, obviously reliving moments from the previous evening.

"So … did everyone stay late? Or …"

Jess looks at the ceiling in thought. "Yeah, I think we all stayed there till the bar closed at about 2:00 or 2:30."

"Huh," says Hannah.

Jess gets up to plunge some coffee and recounts some amusing parts of the evening. They went to the Korean karaoke bar first. Apparently World Bank Dave knows all the words to "Girls Just Wanna Have Fun," which everyone found hilarious except for Pip who said he shouldn't "appropriate" the song, which is an "anthem of second wave feminism." "Poor Dave," Jess says, "He can't win." At the bar, Jess tried to exchange numbers with the Dutch guy – an elaborate ploy to get him to spell out his name – but as she opened up a new contact, he just said, "It's okay, I just give you missed call." At this point in her story, Jess put on a funny and probably inappropriate Dutch accent. The upshot of this is that they *still* didn't know his name. "I mean, it's getting ridiculous," she says. The group then moved to this sleazy night-club, before, predictably, ending up at O'Hannigan's.

"Sounds like fun!"

Jess smiles as she presses down on the plunger.

Hannah affects a light casual tone. "Hey, so … what do you think of Michelle?"

Jess thinks for a moment. "I really like her, actually. At first I thought she was kind of spoiled and annoying. But she's actually pretty sweet. And she can be so funny. Has she told you about that time she went to the full moon party in Bangkok?"

"No."

"You should get her to tell you some time. It's hilarious. Why do you ask?"

"No reason."

"No, why?"

"Nothing, no, she's nice."

Jess takes her coffee with her as she goes to retrieve her phone from her bedroom. Hannah tries to concentrate on her notes. From the sofa, Hannah hears Jess greeting Brad on FaceTime. There's an awkward three-second delay. "Hannah's here, too!" Jess says and turns the phone around so Hannah can see her small, pixelated boyfriend.

"Hey, Brad." Hannah waves at the phone dutifully, at the same time Brad says something like "How's it going, Hannah?" Then she replies, "I'm good, and you?" at the same time he says something like "All good," but Jess has already turned the phone back around to her.

"Soooooo, had a bit of a big night last night," she says, and tells him all about it. Except, Hannah notices, for the pole dancing.

ISIKELI PULLS Eta across the main street in Suva, weaving her between the gaps in the slowed traffic. The girl giggles and splashes in the puddles, and Isikeli grips her hand more tightly. Reaching the other side of the road, they shelter under a shop awning. Isikeli grabs her harshly. "You have to *listen to me*." She nods, her eyes smarting with tears. His voice softens. "It's dangerous, eh?"

They walk down the street toward the hardware store, with Eta trotting along next to Isikeli's long-legged strides. The store is largely empty. They walk between the aisles, past the lanterns, cooktops, and outdoor furniture, leaving big and little wet footprints behind them. An Indo-Fijian woman seems to appear from nowhere and asks Isikeli if he needs any help. "No, *vinaka*," he says, but the woman follows them closely from aisle to aisle anyway. This is an intimate dance that shop attendants have played with him all his life. As a child, when he used to accompany his barefoot father to the department store, Isikeli used to feel so proud to walk alongside him, hand in hand. It seemed as though his father had an aura of importance and nobility: why else would the staff give him such personalized, attentive service? It was only later that he began to understand the sidelong glances, the tense standoffs, the barely disguised suspicion.

Now, when he steps into the tools aisle to browse the wares, Eta picks up a screwdriver and plays with it, casually tapping it against a container of screws. The shop attendant prises it out of her hands. "Don't touch sweetie," she says unsmilingly, returning it to its place on the shelf. Isikeli raises his eyebrows reassuringly at his niece. *Don't worry about the silly lady*. A sense of tragedy washes through him, that he will not always be able to shield her from the harshness she will experience in her life, this little girl from the settlement.

He glances at the price of crowbars and whistles under his breath – they are too expensive. They will have to borrow one, or will need to think of another way to break into the Chamberlain Street house. Grabbing Eta's hand, he makes his way toward the exit, with the woman still trailing them closely.

Just near the door, though, Eta tugs on his shirt and points at a tub of novelty toys sitting near the checkout, seemingly out of place in the hardware store. A pair of fairy wings sits near the top. She looks at him, pleadingly. He does have fifteen dollars in his pocket, which Mere gave him from last night's earnings to buy some food. His sister is in a good mood at the moment; she even let him use her phone to contact that Hannah girl by Facebook. Isikeli raises his eyebrows and the little girl beams.

At the counter, a *Kai Valagi* customer is in front of them, holding his purchase in a bag, ready to leave. The checkout guy – "Pradeep," according to his badge – is being particularly chatty. "When did you say the plumber was coming?"

"Tuesday," says the expat customer. "Well, he *says* he is. Let's see whether he rocks up or not."

Pradeep rolls his eyes. "Fiji Time, eh?"

Pradeep begins to tell an anecdote about a tradesman he dealt with recently. Isikeli waits while the attendant tells his story. Eta gets increasingly impatient beside him. Eventually, Isikeli gestures to the *Kai Valagi* customer, who makes space for him at the counter. Pradeep looks irritated. He snatches the fairy wings, scans them, puts them in a plastic bag, and holds the bag out in Isikeli's general direction.

It is a relief when they finally step back onto the sidewalk into the fresh air. Eta begs to put her fairy wings on immediately. Isikeli wrestles with the tangled elastic straps, swearing under his breath until he finally gets them on the girl.

They walk to the supermarket, the tall teenager and the little lagging fairy. He cajoles Eta through aisle after aisle, trying to calculate how much food he can buy with the money he has left, leaving enough for the bus fare. Stomach rumbling, he looks wistfully at the seafood – he has a craving for *nakai* the way Bu used to make it, with garlic and chili and soy – but if he buys the shellfish, he won't be able to afford anything else. He eventually decides on a big bundle of two-minute noodles and a tub of ice cream on special, which will at least fill everyone up and cater for any unannounced guests. Aunties and uncles are always popping in to see Bu, and she hates it when she doesn't have anything to offer them.

At the exit, the security guard closely inspects Isikeli's receipt, peering in his bag for an extended time. While Isikeli waits, he can see the orange bus, the one that goes past their corner of Paradise Estate, poking its nose around the street corner ahead. He wills the security guard to hurry up, but doesn't want to seem suspicious. Finally, the guard holds the bag out to Isikeli: permission to leave. Isikeli hoists Eta onto his shoulders and moves quickly toward the bus stop, ducking to ensure her head and wings miss the low-hanging shop signs. The driver doesn't seem to see Isikeli and drives straight past the bus stop without slowing. Like a comical Bad Day, the wheels plow through a puddle that splashes onto Isikeli, saturating his lower half. He slows down, his feet squelching and slipping on his thongs. "*Magai*," he swears.

Defeated, Isikeli spends the bus fare on a warm sausage roll. He breaks off half for Eta and they eat it sitting side by side, leaning up against the wall of the bakery. Fat droplets of rain make their way under the roof and speckle the dirty pavement as pairs of legs walk past them. Eta eats only two bites of her half, which Isikeli was counting on, and he hungrily finishes the rest.

Finally, he puts Eta on his shoulders and begins the long, wet walk home.

RISHIKA IS trying to maintain a pleasant facial expression as she swallows the overly salty pumpkin curry. She is sitting on the sofa at Vijay's aunty and uncle's place while the relentless rain thrums against the windowpane. Aunty is watching her closely, pleased that she is enjoying her meal.

"More?" Aunty says, when Rishika eats the final mouthful.

"*Gee nahi*, Aunty."

"*Khau*. Have some more. Plenty curry."

"*Gee nahi*, Aunty, I'm full." She smiles and pats her stomach.

Aunty sits back sulkily. "You're too skinny. You must take some home."

Every few months, Rishika dutifully visits Vijay's relatives, who live in one of the new housing developments in Nasinu, outside of Suva. She looks around at the familiar loungeroom, awash with color; the walls painted a spearmint green, the patterned yellow cloth on the coffee table, the vase of purple and blue plastic flowers with fluorescent leaves. On the wall, big, framed posters of the Bollywood star Ashwariya Rai – Aunty's favorite – look down on the room, just next to a framed graduation certificate from their son Akesh's degree in computer science. Akesh is Vijay's cousin and best friend from childhood.

"So, Vijay is working?" Uncle asks Rishika for the second time that afternoon. He puts another handful of brown rice and boiled vegetables into his mouth – the meal that Aunty has made him eat with matronly stubbornness ever since he was diagnosed with diabetes almost a decade ago – and chews it stoically.

"*Ha*. He says he is very sorry, Uncle. He will come next time." She actually didn't even get a chance to tell Vijay she was coming today.

"*Thik hai*," Uncle says. Rishika knows they hold her responsible for her husband's absence.

The conversation turns, like it always does, to the couple's former sugarcane farm on the northern island of Vanua Levu. She understands why. Years later, they are still hurt about what happened and they need to talk about it. It's just that these conversations always go around in circles.

In the year 2000 – just after George Speight stormed Parliament House and detained thirty-six hostages, including Fiji's first Indo-Fijian prime minister, in Fiji's third military coup – a group of iTaukei men armed with cane knives gave Aunty and Uncle twenty-four hours to leave their family farm. Their farm was on native iTaukei land that Uncle leased, as had his father and grandfather; it was where he had built a house and raised his family. Sugar was in his bones, Uncle always said.

Rishika remembers the coup vividly. She and Vijay were a young couple living with Vijay's mother. Through the television, Speight kept saying, "The Indians treat us like second class citizens! They will take your land away!" A curfew was imposed on the country, and looters took advantage of abandoned shops. The newspaper printed a photo of a young iTaukei boy smiling in the back of a beat-up van with a television set sitting on his lap. Rishika's friends and family spoke in hushed, worried tones about Fiji descending into outright anarchy, perhaps a mass genocide where neighbors hacked each other to death, like the Hutus and the Tutsis, or a forced exile, like their distant relatives in Uganda. Indo-Fijian houses, restaurants, and Hindu temples were burned down. Stories of bashings and brutal rapes spread through the Indian community like wildfire.

The media fuelled the tension. The newspapers kept publishing photos of army vehicles with ominous-looking groups of men wearing berets and carrying guns, although Rishika noticed it was the same photos over and over again. And once, when she went to the market just after the curfew lifted (ignoring Samriti's shrill warnings), she tripped on the pavement in front of one of those bereted militiamen standing on the corner. He bent down to help her up and she flinched. He dropped his hand and said, "Are you okay *marama*? Careful, eh?" Just an automatic reflex from a well-brought-up boy in scary clothing.

The situation reached a boiling point just as Uncle's thirty-year lease was about to expire. The *mataqali* who owned the land did not renew the lease. To be precise, they did not renew it at knifepoint. The most hurtful part about it was that Uncle had known most of those knife-wielding neighbors since they were children. They used to play with his sons, giggling as they chased each other through perfectly straight rows of sugarcane. Aunty used to give them handfuls of Indian sweets every Diwali. The village used to invite Uncle and Aunty to their big weddings and first birthdays and Fiji Day *lovo*s.

Uncle wrongly assumed that the "tension over land rights" didn't apply to his situation, that the lease renewal process was just going to be a formality. As he stood facing those young men, he protested using all the Fijian swear words he knew. The altercation ended with one of the boys hitting him on the forearm with the blunt side of a cane knife. Over the years the tale was embellished. These days, Aunty talked bitterly about "that savage" who hacked at her husband's arm and "nearly chopped it off at the elbow."

The couple packed up what they could of their belongings and piled them into a cousin's van, shedding fat, silent tears as they caught their last ferry to Suva. Everything they had built and worked for was left behind. They moved in with their son, Akesh, crowding the small house he shared with two other university students. Uncle took on a taxi license and drove and drove and drove – night shifts and day shifts – until they accumulated enough savings to put a down payment on a small house in the outer suburbs of Suva.

Uncle is saying to her now, "My brother went past the farm the other day."

"Oh. What is it looking like now?" Rishika asks, although she can almost recite his answer by heart.

"It is fallow," he spits. "Completely overgrown."

"What a shame," she intones sympathetically.

"Those idiots have no idea how to grow sugarcane," Uncle continues.

Aunty's lip curls. "*Bahut* lazy."

"What a waste!" Uncle shakes his head.

Rishika is never quite sure what else to say. In the years since that coup, Indo-Fijians have rebuilt the burned temples, scrubbed off the hurtful graffiti, and restocked their shelves, but they will never entirely heal from that feeling of betrayal. And recently, they have been looking over their shoulder again, as murmurs of another coup are getting louder.

Suddenly, a key turns in the lock and the door opens to reveal the couple's very wet son, Akesh. Standing in the doorway, his T-shirt sticks to his chest, rain dripping off his hair and nose.

"STOP!" Aunty shrieks. "Don't you dare come a step further."

"Nice to see you too, Mum," he says, making Rishika laugh. She hasn't seen him for weeks, but then Vijay hasn't invited any of his cousins or friends around lately.

"I'll get you a towel." Aunty bustles to the bathroom disapprovingly.

Rishika adjusts her blouse. "I didn't know you would be here."

"Mum said you were coming over, so I thought I'd come and say hi." His mother hands him a towel. He dries his hair roughly and hands it back.

Uncle asks him what the roads are like.

"*Bahut* dangerous, and it's hard to see through the downpour. There was a minor accident near the gas station. No one was hurt, but the traffic is slow."

Uncle nods, vindicated for deciding not to take the taxi out today. Akesh says he just heard on the radio that the cyclone has been upgraded to a category three, and it's likely to hit Fiji on Thursday. Probably only the outer islands, like usual.

"Eat, eat!" His mother shoos him toward the kitchen.

He grabs a plateful of curry and three roti and sits down on the other side of the sofa from Rishika.

"How is Vijay?" he asks her.

"Right *hai*," she says. She looks down, ironing out the material of her jeans with her hand.

Akesh looks unconvinced. "He's working too much, *haana*?" he says, tearing off a piece of roti.

Akesh always disarms her slightly, with his incisive questions and smiling eyes. He is the only one of Vijay's cousins who treats her like … well, like she is his friend, too. She shrugs now and tries to change the subject.

Akesh's first marriage ended in divorce and no children, much to his mother's chagrin. His aptly named ex-wife Priti *was* a very pretty girl (Rishika never liked her). Priti emigrated with half his money and is now married to an Australian man and living in Brisbane.

Akesh takes his first bite of the curry and winces. Behind his mother's back, he mouths, "Waaaay too much salt." Rishika dissolves into giggles, which she politely turns into a cough. Akesh leans over and pats her on the back, while telling his mother, "I was just saying, no one makes *kadoo* curry like you do, Mummy."

Aunty nods. "You must take some home too," she says to her son. "Plenty curry."

After Aunty makes everyone a cup of *masala* tea, and Uncle returns to the newspaper, Akesh looks at Rishika and says, "How is the research going?"

"What research?" she asks.

"Your ancestor? The *girmitiya*? You were writing a biography or something, weren't you?"

Rishika looks at him in surprise. She can't even remember telling him about this. "It's just a short history of his life," she says bashfully.

"So?"

"So, what?"

"How's it going?"

"I've finished it," she says. Pride accidentally creeps into her voice.

He turns to her, giving her his full attention. "Amazing. Tell me about him."

NONE OF Hannah's volunteer friends want to venture out in the dreary weather. Some vague plans to go to the cinema amount to nothing, so Hannah and Jess stay in and download a movie. Hannah wants to watch something familiar and comforting, like a romantic comedy, with warm saturated colors and a happy ending. But Jess keeps suggesting disquieting arthouse films with subtitles, and they eventually begin watching a slow-moving film by an Iranian director. About halfway through, Hannah can hear Jess snoring on the couch, so she gets up and shuts the laptop down, lays a blanket over her friend, and retreats to her room.

When she and Jess first moved into this house, they lovingly adorned it with furniture they sourced from other expats: wicker chairs, white cushions, oak coffee tables. They inherited Fijian paintings and woven mats; local artifacts that were too unwieldy for the outgoing tenants to ship back home or that weren't properly treated wood and wouldn't get through customs. They filled a bookshelf with books that Hannah bought second-hand from the Sunday market – old John Grishams, the Jane Austen collection, orange and beige Penguin Classics. On their first days in this house, Hannah loved the hard-wood majesty of her bedroom as she lay on the covers. The sunlight swept through the open window shutters and emphasized the stark white of the sheets that Ili washed twice weekly. Today, however, the gray weather casts a leaden shadow on the room, and she feels stifled by the oppressive darkness of the floorboards. She is surrounded by belongings that aren't hers – second-, third-, or fourth-hand items imposed on her as Things Expats Should Like.

She hears the buzz of her phone vibrating with a message. She looks at it with a flicker of hope, but it is only her telecommunications provider, PacFone:

Gr8 dealz on calls! $30 free money wen
u recharge on $10 or more. 4 more info,
go 2 pacfone.com.fj

Hannah throws the phone on the bed.

The last time she felt like this, she realizes, was in those first few days at college, when she was an eighteen-year-old country girl who made the big move to the University of Western Australia. It was before the orientation activities began, just after her parents unloaded her belongings from their dusty Subaru Outback, her dad trying to hide his tears as they drove away. Hannah sat in that unfamiliar room on her narrow single bed, staring at the framed photo taken at her year twelve formal. All her high school friends dressed in novelty moustaches and wigs smiled back at her and she felt desperately homesick.

Now, eight years later, the bed she sits on is luxuriously large in comparison and the location is much more exotic. And yet she feels the same yearning to be surrounded by original things, things she grew up with, the voices of friends who have known her since childhood. She grabs her phone again and opens messenger to see which of her friends are online: Lauren Jones or Renee Murphy or Mike Hertz, who she hasn't spoken to in years. None of them are there. She doesn't even really know where they are living these days (hasn't she seen a recent Facebook photo of Renee somewhere in the Northern Territory with that guy she's been seeing?). She lies back on the bed, feels a sting of tears, and eventually gives way to aching, self-indulgent sobs into her pillow.

Eventually, she wipes her eyes and starts dialling the number of home. She imagines the old phone ringing on the bench in the corner of the kitchen in the little brown brick house she grew up in, in the sleepy, orchard town of Donnybrook.

She hears the click of the phone being picked up.

"Hello? Craig Wilson speaking."

Hannah smiles shakily. "Hi, Dad."

Craig is Hannah's stepdad, the realtor who swept Hannah's mum reluctantly off her feet when Hannah was four years old. Hannah's father, Grant, left when she was a tantruming two-year-old. According to the letter he wrote Hannah when she was twelve – handwritten, but on his company's letterhead – he will "never forgive himself for walking out that door." Grant now lives in Perth with his long-term partner, Mel, who Hannah's mum feels certain has "had a bit of work done." Hannah visited them once during school holidays, and Grant always sent generous Christmas money. He surprised her for her eighteenth birthday party with a massive bouquet of balloons and a lavish voucher to David Jones. Her father has a charm that seems superficial at first, but she has come to realize it is actually quite sincere. He pays for expensive dinners accompanied by vintage wines, which don't taste that different to her. She enjoys the novelty of visits with her father, as though he is a nice family friend.

But Craig is her *dad*. It is Craig who taught Hannah how to ride a bike without training wheels, who turned up to year eleven parties in his UGG boots an hour earlier than the agreed pickup time, and who had an innate talent for jokes that were predictable and unfunny. As recently as last year, when she said, "I'm hungry," he would reply, "Oh hello, Hungry, I'm Craig."

"Hannah Banana!" he says now. "Great to hear your voice. How's it all going over there?"

"All good!" she says, quickly changing the subject. "It's bucketing down. How's everyone there?"

"Oh, fine, fine. It's been very hot here. We're all on bushfire alert. Your brothers are driving me up the wall of course."

When Hannah was ten, her twin half-brothers, Hayden and Jarod, were born. She was suspicious of the babies at first, repulsed by their smelly, rotting umbilical cords and their endless oozing of bodily fluids. But Jarod and Hayden grew up and grew on her. As two-year-olds, they obediently wore the princess outfits she dressed them in. When they were three, they were minor characters in the three-act plays that she made her parents sit through. When she was fifteen, Hannah began to enjoy her friends saying, *your little brothers are so cute!*

Craig continues, "They don't talk anymore. They grunt. I say, 'How was your day?' – *'grunt'* – 'What did you do at school?' – *'grunt.'* And that's if I'm lucky! I'll put them on. See if you can get any sense out of them. Wait, they're on the verandah."

Hannah can hear her dad walking through the house, the creak of the flyscreen door being opened, and a rush of outdoor sounds. The familiar warble of magpies and the *tickety, tickety* of her brothers playing table tennis.

Craig starts commentating for Hannah down the line. "Wilson hits it to Wilson. Wilson to Wilson. Wilson back to Wilson. Wilson shoots, he SCORES!"

In the background, one of the twins says, "Wrong sport, Dad." She can't tell the difference between their voices these days.

"Whatever!" her dad says cheerfully. "Here, talk to your sister."

"Hey, Han," says one of her brothers.

"Is this Wilson Twin A or Wilson Twin B?" she asks.

"Haha. It's Jarod."

"Hey Jaz, what's up?"

"Nothing much."

"Cool, how's year eleven going?"

"S'okay."

She affects a maternal tone. "Studying hard, I hope?"

"S'pose."

"That's good."

A silence ensues.

"So how's chemistry with Mr Giles?" she asks.

"He's ok."

"Is he still wearing those really short football shorts?"

"Lol. Yep."

Silence again.

Surprisingly, Jarod speaks up. "How's Fiji?" he asks.

"Oh! It's good! Not much to report."

"The cyclone was on the news here."

"Was it? Oh. It's not that big a deal. It probably won't even hit Suva."

"Cool. Wanna talk to Hayden?"

"Sure, put him on."

Hannah proceeds to have almost exactly the same conversation with Hayden, although she asks him about the English teacher, Mrs Dunn, who is, apparently, still sneaking off in the middle of class and coming back reeking of cigarettes and chewing gum.

When Hayden gives the phone back to Craig, her dad says, "Now let's go find your mother." He pulls the phone away from his mouth and yells "SUE!" and then back to Hannah, "I think she's in the sewing room. She's making a cover for my bike. She's amazing, your mother."

Craig and Sue visited Hannah in Suva a few months back. It was her parents' first trip overseas. Craig's look of childish awe at everything Fijian made Hannah think of *Crocodile Dundee*, the sequel. When Hannah taught Craig how to say *"bula"* and *"vinaka,"* he overused it.

"BOOLAH," he waved to every single person he saw on the streets, including busy looking businesspeople on their phones. "VINARKAH," he said over and over again, often out of context.

When Dr Sireli heard Hannah's parents were visiting, he kindly insisted that Hannah bring them to meet him. Her boss spent a lunch hour with them, taking them to his favorite café. After the lunch, Craig said, "He's a great bloke, isn't he? Just so down-to-earth. Reminded me of a young Nelson Mandela." (When Hannah recounted this story to Ethan, he laughed until tears streamed down his face. "Because he's got a brown face and he's nice, presumably?! Is that the connection he's making there?")

Now Craig is chatting down the phone about his mother, who is in her nineties and at a nursing home. This is Hannah's favorite grandmother, who used to swear like a trooper and have an entire fridge-drawer full of chocolate whenever the grandkids came over. The family was reluctant to leave her in a care facility, but Gran was becoming a danger to herself and others, leaving ovens on and becoming disoriented in the freezer aisle of the supermarket.

"She still recognizes me sometimes," Craig says, and Hannah can hear his voice crack slightly.

"Poor Gran."

"She's had a good innings, though."

"Yeah. I hope she, you know, holds out until I get back."

"I hope so, too."

"Give her my love next time you see her."

"Will do, Hannah Banana. Now here's your mother." She hears Craig hand over the phone and her mum say, "Hold this will you? Just near the seam."

"Hello love! Near the seam!" her mum says into the phone now.

"Hi, Mum," says Hannah shakily.

"You okay, Han?"

"Yeah Mum, I'm fine, just got a bit of a cold." She doesn't want A Conversation. She doesn't really know how to articulate what she is feeling, and if she tries to tell her mum, she knows she will call in concern every day for the next week. Instead, Hannah tells her about the research project.

"Goodness, Han! You're having some fascinating experiences."

"Haha, yeah."

She eventually hangs up, after reassuring her mother about Cyclone Dorothy. "We're going to stay at a hotel, Jess and me and a few of the other Australians here."

"That sounds like a good idea," her mum says. "Do be careful, won't you, love? We want you back in one piece."

Sunday

ISIKELI CAN hear Eta whingeing in the other room. *Let me sleep.*
But it is too late; his mind floods with memories of last night. He
and Seru walked the wet streets looking for unlocked gates and
open windows. It was another bad night; they came away with
about three dollars each, mostly in silver coins that they found in
a parked taxi after they artfully smashed its window. After several more unsuccessful efforts, Seru cut his arm badly on a barbed
wire fence. The boys walked home in silence, dripping wet. In
the moonlight, Seru's arm was throbbing dark red blood, which
joined up with the rain to make little pink rivers down his arm.

Eta whirls into the room and jumps on his back. "Church,
Momo Keli!" she says.

He twists his arm behind his back and tries to swat her off. "*So!*
Go away."

And then he remembers. It *is* church today. Yesterday, for the
first time in two years, Bu announced that she wanted to go to
the Sunday service. Up until she lost her leg, Bu didn't miss a
Sunday for thirty years. Church used to be the cornerstone of

her social calendar, and, in turn, Bu was once the cornerstone of the church community. She was always secretary of one of the committees, always in charge of catering. She was not loud and showy, but a hard worker, well-liked by everyone. People always listened when she talked. One time as a child, Isikeli was sitting next to her during a lunch with a visiting reverend. She said something out of the blue and the entire meeting burst into laughter – not polite chuckles but deep, tears-falling-down-your-face, throw-back-your-head kind of laughter. Isikeli laughed too, partly to pretend he understood, and partly because grown-ups' crumpled faces were actually kind of funny. He was so proud that she was his grandmother.

After her amputation, it was too exhausting for Bu to attend church. That's why yesterday's request was such a surprise, and Isikeli promised to take her.

He sighs deeply. With Eta still on his back he hoists himself up to kneel on all fours. She squeals with delight as he gives her a half-hearted ride into the living room, a jaded racehorse at the end of his career.

Bu is, surprisingly, already dressed in her best *chamba* and *sulu*. Her hair is wet, meaning she must have already had a "shower." For Bu, this involves dragging herself along the floor to the tap next to the tumble-down outdoor toilet. The outhouse permanently leaks a putrid smell, despite the lurid blue cleaner that Mere sometimes sploshes into it. Using the tap, Bu fills up a bucket with cold water and splashes it onto herself with a small half coconut shell. When she does this alone, the process usually takes forty-five minutes and all of her energy. The room now smells of a mixture of coconut oil and talcum powder; the touching aroma of Bu's dignity.

Isikeli places Eta down. *"Rairai vinaka, Bu,"* he says, standing up. She did look beautiful. His grandmother appears reluctantly flattered and for once does not ask why he got home so late last night.

Isikeli gets ready, putting on his navy blue *sulu* and his hot pink Bula shirt. He helps Eta into her lacy white church dress and allows her to wear her fairy wings.

"*Isa*, little angel," Bu says when Eta appears in front of her. The girl tries false bashfulness at first, and then begins prancing around the room, until Bu reprimands her for nearly knocking over her tea.

Isikeli steps onto the back verandah to retrieve the wheelchair. After the amputation, the nurse said they were on a waiting list for one of the state-of-the-art wheelchairs that were donated by NZAid. That was two years ago, and they are still waiting. In the meantime, however, Isikeli is pleased with his handiwork. The chair is made of a rusted wheelchair frame, which he found abandoned in a pile of rubbish on the other side of Paradise. Isikeli tightly roped a plastic chair on top, and Seru's aunty sewed a custom-sized cushion out of some leftover Bula material. Yesterday, Isikeli borrowed Jone's rugby-ball pump and pumped up the tires. *As good as new*, he thinks, as he wheels it into the loungeroom and parks it next to Bu. "You ready?"

She looks at him slightly fearfully, but raises her eyebrows.

He grabs her under her arms and tries to lift, but his positioning is too awkward. He strains under her weight and quickly puts her back down.

"*Oilei!*" he says. "Too much cassava!" She slaps his arm with a smile. They both know the irony, which is that she hasn't had cassava for weeks, not since Seru's uncle brought some around a few weeks ago. Isikeli hopes that when Mere gets paid tonight, she will go to the market.

Isikeli tries to lift her again, hoisting her onto the chair.

"*Qori*, there you go," he says as she settles in.

He pushes her out the door. Bu pats down her dress proudly with one hand and holds Eta's hand with the other.

"*Gade mada!*" Isikeli says. "Adventure time."

Bu chuckles, sounding more youthful and excited than she has in a long time.

She opens her old umbrella to shield her and Eta from the rain. Two of the umbrella's prongs stick out at the back dangerously, and Isikeli has to duck to avoid being poked in the eye.

Neighbors watch the trio trundle over the rocky path from their verandahs. "*Bula*, Bubu Lia!"

"*Rairai vinaka!*" they call.

"Long time, eh? Going to church?" they call.

"*Isa*, God bless!" they call.

And Bu calls back to them, waving royally.

They arrive at the old wooden church, its wonky cross pointing uncertainly to the left of heaven. The *italatala* comes over to greet Bu, taking her hand in both of his. He knows the family well, having been to school and played rugby with Isikeli's father. "It's been a long time, Bubu Lia," he says in his deep and boomy voice. "It's good to see you." He rests his hand affectionately on Eta's head, then turns back to Bu.

"Are you looking after that leg? Listening to the doctor?"

"*Io*," she says, with a warning glance at Isikeli.

"Is Vera still at the resort in Nadi?"

"*Io, io*, working hard, eh? Very good hotel."

"*Vinaka*. And how is young Mere?"

"*Isa*, very happy. Working for a *Kai Idia* family. Housegirl."

"*Vinaka. Vinaka*," the pastor says. He looks up at Isikeli now, staring into his eyes.

"Isikeli Tiko," he says, shaking the teenager's hand. "Your father was a good man."

"*Vinaka*, Reverend," Isikeli says, looking at his feet.

Old friends and distant relatives flock to Bu's side as Isikeli parks her wheelchair in the aisle. She is happy and animated, asking them about their families and making them laugh.

The church rows are packed, but Mrs Karawalevu makes space for Isikeli to sit at the end of her pew, which is closest to Bu's wheelchair. He wedges in between the hard wooden edge of the bench and Mrs Karawalevu's ample hip. Eta sits on his lap.

The crowd hushes when the *italatala* takes to the altar, his purple stole contrasting elegantly with his crisp white gown. Eta taps Isikeli's arm, pointing above her at pigeons nesting in the rafters, cooing nervously. He nods and shushes her.

"The Lord made all men equal," the reverend begins, his booming voice reverberating throughout the quietened congregation. Bu closes her eyes and a look of serenity rests on her face. "The material world is harder for those who have fewer possessions. And yet, it is only with hardship that we are granted the opportunity to learn about our place on earth and the life after." One of the pigeons suddenly takes flight, fluttering over the crowd through a hole in the stained-glass window where a pane is missing. There is a tittering of "*Oilei!*"s. Eta was waiting for this kind of excitement and giggles with glee. The reverend pauses and returns to his sermon. "Let us remember Matthew, chapter five, verse three: *Blessed are the poor in spirit, for theirs is the kingdom of heaven.* This does not mean that if you are poor you get a free ticket into heaven! *Sega.* You must be poor *in spirit.* Matthew is telling us that if you are self-effacing, if you are humble, if you submit to the power of The Almighty and are true to His word, then you will be rewarded with blessings in the afterlife."

The congregation responds vocally to the sermon. People say, "Praise the Lord," and "*Emeni.*" Several members walk to the front in the aisle and kneel down low. The *italatala* acknowledges them with kindly compassion.

When he finishes, the reverend raises his eyebrows at the band, who burst forth with a powerful gospel song, and the congregation begins to sway and clap. Beside him, Isikeli can hear Bu's voice immediately fall into the alto line. He harmonizes below her with the tenor part and Eta lifts her little voice to soprano. As always, goosebumps prickle on his skin as he is carried by a river of voices.

The band begins to play a slower hymn and people sit down in their seats again. Everyone takes discreet, sidelong glances at the collection plate as it is passed between the pews. Sitting on the other side of the aisle from Isikeli is a man who used to live in the settlement but recently moved out after experiencing an extraordinary run of luck; he now runs a successful *yaqona* store. He takes out a twenty-dollar note from his wallet, slowly unfolding it and carefully placing it on the plate. People can barely hide their looks of admiration and envy.

Out of the corner of his eye, Isikeli notices that Bu is singing straight ahead and pretending not to look, belying her sense of shame as the collection plate comes closer.

In his pocket, Isikeli can feel the warm coins from last night. He surreptitiously slides the metal into Bu's hand. She looks at him in surprise. The collection plate arrives at Bu and she holds the bowl for a moment, with Isikeli watching her closely. Yet she passes it on without putting anything in it. Isikeli is confused until she slides the coins back into his hand, patting it. Then she whispers in his ear just loud enough so he can hear over the singing, "I know where you got that money from, and so does *Turaga Jisu.*"

For the first time since his father died, Isikeli's chest feels punctured, like it is leaking air, and he struggles to breathe in.

Monday

HANNAH'S FEELING of unease has not lifted. She hopes it will fade after the routine and busyness of a work day. Today, she and her colleagues are attending a workshop on diabetes. It is another one of those on-trend workshops, where representatives from all sectors – trade, health, education – are invited. She is familiar with the lavish hotel conference venue because she has attended several workshops here previously.

Seated in the air-conditioned hall amongst the other delegates, she waits for the formalities to start. An eager-to-please permanent secretary from the Ministry of Health introduces his minister – Hinal Singh – to formally open the event. Hannah has often seen the minister at these events. A tall man in his late fifties, Singh always wears immaculately tailored suits and fashionable spectacles and tends to speak at length about his friends in high places. Hannah never minds too much because he is funny and attractive in a silver fox kind of way.

The first session of the workshop involves the launch of a new exercise app. The CEO of the corporate sponsor – Gupta's, the big flour and biscuit company in Fiji – introduces it to the audience with a snappy PowerPoint presentation:

- *Easy to use*
- *Available in three languages*
- *Free download*
- *Invest in Fiji's health today*

The man leads the audience in an activity, asking the delegates to download the app on their smartphones right now. He makes them stand up and jog around the venue ("On the way, meet three people you haven't met yet!"). Finally, he tells them to look at how many steps they have done on their newly installed pedometers. "See? You've just burned 200 kilojoules. You can have an extra biscuit at morning tea. Just make sure it's not from one of our competitors!" The delegates chuckle. They are accidentally having fun.

The second session involves getting into "mini think-tanks" with people from other sectors. Hannah joins a group with a girl from Nestlé and a guy from the Ministry of Education. They pick up the colored markers on their table and obediently begin to brainstorm "strategies for improving nutrition" on big pieces of butcher's paper. Hannah scribes. By the end of it, she is quite proud of their poster and pleased with the suggestions her group makes to the broader group discussion later, which include "engage all key stakeholders" and "more workshops."

At lunch she waits in the queue to get to the table of finger food. Further up the line, she sees an Australian woman in her thirties who she recognizes from HealthInternational laughing with some of the Ministry of Health staff. The woman is an expat who has lived in Suva for years; her children go to the International School. Hannah always sees her at these meetings and sometimes waves to her at the Hibiscus Inn on Friday nights, where she always seems to be eating dinner with her earnest husband and two quiet children. She treats Hannah with a friendly distance, as though not wanting to invest much time in a short-term volunteer. Months back, Hannah asked her to coffee, listening with admiration to the older woman's stories and gently inquiring about potential long-term job opportunities. The woman answered her questions with perfect politeness, and then apologized for having to cut the meeting short. Hannah can't muster the energy for one-sided small talk with her today. She steps out of the line and decides to escape into town to buy her own lunch.

Outside the hotel, the rain has lessened to a steady dribble, so she walks at a fast pace to a little café tucked away in a dark arcade. It is one of the Australians' favorite lunch spots; it has divine salads with fresh, local ingredients and is run by kindly, earnest Seventh Day Adventists (or, as Ethan calls them, the "body-is-your-temple peeps").

So, as she pushes open the door to the café, she is only half-surprised to see Ethan sitting at a table in the corner. He is dressed professionally, his blond hair combed back for once. He is sitting with a striking iTaukei man she has never seen before. Ethan waves and calls her over, introducing his friend as Peniasi. Peniasi holds out a flexed wrist toward her. He has extremely long eyelashes and is wearing cherry-red lipstick – evidently *qauri*, one of the men who often work in traditional feminine roles around Suva: waitresses, nurses, kindergarten teachers.

"*Isa*, Ethan's told me about you," Peniasi says in a mesmerizing voice; his consonants are crisp and sibilant.

"Oh! Only good things, I hope!"

"Meh. Half and half," he teases, and she likes him immediately.

Peniasi, Ethan explains, is a freelance journalist and political blogger. They met last year when he was reporting on one of

Ethan's cases. They ran into each other again this week, because Peniasi is writing an article on the copyright case.

As he pulls up a chair for Hannah at their table, Ethan says, "Actually I've been meaning to introduce you guys. Hannah works in diabetes, and Peniasi has written a few articles about food imports in the Pacific. So, you'll have things in common."

"Oh, cool," Hannah says, and for want of anything better to say, she talks briefly about the workshop she's just been attending.

"Was the minister there? Hinal Singh?" Peniasi asks.

"Yep. He opened the event."

"What did you think of him?"

"Um …" Hannah isn't sure how honestly to answer. The volunteers have been told never to talk politics in Fiji. The volunteer program doesn't want any diplomatic gaffes or embarrassments on their hands. Suva is a small town and gossip gets around like wildfire. They call it "the coconut wireless." Peniasi is obviously a trusted friend of Ethan's, but you can never be too sure. She settles on saying, "He's really interesting."

Peniasi takes a quick look at the people at the tables on either side of theirs, and then leans in conspiratorially. "What do you *really* think of him?"

She chuckles at the permission to be honest. "Well, he's kind of name-droppy."

"*Ha*! you're telling me. Was the permanent secretary there?" Peniasi asks again.

"You mean the guy who laughs at every joke the minister makes?"

"Mm-mm," Peniasi says. "He's like a skinny little mongoose."

Hannah giggles. Ethan looks pleased that his friends are getting along. "A mongoose? I wish I was there."

Between forkfuls of salad, Hannah tells them about the exercise app that HealthInternational just launched.

Peniasi rolls his eyes. "Of course they did."

"I know." Hannah rolls her eyes too, although she isn't quite sure why that is so annoying. Maybe their apps are notoriously bad.

Peniasi drops his fork on his plate. "I'm sick of the message that Fijians could stop getting diseases if they just tried harder. 'Just download the app!' It's so ... neoliberal, eh?"

"Totally," says Hannah. "*So* neoliberal." Although she has never fully understood what neoliberalism is exactly. It is one of those words that her lecturers used to say all the time during her degree. She even dropped it into the odd assignment to sound sophisticated. And Pip is always arguing with World Bank Dave about it, always saying "trickle down economics this; neoliberalism that." Hannah always loyally supports Pip. Whatever it means, she knows she should probably be *anti*-neoliberalism.

Peniasi continues. "Fijians don't choose to be unhealthy. It's not that simple. I mean, the biggest irony is that tobacco and alcohol and refined sugar came with the Europeans." He points a finger at Ethan accusingly. "Your people."

"Ah, yes," Ethan says. "I've been meaning to apologize for that."

Peniasi laughs. "Apology accepted, bro."

Hannah is impressed with their easy repartee, even slightly envious of Ethan.

"These days," Peniasi says, "when Western governments get all strict about tobacco and slap a tax on cigarettes – and Westerners start quitting – tobacco companies just start targeting the Pacific. Cause we're an untapped market, eh? They just *kerekere* the right minister and suddenly our regulations get withdrawn. Or completely diluted until they don't mean anything."

"Yeah, Big Tobacco can be dodgy," Hannah says, only opening her lips slightly because she is self-conscious about having coriander on her teeth.

"More and more of our adults are taking up smoking now, eh? But no worries, *sega na leqa*," Peniasi continues, "at least we have big billboards that say 'Smoke responsibly! Passive smoking harms your children! Quit for them!'"

"Yeah, that's a bit rich," Ethan says.

Hannah feels herself blush. She is partly responsible for these kinds of billboards. She has worked on countless health promotion campaigns, both here and back home. She always thought she was doing important work, trying to change people's behavior. But now when Peniasi puts it that way, in the context of million-dollar ad campaigns, it does seem kind of feeble to tell people to "just make the right choice."

"And the meat industry, too, eh? You've heard about the meat imports, haven't you?"

"Kind of ..." Hannah says. She doesn't have any idea about meat imports. "Tell Ethan about it, though."

"In the nineties, Australians got all health conscious about fat, right? So the market just dropped for fatty cuts of lamb."

Hannah is reminded of an *Australian Women's Weekly* magazine she found last year in an op shop, dated 1977. One of the advertisements pictured a big fried lambchop with a slug of greasy fat still curled around it. The chop was presented with a dollop of butter melting on top, and no greenery on the plate whatsoever. It looked starkly dated. These days Australian magazines always present lamb as some kind of grilled, lean, French cutlet with rustic-looking vegetables.

"But," Peniasi is saying, "the Australian and New Zealand governments didn't want their sheep farmers to be out of pocket. So they negotiated trade agreements to export the fattiest offcuts to us. So Aussies could still make money by selling us their scraps."

"Genius," Ethan says drily.

"*Io.*"

"That's horrible," Hannah says. She wants to talk to Dr Sireli about this and show him how *outraged* she is about her government's behavior.

Peniasi mentions that his village used to eat mutton flaps all the time, because they were cheap and did have *some* meat on them. The Fijian government banned their import eventually, but not before people started dying.

"Yeah, there's no doubt about it, mate," Ethan says. "That's fucked up."

Hannah squints at Ethan, who has a look of sobriety on his face. For once, he is actually being serious, and she doesn't know quite what to make of it.

Ethan continues, "Not to mention how expensive it is to eat well here. That salad I've just eaten was, what, twelve dollars? That's twice as much as the fried chicken and chips at the food court. No wonder Fijians choose the chicken."

"No, *that*," Peniasi waggles his finger at Ethan sassily, "makes sense. Have you tasted that chicken?"

Ethan laughs concedingly.

Hannah wonders how many other local friends Ethan has. She doesn't have any. Except for Pasepa, but Pasepa doesn't really count because she is kind of Australian-ish anyway. Hannah's Fijian colleagues are lovely, but it seems there is a barrier between them. She feels like a slightly misfitting jigsaw piece. Maybe she should enroll in Fijian language lessons. Her world here is a bit insular. A bubble. Maybe that's why she's been feeling uneasy lately.

Tuesday

ISIKELI IS swiveling on the broken office chair beside the road corner, aggressively shaving the top off a green coconut with an old pickaxe. The shavings fall at the feet of Seru and Epeli who are watching him closely. They are semi-sheltered from the rain by a ripped, blue tarpaulin that Epeli tied to the tree. Cars splash by, pedestrians hurry past them on their way to bus stops and lunch meetings, barely lifting their umbrellas enough to notice them. Periodically, Seru gets up to adjust the stack of coconuts for sale. His conscientiousness is making Isikeli feel even more on edge. His shoulders feel tightly wound, like overtuned strings on a ukelele.

"Where's Jone?" he asks.

"Work," says Seru.

"*Work cava?*"

"Work."

"What work?

"Jone got a job."

Isikeli stares at Seru. "Where?"

"Security, eh? Some hardware store in Lami."

"Jone? Fatarse? He couldn't even fit through the door."

Seru laughs cautiously, wary of Isikeli's volatile mood. His nervousness only grates on Isikeli more.

"How? How did he get it?"

"His cousin worked for them – you know Inoke? – but Inoke got a job in the army."

"How much?"

"Four dollars an hour."

Isikeli makes an effort to seem unimpressed.

Jone has always been different to them. Although he went to the same school, he has never actually lived in Paradise Estate; he lives two streets down on the western side, in a little wooden house with his dad and aunty and cousins. His aunty has a job as a receptionist, and always made him do his homework. The teachers always liked Jone; they pinched his chubby cheeks affectionately. They liked how he listened in class and did well in his exams. The teachers always talked to Jone in encouraging ways, saying things like "potential" and "career." When Jone pulled out of last year's exams, the teachers felt "disappointed" in him.

The difference is, they gave up being disappointed in Isikeli years before. But Isikeli didn't care what the teachers thought; it was the *coaches* he feared and respected. Isikeli used to spend every recess, lunchtime, and after school–hour playing rugby. He returned home each evening at sundown, muddy and exhausted. Bu always muttered disapprovingly, and yet always hand-washed his rugby jersey and never missed his Saturday games. That was when she still had her leg.

Everyone said Isikeli was bound to be a professional rugby player. He had a free-flowing style that bamboozled the opposition. He was fast and strong, aggressive but agile. When he was tackled on the field – just before he landed – he would flick the ball effortlessly behind him to his teammate with perfect accuracy. He would always be exactly where he was needed to receive the ball again, shifting, gliding, and dancing around players to sprint toward the try line. People always used to shake their heads and laugh in admiration at Isikeli and tell him he played just like his dad used to.

He continues to shave the top off another coconut … *ffft* … *ffft* … *ffft*. There was a daydream he used to have when he stared out of the classroom window. His plan was to play for the Flying Fijians rugby team. He used to picture himself sitting on a plane for the first time as he traveled to overseas games. They say the seats recline, and you can order free beer, which is brought to you by pretty Fijian air hostesses. He was going to look up from stadiums around the world and see hundreds of light blue Fijian flags littered throughout the crowd.

After he made a name for himself in the Flying Fijians, he was going to get *noticed* and drafted to Australia, or New Zealand, or France. Of course, he would be sad that he could no longer live in Fiji – and he was going to miss his family – but he would be making so much money that he could come back whenever he wanted.

So. Much. Money. He used to imagine exactly how he was going to spend it. He planned to buy two things. First, he dreamed of building a house in his dad's village on Mataqai, right near the sea. A great big two-storey house made of fat slabs of concrete – impenetrable by cyclones and high enough to avoid the floods. He was going to paint it a beautiful color, like hot pink, or lime green. Bu and Mere would move back there with Eta. His mum would quit her job and come home. She would cook her amazing custard pie like she used to, the one with the thick buttery biscuit base that melted in your mouth. Eta would go to Tiwawa Primary School, and he would make her attend school everyday and do her homework (not like Mere, who was spoiling that girl). In his daydream, Isikeli planned to blindfold Bu and then whip it off to show her the finished house. He got this idea from a "Bank Australia" home loan ad, where the husband revealed a new house to his wife. When Isikeli first saw this ad with the soaring piano music his eyes accidentally welled with tears, and Seru teased him for days.

Second, he was going to buy a loud, sky blue Mazda MX5. He saw one a few years back in a *Pacific Business* magazine discarded on the sidewalk; the pages had fallen open to a photo of the sleek sports car, its driver leaning his elbow casually out the window and flashing a winning smile. Isikeli imagined sitting on those smooth leather seats, with Seru in the passenger seat and Epeli and Jone in the back, nodding in time to Fijian reggae. *Although Jone wouldn't be there*, Isikeli thinks resentfully now. *He'd be at "work."*

Io, rugby was going to be his ticket out of here.

He knew that every Fijian boy dreamed of being a famous rugby player. But for Isikeli, it actually felt possible. Even probable. It seemed just within reach, like a low-hanging *moli* branch on the other side of a fence. His talent was a gift from the Lord Almighty, and if he just kept playing, success was his destiny.

Then last year, just before Christmas, two unfamiliar men appeared at the sideline of one of his rugby games. There wasn't any warning; even the coach wasn't told they were coming. One was a tall, *Kai Loma* guy with an Australian accent, and everyone recognized him from the news as the assistant coach for the Fijian reserves team. Scouts! This was Isikeli's chance. Everyone knew he was the one they'd come to see. Coach came up to him in the changerooms and whispered words of encouragement, finishing with, "Don't fuck this up, boy."

Before the whistle blew, Isikeli looked to the sky and prayed silently, over and over. *Kerekere Turaga Jisu guide my hands and feet. Kerekere Turaga Jisu guide my hands and feet.*

Early in the first half, he rolled his ankle on a small hole in the shoddy pitch. He felt sluggish and off form for the rest of the game. Once, when he flicked the ball behind him to keep it in play, his teammate wasn't there to catch it, and the ball bounced and rolled to the opposition. Another time, when he sprinted toward the try line and attempted to dance around the opposition, they anticipated his move and tackled him easily to the ground.

When the final whistle blew, the scouts talked briefly with the coach and then left, spinning dust behind them in their shiny four-wheel drive. Coach relayed their message back to Isikeli in the dank, sweaty changerooms. His teammates looked away respectfully, pretending not to listen. Coach said something about "talented but needs discipline," "lacking maturity," and "needs to work on technique."

Coach reckoned they would come back again next season. Isikeli, however, was indignant. It was supposed to happen easily. His dream suddenly seemed less possible. Even *unlikely*. And just like that, something in him changed. He stopped going to training, just turning up for games. He started spending nights on the streets with Seru looking for open windows.

One Saturday he arrived half an hour late to the game because he lost track of time, drinking *yaqona* with his cousins. Coach swore at him and told him not to come back until he "grew up." Isikeli swore back, kicking a can as he walked away. He watched the rest of that game from a hill, hidden from view, muttering at his teammates whenever they lost the ball, knowing they needed him. His team lost that game and, for a short time at least, the vindication made him feel slightly better.

That was a few months ago, and he hasn't gone back since then. Sometimes he misses playing rugby so intensely that his legs jump restlessly by themselves in his sleep. He often dreams he is on the field: vivid dreams, in which he leads his team to victory with his usual skillful ease, or nightmares, in which he makes a fool of himself, the ball as slippery as a mango pip. A few days ago he walked halfway to the homeground on training night, before deciding against it and walking home again. He couldn't handle the shame if coach sent him away in front of all his teammates.

So here he is. *Selling fucking coconuts again.* Meanwhile, Jone is moving up in the world. He looks down at the coconut he has just opened, swivels around on his chair, and pelts it against the tree. The nut cracks in half and part of the shell ricochets back, narrowly missing Seru's head.

THE RADIO on the bench is tuned in to the Hindi channel, the lilting rhythm of the *tabla* pulsing throughout the kitchen. Rishika peers over the pot and sprinkles in a large pinch of *masala*. The sizzling cloves and cardamom immediately return her to her childhood, to big family gatherings with aunties and uncles and cousins; her parents in a festive mood. She scoops the pounded garlic, ginger, and chili into the pot and stirs in the chicken pieces until they brown. Three cups of rice, six cups of hot water, and three cinnamon sticks. She replaces the lid and lets the *pilau* bubble away contentedly.

Now for the chutney. She dashes down the stairs and into the garden, braving the fat droplets of rain to pick a sprig of curry leaves. Solomon watches her from the shelter of the balcony.

"*Lamu,*" she teases. He looks away, as though he understood the insult.

She reaches back as a matter of habit to clasp her hair, to twist it and drape it over her shoulder. Except – she is suddenly reminded – there is nothing there anymore. She puts her hand on the back of her neck and caresses the delightfully soft ends of her newly cut hair. It was an impetuous decision this morning, just after she walked out from the market. Laden with plastic bags full of vegetables, she saw the tired-looking beauty salon across the road and made the snap decision to enter. She asked the young gum-chewing hairdresser to cut all her hair off. The girl looked disbelieving and slightly excited, as though she was rarely given such dramatic projects. "What style do you want?"

"I don't mind. Whatever you choose."

Rishika closed her eyes and enjoyed the gentle, metallic tug as the scissors cut through the strands, her head gradually feeling lighter and lighter as the hair fell away.

"There," the girl said when she finished blow-drying. "It's called a pixie cut."

Rishika opened her eyes and stared at her unfamiliar reflection. Her hair was short at the back and sides. An asymmetrical fringe framed her face, and some longer, wavy strands of hair dangled beside her ears.

"Cute?" the girl remarked to her colleague, who looked at the mirror and said, "*Io*, it suits her features," as though Rishika wasn't there.

She feigned appreciation, paid, and left.

She knows Vijay is going to hate it. When they were first married, he loved her long, silky hair. In those early days, when they lay together, talking and laughing in the darkness, he used to absent-mindedly comb his fingers through her hair, curling it and twisting it behind her ears. Once, he whispered, "How did I ever get you? You're so out of my league." She laughed and agreed with him. Thinking about it now, she almost wonders if this memory actually happened. The younger Rishika must have been so sure of herself – so comfortable in her marriage – to be so playful.

She throws the onion in with the cumin, mustard seed, and curry leaves and waits for it to become translucent. She pours in the can of chopped tomatoes and stirs the wooden spoon in a smooth figure eight.

Akesh is coming to dinner tonight. At his parents' house the other day, he invited himself over in his usual affable way. "I should come around and see Vijay. It's been too long. What about Tuesday? Make your famous *pilau* for me, *acha*?" She laughed and agreed, of course. She reminded Vijay this morning that his cousin was visiting tonight. He promised to come home in time, but it is always possible that he will cancel at the last minute. He usually does.

She waits for the chutney to boil down, wiping a thin layer of sweat from her forehead. On the radio, the song fades into the news. Rishika always likes the newsreader's voice. Confident, mellifluous, official, it is he who tells her about all the world's happenings and warns her about the weather. He begins with an update on a case being heard today in the High Court. It's about copyright – something about pirated DVDs and intellectual property. Rishika has an image of the police blasting down her front door and raiding the cupboard beneath her television, filled with discs in plastic sleeves and badly photocopied covers. She feels slightly thrilled at the drama of being arrested. She would make her phone call to Vijay. Perhaps he would leave work immediately and arrive at the police station breathless, hugging her in relief.

She tunes back into the newsreader, now updating listeners on Tropical Cyclone Dorothy. Dorothy has drifted west again and picked up force. She is officially upgraded to a category four.

The newsreader is saying that weather conditions are likely to intensify throughout Fiji over the next few days, and people are advised to remain on high alert. Rishika regrets agreeing to stay at Lakshmi's on Wednesday night. If Vijay is working late, Solomon will be left in the compound alone, and the poor dog will fret in the worsening weather.

Vijay's little hatchback pulls into the driveway at half past five, a perfectly reasonable hour. On a whim, she decides to go and greet him at the top of the stairs.

"*Kaise?*" he says when he sees her.

"Right *hai*."

"You cut your hair."

"*Ha.*"

"Looks nice," he says, walking past her. "I'll get changed."

It is only then that she realizes that she wanted him to dislike it, to get angry, to *say something with conviction.* She doesn't know how much more she can endure of this cold indifference. He retreats down the hallway. With every fiber of her being she wills him to turn around, and even considers screaming at his back. This is the last ounce of fight she has, before she too stops caring, and then there will be no one left in their relationship. When he disappears into the bedroom, she imagines flying after him with a flurry of words, throwing a teacup against the wall. The intensity of her anger consumes her, taking control of her body like an external force.

And yet, suddenly, a tinkling sound is coming from the gate. Akesh must have arrived early. She leans against the wall and takes a deep, shaky breath. She goes to collect her gate keys from the hook and walks onto the balcony.

Akesh's business shirt is already saturated in the rain. He calls out as soon as he sees her. "Whoa! What happened to your head?!"

She laughs ruefully.

"Your hair has all gone! You look like … what's that actress's name? Halle Berry. You look like a *Hindustani* Halle Berry!"

She dashes to let him in, her tears splashed away by the rain.

THE FRIENDSHIP Restaurant in downtown Suva is largely empty, dimly lit by low-hanging red lanterns. Hannah and Jess are seated alone at a large round table, surrounded by empty chairs. They are already tipsy from a glass and a half of wine, laughing at the poorly translated menu items. They try to outdo each other by finding the most outlandish one. So far, their favorites are *Happy family in casserole* (number forty-two) and *Glamorous spicy chicken ideas* (number eleven).

Jess is taking photos and uploading them to Facebook, where she has an entire album dedicated to "Chinglish and Other Typos in Fiji."

Hannah wipes her eyes. "How can they get it *so* wrong?"

"I know, right?"

"A copyeditor has looked over this and nodded sagely with approval."

An iTaukei waitress appears, standing at their table and holding a notebook.

Jess says, "Could we also have number thirty-two, please? The *Friendship meat rices noodle?*"

Hannah dissolves into giggles again. Unamused, the waitress writes their orders down. Hannah hopes she doesn't think they are laughing at her, so she composes herself and says "*Vinaka!*" with sincerity as she hands over her menu. The waitress gives her a forced smile before withdrawing to the kitchen.

The food arrives. As she dishes the rice, Jess recounts a story about a workshop she went to recently, where she was placed at a table with a Chinese woman. "We were discussing challenges facing women in business, right? And I was talking about stigma, and she didn't understand what I was trying to say. So she got out her phone and asked me to speak into it, for Google Translate? The one where you speak into it in English, and then it speaks the word back in Chinese? So I said 'stigma' into the phone, and then she held up the phone and looked really confused, and then cracked up laughing. Turns out the app translated the other meaning of stigma – you know the germination part of the plant?"

"Ha!" laughs Hannah. "Of course! I remember that from primary school science classes."

"It's, like, the flower's vagina or something."

"Ovaries, I think."

"Whatevs. I couldn't stop laughing."

They only eat half of their enormous servings. Hannah pushes the remaining balls of batter around the plate, slightly repulsed by the lurid pink of the sweet and sour sauce she has just eaten. The girls sit back in their chairs, full and a little bit drunk. Hannah's feeling of claustrophobia from a few days ago has dissipated, and the gleam of her Suva life is somewhat shiny again. Perhaps she does live in a bubble, but at least it's a fun one! A buzz in her handbag prompts her to check her phone. There are two messages on there, the first from PacFone:

Gr8 dealz on data – recharge $10 or more with PacFone 2 get 24hrs free facebook, insta and twitter! Offer endz midnite Sunday.

"Fuck off, PacFone!" she says happily.

The second message is from Ethan.

Coming to O'Hannigans?

She looks up. "Hey, the others are at O'Hannigan's."

"Let's do it," Jess says, and they get up to pay.

They push open the restaurant's heavy door and step into the blustering rain, walking arm in arm under the shop awnings of Suva's night strip. Black-clad security guards lean against the wall of a nightclub, the muted thrum of drum and bass leaking onto the street. The men raise their eyebrows at the girls.

"Not tonight!" say Hannah and Jess, tottering past in their high heels as they continue down the street.

The security guards of O'Hannigan's give them a smile when they arrive and open the door, unleashing a fog of warmth and the smell of stale beer. Loud R&B bass reverberates through Hannah's body. The crowd inside has crystallized into little iTaukei or Indo-Fijian groups, talking and laughing loudly. Hannah looks past the bobbing heads on the dance floor and scans the back of the bar. At her friends' table, she sees Pip, Ethan, Aaron, Pasepa, and World Bank Dave. She keeps scanning. Finally, her eyes land on Jean ordering a drink at the bar, his wavy, shoulder-length hair hanging down, a thin shadow of a beard darkening his chin. He looks up at that moment and catches her eye.

Emboldened by the wine, Hannah walks up to him and kisses him on the cheek, and he disarms her by kissing her twice. She forgot about that French thing.

"A drink, *Poisson*?"

"Yes please. A cab sav, thanks."

He gives her a wry smile. "You mean a cabernet sauvignon? You *Australiennes*."

"Haha!" she laughs, although she doesn't like the generic sound of that.

They return to the table with drinks in hand. The group is in an animated discussion about their planned stay at the Hibiscus Inn during the cyclone, discussing what they should stockpile. It is a little sobering to be in an *actual* natural disaster. Pip sensibly suggests canned foods and bottled water. World Bank Dave says coffee and booze are non-negotiable, and Aaron says he will "source some good weed."

Ethan stands up suddenly from his chair – Peniasi has just arrived. "Peni! Glad you could make it down, mate." He is wearing a loud orange Bula shirt that hugs his chest. Hannah kisses him

on the cheek, proud to show the others that she knows him too.
The volunteers are discreet about noticing his lipstick and jump
over each other to welcome him into the circle. Peniasi, it turns
out, is an old university friend of Pasepa's; just another little coincidence in small-town Suva.

Hannah tries to engage Jean in a more intimate, one-on-one
discussion. She turns to him and speaks loudly over the music.
"So, have you traveled much Jean? Before coming to Suva?"

He nods as he takes a sip of his red wine. He has done South
America, he says, and Africa, Southeast Asia, and Europe.
He has no interest in North America. She asks him about his
favorite part of the world, and he says he can't decide between
the trek through the Andes and the backpacking he did in Southern Africa.

It is late now, and Hannah should be getting an early night's
sleep before her second day in Paradise tomorrow, but she is
happy listening to Jean's stories. When he begins to tell her she
should visit Indonesia, Hannah can't find the right moment to
tell him she has already been there. "That sounds amazing," she
hears herself saying a lot.

Later, when the crowd thins out, the volunteers are the last
table remaining. A tired-looking woman comes to collect their
empty beer glasses.

Pasepa is asking Peniasi about their mutual friend who, apparently, was elected to parliament last year.

"He's good, eh?" Peniasi says. He then quietens his voice so
that it is just audible to those at the table. "But there'll be another
coup soon."

Pasepa laughs. "Here we go."

"You reckon a coup is on its way, mate?" Ethan asks.

"*Io.* The writing's on the wall."

Pasepa rolls her eyes as she interrupts him. "Bullshit. Fiji's doing great. Suva's booming. Come on, we're the hub of the Pacific!"

Peniasi rolls his eyes. "Such an economist, Pa. 'Hub of the Pacific'? What does that even mean?"

Everyone at the table begins to listen in, intrigued to hear two Fijians debate about the state of their country.

"A hub," Pasepa repeats. "All the big businesses, multilateral agencies, and NGOs have their Pacific headquarters here ..."

"But what about Fijians?"

"What do you mean, what about Fijians?"

"How does this benefit everyday Fijians?"

Pasepa looks incredulous at his question. "Development, obviously."

"But this is the question, eh? What does development actually do?" He looks at the Australians at the table and says, "Aside from bringing in cool Australian volunteers, obviously. No offense," and everyone laughs.

"It brings in money, of course," Pasepa says.

"Yeah, but where does that money go?" Peniasi takes a sip of his wine, flashing his long eyelashes at her.

She laughs. "More jobs!"

"Oh goodie," Ethan says. "At four dollars an hour?"

"Exactly," Peniasi adds.

World Bank Dave shrugs, unconvinced. "It's all relative," he says. He tells them a story about his last posting in the Philippines. "You haven't seen desperation until you've been to the slums in Manila. The poverty and unemployment there are horrendous. I'm talking human trafficking. Sex slaves. Men came up to me asking me if I 'wanted a twelve-year-old.' You know, it's *icky*. Fiji's a fucking utopia in comparison."

Aaron nods. "Yeah, Fiji's doing pretty well. We put out a report yesterday. Fiji's rising out of poverty. The number of people living below the line has decreased."

"I read that, too." Peniasi pursed his lips skeptically. "It's based on vague estimates and, you know, patchy figures. No one's actually stepped out of their offices to see what's happening on the ground. Poverty is bad in Fiji and getting worse – it could very easily become a Philippines."

Ethan leans back on his chair. "I'm with Peni. I don't trust the modeling. The poverty line they use is, like, what, six dollars a day or something? That means if someone earns seven a day, they're not counted as poor anymore. Besides, six dollars buys you jack shit."

People begin to talk over each other loudly, alcohol taking the edge off their usual cautiousness about open political discussion in Suva. Everyone agrees that living in Suva *is* expensive for a de-veloping country: house prices, rent, food, and building supplies are all surprisingly steep. German Jana, who always likes to re-mind everyone that she has been in Fiji the longest out of all the volunteers, confirms that she and Pip are paying much more rent now than she was paying for the same house several years ago.

Pasepa remains skeptical. "Sure, sure. But people can lift them-selves out of poverty too, right? It's always the lazy ones who complain. Take my taxi driver tonight, eh? He grew up in the settlement, but he's been working three jobs and he's just put a down payment on a mortgage for his first house. I was like, *isa* man, good for you."

"And now he's a slave to the bank," says Peniasi.

Pasepa laughs. "Don't give me that Marxist bullshit." She takes a sip of her drink.

Ethan changes the direction of the conversation. "So, Peni, what do you mean, a coup? Who do you actually think is going to storm the streets? Take over parliament?"

"There are a lot of people who don't like Lewanivanua. I mean, he's no saint but he's trying to make big changes in Fiji. He plays hardball for Fiji in trade negotiations."

"Tell me about it." World Bank Dave shakes his head. "It's called 'alienating Fiji from the rest of the world.'"

Ethan ignores Dave and keeps talking to Peniasi. "But who would be behind this coup?"

"Overseas interests, but they'll fund some ethnonationalists to front it. Big business doesn't like the changes, eh? They want a different man in power. Someone they can control. Rumors are that some of the people in Lewanivanua's own government are turning on him. He formed a coalition to get over the line after the election and it's starting to crack."

The waitress interrupts to say that if they want a final drink, they need to order it now. They all nod and thank her.

Hannah is intrigued. "So how does a coup, you know, *happen?*" she asks.

Jean steps in. "The CIA usually gets involved; I've seen it happen."

World Bank Dave rolls his eyes. "Bullshit. The CIA? You believe that shit?"

Jean looks him straight in the eye. "Look at Egypt. Look at Libya. Look at most of the countries in Latin America."

"Oh come *on*," Dave scoffs. "They were civilian uprisings. The people overthrowing dickheads. Not some kind of international plot."

Jean cocks his head patronizingly at Dave. "Is that what you think?"

"Er, yes! Because it's what bloody happened!"

Jean and Dave go on to argue about "what happened in Egypt." Hannah laughs nervously, feeling out of her depth. She has no idea what happened in Egypt. It's slightly uncomfortable how heated her two friends are becoming. The alcohol has made Dave cantankerous and Jean righteous and defensive.

The volume of the music plummets suddenly, a message from the staff that they are tired and want to go home. The overhead lights flash on, illuminating the scuffs on the dance floor and sticky patches of spilled beer. The waitress is mopping under the tables, circling ever closer.

"I wouldn't rule out the CIA again," Peniasi says cryptically. "They were involved in '87."

Jean leans back in his chair in huffy vindication.

Pasepa laughs. "Peni, you're such a hack. You do know there isn't a conspiracy around every corner?"

Peniasi smiles, raising his eyebrows. "You'd be surprised."

Aaron stands up, defusing the tension by pouring what is left of the jug of beer into people's glasses.

Jean, however, remains evidently annoyed. He gets up to leave, walking out of the bar without much of a goodbye.

When he's gone, Dave addresses the table. "He's a bit intense," he says.

Hannah feels a prickle of irritation and shrugs defensively. "Oh, Jean? He's pretty passionate about global politics. He's very well traveled."

Ethan guzzles the last of his beer and places his empty glass heavily on the table, standing up to leave. "So he likes to keep telling us."

Wednesday

ISIKELI WATCHES the people across the road sprint for shelter under the bus stop. Their limp, wet hair makes them look skinny and vulnerable, like wet rats. He can aready tell that Dorothy is going to be a bad storm, the worst one in years. He can tell by the shape and movement of the clouds and the way the wind is swirling the rain in different directions. It was his dad who taught him how to read the weather. As a child, Isikeli sponged up his father's teachings until he too could interpret the sky and listen to the wind. Bu says Isikeli's talent is spiritual. She thinks he has *mana*. She says when he's older he will be able to harness the weather's power and use it for good. Isikeli isn't convinced of that, but he likes it when she says so.

Eta sits barefoot on the concrete next to him. They're waiting outside SupaValu for the Australian woman and the nurse. It's been a while, and the supermarket's security guard keeps looking over at them.

Isikeli's stomach is rumbling with hunger. There was nothing for breakfast this morning. He tries to take his mind off the shopping bag in his hand with the two loaves of fresh white bread and the bottle of lime-flavored Island Cola. He would love to break off a hunk of bread and eat it hungrily right now, but he needs to cater for his guests properly, the Fijian way.

He looks down at his niece again. He flicked her ear this morning when she whinged for peanut butter. She screamed melodramatically and didn't talk to him for a while. But that all seems to be forgotten now. She is flapping her fingers in the air, gently singing the tune that Bu used to sing, the one about catching fish by their tails when the tide went out.

Teitei Ulavi
Tei Balagi
Tei Tivitivi
Tei Robono

He suddenly feels as though he is a bit harsh on her sometimes.

Finally, the *Kai Valagi* girl and the nurse appear stepping out of a taxi across the road. He watches Hannah look around, until she locks eyes with him and waves. She says something to the nurse, and they begin to run toward the supermarket.

"*Bula*, Isikeli!" she calls, in that eager Australian accent. The security guard can barely hide his surprise.

Eta hides behind Isikeli's leg.

"And who's this?" Hannah bends down, squatting at eye level with his niece.

Isikeli pulls the girl in front of his legs. "Stand up properly. Speak nicely to the lady."

"*Bula*, Aunty," Eta whispers.

"Naww, and what's your name?"

The girl looks up at Isikeli uncertainly.

"*O cei na yacamu*?" he translates.

She looks at her feet bashfully. "Eta."

"Hello, Eta, I'm Hannah," she says, shaking the girl's hand in faux formality. Eta smiles coyly. Hannah stands up. "She's a cutie!"

He raises his eyebrows.

Isikeli leads the way behind the supermarket through the paths of the settlement toward his house. They pass a street dog, a large growth on its leg, nosing through a rubbish bag in the rain. The guts of the bag have spilled out into a muddy circle of nappies, chicken bones, and cigarette packets. Isikeli takes a step toward the dog and she cowers, growling and moving away quickly, seeking shelter under the stilts of a nearby house.

"Here, eh?" Isikeli says when they reach Bu's house.

"Oh, lovely!" says Hannah, but he sees her take in all the details of the home: the rusted patchwork of corrugated tin; the leaning angle of the side room; the rotting wooden step to the doorway. He notices, too, that Bu has spread out the colorful doormat that she keeps for special occasions. The one that says WELCOME.

When he told Bu this morning that he had invited the *Kai Valagi* girl and the nurse, his grandmother flew into an angry rage, or, rather, remained seated and pointed at him furiously. He'd been expecting it. Bu is petrified of doctors and nurses. The last time she went to a hospital she came back without a leg. She suspects them of witchcraft. She doesn't blame them, per se, but she thinks they are possessed by *tevoro*. Isikeli isn't so sure – he wants her to try anything that will work, even Western medicine. So he weathered her anger stoically and went to greet the visitors. It will be worth it. He is confident that the Australian woman is going to be able to help them.

Bu is sitting on the mat, half lit by the small window, waiting nervously. She has brought out the special tea set that she reserves for visitors. The china set was a parting gift from the

Reddy family thirty years ago. She started working as a house-girl for the Reddys when she was eighteen years old and stayed with them until the family migrated to Canada. *Bosso* and *Marama* have long since died, but Bu still receives a Christmas card each year from their oldest daughter, now a dentist in Vancouver. Bu always displays that Christmas card on top of their toaster oven until at least Easter.

"*Bula*, Aunty, I'm Sister Ruci," the nurse says. She sighs as she sits cross-legged on the mat in front of Bu, getting out her blood machine from her sequined bag. "Usually you see my colleague, Sister Nidhya, don't you? I'm doing your check-up for today. This is Hannah, she is from Australia. She's doing research with FijiHealth. She is going to *talanoa* with you afterwards."

"*Ni sa bula vinaka*, Hannah," Bu says quietly.

Hannah bows. "*Bula*, Bu, thank you for having me."

The nurse places a peg on Bu's finger and continues. "Now, have you been taking your medication? The pills?"

"*Io*," Bu says, avoiding eye contact with Isikeli.

The machine beeps, Ruci looks at the screen, and looks distrustfully at her patient. "Your blood sugar is still very high, eh? Have you been cutting back on the sugar?"

"*Io*," she says obediently. "No sugar."

"How is your leg?"

"*Vinaka*, it's very good, eh?" she says.

The nurse goes on to ask a series of questions, with matronly efficiency, while Isikeli gets up to prepare morning tea: a plate of thick slices of bread, layered with margarine and strawberry *jamu*. He heaps three teaspoons of sugar into Hannah's cup of tea and then decides to add another one because she is a special guest.

The nurse examines Bu's half-leg. It has healed well; the skin has stretched tightly over the knob, which ends just above where her knee used to be. The nurse completes her check-up – or, at least, gives up trying to get honest answers out of Bu – and says she will leave Hannah here while she completes several more of her home visits close by.

"*Vinaka*, sister," Bu says, visibly relieved to be rid of the nurse at last.

Hannah hands Bu and Isikeli a sheet of paper each. She begins to talk to his grandmother loudly and slowly, gesticulating extravagantly. Isikeli hides his smile; Bu has the best English of anyone he knows.

He looks down at the sheet and glances at the thick paragraphs of writing, recognizing phrases from research he's participated in. Bu scrawls her signature on the consent form and tucks the information sheet away in her handbag.

Hannah begins to ask Bu a series of questions. Bu answers like she always does. Little white lies; the good patient.

After three questions, Hannah takes a deep breath. "Bu, I am not a nurse or a doctor. I'm not going to get angry. I won't tell the nurse or anyone else what you say. But I want to hear honestly about your experiences, and about your life before and after diabetes. And with that information, we can help other people with diabetes."

Bu remains silent for a minute.

Hannah continues, "You are very important to this project. We need people with your kind of experience to tell us what it's like."

Still Bu looks reluctant. A minute later, after a long, thick silence, Bu raises her eyebrows at Hannah. Isikeli can see in her eyes that she has decided to trust her.

"I tell you, eh?" And so Bu begins her story.

While Hannah and his grandmother talk, Isikeli feels the tension build in his shoulders again. He realizes, now, that Hannah is no different from the other researchers. She is not a doctor. She has no way of fixing Bu or providing them with new treatments or a wheelchair. She just wants information from them. Private, intimate information, which Bu is happily sharing. He slips out of the house and sits on the step.

When he returns, the girl has finished her questions. The cup of tea sits beside her, still full, now cold. Perhaps he didn't put enough sugar in it. She is saying *"Vinaka vakalevu!"* She rummages around in her handbag and eventually finds what she is looking for. "This is just a little thank you," she says, handing over a five-dollar PacFone recharge card.

HANNAH FLIPS open her umbrella and tiptoes through the settlement to meet Ruci at the agreed place. She is exhilarated by such an unfamiliar research experience. It has rubbed her emotionally raw, somehow. She can't wait to write up her story. Finally, she has established an honest rapport with a participant. It feels like the first genuinely rewarding moment in her career.

Each time Hannah asked Bu a question, the old woman remained silent for what seemed like minutes, a silence that extended until Hannah began to feel uncomfortable. Whenever she was about to move on awkwardly to the next question, Bu always surprised her by beginning to tell a story, a roundabout tale that spanned years and seemed irrelevant initially, but later revealed itself to be an intriguing insight.

Bu grew up in a village between a mountain and the sea not far from the town of Tiwawa on the island of Mataqai. Bu was the first child in her family. Every time she did something new, like had her first birthday or caught her first fish, the whole village celebrated with a big feast. She grew up thinking the world was made for her. When she was sixteen, her father sent her to Suva to live with her aunt and uncle. Her uncle got her a prestigious job as a housegirl for Mahendra Reddy, the shipping tycoon, whose wife was pregnant at the time. When the baby boy was born, Bu was asked to be their nanny and she was delighted.

Bu lived in the maid's quarters below the Reddy estate. She married the night watchman, Netani, because he was funny and charming and because he traveled to Mataqai to present four whale's teeth to Bu's father, which was very flattering since most girls were exchanged for three.

Bu and Netani had three children of their own, two girls and – finally – a boy, much to Netani's relief. Bu always felt as though she had six children – she loved those Reddy kids like her own. She took them to school every morning and picked them up every afternoon. They came with her to Sunday school, and she sometimes took them back to her village on school holidays. The youngest boy's first words were in Fijian, much to Mrs Reddy's consternation.

Bu's son, Mosese, used to play soccer with the Reddy boys in the front yard and climb the fence of the neighboring mansion to collect lost balls from wayward kicks. She used to watch them from the kitchen window, always marveling at her son's friendship with the young heirs to the Reddy fortune: the only difference was the Reddys' crisply starched private school uniforms.

Bu and Netani used to help prepare for the Reddys' lavish garden parties throughout the seventies and eighties. Extravagant affairs attended by bank managers, prime ministers, and governor generals. Big pots of lamb curry, pigs slaughtered by Netani and roasted in the *lovo*, and never-ending bottles of whiskey. The proudest moment of Bu's working life was when the American ambassador went back for seconds of her *kakoda*.

While Bu told these stories to Hannah, little Eta sat listening to her great-grandmother in awe, giggling at the funny bits, scrutinizing Hannah for her reactions. The girl's laugh was sweet and infectious, but Hannah couldn't help but notice the two baby teeth rotted black on her bottom gum.

The Reddys sold up and emigrated from Fiji when the money dropped out of the shipping trade after the '87 coup. On the day the Reddys flew to Canada, Bu and Netani caught a bus to the airport and waved them off. All of them – even Mrs Reddy – had tears in their eyes as the family disappeared through the security gates.

Bu and Netani were left unemployed and homeless. There were no jobs back home in Mataqai, so they *kerekere*'d one of Netani's cousin-brothers who lived in Paradise Estate, who let them build a shack on the land behind his house. They moved in with their three teenage children.

Mosese married his young bride, Vera, and they stayed in the house, too. Bu helped to raise their children, Mere and Isikeli. Two days before Isikeli turned eleven years old, his father dropped dead on a factory floor. Mosese was thirty-six. (When Bu told this part of the story to Hannah, her eyes welled with tears. Hannah glanced discreetly at where Isikeli had been standing, but the boy had slipped unnoticed out of the room.) The doctor said it was most likely lung complications from asbestos exposure. They didn't even know he had it.

Netani was *kavoro* when Mosese died, Bu said.

"Sorry, what's *kavoro*?"

"Like the glass, eh?" She mimed something being smashed.

"Oh." Shattered.

Bu's husband died two years later.

Stripped of the family's two breadwinners, Vera *kerekere*'d a distant relative and was lucky to be offered a job as a maid at a resort despite not having any experience nor references. She had to take the job, even though it was far from her family. She sends money back to Suva, while Bu looks after her kids.

Bu summed it up for Hannah. She has raised thirteen children: three of her own; three of the Reddys; two neices; four grandchildren; and one great-granddaughter, Eta. She counted them out on her wrinkled fingers, one by one, the little bodies that she has fed and bathed and fanned to sleep.

Bu didn't know she had *na mate ni suka* until the doctors told her that her leg was infected and it needed to be cut off. The doctor said it was because of too much bad food, but Bu knew it was really from *tevoro* – witchcraft. She didn't entirely trust the doctor. But she had also seen the neighbor look at her jealously through the window, listening to her conversations. After all, Bu worked with the Reddys; who wouldn't be jealous of that? (Hannah nodded when Bu said this, thinking, *she actually just said "witchcraft"!)*

Bu didn't take the medication the nurse gave her because she knew it wouldn't work. Instead, the prayer group came around to exorcise the bad spirits.

"Now I'm better," she said. "The Lord Almighty is good. I still got this leg, eh?" The old woman chuckled.

When Hannah asked if her diet had changed over her lifetime, Bu sat quietly, the silence extending until Hannah felt sure she had not heard the question. But soon enough, Bu began to tell a winding story about her village on Mataqai.

The men in Bu's village used to go fishing on bamboo *bilibili*, bringing home the fresh catch for the women to cook. Then a big Japanese fishing company set up a tuna cannery in Tiwawa town. Everyone celebrated and yearned for a job there – night shifts or day shifts, they paid good money. The men left the land, the women left their children with their family. "When Pacific-Tuna was in town, we all had incomes," Bu said, emphasizing that last word, as though it meant riches. Everyone began to get phones and pay television dishes.

When there were fewer fish in the waters around the island, the workforce was laid off and the Japanese company left. "But we forget how to live the traditional way, eh? Like our old people. Now we're just lazy. We don't fish anymore, we just eat tinned fish. Watch TV. We have lost the Fijian way."

There is that word again: "lazy." Hannah has heard it so often lately, as though it belongs to iTaukei.

Now, Hannah rounds the corner of the settlement and sees Ruci waiting under a bus shelter for her. Together they begin the walk back to SupaValu. Hannah has so many questions that she wants to ask Ruci – little things that need explaining. *What does* kerekere *mean? Has she heard of the Reddys? Does asbestosis have any symptoms?* The nurse answers them tersely. The final question Hannah asks is, "What are those tablets Bu is supposed to be taking?"

"Metformin and Glipizide, for controlling the diabetes."

"Right. And if she doesn't take that medication, is that … bad?"

"*Io.*"

"Bad in what way?"

Ruci shrugs. "Kidney failure. Blindness. Losing the other leg. She could die."

"Oh," Hannah says. "Oh, right."

LAKSHMI LUNGES at Rishika with a squeal. "You've cut your hair off!" She rubs the shortened ends at the back of Rishika's head. "So cute!" As the electric gate screeches shut behind them, Lakshmi pulls Rishika beneath her umbrella. "Come find the garden boy with me," she says, leading her around the side of the house.

"SIMONI!"

They find Simoni, a short, stout man in his sixties, perched precariously on an old wooden step ladder in the pouring rain, screwing in the last of the heavy wooden cyclone shutters on the back window.

Lakshmi waits until he steps down from the ladder to hand over the money for his day's work.

"*Vinaka, Marama,*" he says.

"You'll come Saturday?"

"*Io,*" Simoni says softly, a fat raindrop hanging on his nostril before plopping off.

"Take the ladder back to the shed before you go."

"*Io.*"

Rishika smiles at him from under the umbrella as he walks past, but he doesn't seem to notice.

Inside the house, Lakshmi prepares dinner in the kitchen. Rishika finds Arveen and Karishma staring blankly at the TV to the boom! bap! pow! of *Tom and Jerry*. She tickles Arveen, who looks annoyed at the interruption and then squirms with a reluctant smile. Little Karishma huddles in closer to her brother.

Lakshmi calls out from the kitchen. She reminds Rishika that tonight they are observing the Hindu vegetarian custom, so there is no meat for her guest.

"What did you make?" Rishika calls back.

"*Bindi* curry," Lakshmi replies.

Rishika browses the photos on the display cabinet next to the television. Photos of the boys when they were younger at Gold Coast theme parks splashing to the bottom of water slides, screaming down rollercoasters, being hugged by Mickey Mouse. A photo of a solemn-faced Sachin at a wildlife park, a python coiled around his neck. The kind of photos you are encouraged to buy just before the gift shop.

Lakshmi's two older sons come out of their room for dinner. They dutifully answer Rishika's questions about school and study and soccer. She tries to cajole a smile out of them.

Arveen is unusually quiet, chewing his roti.

"Aunty?" he says eventually.

"*Haan*?"

"Why aren't you a mummy?"

Lakshmi looks mortified and tries to hush her son. But Rishika doesn't mind this question when it comes from Arveen. Lakshmi herself hasn't mentioned Rishika's miscarriages for years. She thinks about how best to put it to the little boy.

"My body didn't let me have babies."

Arveen continues chewing, thoughtfully. "Are you angry with your body, Aunty?"

Lakshmi looks horrified. "Arveen!"

"It's okay." Rishika smiles. "*Haan*, a little bit."

Arveen looks pensive, and then puts his roti down solemnly. "You can have my transformer."

Rishika laughs spontaneously. "Thank you, *Babba*. But you keep it."

Arveen can't hide his relief.

Later, Rishika stacks the dishwasher and Lakshmi puts the younger kids to bed. The house falls silent. The two cousins sit cross-legged on the couch, each nursing a cup of ginger tea with a Hindi drama playing in the background. They talk of their old school friends.

"You should join Facebook," Lakshmi says. "Everyone's on there. Lalita, Deepika ... even Master Maharaj."

At this, Rishika swallows a gulp of hot tea, which scalds her throat. Master Maharaj used to smack left-handed children with a ruler and then smack them again if their writing was not impeccable. He used to disappear out of the classroom for significant periods of time whenever he got a chance. The idea of befriending him on Facebook was bizarre.

Rishika is ambivalent about the idea of social media. Friends and cousins have tried to show her how to use it. On the one hand, she loves the idea of searching for old acquaintances; mapping the degrees of separation between friends – a modern form of archival history. On the other, she wants to protect herself from the little stabs of envy she will experience as she scrolls through pages and pages of photos: her friends with their smiling children; their careers; their engaged, present husbands.

"Just the other day," Lakshmi continues, "I got a friend request from Julia Morris. Do you remember her? That Australian girl?"

Rishika's head whips up. "Julia Morris?" She decides not to mention that she often thinks of Julia and her mother, Wendy. "*Haan*. I remember," she says casually. "Where is she now?"

"Brisbane. *Dekho*. I'll show you." Lakshmi scrolls through her phone to find Julia's profile.

"Here." She hands the phone over to Rishika. "You can swipe right to see more photos."

This is a surreal moment for Rishika. Her first thought is that Julia Morris looks so *old*. The last time she saw Julia, she was thirteen years old, and now she is in her forties. It takes a moment for Rishika to remember that she is, too.

As she swipes, she sees an earlier photo of Julia, perhaps when she was in her late twenties – with a short man with very pale blond hair. They are standing either side of a real estate sign with a SOLD sticker, in front of an old weatherboard house, looking happy and invincible. Photos of Julia in a business suit, sitting amongst a team of colleagues. Photos of Julia with that blond man again, arms proudly around their two children, one little girl with white-blond hair, one little boy with red hair and freckles. The stab of envy is not as painful as Rishika thought it might be. She is happy for Julia.

As she swipes through, she sees less and less of the blond man. In the more recent photos, he isn't there. She clicks out of the photos and begins to look back through Julia's posts: newspaper articles she has shared, birthday messages for her children. Then she finds it: "Dear friends, it is with great sadness that we announce that Steve and I are separating … we remain friends and are deeply committed to coparenting our children … thank you for your support." The post accrued fifty-one comments ("Sorry to hear that Jules and Steve. Heaps of love xxx"), seventy-six sad-faced emojis, and one "like" from an insensitive friend who probably didn't realize how that might come across.

Lakshmi peers over Rishika's shoulder and makes gleeful sounds of interest at the scandal. "That's the problem with *gora* marriages!"

Rishika just feels sad. Poor Julia. Poor blond Steve.

In the most recent photo she can find, Julia's red-haired boy is beaming in front of an indoor pool, goggle marks etched around his eyes. A comment underneath catches her eye – "Can't believe how tall Max is getting! Love Mum xxoo."

Rishika stares in amazement. She clicks again, and there is Wendy Morris – strong, kind, wise Wendy – silver hair, but definitely the same woman, gentle wrinkles like parentheses around her smile etched more deeply now. Rishika thinks she can see a glint of sadness in Wendy's eyes that she can't remember from before.

A series of metallic sounds rings outside the house. Lakshmi looks at her with widened eyes, until they both realize it is only the front door being unlocked. They are surprised to see Sachin appear down the hallway, the smell of whiskey emanating from him.

"*Kaise*, ladies?" he says woozily.

"Right *hai*," they say in unison, sitting more erect now.

"Meeting finished early?" Lakshmi asks warily.

He ignores or doesn't hear the question, instead looking at the windows. "Simoni put the cyclone shutters up," he states. "That's good."

He flops onto the armchair.

"Rishika," he breathes after a brief silence.

"*Haan*, Sachin?"

"*Kaise?*"

Lakshmi laughs at his repeated question.

"Right *hai*," Rishika says again. "*Tum kaise?*"

"Ok, ok, ok." He closes his eyes, and fumbles with the armchair lever to recline it.

Lying almost horizontally now, he breathes raspily. The cousins look at each other, wondering if he has fallen asleep, but he begins to talk with his eyes closed.

"Your husband never comes drinking anymore," he says.

"*Haan*," says Rishika slowly. She's not the only one he has been avoiding.

"Takes himself too seriously," Sachin continues. "He used to be fun."

Rishika doesn't respond.

"Do you know what his problem is?" He pauses. "He likes that fucking *jaati* prime minister too much."

Lakshmi immediately stands up and loudly grabs Rishika's empty tea cup, pulling at Rishika's arm to indicate bedtime, bustling her to the spare room.

Later, Rishika lies awake listening to the wind rattling the cyclone shutters, feeling a rising tide of resentment.

She couldn't help but think Sachin was right. Vijay isn't much fun anymore.

THE DRONE of the mosquito is surprisingly loud in Isikeli's ear, even audible above the din of the rain on Bu's creaking tin roof.

Isikeli looks over at his family, their chests moving up and down slowly, finally asleep. Eta lies on the mat next to Bu, arms splayed restlessly above her head. Aunty and Uncle are asleep on the rolled-out mattresses in the adjacent room.

Tonight, Isikeli and Seru are going to break into the Chamberlain Street house again. They finalized the plans last night when they were sitting in front of the television at Seru's uncle's house, watching the Flying Fijians lose miserably to the All Blacks. They always watch rugby together. They shout at the television, swearing at the questionable decisions from the referee. They used to go and see the games live with their dads at National Stadium. They would sit on the grassy slope, jumping up and down at every try, calling out the same injustices and triumphs in unison. One memorable occasion was when they were ten years old, watching Suva versus Mataqai. They all cheered for their home province of Mataqai, even though Isikeli's dad had spent many years playing semi-professionally for Suva City. The Mataqai team won convincingly (67–12) and they all went back to Seru's house to celebrate. That party – Isikeli remembers – went long into the night. The men got out their guitars and the women danced, laughing when the men rolled up notes and placed them flirtatiously in their *sulus*. Isikeli's mum grabbed him and twirled him around while he pretended he didn't enjoy it. Later in the evening, the boys stole a can of beer and took it behind the outdoor toilet block, thrilled at the sound of it opening: *click-fizz*. They both had one sip and spat it out in disgust. Isikeli was genuinely disappointed. *When will I taste what the grown-ups do?* They poured the rest of the can out and kicked it to each other along the path to the other side of Paradise, where they climbed to the top of the mango tree. You could see the city from there.

When they returned to the party on the verandah several hours later, the mood had darkened. Seru's mum was in tears in the corner, holding a bag of frozen peas against her nose, blood trailing down her cheek, while Seru's dad was being held back by Isikeli's. Seru's aunty was comforting her sister and shouting back. Isikeli and Seru slunk unnoticed through the door. They watched cartoons on the small television, turning up the volume as loud as it could go to drown out the adults outside.

Seru's mum's nose was permanently wonky after that night.

That happens sometimes with Seru's dad. He gets angry. Isikeli finds him frightening and he can tell that Seru does, too.

The truth is, over the last few days, Isikeli has been troubled by his own anger. It is an all-consuming, intoxicating feeling. It makes him manic, out of control, a feeling he doesn't enjoy.

He looks over at Bu now. He doesn't want her to look at him with disappointment anymore. He doesn't want to feel bad every time someone tells him his father was a good man.

I don't want to break into houses anymore. Just thinking about it makes him feel lighter. Maybe he can ask Jone to put in a good word for him at the hardware store.

And yet. Seru is out there right now, waiting for him at the corner of Chamberlain Street as planned. Isikeli has no way of contacting him. Seru is so excited about this one, so confident that this is the night they will find something valuable – a laptop, for example, or a big fat diamond ring. It might be the break they need.

He will do this one last job for Seru's sake. He looks over at Bu. *I promise this will be my last.*

He bends down and brushes the mosquito away from where it is lurking on Eta's forehead. Then he puts on his black floppy *Magpies* hat and slips out the front door.

Thursday

RISHIKA WAKES with a start. Eerie blue light fills the unfamiliar room. It takes her a moment before she recognizes the sparse furniture of Lakshmi and Sachin's spare room. The wind has died down for now, soft rain quietly pattering against the window. *Is that what woke me?* Reaching back into the last moments of sleep, she is sure it was something else – a loud, specific sound. Perhaps she was dreaming.

No, there it is again. *Ding. Dong.* She has never heard the gate intercom from inside this house before, although she has rung it from the outside many times. She almost laughs. Of course, Sachin would choose that sound; loud and cliché, like doorbells in American movies.

She briefly considers going to answer it, and then realizes that would be inappropriate because it isn't her house. Who could possibly be visiting at this hour? Ane? Simoni? Vijay? But it wouldn't be Vijay; he knows she is here, and he would be fast asleep right now.

She hears the bell ring again, more urgently this time, as though to say *Ding DONG for God's sake!* She is relieved to hear stirring in the bedroom next door: Sachin muttering, footsteps up the hallway, the clinking of the lock on the front door, and the screech of the electric, heavy metal gate sliding open. Muted voices. She relaxes and closes her eyes. She will find out who it was later.

She drifts back into a shallow sleep.

Two sharp knocks on her bedroom door jolt her awake again. She sits up, slightly dazed. "*Haan?*" she says tentatively.

Sachin pokes his face around the door, sober now. He is wearing a checkered flannel dressing gown, his hair tousled and spiky like a bird's nest. It makes him look younger somehow, more vulnerable. She is reminded of the first time Lakshmi brought him to her house, pushing him in front of her like a prize goat, desperately wanting her cousin's approval of her new boyfriend. Rishika did like him, the young accounting student who wore dowdy clothes and didn't speak much. That was before he got the job at Jogia's, before he developed his expensive taste in men's fashion and rehearsed charm.

It takes Rishika a split second to realize Sachin's face is extraordinarily pale. In fact, he is struggling to speak. "The police want to speak to you," he says eventually.

It's funny, the way the mind tricks itself when it knows very bad news is coming. Rishika's first thought is, *Solomon must be wandering outside the compound again!* She adjusts her pajamas and stands up.

Then something very odd happens. Sachin breaks down in tears. Surprisingly high-pitched, feminine sobs of grief, so violent that he has to hold onto the door handle for support. She almost feels embarrassed for the poor man. And yet, a foreboding feeling begins to take root at the bottom of her stomach.

She leaves him sobbing and walks alone down the hallway toward the police officers standing in the living room. She

approaches them hesitantly, noting the little details like the zig-
zag hem of their white *sulus*. She feels herself taking in their
drawn, somber faces. It occurs to her, then, that something quite
bad might have happened.

꙲

THE CHIRPY voices of breakfast radio hosts are all but drowned
out by the frantic sweeping of the taxi's windscreen wipers. In
the back seat, running late for work, Hannah is fixing the strap
on her shoe and Jess is trying to apply dark, blood-red lipstick.
The driver – one of the rare female taxi drivers in Suva – re-an-
gles the rearview mirror so that Jess can see her reflection.

"*Vinaka.*" Jess smiles gratefully, baring her teeth to confirm
there are no embarrassing lipstick stains.

"Woman's problem, eh?" the driver says. "Same everywhere,"
and Hannah and Jess politely chuckle with her.

The driver turns up the volume on the stereo as the news begins. A body has been found at a house on Chamberlain Street.
An Indo-Fijian man, aged forty-six, has been beaten to death in
what appears to be a violent home invasion. A relative of the
man made the grisly discovery in the early hours of the morning.
Further details will be released at a press conference later today.

Hannah shudders. Home invasions are a relatively common
topic of conversation amongst the volunteers in Suva. Everyone
knows someone – or at least knows someone who knows someone – who has experienced a break-and-enter. Second-hand stories
about burglaries are passed down from outgoing expats, along
with the furniture, the books, and the hired help. A few years back,
one couple who worked for the UN were tied up with twine while
machete-wielding thieves looted their house. Just last year, one
of the Australian volunteers had their iPhone stolen from beside

their bed *while they were sleeping*. According to German Jana, the girl woke up coughing uncontrollably, which meant they must have used gas to make their victims sleepy (although, as Ethan says, "German Jana says a lot of things"). As the story goes, the police were reportedly *hopeless*. When the girl called them, they said they were on their way. An hour later she called back, and they still hadn't left the station. They admitted they didn't have any cars available. The girl eventually caught a taxi to pick up the police and bring them back to her house.

"*Isa*," Pasepa said when she heard that story, "that's *so* Fiji."

The volunteers laughed cautiously.

Most of the time, Hannah brushes these stories away as urban myth, as fear-mongering. She and Jess have three padlocks on their door, security grills on every window, and a sticker on the gate that says "*Smile, you're on CCTV*." Their house has passed the safety threshold of the volunteer program and has been cleared as low risk by the Australian authorities. But every now and then, she can't help but mentally scroll through the weak points in their security, casing her own joint. She said to Jess and Ethan once, "A robber could climb up through the bathroom window, or wedge open the security grill, if he really wanted to."

"Or she!" Jess reprimanded.

"Han, did you just say 'robber'?" Ethan said. "That's cute." Needless to say, they didn't take her very seriously.

But this news of the Chamberlain Street murder unnerves her. Ever since her meeting with Bu she has been thinking about how fragile lives seem in Fiji, how breakable bodies are. She has started to feel a subtle, ever-present foreboding, like thunder rumbling quietly in the distance.

"Thank God there aren't any guns here," World Bank Dave said at O'Hannigan's a few weeks ago. "Otherwise, Fiji would easily descend into South Africa."

Hannah marveled at the way boys always seemed to make such confident calls on things. Did they actually know more, or did they just have more opinions?

The driver pulls the taxi in beside Hannah's work and smiles back at the girls, one gold tooth glinting. Jess rummages in her wallet for coins, giving her an extra fifty cents.

"You okay?" Jess asks, putting her hand on Hannah's arm.

"Totally! I'm fine!"

They jump over the running water in the drain and dash into their workplace.

But Hannah can't stop thinking about it. Chamberlain Street is just a few streets down from theirs.

A *FIJI HERALD* vehicle pulls up outside Rishika's gate. A photographer steps out, shielding his camera from the rain, his camera angled toward Rishika and Solomon on the balcony. Solomon tries to bark, but it comes out as a wheezy whimper. The poor dog has been fretful all day.

A kind-faced detective runs to the gate and shoos the cameraman away, swearing at him in Fijian. The photographer gets back in the car, but not before taking one last photograph of the crime scene.

Rishika is sitting on the balcony to escape the crowd inside the house, which includes Vijay's mother, Samriti, his two brothers, his cousin Akesh, and a mix of aunties, uncles, neighbors, and friends. Because the cyclone is hurtling toward Suva, a few family members have decided to stay with Rishika for several nights. She was not consulted. Spare beds have been made and mattresses rolled out.

Akesh opens the door now and hands her a cup of tea. His presence gives her a sense of calm.

"Thank you," she says, and gestures for him to join her on the wooden bench. He sits down beside her gingerly. She takes a sip and swallows the hot liquid, surprised to find it gritty and metallic. Everything seems to have lost its flavor.

She looks sideways at Akesh. Tears have welled in his eyes again, and he wipes them away with an angry sniff, his handsome face now slightly blotchy. He has changed into a white shirt – the traditional color of mourning – and beige slacks.

Rishika has learned two things so far about death. The first is that the people around you cry. A lot. And they cry in different ways. She has categorized them into four types: the silent, tearful ones; the snivelers; the sobbers; and the wailers.

The second thing she has learned is that people like to keep busy while they cry. The aunties have bustled and fussed, cleaned obsessively, and cooked enormous amounts of food, none of which seems to have its usual taste.

The detective mounts the steps with another officer who looks barely out of his teens. They gently inquire if they can ask some questions. Receiving no response, they walk past Rishika and Akesh to sit on the plastic chairs with a respectful "*tulou, tulou*" as they pass.

The detective asks the questions while the young officer takes notes in a little book. Rishika feels strangely comforted by the fact that police officers are still handwriting notes at crime scenes. She is pleased that they don't whip out iPads or something. That would seem crass.

At the behest of the detective, Akesh retraces his steps again. He spoke to Vijay early yesterday evening at about 7:00 p.m. He pulls out his phone and checks the log of recent calls, confirming that the call was at exactly 7:17 p.m. and for thirteen minutes. The main topic of conversation was the recent football game between Liverpool and Manchester City. He was teasing his cousin because the score was 3–1 to Liverpool (Vijay was a die-hard City fan). The game was going to be replayed on SportsCentral after midnight, and they decided to watch it together. Akesh was on a deadline to finish something at work but promised to try to get there in time for the second half. Vijay told him he was tired, but to wake him up when he got there.

When Akesh arrived outside the gate at about 12:30 a.m., he was surprised to see the door wide open with the grill unlocked. He called out, but there was no movement from inside the house. Akesh tried calling Vijay's phone, but it went straight through to the message bank. *"You've called Vijay. Leave a message."* Rishika knows this sound so well.

It was the dog who came to greet him at the gate, whimpering and agitated. Rishika hates this part of the story; *poor, poor Solomon. What did he witness?*

Akesh hoped desperately for a simple explanation, but he knew instinctively that something was very wrong. He jumped the fence and ran up the stairs. It was immediately obvious that the house had been ransacked – chairs had been toppled over, drawers were half open, and papers and clothes were strewn across the floor.

As Akesh entered the kitchen, it was there that he found Vijay, crumpled near the table.

Akesh trails off at this point in his story, choking slightly.

"I'm sorry, sir?" says the detective. "You need to tell us again what you saw when you found his body, eh?"

Akesh looks at Rishika uncomfortably.

"It's okay. Tell him. I'm fine," Rishika says.

Akesh explains that Vijay was still warm, but there was no pulse. His left eye was blackened and bruised, and there was a deep cut to the back of his head. Thick dark blood matted his hair.

Rishika stands up suddenly. The men all look up at her.

"Carry on, carry on," she says, waving away their concern. She excuses herself and walks back into the house, past the relatives in the living room, hastening toward the bathroom. She arrives just in time to heave the contents of her stomach violently into the basin. She wipes her mouth with the back of her hand. Maybe she isn't fine after all.

They have all kept the details from her until now. Vijay's body was removed by the time she returned with Lakshmi late this morning. "Forensics" had apparently taken all the photographs and gathered all the evidence they needed. Nadi Uncle took Samriti to the morgue to formally identify that the body was, indeed, Vijay. The scene was professionally cleaned before Rishika's aunties got there to tidy, clean, disinfect, and clean again before Rishika arrived.

Now she bends over and drinks directly from the bathroom tap. She wipes her mouth and stares at herself in the mirror. It is the same Rishika from yesterday who looks back at her: short pixie hair, slender nose, honey-brown eyes.

She knows she is expected to be crying. She knows that everyone around her thinks it is strange that she isn't. And yet, her eyes feel dry and gritty, as though she has been for a long swim in saltwater.

The phone in her pocket buzzes with a message. Her immediate thought is that it might be Vijay. The realization comes flooding back that her husband is, in fact, dead. It is followed quickly by the realization that she is being extra silly because he hardly ever texted her anyway. On a whim, she looks back through the little texts she has sent him over the last few months.

Duck curry for dinner ☺

Just finished my history of Arjun!

What time will you be home tonight?

To all of them, she received monosyllabic replies, and sometimes no response at all. To be honest, Vijay was so cold and un-
communicative lately that the lifeless body lying in the morgue
right now is *not that different* to her husband at the breakfast table
yesterday!

Rishika does not smile at her own joke. She sits down on the
cold porcelain of the bath.

The phone vibrates again against her leg, reminding her about
the text she just received. She glances at the screen. It is only
PacFone:

**Want 2B safe in da cyclone? Text UPD8
to #132 for hourly news on TCDorothy
(regular charges apply)**

She shuts the bathroom door quietly and walks toward the
loungeroom. She can hear her aunties whispering urgently. Nausori Aunty is wringing her fingers. "His soul is waiting," she
hisses, worried that the timing is all wrong for the funeral rites.
The *pundit* is not going to be able to come today because of the
weather, and the need for an autopsy means that Vijay's body
can't be cremated until tomorrow.

The conversation hushes as soon as everyone sees Rishika.
They all affect shaky, pretend smiles. All except Samriti, who
doubles over in a howl of fresh grief, surprisingly loud for the
diminutive woman. Vijay's mother is definitely a wailer.

Rishika blinks at them. Suddenly, she likes the thought
of hourly communication from someone who isn't crying.
She looks down at her phone and types out a quick reply to
PacFone.

Back on the balcony, Akesh is looking at the young police officer writing up his notes. The older detective has disappeared.

"So, do you ... what happens now?" Akesh sounds very tired.

The officer runs through a well-rehearsed piece about following any leads, keeping them updated. "But the investigation might be delayed, eh? Because of the cyclone. We can't do much when there's a curfew."

Rishika used to associate cyclone curfews with a childish sense of cooped up excitement. School used to be canceled for days and her father would have to stay home from work. They would sit inside and play cards – hundreds of games in a row: Trump Ten; Five Three Two; Rummy. Her brother would write up a score chart and always won by a dubious landslide (it was much harder to tell if he was cheating by candlelight).

She wishes her brother were here now. She mentally clocks what time it is in San Francisco: he would have just gone to sleep.

Just then, the detective appears on the stairs, holding something in front of him.

"Excuse me, ma'am? We just found this outside the fence. Does it look familiar?"

He holds out a ziplock bag with an evidence number written on it in permanent marker. It contains something muddy, sodden, and black. "It's a hat, eh?"

Rishika looks closely and can just make out the words *Wagga Wagga Magpies* sewn into the material.

She and Akesh both shake their heads slowly. They have never seen it before.

Wagga Wagga Magpies. What language is that? Rishika makes a mental note to look it up later.

THE SIGN in the shop window says:

UPSTAIRS FOR CHEEP INTERNET
PRINTING

PHOTOCOPING
GAMES

"*Mai*," Isikeli says to Eta, and leads her up the narrow wooden staircase. His new black backpack is slung casually over his shoulder, giving him temporary satisfaction. He likes the bag's sleek professional look: all those little pockets designed for business cards, pens, and a smartphone. Now all he needs is business cards, pens, and a smartphone.

Eta walks up the stairs in front of him. She is wearing her fairy wings again, misshapen from overuse. At the top, he pushes the door open to reveal the barely lit, dank room inside. The booths are largely empty except for three teenage boys gathered around one of the computers. One is playing a video game, killing off enemy combatants, while his friends bark instructions. The gunshots make Isikeli feel jumpy. He thought he was going to feel better after last night. He thought his shoulders were going to feel relief, but they don't. The evening didn't go how he expected. He can't shake off a feeling of paranoia.

A *Kai Idia* has his feet on the counter, scrolling through his phone. He looks up at Isikeli, and then down at Eta. "Two dollars, half an hour, pre-pay," he intones before returning to his phone. Isikeli places a two-dollar coin on the counter. Without looking up, the man places his finger on the coin and slides it over to his side of the desk.

Isikeli leads Eta to the computer near the window so that he can watch for the bus on the street below.

He can probably count on the fingers of one hand the times in his life in which he has sat down at a computer. His high school had an "Information Technology" room with two desktop computers. When he attended the compulsory computer classes in Form One, his classmates took turns on the computers, while the rest of them sat on the edge of the room and looked on. Isikeli paid little attention, instead sitting next to Seru and arguing about rugby tactics.

More recently, though, Jone purchased a laptop from a pawn-shop in town, a heavy white one that took about ten minutes to boot up. In the corner of his house, Jone showed Isikeli and Seru how to play *World of Warcraft* and wait for porn to slowly download. They squealed with laughter when the little spinning wheel kept pausing on the generous breasts of a beautiful but pixelated woman. When Jone's aunty came into earshot they hastily slammed the screen shut.

Now Isikeli fires up the internet browser, typing slowly with his index finger to find *Dora the Explorer* on YouTube. Eventually, he clicks on an episode and the little girl becomes entranced by the cartoon, kicking her shoes off and sitting perfectly still on her chair.

Isikeli slinks into the booth beside Eta's. Placing the backpack at his feet, he unzips the pocket and looks inside at its contents again, hoping in vain that he might have missed something valuable. The same useless things are in there – a lunchbox, an instruction booklet of some kind, a folded newspaper. What a waste.

He takes a sidelong glance at the attendant who is still en-grossed in his phone, and boots up the computer in front of him, adjacent to Eta's. He reaches into his memory for the login de-tails of his Facebook account, trying twice unsuccessfully before he lands on the right password. *Fuck you, Jone, for laughing at how slowly I typed and calling me* kai colo.

On his Facebook feed, several of his friends have shared a news item about a murder in Suva last night. His eyes catch the words "Chamberlain Street," and his fingers immediately begin to shake. He double-clicks on the news item. It seems to take an eternity to load, millimeter by millimeter.

Before it appears, Eta shrieks, "*Na busi!*" and sure enough, he can see out the window below that the orange bus is making its way around the corner earlier than expected. Isikeli knows that it is probably going to be the last bus running before the curfew descends on the town. He tries to do Eta's Velcro straps up, but the girl is wriggly. Eventually, he gives up and throws the shoes in the backpack, grabbing her under his arm and running down the stairs and into the windy street, awkwardly carrying the little fairy in order to reach the bustop in time.

The bus driver kindly waits for them as taxis honk impatiently behind. When they finally board the bus, he sees that it is crowded and that there are no free seats. An elderly iTaukei stranger holds out her hands and Isikeli hands his niece over gratefully to sit on her lap. He holds a seat handle and sways in the aisle as the bus gets moving. Isikeli's anxiety hasn't dissipated. The passengers around him also seem a little manic – smiling at each other nervously, homeward-bound, acutely aware of the cyclone hurtling toward them, probably all praying that it won't be as bad as Winston.

WHEN THE detective has finally finished his questioning, Akesh excuses himself from the balcony. "If you don't mind? I'm exhausted …" He touches Rishika's arm gently and walks back inside the house, where a neighbor is handing out containers with *chana dal* for the officers to take back to the station.

Rishika stands to take her leave too, but the detective stops her.

"Excuse me, ma'am? One more thing …"

"Yes, detective?"

He quietens his voice so that there is no chance that those inside will hear. "Did Mr Vijay and Mr Akesh get on?"

"Vijay and Akesh?"

"*Io*."

"They were cousins."

"*Io*. But was there any … any bad blood between them? Anything unusual that had happened recently? Any arguments?"

Rishika immediately understands what he is getting at. It should have occurred to her that Akesh would be a Person of Interest.

"*Nahi*, never. Nothing. Akesh and Vijay were good friends."

The detective raises his eyebrows. His silence makes her feel like she needs to convince him further. "Akesh wouldn't hurt anybody, if that's what you're thinking!" She trails off, not sure what to say. *Should I mention he's a really good listener?*

He raises his eyebrows again. "What about your relationship with Akesh?"

"Me? He's my cousin. In law. My husband's cousin."

"And how long have you known Akesh for?"

"Well, ever since I've known Vijay." She can hear her tone getting high-pitched.

He just raises his eyebrows.

A deep rumble of thunder gurgles in the distance, so far away that it sounds like an amateur sound effect; someone backstage rattling a sheet of metal. Dorothy is fast approaching.

"We'd better go," the detective says, hurriedly getting ready to leave. "Thank you for your cooperation, ma'am. And sorry again for your loss. We will continue the investigation as soon as the curfew has lifted." He summons his colleague, who emerges from the house laden with steaming ice cream containers of curry to take away.

A FESTIVE feeling zings in the Hibiscus Inn when Hannah and Jess arrive. The reception area is crowded with expats, tourists, and wealthy-looking locals checking in. Two blond children already with cabin fever scream excitedly as they race around the lobby. At first, their parents reprimand them ineffectually – "Finn! Careful of the lady! Ava! Slow down!" – but soon give up. Everyone is giving supportive, knowing smiles to each other, strangers united in crisis. They are going to get through this cyclone together. In comfort.

Through the sliding glass doors, Hannah can see the outdoor area in which she has spent so many warm evenings. It is now eerily empty, the furniture packed away. The pool is overflowing, sloshing over the edges.

At the check-in counter, the woman hands Hannah and Jess the key cards for their room. She surprises them with personalized service. "Your friends have already arrived, eh?"

"Oh! Thanks."

"And there is a message for you."

"Is there?"

"Mr Aaron said for you to come to room 309."

"Oh, haha, *vinaka vakalevu.*"

They drop their bags off in the small hotel room that will be their home for the next two nights and quickly get changed.

"You look *hot* in skinny jeans," Jess says, as she anoints her eyelashes with mascara. Hannah waves away the compliment gratefully.

When they knock on the door of room 309, Pip flings it open. "Yay! You're here!" she shouts. Behind her, Aaron's small room is teeming with their friends talking and laughing, sitting in any space they can find, on the desk, the bedside tables, and the floor. Bottles of alcohol and bubbly mixers are already open.

Ethan and Aaron sit on the edge of the bed poring over a laptop, arguing over the Tropical Cyclone Dorothy playlist. "Good name for an album," Ethan says.

Hannah's eyes rest on Jean leaning casually against the window. Michelle is beside him, chuckling huskily at something he has just said. Hannah's shoulders droop. *Why can't he see past Michelle's intriguing upbringing and ethical face to recognize that she's actually very superficial?* She is pleased when he lifts his gaze to meet hers, his dark eyes shining. She smiles back and then drops eye contact, busying herself at the bar fridge, some power regained.

Ethan and Aaron seem to finally agree on some music. Classic Australian rock begins to play from portable speakers on the bedside table, with Jimmy Barnes singing about flame trees and weary drivers.

Ethan gets up from the bed and joins Hannah at the bar fridge. "If we're gonna die tonight, Han, at least it'll be to Cold Chisel and not that house shit that Aaron listens to."

She laughs and asks him for an update on the copyright case, which seems to be the talk of the town. He tells her that the first hearing went as well as could be expected. Ethan feels the judge was sympathetic and "wasn't taking any shit from the prosecutor."

"That sounds good, I guess?" she says. She hands him a red plastic cup full of beer, and they plink cups together.

"Cheers," she says.

He looks her in the eye. "I don't know why I have the guts to say this all of a sudden."

"Pardon?"

"Han, I really like you."

Hannah starts to laugh and then stops immediately. His quicksilver eyes are serious.

"I have for ages. I think you're gorgeous."

Hannah takes a long sip of her beer while she tries to remember what the right facial expression is in this situation. This is

Ethan, who hardly takes anything seriously. Ethan, who mocks everyone relentlessly. She has only ever thought of him as funny but kind of annoying, like a cousin or a neighbor across the road when you're growing up. She suddenly feels deeply embarrassed for him. It is not his style to be honest and vulnerable. But also: *how irritating! How inconvenient!* She doesn't have the mental space to process such an absurd revelation right now.

In the background, everyone in the corner is laughing at something Aaron just said, and Jimmy Barnes is still crooning in the speakers. It takes her a second to realize how to react. She puts her beer down.

"Naww, thanks Eth! I think you're great too. I love all you guys!" She gives him a flippant hug, her arms flinging lightly over his shoulders, careful not to press her chest too closely against his. "Now come talk to Michelle and Jean with me!"

As she pulls away from the hug, she thinks she sees a brief flash in his eyes – of confusion? of hurt? – but it disappears instantly and his face reverts to its usual look of casual friendliness. Same old Ethan, dignity intact.

"Cool. Yep." He takes a gulp of his beer. "You go, I'll join you in a sec."

BU'S HOUSE rattles and contracts as the wind howls through the narrow gaps in the settlement. Eta squirms on her great-grandmother's lap. Bu adjusts the blanket over her. One overhead bulb – its filament visible – emits a dim light in the room. Uncle is lying down on the rolled-out mattress. After a standoff with Bu and Uncle, Aunty has followed a group from the settlement to a cyclone shelter at the local school. Mere has gratefully accepted a last-minute offer of a one-night job as a maid at a hotel in town.

Isikeli places towels under the door to block the draft and a bucket in the middle of the room to catch the leaking water from the roof. He sits down again. Speaking loud enough to be heard, Bu tells a story about the *kalou vu*. They have all heard it a thousand times, but it takes on a particularly dramatic tone tonight. Isikeli closes his eyes and listens to Bu's deep voice rolling over the words about the origins of life. It is the story of Movua, the ancestral spirit of the people from Mataqai. When Movua first landed on the island, he settled on the steep mountain behind Bu's village. "The mountain has three mounds on top, big sandy mounds, and the one on the left is where Movua lives."

When Isikeli was seven, his father took him up to the top of that mountain to pay respects to Movua and present the spirit with gifts. The climb was exhausting, almost too much for the boy, the sharp foliage scratching at his legs and arms. But he didn't complain, his heart singing with the honor of being invited to such a *tabu* place. When they reached the top, puffed and exhilarated, his father rested his hand on his shoulder. Isikeli breathlessly scanned the full view of the island, all the way down the lush green mountain and across the Pacific Ocean as far as the eye could see.

"And now," Bu is saying as she looks between her brother, her grandson, and her great-granddaughter – eyes resting on each person before she moves to the next – "Movua lives in the owl. Whenever you see the owl, Movua has a message for us. Someone is going to die." She stresses the last word, enjoying the effect it has on her audience.

Eta gasps, "I saw an owl today!"

Isikeli shooshes her. "*So*! You don't even know what an owl looks like."

Eta settles back into Bu's lap, appearing only slightly reassured.

Uncle chuckles from where he lies on the mattress. "Those spirits are just myths, eh? Ghost stories for the kids. God is in charge."

Bu raises her eyebrows skeptically. Uncle is a New Methodist. His reverend preaches against the "dark heathen" beliefs of the past. He often gets in heated arguments with Bu, saying, "We were created in the image of God, eh? Not by animal spirits!" But Bu isn't convinced. She has seen the ancestral spirits work their magic too many times. For Bu, threads of Christian faith are only ever woven in and around the power of the ancestors.

As the elderly siblings begin the same old argument, there is a thwack against the roof, a tree branch so heavy that it dents the tin just above the toaster oven. Uncle startles and sits up. He takes off his glasses and rubs his eyes. He begins to pray, his back bent over, mumbling his prayers over and over again. Isikeli hears him ask the Holy Spirit to protect his family and all the people in Mataqai. Then, in a quiet whisper that Bu can't hear, Uncle adds a little word of respect to Movua, the owl spirit, just in case – spiritually hedging his bets.

Isikeli isn't quite sure where he stands between Uncle and Bu on this. He doesn't know how he is going to reconcile *vanua* and God; he's still figuring this out. But there is one thing that he has never told anyone: when he was eleven, Isikeli saw an owl. He and Seru were playing rugby with the older boys on the pitch in the corner of Paradise Estate. Just as he caught the ball from a hurtling torpedo pass and began to sprint toward the try line, he saw a tawny bird in his peripheral vision. It was sitting on a tree branch, its large eyes staring straight at him. After his team won the game, he looked back at the tree and the bird had gone. He brushed the vision from his mind – it was possible he imagined it, and besides, he wasn't sure he believed in that stuff anyway. He forgot all about it. But twelve days later, his father dropped dead suddenly. Sometimes, Isikeli couldn't help thinking that if he had told someone, if he had just warned his dad, maybe he would still be alive today. Sometimes this guilty secret feels like a swarm of white ants eating away at him slowly.

Over near the door, the towels are soaked with rain. The intermittent drops from the roof have turned into a steady dribble, and Isikeli knows he will have to empty the bucket soon.

All of a sudden, the light cuts and everything goes pitch black. Eta begins to cry.

"IT'S ACTUALLY kind of mesmerizing," Jess says, her nose pressed up against the window. Hannah, Jess, and Pip are looking out at the harbor from Aaron's hotel room. In the muted moonlight, they can see the palm trees along the beach thrashing back and forth, as though dancing manically to heavy metal music. Beyond them, enormous waves rock the container ships in the port, the large contraptions of iron bobbing like plastic boats in a bathtub. Every few moments, a mercurial bolt of lightning zaps, lighting up the whole scene.

"It's so intense," says Pip.

"Dorothy is grumpy," Hannah muses.

"Dorothy needs a good shag!" Jess slurs, and Pip giggles.

Hannah is relieved to be facing the window. It allows her to let her smile drop for a moment, a brief respite from the tangled politics of the party happening behind her. All evening she has been acutely aware of Jean's movements, tracing him in the corner of her eye. Whenever she stands near him, she mentally rifles through her repertoire for good questions to ask and funny, intelligent things to say. Michelle has remained at his side all evening, complimenting Hannah on occasion – "cute earrings" and "you're funny!" To the untrained ear, these comments are charming and gracious, but Hannah knows they are strategically patronizing. "Thanks," she responds thinly.

Ethan, meanwhile, is avoiding her entirely.

A Cat Empire song is playing now, and people have broken off into little groups, arguing and laughing.

When the power dies and the room suddenly goes black and silent, conversation fades to a close. For a brief moment everything is deathly still. Muted thunder is just audible through the triple-glazed windows.

"The power's gone out," World Bank Dave's voice pierces the darkness.

"D'you think?" says Pip, and everyone laughs nervously.

"Generator should kick in soon," someone says.

One by one, people pull their phones out of their pockets and swipe them on. Someone makes the comment that Wi-Fi is still working. A ghostly artificial light from the screens illuminates everyone's faces, seemingly beheaded from their bodies. Hannah feels a strange sensation, a rush of acute existential awareness. *I'll remember this moment for the rest of my life.*

THE WALLS between Isikeli and the screaming winds seem paper thin, the sound around him unbearably loud.

He moves his legs slightly and they meet a subtle resistance. They are sploshing. In water. *Magai!* He thinks. *The bucket, I didn't empty the bucket!* He gets on all fours and crawls toward where he thinks the bucket is. On the way, he feels the warmth of a sleeping body beside him – Bu, or Uncle maybe – and keeps crawling. Finally, he feels his way to the bucket.

But it hasn't overflowed yet. He remembers, he emptied the bucket. The bucket is not the reason for the water. It is coming from somewhere else.

Bu's house is filling with water.

THE VOLUNTEERS hear the whir of the hotel's generator kicking in. The warm bedside lamps illuminate Aaron's room again, and the speakers burst into life with a funky Latin trumpet solo. "Thank God for that," Aaron says. "Is anyone else hungry?"

There is a roar of approval and they order room service.

The service is surprisingly quick. The food is delivered by a tall iTaukei man, whose name tag says "Kenny."

"*Bula*, Kenny!" they greet him as he wheels in the trolley. They begin opening silver domes to reveal bowls of potato wedges and large cheesy pizzas.

They are all slightly feverish with the novelty of someone else in the room and quiz Kenny amicably while he gets Aaron to sign the receipt. Where is he from? (A village in the interior of Viti Levu.) How long has he worked at the Hibiscus Inn? (Six years.) They try to squeeze some gossip out of him about other guests at the hotel. (Apparently some drunk New Zealanders snuck out, ignoring the curfew, and were returned by the police.) "I'm not surprised at all," Aaron says through a mouthful of pizza. "You can never trust a Kiwi."

"Racist!" calls Pip cheerfully, placing a New Zealand accent on the "i."

Aaron rests a hand on Kenny's shoulder. "Do you want some pizza, Kenny? Help yourself. We won't tell anyone." He woozily pretends to zip his lips.

"*Vinaka*," Kenny declines, politely extracting himself from Aaron's arm.

Hannah watches Kenny leave. Something about his facial expression as he gently pulls the door closed triggers her. She hasn't really thought about the staff. Does Kenny have children, a lover, or parents at home? She has a sudden pang of guilt. Here she is obsessing over her love life when people beyond those walls are in danger. She dips her wedge into sweet chili sauce and sour cream. She forces herself to think about all the people she knows that are somewhere out there, beyond the weather, in houses of varying structural integrity. Dr Sireli; Peniasi; Ili. And what about all the people she visited in the settlements? How could those shabby, tumble-down houses possibly withstand that wind, if that's what it does to container ships? She thinks of that Isikeli boy and his grandmother and the little girl. She closes her eyes and wills them all to remain safe and dry, a little secular request to the universe.

When she opens her eyes again she sees Jean and Michelle directly in front of her. They are sitting on the bed eating pizza – him hungrily and her daintily, in small bites. Hannah suddenly feels overwhelmingly tired. She is sick of drafting clever things to ask and funny things to say so that Jean will like her most. She wonders if Jean has thought about those in danger beyond these walls tonight.

A thought suddenly occurs to her – *has Jean ever asked her a question?* The answer causes a sudden moment of clarity. *Not once.* He knows nothing about her. He seems to enjoy her company, but only because she listens to him. It is almost like she holds up a mirror for him to fall in love with himself. And Michelle is doing the same thing. The realization makes her feel swindled and small.

Aaron has taken control of the playlist now, and the room pulsates with techno music – *Oonce oonce oonce*. The alcohol is making her thoughts foggy, and the room suddenly feels claustrophobic. She scans the room for Ethan, suddenly craving the reassurance of his no-nonsense affability and his kind, inquiring questions. She wants to tell him that she also hates Aaron's taste in music.

She can't see him anywhere.

"Hey, has anyone seen Ethan?" she asks, but no one hears her question.

⁂

ISIKELI CRAWLS to the door and begins to open it slowly. The wind catches it and flings it out of his grip, banging it against the side of the house. More water rushes against his legs.

The sound is deafening now, rain thrasing in different directions. His eyes adjust to the darkness and he sees the trees above the settlement, silver-wet in the moonlight, violently flinging themselves at each other. A sheet of tin flies through the air and hits the side of his neighbor's house.

Finally, he understands. Coming down the hill above their house is gushing water, rushing down through the alleyway. It is pooling in the small valley where Bu's house sits, small waves splashing onto Bu's and neighboring houses.

It's a flood and it's rising.

They need to get out of here.

⁂

AARON IS playing Jenga with World Bank Dave. They are both very drunk and the tower keeps falling over and having to be rebuilt. No one knows where Ethan is.

"Don't worry about it, Han," says Aaron, clumsily withdrawing a brick from the stack. "He's probably just chilling in his room."

But Hannah has tried calling Ethan's room number. Four times. He hasn't answered. What if he left the hotel, upset? What if he is out *there*? A wrench of dread twists in her stomach.

She opens the door of Aaron's room and runs down the hallway. She presses the button for the lift but it is not working. She races down several flights of stairs to the lobby.

The reception is unattended and ghostly quiet. Cheerful music still playing in the lobby provides a creepy soundtrack to her spiraling thoughts. She walks with haste through to the hotel restaurant, where a bartender is absentmindedly staring out the window. She follows his gaze. Two palm fronds, battered by the rain, are pressed up against the windowpane, as though begging to be let inside. She looks around the restaurant, empty except for an elderly couple sitting in the far corner, staring at the scene outside, the man clinking ice in his glass.

"Excuse me?" she says to the bartender. He spins around and gives her a warm smile.

"*Io.*"

"Have you seen …" – she stumbles – "my friend Ethan?" It's the first time she has described him to someone else. He *is* her friend. One of her *best* friends here, really. The bartender keeps smiling but his eyes narrow in confusion.

She explains. "He's tall, he's Australian, he's got blond hair? It's pretty messy?"

He raises his eyebrows. "Messy hair, eh?"

"Yes!" she feels a glimmer of hope.

He subtly shakes his head. "If I see him, I'll call you, eh. What's your room number?"

Hannah leaves her room number with the bartender and makes her way back to Aaron's room. Surely Ethan will have returned by now. Surely there will be some simple explanation. As she climbs the stairs again, she crosses her fingers on both hands, even though she has never done that before. She's not the superstitious type.

Pip is waiting for her in the corridor. She too looks concerned now. Ethan still hasn't come back.

❦

EACH CANDLELIT room in Rishika's house has its own weather system quite independent from the storm that rages beyond the sturdy cyclone shutters.

In the spare room, her aunties – still red and puffy around the eyes – are a whirlwind of nervous energy. Their husbands have told them to sit and relax but they insist on fussing industriously between cupboards and drawers, digging out Vijay's old soccer shoes and faded business shirts and throwing them into black plastic rubbish bags. Their movements make the candles flicker, their shadows dancing upon the walls. Every now and then, one of the aunties seeks Rishika out and holds something up, asking if she wants to keep it. Rishika stares at each item, struggling to place it in the archives of her life. Oh, that's the etched cowrie shell that Vijay brought back from Vanuatu; that's the novelty Spider-Man tie she bought him for his thirtieth birthday. She must be staring at each item for slightly too long, because the aunties keep looking at her sadly and making swift, executive decisions on her behalf. Apparently, she can keep the tie but the shell must go.

She actually quite liked that shell. It had been given to Vijay by a traveling UN delegate, an odd parting gift after Vijay had driven him around the main island for two weeks. When Vijay returned from the trip, Rishika was excited to see him back. He gave the shell to her in irony, making her laugh. "But *this* is your real gift," he winked, and began to unbutton his shirt in an effort to be alluring. He flung his shirt over his head, but a button got caught in his hair and the shirt hung limply from his head like a veil. She laughed and made him sit on the bed as she prised the button free, teasing out the knot. As she worked, his hands traced the curve of her hips, impatient and aroused. He pleaded with her to just get the scissors. When the button was finally released, they fell onto the bed together. *When was that?*

She doesn't have the energy to turn back the tide of her aunties' made-up minds, so the shell is discarded into the rubbish bag and instantly rendered meaningless, an artifact separated from the only archaeologist who understands its historical significance.

The loungeroom, by contrast, is an entirely different climate, the atmosphere broody and stifling. The men gulp at cups of tea, unable to indulge in the whiskey they crave because of age-old Hindu funeral customs. Rishika has heard them speaking in whispered tones about the death of their brother, their nephew, their friend. They make amateur observations about the likely perpetrators – definitely iTaukei, probably from the squatter settlements. They spit out these assumptions as though it vindicates them; as though they have always known it was only a matter of time before this happened. They try half-heartedly to impress each other with the violence that they will inflict on the culprits if they ever get their hands on them, their chests puffed with empty threats. But their bravado soon dissipates, leaving only a bitter silence. Periodically, Nadi Uncle offers opinions about the Premier League – "Crystal Palace has no chance against Manchester United," and "aren't Brighton a wild card this year?" – and the others grunt in agreement for once. Gone are their usual playful disagreements.

Different again, a frosty chill emanates from Rishika's mother-in-law in the main bedroom. The little woman – momentarily deplete of tears – is seated on Vijay's side of the bed, stroking the quilted cover, smoothing out wrinkles that are no longer there. Her legs are dangling over the side of the bed, heartbreakingly child-like, her feet not quite touching the floor. Every time Rishika enters the room, Samriti seems to sense her presence without looking up. She asks pointed questions in an unusually low monotone, leaving no ambiguity about who she holds accountable for her favorite son's death. *Why were you not staying with your husband on Wednesday night? When was the last time you brought him to come and visit his family? Where are your tears?* Rishika answers them all with steely patience, using every ounce of her self-control not to scream at Samriti. *He's barely been home for months! You have no idea what I'm feeling right now!* In Samriti's defense, though, Rishika doesn't have any idea what she is feeling right now either. Whatever it is, Rishika knows she isn't feeling sadness in the clean, uncomplicated way she probably should be.

THE VOLUNTEERS turn the music off. Everyone is panicking that Ethan is missing, but their conversation is going around in circles and no one is making much sense. World Bank Dave stands up from the bed, swaying, and says he's going to start searching for his friend outside the hotel. Pip pushes him back onto the bed and he falls easily. She tells him not to be an idiot, but her reprimand has an unusual softness to it. Aaron leaves the room yet again to check in the lobby and ask at reception. The restaurant is now closed, and the hotel has an eerie silence to it.

Hannah catches a light emanating from the bathroom. She realizes she hasn't checked there yet. In desperation, she hopes

Ethan's been passed out in there this whole time. She strides quickly and pushes open the door, wincing, hoping.

It is not what she is expecting. Michelle is sitting on the edge of the bath, while Jean is leaning over the bench beside the sink. He is snorting a small heap of white powder with a rolled-up ten-dollar note. Michelle looks up at Hannah and giggles, somehow managing to look manic, beautiful, and smug all at once.

Jean gives an exhilarated shudder and turns to see Hannah. He holds out the note to her. "Want some, *poisson*?" His pupils are dilated, his black eyes sparkling.

Half an hour ago, this scene would have made Hannah feel dowdy and left out. She probably would have agreed to a line of cocaine in an effort to seem sophisticated. But now, the whole scenario feels smutty and B-grade. Jean's casual disregard, which seemed so sexy just moments ago, now seems pretentious and, frankly, self-absorbed.

She can't even think of how to respond, so she simply walks backwards, closing the door on them.

It is then that she hears Aaron's voice cutting through the room.

"IT'S ALL OKAY!" he shouts. "Ethan's in his room."

Hannah's head whips around, confused. She called his room and he didn't answer.

"He's in his room," Aaron repeats. "He was watching the cyclone from the top floor window for a while, but now he's gone back."

Hannah's body feels weak with relief. She sits down on the sofa.

"I woke him up." Aaron laughs. "He wasn't happy."

He immediately begins pouring everyone a celebratory drink. The music and the laughter restart.

Hannah can't get back into the groove of the party. It feels like something has shifted in her, a heavy and fundamental shift, like tectonic plates resettling. She tells Jess that she is tired and is going to sleep. She walks slowly down the hallway to her room and lies back on her bed, fully clothed and wide awake.

EVERYONE IS awake in Isikeli's house. His uncle fumbles around in the dark for his glasses but doesn't find them. Isikeli leads him to the open doorway where they squint out at the chaos. Uncle shouts at Isikeli, "We need to make our way to Mrs Karawalevu's house!"

But Isikeli has a feeling, deep in his bones, that Mrs Karawalevu's house will not survive this storm. "*Sega*! We need to go the other way, further up the embankment."

"That's crazy!" Uncle shouts. "We can't cross that water!"

"We have to," Isikeli yells back. He is surprised at how decisive he sounds.

He scrambles blindly back into the house and makes his way toward Bu. Her body is rigid with fear, sitting up with Eta still asleep on her shoulder. The water is now up to her waist when seated. She clenches his arm. "Leave me, Keli." Her voice is stoic, resolute. "Please Isikeli. Go without me. Just keep Eta safe."

RISHIKA FINDS Akesh sitting on the floor of the study, typing on his laptop beside a small torch. He looks up when he sees her. "Just some work emails," he says apologetically, and begins to shut the computer screen.

"Carry on," she says. "I'll just sit beside you, if you don't mind."

She rests her head against the cupboard, comforted by the normalcy of his quiet tapping of the keys.

Eventually, he gives a decisive tap tap on the mouse pad and closes the screen.

"Done," he says. "Sorry about that."

She shrugs. "I don't mind."

"The Houston office now feels guilty about hounding me. It turns out that 'cousin murdered' and 'category five cyclone' does get people off your back." He smiles weakly.

The two of them listen to the muffled roar of the weather outside. Rishika is grateful for Akesh's stillness. It is getting late, but the bedroom that Akesh was going to sleep in is inexorably busy with aunties, and Rishika's bed is being guarded by a wounded mother-in-law who, it seems, might pounce at any moment.

She has an idea. She can feel Akesh's eyes watching her as she moves to the desk. She rifles through the top drawer – paperclips, Post-it Notes, pens – and then the second drawer – warranties and instruction manuals for various appliances. Finally, she finds the little box she is looking for. She holds it up for him to see.

"Will you please play cards with me?" She can hear the plaintiveness in her voice.

They play four games in a row of Rummy. She wins each time due to an unusual run of luck. On the fourth hand, she fans out her cards to reveal all four aces. She realizes he has been secretly dealing her the best cards, like a kindly big brother.

"Akesh!" she says, a smile accidentally creeping into her voice.

"What?" He holds up his hands innocently.

Samriti walks past the study at that moment and Rishika quickly drops her smile.

❦

ISIKELI FEELS motionless. What if he isn't strong enough? He closes his eyes and pleads with *Turaga Jisu* to guide him. He promises the Lord Almighty that if He spares their lives tonight, Isikeli will turn his life around. And gradually, for a moment at least, he feels a little stronger.

"Eta!" he shouts at his niece. "Tonight you have to be a brave girl. Uncle can't see. He will hold your hand but you will need to be his eyes, eh? We're going up the hill. Show him the way, like a fairy." Isikeli can barely see her in the darkness, but he can hear that the girl has stopped crying.

He then moves back toward his grandmother and squats beside her, placing one arm under her leg, the other under her back. When Bu realizes what he is doing she squeals and slaps him – "*Oilei*! Put me down!" – but he ignores her and lifts her over his shoulder. She is heavy. He musters all his strength to hold her in place.

Outside now, forks of lightning flash above the surging flood.

Isikeli can hear Bu on his shoulder praying over and over again. He shouts instructions to Eta and she leads the way – the water up to her waist. She holds Uncle's hand, with Isikeli and Bu close behind. And like that, they begin to traverse the waters, wading step-by-step.

"Uncle!" Eta shrieks suddenly. The old man moves back quickly and a sharp piece of floating metal debris speeds past. Isikeli catches sight of it, a flash of metallic light. That piece of metal could have sliced Uncle in an instant. His concentration intensifies.

Finally, Eta and Uncle reach the embankment on the other side and make their way up the incline, just as another clap of thunder booms. Still wading through the water, Isikeli is weak with exhaustion. At any moment, his shaking arms could simply drop Bu heavily to the ground. Summoning all his reserves of strength, he trudges through the mud up the slope.

They make their way, slowly, slowly, up toward their neighbor's shack. When they reach it, Uncle bangs urgently on the door, wheezing. The woman's face appears, shocked to find the bedraggled guests. She welcomes them in and immediately goes to the cupboard with blankets and towels and makes them a cup of tea on the gas stove. Bu huddles Eta in close, her eyes shining gratefully. Isikeli collapses, finally, in the corner. Outside, the violence of the wind has died down, the rain dulling. A strange quiet descends on the settlement, a brittle truce. For now, at least, they are safe.

PART II

Friday

AS THE pinky hue of dawn filters through the window, Isikeli watches his grandmother's chest rise and fall, confirming she hasn't slipped away in the night.

When she was her full two-legged self, Bu was widely known as the best at three things: gutting fish, beheading chickens, and getting screaming babies to sleep. When the doctor delivered the striking blow that her leg was infected and that it needed to be amputated if she was going to survive, Isikeli watched his grandmother double over, her body wrenching in sobs. They did not even know she had *na mate ni suka*. She was wheeled into surgery, and he sat for hours in the waiting room, fretfully scrunching a leaflet about breastfeeding. At one point, the Muslim surgical nurse came to talk to him, her cheeks smiling under her headscarf. She gave him a long list of information about medications, dietary dos and don'ts, and what to expect from the condition. "The most important thing is we need to look after the kidney. Because her kidney is not good. If her kidney fails, she will need dialysis."

Fifteen-year-old Isikeli tried to concentrate. The nurse's face swam before him.

"If she needs dialysis ..." the woman continued, "she will need it three times a week."

Isikeli raised his eyebrows.

"Now, it's subsidized, so it costs $250 a time."

"$250 a week," Isikeli repeated.

"No, $250 per *time*. That's $750 per week. Or she could always travel to India to get a kidney transplant. We don't do transplants here. Some people choose to go to India."

"India, eh? How much for a transplant in India?"

"It can vary, but it's about the equivalent of forty thousand dollars."

Isikeli raised his eyebrows again. Down the corridor, a receptionist held a manila folder up, gesturing to the nurse.

"Your other option," the nurse said, getting up to leave, "is to get sponsored by the Rotary Club. They sponsor a few people for their dialysis each year."

Isikeli knew the Rotary involved *Kai Valagi*. "How do we do that?"

She shrugged. "I don't know, sorry. You have to ask them."

Ever since, he has kept his eye out for someone in the Rotary, with no luck yet.

Shafts of light are now flooding through the window. Isikeli creeps out of his neighbor's house, his body aching from the night before. He winces at the loud creak of the door, but the bodies behind him remain still, sleeping.

The settlement outside is surprisingly busy. Neighbors are emerging from their houses, stepping carefully through floodwaters and over branches across the path. Little black silktails fly down and flitter amongst the water-swept rubbish, finding things to renovate their dislodged nests. Isikeli peruses the damage to the houses he knows so well. He looks down at Bu's house. It is intact, but a meter deep in water.

People start gathering from all over the settlement to help move each other's soaked furniture into the sunshine on drier patches of ground.

The entire roof blew off Mr and Mrs Karawalevu's house. The couple tell the story to their neighbors, wide-eyed and clearly shaken. They knelt behind a couch in the corner with their heads just above water, praying for the storm to pass. One jagged sheet of metal slid off the roof, falling inwards only inches from Mr Karawalevu. Isikeli and three other neighbors try to salvage the sheets of tin from the Karawalevu's roof, lifting them back on top of the house and securing them down with heavy old tires that one of their other neighbors has been keeping for just such an occasion.

With tears in her eyes, Mrs Karawalevu offers around a packet of Gupta's Scotch Fingers that somehow survived the storm. "*Vinaka vakalevu*, Isikeli," she says, when she gets to him. He likes the way her eyes soften, like she is proud of him. People don't look at him like that very often.

He feels a spark of hope, his stomach fizzing with possibility. The storm has passed and things are going to get better now, he is sure of it. *Praise Turaga Jisu.*

HANNAH TRIES over and over again to reach her parents but keeps getting the *all the lines are currently busy* message. After the tenth try, she hears a dialtone. It rings once, before it is snatched up. "Oh, thank God, love," her mum cries. The line cuts out before she gets to speak to her dad, but at least they won't be sickened with worry anymore.

She declares herself officially safe on Facebook and writes brief, reassuring replies to the thirteen messages she has received from worried friends back home. She doesn't have much time because the Wi-Fi keeps dropping. Jess sits on the single bed next to her with her phone against her ear, talking to her dad in Sydney in hushed tones.

The gravity of the cyclone now seems soberingly real. Through the window, the world seems to have negotiated a fragile peace. The sea is glassy, and the container ships are acting as though nothing has happened. The palm trees on the beach look traumatized and beaten, many of their branches dislocated at impossible angles. The usually manicured lawn of the hotel is hardly recognizable under a layer of strewn, broken fronds. Hannah and Jess marvel at how close the water came to the hotel in the night – the waves that violated the sea wall left a trail of refuse in their wake, a ghostly tide of leaves, seaweed, and plastic rubbish.

Jess swipes her phone off. "My dad says it's all over the news there. The death toll is nineteen or something and rising."

Hannah leans back against the headboard and tries to get her head around this. Nineteen bodies. Nineteen people with families and histories and futures cut short.

The maid who comes to service their room replaces their complimentary bottles of water. She tells them about two men in Kadavu who were ripped away in a king wave and drowned, and a woman in the settlements whose arm was cleanly amputated by a flying sheet of metal when she was trying to run to safety.

"Ew," says Jess.

"That's *horrible*," Hannah remarks.

The volunteers visit each other's rooms down the corridor, giving each other tight hugs, sharing snippets of news they've heard. They receive instructions from the Australian High Commission to remain where they are throughout the curfew. The curfew isn't expected to be lifted until tomorrow at least.

Hannah feels jittery from too many cups of instant coffee. It makes her prickly and irritable. Her change of heart last night has not faded. If anything, she feels more acutely aware of the shallowness that surrounds her. Her friends' sense of humility and relief for having survived the cyclone seems to wear off as soon as the inconvenience of their confinement becomes apparent. They lie around on each other's beds, heads aching from too little sleep and too much alcohol the night before. Their topics of conversation are increasingly vacuous. Aaron helps himself to a cup of tea in Pip's room, saying, "What is this creamer shit they always give you in hotels? It's nothing. It's like white food coloring." Later, Pip asks randomly, "Since when did Toblerone become the duty-free chocolate of choice?"

When the generator stops working and the air conditioners whisper to a halt, the hotel rooms fill quickly with repressive, muggy air. They open shutters to let in a light breeze, but mosquitos find invisible holes in the netting. Aaron warns them about the increased risk of dengue, and they all lather themselves in searing chemical repellant.

"I can't help but feel kind of annoyed," World Bank Dave says, sitting on Pip's bed. "We're paying for that generator. It's the reason we came here."

He walks down to complain at reception. He reports back with the manager's response to the group. "It's broken. Apparently Viliame could fix it, but he's not working today."

"Who the hell is Viliame?" Aaron asks, wiping sweat from under his cap.

"No idea. The maintenance guy?"

"And he's not working on the one day of the year where most maintenance will be needed?"

"Seems like it."

"Is there no one else who can fix it?"

"Apparently not."

"This is *so* classic Fiji."

In a quiet moment Hannah retreats to her room to be alone. She lies spreadeagled on the bed, staring at the ceiling, feeling the ineffectual waft of air from the fan. It's not long before she hears a knock on her door, opening it to find Jean, leaning against the doorframe.

"Hello, *poisson*," he says. The nickname sounds jarring now, overly familiar. He hugs her for slightly too long, until she pats his back twice and extracts herself. "I'm just reading my book, so ... I'll catch up with you later," she says. He looks momentarily surprised. "Okay." He shrugs and walks up the hallway.

The only person whose company Hannah craves right now is Ethan's. He doesn't know about the panic she felt for him last night. The opportunity to tell him hasn't presented itself.

The group is now gathered in Aaron's room, talking about the cyclone. "It's actually really heartwarming," Michelle says, fanning her face with a brochure and reading about the international response to the cyclone.

"What is?" Ethan snaps. "The rising death toll?"

"No, of course not. I mean, in light of that. It's touching how the world unites when there's a crisis."

"What gives you that impression?"

"Well," she starts defensively, "the Red Cross has set up a cyclone relief hotline, and Australians have already donated something like two million."

"Naww, that's lovely," says Pip.

Michelle continues, "It sounds cheesy, but it makes me feel hopeful about humanity, you know?"

Ethan gets up from his chair. "I think that your kind of humanity has a lot to answer for."

"Eth!" Michelle laughs nervously. "What's that supposed to mean?"

He walks toward the door, a flash of anger in his eyes. "You can't talk about humanity when you're surrounded by room service and ... and bloody *laundered towels*."

Hannah feels a delightful sense of vindication. She tries to catch Ethan's eye, but he looks straight past her and leaves the room.

Her friends exchange glances.

"Don't worry about him, Mish," Pip says.

"I know! I'm like, what's his problem?"

Aaron chuckles, "Ethan's always a grumpy bastard when he's hungover."

Saturday

THE AUDIENCE in the small hall is quiet except for the soft flapping of woven fans and the muted coughs of a man in the front row. Isikeli strains to hear the presenter, a softly spoken iTaukei man from the disaster response team at the Suva Town Council. Isikeli hears snippets of his instructions: some basic first aid; how to minimize the spread of rubbish; how to dig your own drainage. The man finishes with a reminder to "chip in and do your little bit to rebuild Suva."

When he finishes, hands fly up with questions. A man in the front of the audience stands up. "*Vinaka* for coming to talk to us," he begins, and Isikeli immediately recognizes the booming voice of the *italatala*, looking strangely unfamiliar without his robes. "Can the council promise us that the settlements won't languish without running water and electricity long after the rest of the city, like we usually do? We too have rights to this city's resources!" A cacophony of agreement rings out from the crowd. A scattering of voices call, "*Emeni!*"

The council employee looks slightly nervous. He answers the question cautiously – something about "emergency services working as fast as they can" and "we thank you for being patient at this difficult time." His assistant hands out some leaflets on Zika virus and they drive off in their four-wheel drive, mud splattering out from under the wheels.

Isikeli is thirsty. He breaks away from the disgruntled crowd and exits the hall, his backpack resting on his shoulders. He salvaged the bag this morning when he crept back to Bu's dank, flooded house to find Uncle's glasses and Bu's bible.

He calls into the corner store and browses the bottles of water. He eventually decides on a bottle of Island Cola because it is cheaper, choosing passionfruit flavor, Bu's favorite.

When he returns to the neighbor's house and opens the creaking door, Eta runs to hug his leg. In the dark interior he can see Bu is sitting with guests. On closer inspection he sees it is Epeli and Aunty Ria, an enormous woman both in figure and temperament. Isikeli greets his aunty respectfully and holds out his hand to his cousin-brother. "*Set, Tavale?*"

"*Set,*" Epeli says, refusing his handshake.

What now? Isikeli thinks.

He unzips the cola from his backpack and holds the bottle up, asking if anyone would like a drink. Eta shouts, "*Io, io, io!*" He places his backpack in the corner near the door. Epeli is watching his every move.

Bu appears about to accept the offer of a drink but Aunty Ria pipes up, "Bu Lia won't have any. Too much sugar."

Bu nods obediently and says, "*Vinaka.*" Isikeli feels a prickle of irritation, his gift undermined.

He pours the glasses while Aunty reports details from Mataqai — no one has been seriously injured, thank the Lord, but two uncles' houses were flooded.

While Bu and Aunty Ria continue to talk, Epeli turns to Isikeli.

"Did you see the news?" he asks softly.

"*Sega.*"

"There was a murder on Chamberlain Street."

Isikeli remains deathly still.

"An armed burglary," Epeli continues, "on Wednesday night." He stares at Isikeli, interrogating his reaction. "You and Seru said you went to Chamberlain Street the other night."

Isikeli takes a long sip of his cola until the bubbles burn the back of his mouth. Tension rushes back into his shoulders. He shrugs. "There are lots of houses on Chamberlain Street."

"Looks exactly like the one you said."

Fear grips Isikeli by the throat.

"You sure you don't know anything about it?"

"*Sega!*" he whispers. Trapped by Epeli's glare, he feels like lashing out. He utters his old taunt under his breath, "*Lia lia Kai Idia.*" He knows he is being juvenile. Epeli's eyes flash in anger.

Aunty Ria soon gets up to leave. She asks Epeli to help her up off the mat and her son nearly falls over under her weight, then tries again. As they walk out the door, Epeli points toward Isikeli's backpack in the corner.

"Nice bag," he says loudly enough for everyone to hear. "Where'd you get that from?"

Isikeli takes another long sip of his cola, feeling everyone's gaze upon him. "Found it."

Epeli raises his eyebrows and then disappears through the door, a charged silence lingering behind. Afraid to look Bu in the eye, Isikeli can tell she is looking at him with renewed disappointment. He makes another silent vow to make her proud again.

Thankfully, Eta spills her drink at that moment, drawing his grandmother's attention to the mess in the middle of the room. Their neighbor bustles to clean it up.

When they are alone again, Bu gestures urgently to Isikeli.

"Keli," she whispers, pointing to the Island Cola. "Pour me some, quickly!"

A LOUD cheer can be heard throughout the Hibiscus Inn when the generator comes back on. Air conditioners whir into life, televisions begin blaring mid-sentence, and residents give high fives to the staff in the breakfast buffet.

Back in her room, Hannah sits with Jess and Pip on her bed, poring over meteorological pictures of Cyclone Dorothy on her laptop, trying to decipher what the little yellow arrows and angry whispy streaks mean. In horror, they watch helicopter footage posted online of the islands that were decimated by the storm. Suva did not get the full brunt of its wrath; many villages on the other big island were flattened as though a massive circular saw spun right through them. Villagers emerged from their shelters with ghostly faces to find very little left of their homes.

They scroll through the Australian headlines:

DEADLY DOROTHY: 22 dead, 7 still missing in devastating category five cyclone. No Australians believed to be among the injured.

OPERATION DOROTHY ASSIST: Aussie Army touches down in Nadi; HMAS Melbourne sets sail with humanitarian relief

STRANDED AUSSIE TOURISTS BREATHE SIGH OF RELIEF AS FLIGHTS RESUME IN AND OUT OF NADI

Hannah rolls her eyes at the Australian-centric focus of the media. "How predictable."

"I know," Pip says. "God, I hate tourists," subtly missing Hannah's point.

The rest of the expats have not yet emerged from their rooms. According to Pip, most of them were drinking at the hotel bar last night, well into the early hours of the morning, long after Hannah went to bed. They befriended the manager, who sneakily opened the bar for them. The volunteers decided to drink a heady cocktail of more unorthodox liqueurs – absinthe, chartreuse, crème de menthe – and eventually passed out.

They still haven't emerged at ten o'clock – checkout time – and neither a knock on their doors nor a phone call from reception can rouse them. Ethan's room is empty, and he is nowhere to be seen. Apparently, he was not at the bar last night, and Pip thinks he might have already left the hotel. In the past, Hannah would have just texted him, but things feel different with him now.

The foyer is crowded and manic, everyone seemingly checking out at once. As Hannah, Jess, and Pip make their way to the door, a woman rushes over to them. Hannah immediately recognizes her as Sarah, the Australian woman from HealthInternational. Today, Sarah is surprisingly warm as she asks after Hannah in concern. She tells them about a local relief effort, which is being organized through the arts center that afternoon. "We need volunteers," she says and thrusts a little note with the details into Hannah's hand. "You should come."

"Great," Hannah nods, looking down at the address.

"We'll definitely try!" Jess adds, although she is already beginning to wheel her suitcase to the front of the hotel.

There aren't many out on the roads, but the porter eventually hails a taxi.

The drive back to Pip's house is slow and dream-like. They come across fallen trees that block the roads, and the driver takes them on long detours through abandoned, ghostly streets.

They pass a military checkpoint, and the car slows right down. Bereted officers stare solemnly through the window at the girls in the back seat, and Hannah feels for a moment as though everything is in slow motion.

Jess, however, waves at the officers.

Pip elbows her in the ribs.

"Ow! What?!" Jess says.

"I don't know, maybe because *it's the army!*"

"I'm just being friendly."

The young officer at the rear of the checkpoint smiles back at Jess, a big grin, the stark white of his teeth contrasting against his dark skin.

"See?" Jess says, still waving. "They like it!" And Pip chuckles.

After seeing Pip safely enter her house, Hannah and Jess ask the driver to take them to theirs. On arrival they can see that the damage is minimal. Some rain seems to have made its way under the gap of the front door, creating a small puddle in the entryway.

They unpack their suitcases, get changed into fresh clothes and make a cup of coffee. The power in Suva is still out, which renders the kettle useless, so Hannah boils water in a saucepan on the gas stovetop, feeling impressed at her own resourcefulness.

They nurse their hot drinks on the sofa in silence. Jess begins checking her phone and Hannah pulls out the note about the relief effort.

She reminds Jess about it.

"Oh, Gawd," Jess sniggers. "It's probably organized by the Ladies Who Lunch."

"I know. But part of me thinks at least they're doing something, you know?"

She looks at Jess, but Jess has looked back down at her phone. Hannah feels restless and ineffective. She has a strong desire to do something physical. Anything really. On a whim, she decides to go, and Jess reluctantly agrees to come.

Hannah hurries around getting ready. She slaps on some tracksuit pants and an old T-shirt with holes under its arms. She feels more humbled and wholesome, somehow, than she has in a long time. This quickly turns into an ashamed calculation of how many hours she has recently poured into her appearance in the hope that Jean would take notice. And right now, Jean is passed out in a hotel room while the country around him tries to rebuild itself after the devastation. *Fuck you, Just Jean.*

Jess interrupts her train of thought, calling out from the sofa. "Actually, Han, do you mind if I don't come?" she says. "I'm exhausted."

In the bathroom, Hannah's shoulders drop. "Oh. Okay."

"I know I'm not really entitled to be exhausted. But I am. I think I just need to FaceTime Brad."

"No, no, that's cool."

"Will you be okay by yourself?"

"Sure! Yeah, don't worry about me."

"Take your phone."

"I'll be fine. Totally fine."

Hannah grabs her handbag and walks out the door before she has a chance to change her mind.

Droplets of sweat form on her forehead as soon as she steps into the clammy afternoon air. The humidity is so unpleasant that she almost reconsiders. She forces herself to continue. *Come on Hannah Wilson, Fiji needs you.*

The detritus from the storm is already beginning to decompose in the heat. Odors of decay layer one on top of the other: the rotting mangoes on the sidewalk, the wounded rubbish bags on the verge.

Hardly any taxis pass by. Those that do ignore her, either occupied with passengers or driving for another purpose. She comes across a dog sitting beside the road, teasing a chicken bone apart with its teeth. Hannah circles past the dog as it tries to get a better grip on the bone, the polystyrene container swarming with maggots. A swell of nausea rises in Hannah's stomach, and she keeps walking, faster now.

Her phone soon buzzes with a call. It is Ili, their quote-unquote-housegirl, who kindly asks if Hannah and Jess are okay. Hannah feels guilty, because she probably should have called Ili for the same reason. Ili's voice then gets quieter and more reverent. She asks – *kerekere* – for some money to help restore her mother's house, which has been badly hit by the storm.

"Absolutely!" Hannah says, genuinely pleased to be able to do something concrete. She agrees to send through some money as soon as she can get to a post office.

She ends up walking all the way. By the time she arrives outside the old arts center – an enormous turn-of-the-century house in town, repurposed into an arts hall – her underarms are dark with circles of sweat. The front room is buzzing with industry – several people walk into the hall carrying boxes, two people are standing at a desk, working with a laptop and mobile printer, and another small crowd is standing around a map, drawing routes.

An iTaukei man notices Hannah. "*Bula*," he says. "Are you here to volunteer?"

She nods and he gives her a warm smile, shaking her hand. He takes her into the hall, which is scattered with about twenty trestle tables. At each table, four or five people sit around it, leaning over each other and packing boxes. The man leads her to one table at the side of the room and introduces her to a blond woman.

She offers Hannah a hand to shake. "Hey, hon! I'm Bex."

"Nice to meet you, Bex. I'm Hannah," says Hannah, discreetly taking in the woman's age (in her forties) and heavy makeup. In turn, Bex kindly pretends not to notice Hannah's homeless appearance. Bex's smile suddenly drops in sincerity. "Isn't it just ghastly what's happened? God, I can't stop thinking about it," she says.

"It's horrible," Hannah replies.

Bex turns and gestures to the four women around the table.

"Ladies, this is Hannah. Hannah, ladies!" She beams. Hannah sits down at the trestle table and receives instructions from the women: each package should be filled with five tins of tuna, two large packets of white rice, and two boxes of Arnott's Tiny Teddy biscuits. "Just a little treat for the kids," explains a New Zealand woman who introduces herself as Jen. "My friend sources these."

Hannah can't help it – the public health professional in her is slightly concerned about the packages' nutritonal value: such high sugar, salt, and starch content. She also knows her volunteer friends would scoff at the paltry size of the packages. How far would this food go in one Fijian household, let alone a village? However, most of her friends were probably still asleep, so they aren't really entitled to comment right now. And there is something endearing about the earnest efforts of these women.

So Hannah stops being hypercritical and joins the production line. As she works, she is pleasantly surprised at how open and welcoming the women are to her. She accidentally finds herself swept up in their energy. The women ask her questions and gush about how impressed they are by her volunteering at FijiHealth. Some of them, Bex explains, are wives of diplomats from various high commissions here. Their husbands all whizzed off to urgent meetings this morning after the curfew lifted, negotiating with foreign ministers back home and managing million-dollar relief efforts. "They're doing the important work of course!" Bex says.

"We just wanted to do our little bit." They left their children with nannies and came here as soon as they could.

When all of the boxes have been packaged, the volunteers gather around one of the coordinators to listen to the instructions for the next phase. Each group is given a map, with directions to the villages that were hardest hit by the storm. Bex has offered to use her Land Rover for the relief effort. She reverses it close to the entrance and Hannah helps her pack the trunk full of boxes. Once the boot is full, Hannah begins to return to the hall, but Bex protests. "No! Come with us!" Hannah doesn't feel able to say no. Hannah sits in the back seat alongside Jen while Bex and another woman get in the front. The rest of the women step into another four-wheel drive parked outside, full to the brim with boxes, which is going to follow along behind them.

"Convoy!" one of the women cries out as she fumbles to put her seatbelt on. "We should have walkie talkies!"

As they drive, the adrenaline Hannah felt earlier begins to wear off, and she starts to feel uncomfortable. She isn't sure how they are going to choose which families to give the packages to, because presumably everyone desperately needs them – it is just a matter of scale. And she worries that rocking up in four-wheel drives is a little ostentatious, given the circumstances.

She tells herself to relax and winds the window down to feel the wind in her hair. She watches the disheveled streets of Suva reel past, unable to look away from the carnage. A severed powerline fizzes on a side road. Everything seems broken: trees, roofs, walls, shops. A police officer slows the cars down to make way for a group of men clearing a tree off the road. While they wait for the tree to be removed, Hannah scans the landscape, her eyes resting on the squatter houses on the hill, which seem to be leaning even more precariously than usual. She recognizes a familiar settlement on the riverbank: a little row of about ten shacks on stilts, painted in brilliant colors. Ethan drew her attention to this settlement months ago. (One of his clients lives in the orange one and had invited him there for roast pork once. It was, apparently, the best roast Ethan ever tasted, but he had been shocked to realize the pig was still alive when he first arrived, digging its heels in and knowing full well what grisly fate awaited it.) When Ethan first pointed the settlement out to Hannah, she mentioned that it reminded her of the boathouses on Melbourne's Brighton Beach. "Yep," Ethan said. "Except that instead of small yachts and picnic baskets, they house entire, extended families." She laughed at the time, but she now blushes at how naïve and spoiled she must have sounded.

Looking at those shacks now, Hannah can see that the small orange house that Ethan visited has collapsed on its stilts in the storm. A group of young iTaukei men are working around the house, carrying poles of wood and lifting sheets of tin, presumably to repair it.

All of a sudden another young man appears behind the house, pushing a rusted wheelbarrow. It is only when she looks closer at his sandy hair and tanned shoulders that she realizes that she is, in fact, looking at Ethan. Presumably helping his old client. She sees him turning his head, looking in the direction of Bex's car. Hannah gasps and sinks deeper into her seat. She presses the electric window button repeatedly, willing it to rise faster.

From behind the safety of the tinted glass, she keeps watching Ethan on the riverbank. It is the second time this week he has profoundly surprised her.

She realizes that the other women in the car are also watching the scene with interest. All the young men have taken their shirts off – including Ethan. Their chests glisten with sweat in the mid-afternoon sun.

"Well, he*llo boys!*" Bex says. The ladies dissolve into giggles. Forgetting about the devastation for a moment, Hannah can't help but grin.

꒰

"I BET we don't hear from the police again," Nadi Uncle spits. "They won't do anything." He and Sigatoka Uncle are sitting cross-legged on the balcony floor, whipping each other into a state of indignation. They have just returned from the second-day mourning ritual, in which they scattered Vijay's ashes in the Rewa River. Now Solomon sleeps fitfully beside them on the balcony, legs jutting out.

Sigatoka Uncle nods. "The police will be too busy after the cyclone. All the looters."

"*Nahi*, it's not that. It's easier for them to write it off as another unsolved burglary. Less paperwork, eh? They're lazy."

Sigatoka Uncle grunts in agreement.

Rishika remains quiet. It isn't proper to argue with your uncles.

"Besides," Nadi Uncle continues, "they're probably related to the fella that did it. A little bit of *kerekere* and they'll forget all about it."

They sneer.

Her uncles' jokes about laziness and corruption are always directed at organizations that are mostly iTaukei. The police. The army. The government. And the Fijian 7s rugby team, but only when they're going through a losing streak. (When they're winning, the uncles have a strong solidarity with their iTaukei brothers. "*Toso Viti!*" they cry proudly at the television. The contradiction used to drive Vijay mad.)

Rishika tries to turn her attention away, focusing instead on the insect life surrounding her. Hidden civilizations seem to have been unearthed by the storm. Armies of ants are marching to and fro along circuitous routes on the balcony, while an airforce of mosquitos cruise and dive-bomb in the swampy air.

Up the street, a scattering of her neighbors can be seen in their separate compounds, dragging broken branches and raking their lawns, reinstating order in their little patches of earth.

In her own garden below, Nausori Uncle and Akesh are raking her lawn. The aerial view emphasizes how similar Akesh's figure is to that of her late husband's, the cousins both tall, slim, and muscly, with an attractive salt-and-peppering of hair – their bodies not too dissimilar to those of their ancestors, shown in the black-and-white photos, who arrived on boats from India, except the muscle tone is caused not by laboring on sugarcane plantations but regular trips to the university gym and the odd game of soccer. Their physique is following the genetic destiny of most Indian men: a perfectly rounded potbelly pregnant with curry, roti, and beer. Just last week at dinner, Akesh teased Vijay about his growing paunch.

Surely that wasn't just last week! It was the same day that Rishika got her hair cut. It feels like years have passed since that moment. She feels nauseated, chronologically dizzy. She stands up, steadying herself against the chair, feeling the need to busy herself immediately.

Back inside the house, Nausori Aunty is in the kitchen, unwrapping the roti brought by a neighbor in a tea towel. Samriti is sitting on the sofa, eyes puffy and red and staring at nothing in particular. Rishika has been respectfully avoiding her mother-in-law all day, and again she gives her a wide birth as she walks to the bookshelf.

While she scans the spines of the books, she can hear Nadi Aunty plopping down on the sofa next to Samriti. Aunty places her arm around her sister and whispers words of solace, cooing that Vijay was a good man during his lifetime and his spirit would be reborn – "His karma was the very wonderfullest, *haana*?" Tears well in Samriti's eyes, and her whisper comes out raspy and foreign; she has not spoken all day. "Who made the roti?"

"The neighbor from across the road," Nadi Aunty whispers back.

Samriti sniffles. "I bet they'll be dry."

Nadi Aunty rubs her back soothingly. "I know, *Babbi*. I know."

Rishika tunes them out and scans the books on the shelf. She pulls down the *Readers' Digest Atlas of the World* and takes it into the study. Sitting at the desk, she rifles through to the index, welcoming the dusty fragrance of its pages, and scrolls down to "W."

Wagga Wagga is, she learns, a regional town in the Riverina region of New South Wales on the eastern side of Australia. A quick Google search on her phone tells her that the word *Wagga* means "crow" in the language of the Wirudjeri people. Rishika runs her finger down the page of the atlas, over nearby mountains and rivers, and rolls her tongue around their exotic sounding names. Murrimbidgee. Murray-Darling. Kosciuszko. She imagines they are the usual mix of self-promoting European explorers and mispronounced Indigenous words. She likes the idea that the latter might be in-jokes that the First Nations peoples are still laughing about. Perhaps these names *really* translate as "please leave us alone" or "go back to where you came from."

This is her strength – methodical research. This is when she is at her best, her most focused. She is, after all, a historian. The last time she compiled a list of sites was in her third year historiography course. It was for an assignment that required her to devise her own research question. She trawled through letters from missionaries, colonial reports, and old newspapers in the Fiji archives to find out why, exactly, Fiji was ceded to the British.

She had never quite believed the official story that Fijians simply handed the country over.

The truth she uncovered was more outlandish than she'd expected. A drunken American man burned down his own trading store with stray canonfire during a jovial night of Fourth of July celebrations. He blamed the locals for the damage and lumped the debt on the self-proclaimed Chief of Fiji. The chief felt backed into a corner, and gave Fiji – *the whole country* – to the British to pay off his debts. There were reprisals, but nothing the British couldn't handle. To Rishika, it was a permanent reminder of the arbitrary and sinister way in which history is determined. Just little boys in a big playground making up rules. Rishika's heart was beating when she finally stapled and slotted that essay through the submission box, and then again three weeks later when she went to pick it up after it had been marked. Her lecturer, an unapproachable-seeming English man on sabbatical from Oxford University, had scribbled an A+ in the margins. Underneath, he'd written, "This was one of the best undergraduate essays I have ever read. Have you considered doing honors?"

That was a couple of months before her wedding.

Now, twenty years later, she has devised another research question for herself: *Who murdered my husband? And what does this strange inland town of Wagga Wagga have to do with it?*

᠅

THE PORTER opens the door of the taxi with one hand while his other arm is bent behind his back in royal servitude. He wears a colonial bellhop uniform, with a long red stripe down each pant leg. "*Ni sa bula vinaka, ma'am,*" he bows as Hannah steps out of the car.

Tourists who venture out of their resorts love the Old Victoria Hotel for its ornate white pillars and excellent high teas. It is where the royal family stay on their visits, and the foyer is adorned with a large photo of Prince Harry and Meghan waving to the crowds from the central wrought-iron balcony, an adoring crowd of subjects on the tree-lined street below. Hannah has hesitantly accepted a last-minute free pass to attend a charity auction here tonight. The event is being organized by her new friends, The Expat Mummies Group, spearheaded by Bex, of course. Apparently, the expensive tickets sold out fast with the help of their well-networked husbands.

Gentle ukelele music is playing in the lobby. Hannah immediately relaxes in the air conditioning amongst the wicker furniture and vases of fresh tropical flowers. Thankfully she can forget – for a moment – the dirty, decaying reality of the cyclone-damaged Fiji beyond those walls.

A sign at the bottom of the mahogany staircase says *This way for the Tropical Cyclone Dorothy Victims Benefit*. She makes her way up to the ballroom in her strappy high heels and a tight-fitting black cocktail dress that she borrowed from Jess, who is currently at home on the sofa in her tracksuit.

Through the tall, art deco doors mills an elegantly dressed crowd. Hannah is relieved that she at least got the dress code right.

An Indo-Fijian waitress stands just inside the entry with a tray of glasses fizzing with orange Aperol Spritz, which she holds out to Hannah. Hannah squints at the tray in indecision. She has been drinking a lot over the last two days.

"Oh, fine, twist my arm," she says to the waitress, who smiles in a way that thankfully seems non-judgmental.

The atmosphere in the crowded ballroom is one of restraint. There is the odd burst of laughter, quickly subdued again. People seem a bit frenzied. They have, after all, just confronted their own mortality, albeit in a vicarious way.

Hannah scans the room for Bex. She eventually sees her across the hall, dressed in a stylish, full-length gown, throwing her head back in laughter at something a besuited Indo-Fijian man just said.

It is a bit ironic, really. After becoming irritable with her hipster friends, Hannah seems to have accidentally swapped them with a group she finds just as ideologically grating. From fashionably ironic to uncritically enthusiastic. She takes a gulp from her glass, and then another, and approaches Bex's circle. Bex welcomes her with the affection of an older sister and warmly introduces her to everyone in the group – a multicultural mix of ambassadors, businesspeople, and university lecturers.

Hannah nods politely and smiles in all the right places. After a little while, she feels a hand on her back. She flips around and sees a familiar face – it's Peniasi. She flings her arms around him with a spontaneous hug of relief. She looks over his shoulder, disappointed to see that Ethan has not accompanied him. By way of explanation, Peni holds up his "Media Pass" lanyard. He is writing an article about the aftermath of Dorothy.

The crowd around them soon hushes as a group of bare-chested iTaukei men appear on stage with painted faces and grass skirts. Hannah and Peniasi face the front, shoulder to shoulder. The men begin a traditional *meke*, dancing and chanting with aesthetically pleasing masculine aggression. Hannah catches a little glimpse of boardshorts beneath one of their grass skirts.

Tears well in the audience's eyes as they applaud the dance troupe, hearts touched by Fiji's resilience in the face of adversity.

When they finish, the master of ceremonies requests that everyone observe a respectful minute of silence for the deceased. Hannah closes her eyes and listens to the sound of people trying to be quiet. The Australian high commissioner then makes a speech, a compassionate talk about the importance of neighbors and shared interests at a time like this. "Australia's aid," he says, "is offered in a genuinely unselfish and humanitarian spirit," and the crowd claps loudly.

"What he really means," Peniasi whispers in Hannah's ear, "is *don't trust China.*"

The cocktails flow and the crowd settles in for the main event, the auction. Pretty iTaukei girls walk on stage modeling clothes by local designers; dresses made of muted Bula designs that will be considered tasteful to Australians. Bex holds up large, beautiful paintings by local artists – turtles painted in Picasso-esque cubism, stylish etchings of tropical landscapes. The items are bid for at ostentatiously generous prices. Peniasi leans into Hannah's ear and points out the bidders in the crowd: "that's Gupta from Gupta's Biscuits"; "that's the real estate agent who sells all the freehold land to Australians and New Zealanders"; "that iTaukei fella is a businessman, big in the mahogany industry"; "that guy over there? CEO of PacFone." Hannah feels privileged to have her own personal political guide.

A bidding war unfolds between two people – well-known socialites according to Peniasi. They comically try to outbid each other on a tea towel. The small piece of cloth – albeit with a pretty *tapa* design – is sold for $2,300, and the audience roars with laughter and admiration.

Peniasi whispers, "I think I'll call this article 'Gala Glitters with Glamorous Giving.'"

"Nice," she whispers back.

While they listen to the auctioneer, an American man approaches Peniasi, obviously known to him. They have a quiet chat; she can't hear what they say. Peniasi giggles – nervously, Hannah thinks.

The man walks away into the crowd, and Peniasi does a startled jump.

Hannah looks at him in surprise.

"Did he just grab your arse?"

"*Io*," he whispers, staring at the man's back as he walks into the crowd. "He's always like that when his wife's out of town."

"That's harassment!"

He raises his eyebrows.

Hannah is horrified. When she first arrived in Fiji, she was impressed with how *qauris* seemed to be accepted as one of the ladies here. To her eyes, they were treated as funny and loveable men who were good at cleaning, caring, and gossiping. She thought Fiji seemed progressive in its inclusion of alternative genders. But over time, the ambivalent treatment of *qauris* unraveled to her. They are sometimes leered at in the street, the butt of "poofter" jokes. Some of them are used for sexual experimentation by gay and straight men: Fijians, expats, and tourists alike. Some seem to be offering sex services by choice, some by coercion, and some because they need the money and don't have other options for employment. Some, like Peniasi, have brilliant careers. And yet, some men still feel entitled to grab their arses.

The dance troupe returns to the stage with a more contemporary piece. Hannah feels a vibration in her handbag. She takes a discreet look at the screen and sees an unfamiliar local number. Intrigued, she excuses herself from Peniasi and walks out of the ballroom.

"Hello, Hannah speaking."

She can't hear anything and walks further away from the doors of the ballroom.

"Hello?"

This time, she thinks she hears muted sounds on the other end but can't be sure. "Hold on a second, I'll just go somewhere a bit quieter."

She walks toward the top of the staircase. "Sorry, I didn't catch who it was?" She holds the phone closer to her ear and puts a finger in the other. Finally, she hears a soft, deep female voice. "Ana?" It is her own name with an iTaukei accent.

"Yes, this is Hannah."

"It's Lia."

"Who, sorry?"

"Bu Lia. Isikeli's grandmother."

"Oh! Hello," Hannah says hesitantly. *She's going to ask for money.* The realization makes her sigh quietly. A request for money will taint the conversation they had – changing it from a mutually rewarding research moment into a *transaction.* How disappointing. A further realization dawns on her. Of course. The participant information sheet. She handed that document out to all those people in the settlements with her personal number on it. A stupid, rookie error.

Suddenly, she realizes that Bu is, in fact, crying. Soft, husky weeping. Hannah is horrified, immediately feeling guilty that she has been so ungenerous. The poor woman has just been through a cyclone. She sits down on the top step of the staircase and looks at the ornate wooden balustrade. "Oh, Bu, what's happened?"

She waits for the elderly woman to compose herself.

"Ana. It's Isikeli."

"Oh!" Hannah's mind spins, imagining what might have happened to the boy in the storm.

Bu continues, "He's been arrested."

"*Arrested?*" Hannah sees a small group of people milling at the bottom of the staircase and lowers her voice. "What for?"

Bu's voice breaks on the other end. "Chamberlain Street. On the news, eh?"

Hannah's heart begins pounding in her chest.

Bu begins to sob. "I know Isikeli is cheeky."

Hannah doesn't know what to say.

"But he would never kill anyone. Believe me. *Please*. Please can you help him, Ana?"

THE CELL stinks of stale sweat and fear. No breeze seems to be making its way through the security bars of the small open window. Isikeli sits cross-legged on the concrete floor, struggling to breathe. Around him he can count six other men, lying in whatever space they have carved out for themselves. Unlike him, they seem able to sleep.

The silence is unbearable. Isikeli's thoughts are spinning around, loud and out of control, running repeatedly over the events of the day.

He was with Seru and Save at the usual street corner. It turned out to be a surprisingly good sales day. Customers were feeling sentimental. Quite a few people stopped by to purchase a coconut drink and kindly ask how Paradise Estate fared after Dorothy. Army personnel from the military checkpoint up the road walked down to buy a coconut. They even engaged in witty banter with the boys while they drank. "*Toso Viti!*" one of the soldiers called as they walked back up the road. The mood was generous in Suva.

When a police car pulled in at the curb, fear immediately bubbled in Isikeli's stomach; it always does. He hoped the officers were just thirsty like the soldiers. Perhaps they too would be abnormally friendly toward them.

Two officers stepped out and shut their car doors. Seru stood up from where he was adjusting the pyramid of coconuts as the men walked toward the boys.

"*Bula*, officers," Seru said. "Coconut?"

The policemen didn't respond, letting the silence drag out.

Eventually, the taller officer said, "Which one of you is Isikeli Tiko?"

Isikeli's knees weakened. Out of the corner of his eye, Seru and Save remained deathly still.

"Never heard of him," Seru said finally, his voice high-pitched.

A hysterical giggle threatened to emerge from Isikeli's throat.

The shorter police officer gave a slow smile. "That's a shame," he said. He took out his wooden baton from the sheath on his belt and took a step toward the stack of coconuts. He lightly pushed the top one off, making it topple over. The pyramid collapsed and the coconuts jostled and rolled over each other, tumbling down the road.

Isikeli felt a burst of physical energy, like the feeling he used to have just before the whistle blew on the rugby pitch. He imagined balking in one direction – fooling the police officers – and then doubling back around, dancing between them and sprinting down the street. He was fast and agile; he knew he could outrun them.

But then what would he do? Where could he go? And *what would they do to Seru and Save?*

"It's me. I'm Isikeli Tiko," he said finally. Seru flashed him a look of fear.

What happened next was a blur. One of the officers grabbed his hand, whipping him onto the ground. Isikeli felt the baton pressed sharply against his back. They said something about him being "under arrest" and something about "rights," but he was too dazed to listen. They dragged him to the police car and thrust him into the backseat of the sedan.

As the car pulled into the road, Isikeli's heart was drumming in his ears and his whole body was shaking. The drive to the station was eerily smooth through the ravaged streets of Suva. The policemen in the front seat ignored him. At one point the officer in the passenger seat told a joke, a silly play on words, which the driver didn't get. His partner explained it again and the driver chuckled this time, but he obviously still didn't think it was very funny.

All Isikeli could think about was *how did they know*? Other than Seru, the only person who knew about the Chamberlain Street job was Epeli. And Epeli would never snitch on him. Would he?

When they were sixteen, Epeli used to visit from Mataqai during the school holidays. Isikeli once dragged his reluctant cousin-brother to a nightclub in town with Seru. Seru knew a bouncer who let the underage boys in through the back door. The three of them got pleasantly drunk for the first time. Alcohol, it turned out, made Isikeli quiet and contented, Epeli became smiley and affectionate, and Seru became louder and more facetious. They weaved through the pulsating dance floor together, with Seru advancing on older girls with no success. They stood in the queue to buy a beer, behind three Maori men. The men were not as bulky as some of their compatriots but were nonetheless lithe and muscly. Seru said something deliberately loud about the Flying Fijians' recent win against the All Blacks rugby team. The men looked back at the teenagers, and one of them said "Careful, bro," ominously. They were, they said, semi-professional boxers here for the Pacific Games. Isikeli and Epeli placated them with smiles of admiration, and the guys eventually turned back toward the bar. Then Seru said to their backs, "You must be featherweights, eh?"

The men turned in a flash. It was Epeli they saw first, smiling goofily, accidentally looking guilty. They launched on top of him. The crowd spread out, circling around the fight. Without thinking, Isikeli jumped on top of the Maori guys, throwing punches however he could, giving Epeli space to escape the scrum. The fight was, of course, hopelessly unequal; Isikeli got pummelled that night until his nose was crooked and bloody. But Epeli escaped injury free, which was, in Isikeli's eyes, victory in itself.

Io, Epi and him are solid. They annoy each other sometimes but they're cousin-brothers. They have each other's backs.

Isikeli has a headache now that is pounding just behind his eyes. Epeli would never betray him. *Surely he wouldn't.*

WHEN HANNAH returns to the ballroom, Peniasi immediately notices she is pale. "What happened, *lewa*?" He leads her to one of the chairs on the side of the hall, and Hannah tells him about her phone call.

"He's one of the guys who sells coconuts on the side of the street. You know, down near SupaValu?"

"*Io*. The coconut boys."

Hannah nods. "It makes me feel sick. I hung out with the guy. I mean, he *seemed* nice. And his grandmother is sweet. But who's to say he didn't do it? I don't know him at all, really."

The two of them sit in sober contemplation. Around them, alcohol has loosened up the atmosphere of the charity event. There is a rare freedom in the way everyone is dancing together.

"That murder didn't sound like the work of a teenager from the squatter settlements," Peniasi says suddenly.

Hannah looks over at him questioningly.

He shrugs. "It's easy to blame things on the coconut boys, eh?"

She thinks about this for a moment. "Why are they coming to me?" she says weakly.

"Because you've got connections, eh? You've got money."

"I don't really. Not much."

"You've got more than her."

They watch a couple dancing in front of them, the man flinging the woman with dramatic flair.

Peniasi looks up. "What about Ethan?"

Hannah feels confused by the question at first, and then her eyes widen. "Of course! Eth might know what to do."

She feels immediately lighter.

But then she remembers. "Actually, things are a bit, um, weird between him and me right now. Can you call him?"

HE HEARS a loud clanging of metal against metal. The men in the cell all gasp into consciousness, their big bodies flinging awake. Two officers are at the cell gate.

Isikeli doesn't know what is happening. The policemen call his name and, slowly, he finds himself walking toward them. One of the officers grabs Isikeli roughly, pulling him through the gate and clasping handcuffs on him, while the other clangs the gate closed and locks it. They start pushing him up the dimly lit stairs and into an empty hallway, harshly lit by fluorescent lights.

He is thrust into a dark room and the door is closed on him. Pitch black engulfs him again. He stands immobile for a while, and then feels his way toward a wall. Tentatively, he slides down it and sits on the cold floor. The faintly dusty smell of this room, at least, is a pleasant relief from the last one.

Left alone with his thoughts, Isikeli thinks again about Bu. After the arrest, Seru and Save would have gone to the settlement and found her in the neighbor's house. He imagines her face as she heard the news. He has dishonored her. She will not want to show her face anymore – in the settlement, in church, on the island. After everything she has been through, he has burned her with shame. He cannot bear to think about what this might do to her fragile body.

And what about little Eta? What will they tell her? He punches his hand as hard as he can against the concrete floor, wincing at the instant throbs, but finding strange solace in the immediacy of the pain.

The door of the room clicks open and the fluorescent light flickers on. Survival instinct kicks in and Isikeli quickly scans his surroundings. Two plastic chairs and a table sit in the middle of the room. A stained yellow fan stands in the corner, its unplugged cord slithering away.

Standing in the door is a police officer that Isikeli hasn't seen before. The officer has a clipboard.

"*Bula*, Isikeli. I'm Detective Seki," he says. His eyes have lines around them as though he smiles a lot. "Please join me at the table, eh?"

Isikeli lets out a long breath. He gets to his feet and makes his way to the chair, sidling into it. The detective speaks in a gentle, reassuring voice, smiling at Isikeli. He begins to ask questions – easy ones, about where Isikeli lives, how old he is, where he went to school. Isikeli answers hesitantly at first, and then with more confidence. The detective nods encouragingly, as though Isikeli is doing well. "New Methodist High School, eh? That's a good school."

The policeman then looks down again at his notes. "Now," he says. A long pause follows. "Tell me what happened on Chamberlain Street on the night of February the sixth. Late last Wednesday night. Walk me through it. It was an accident, eh?"

Isikeli stares at him. He doesn't know how to explain. "I don't know what you mean," he says quietly.

The officer's smile drops. "Think harder, eh?"

"I've never been to that street." He doesn't know why he said that. He knows he's making it worse for himself, but he can't seem to say the right thing.

"Isikeli, don't lie to me. We found a hat next to the house. The boys said it's yours."

The muggy air encloaks him. He wishes they could turn the fan on. He tries to gather his thoughts – *which boys?* The officer tries again, but still Isikeli's tongue feels thick in his mouth. He tries to unjumble his thoughts and articulate a response, but nothing comes out.

And that's when the nice officer leans across the table, grabs a tuft of Isikeli's hair, and slams his face into the laminate.

When Isikeli lifts his head again, he feels a thick, warm liquid running from his nose. A searing pain begins to pierce his cheekbone.

The officer sits back down, readjusting his uniform. He continues to speak, soft and kindly, as he did before. "There's an easier way to do this, eh? Now tell me why you killed the *Kai Idia*."

Sunday

IT'S NINE o'clock in the morning. Through the window of a café, Hannah can see Suva beginning to return to a fragile version of its former self. More traffic has begun to dribble back onto the roads. Shopkeepers are opening their doors and emptying freezers full of food spoiled in the power outage – melted ice cream and rotten seafood. Jovial men in high-visibility vests are doing their first round of rubbish collection since the cyclone, shouting to each other and hauling large black bags into the truck, thankfully taking the stench with them.

Hannah's coffee is brought to her by the cool-looking iTaukei barista that works here, the one that Pip and Jess think is hot. He makes the best coffee in Suva, and urban legend is that he was trained at a café on Lygon Street in Melbourne. Hannah doesn't make small talk with him today; her nerves are too frazzled. The Iskeli situation is making her anxious. Bu seems to have faith that Hannah can pull strings, a faith that Hannah worries might be deeply misplaced.

Calling Ethan, at least, was a good idea. He agreed to meet her and Peni here this morning. That's the other thing she's nervous about – seeing Ethan again. Her ankle keeps jiggling.

Ethan arrives before Peniasi, a briefcase in his hand. Hannah is slightly taken aback by his scrubbed appearance. His hair is combed with a neat part to one side. Below his suit jacket and collared shirt he wears a dark gray *sulu*, his tanned calves tapering into white socks and pointed, polished black shoes. He is a completely different man from the one she saw laboring with the wheelbarrow yesterday. It makes him look endearingly exposed, like a shorn sheep. He sees Hannah and gives her a small wave across the café, gesturing that he is going to order a coffee.

Hannah smiles casually and looks down at the *Fiji Herald* in front of her, pretending to concentrate. It is dominated by reports of Dorothy's carnage and the international aid response. But she can't help but take the odd discreet glance at Ethan at the counter. Amongst the Australian volunteers, he is the only one who wears a *sulu*. He's been given endless grief from the others about it; Aaron teases him for being "gimmicky." Pip says she, at least, will never wear a Fijian outfit because she thinks it is cultural appropriation and she doesn't have the right. But in typical Ethan style, he has remained cheerfully committed to it. He always maintains that his colleagues and clients are "totally chuffed" when he wears it.

He joins her at her table now. He looks down at his cappuccino and stirs it for a little too long, tinkling the teaspoon around the cup. They decide to wait for Peniasi before they talk about the case, so Hannah makes small talk with him about the post-disaster weekend. He answers her questions politely. He doesn't mention his helping at the squatter settlement yesterday. He is amicable enough, but there is a distance in his eyes that makes her miss him. *Come on, Eth!* she feels like saying. She keeps the smile fixed on her face and tries to squash the feeling.

ISIKELI'S BODY aches for the relief of sleep but he knows he needs to remain alert. He has no idea what time it is in the windowless room. All night, Detective Seki has come in and out of the room. Sometimes he offers him water and makes small talk about people he knows in Paradise Estate. Sometimes he asks questions. He always seems to be disappointed by Isikeli's answers. His bursts of violence are always unpredictable, always when Isikeli least expects it. Isikeli wonders if he may, in fact, be in a nightmare that he cannot wake himself from.

The faint sound of male voices in the hallway is getting louder. His heart quickens. The light flashes on and there's three of them now. It's the smiley detective and the two policemen from the arrest. The tall one sits at the table across from him. He has a clipboard and a pen. The shorter one leans against the wall, hands in his pockets. Seki paces around the table, hovering whenever he gets close to Isikeli, and then continuing to pace.

"We have your friends in the room next door," the tall man says to Isikeli. "The other coconut boys."

Isikeli's stomach churns with dread. *He's lying*, Isikeli thinks. *Please be lying.*

"They didn't hold out long. They've told us everything. So there's no point in you staying silent now, eh?"

The man keeps flicking the corner of the page at the top of his clipboard. Seki keeps walking. "We know you killed the *Kai Idia*. It was probably an accident, eh? He found you in his house, you pushed him too hard?"

Isikeli wants to explain. He wants to tell them what happened. But the pain is still aching at the back of his head and he cannot think of how to start. He looks up, helplessly, unable to speak.

The shorter policeman crosses the room with speed. He strides around the table and pulls Isikeli's chair back with surprising strength. He lands a fist on the boy's ribcage, knocking the wind out of his lungs.

That's when Isikeli has a strange feeling of rising above his own body. He watches himself down below, grabbing onto the table, gasping for breath, and then getting punched again. But he is able to leave that behind him now, and float back to his childhood. Back to happy moments when things weren't broken yet. He and Mere are sitting on one side of a booth, and his mother and father are sitting opposite. He is nine years old. His dad has just received his first paycheck from the factory and has whisked them all out for fried chicken and chips. Na isn't worried about money for once; they get the "all-you-can-eat" deal. When Isikeli has eaten all that his stomach can possibly hold, he sits back against the booth, satisfied. He looks at his dad, who is laughing at something Na just said. Na looks especially beautiful tonight; she has dressed up to come out. Isikeli soon gets bored and dollops a spoonful of his leftover soft-serve ice cream into Mere's cup of water. Mere squeals in outrage and sploshes the cup back his way, spilling it on the table. Na gets angry with them both and apologizes to the waitress. She bundles everyone up to leave and pushes her children onto the sidewalk. When they step onto the bus, Isikeli can see his parents stifling smiles and holding hands. At bedtime, his father tells them the story of Movua the owl spirit again.

Back in the interview room now, eighteen-year-old Isikeli is clutching at his stomach in agony. The tall man slides the clipboard over the table to Isikeli and places a pen on top of it. Through Isikeli's slightly blurred vision, he can see the leather shoes, black socks, and bare calves of Seki standing beside him.

"Here's what happened," Seki says, pointing to the paper in the clipboard.

Isikeli lifts his head slowly. In front of him is a half-page of writing. The words on the page swim before him. The scrawled handwriting is much neater than his own. "Your confession. Sign it by the time we come back. You don't want to know what will happen if you don't." And with that, the officers leave the room.

Isikeli is too exhausted to even form a prayer. He wonders whether he might die tonight. He imagines someone breaking the news of his death to his mother. She would get the call while she is cleaning a room at the Tribe Resort. Would she sit down on the bed? Would she cry? Would she help herself to a small drink from the mini bar, to numb her humiliation? What an embarrassment her son turned out to be.

WHEN RISHIKA'S aunties try to engage her in conversation, she never seems to get the tone right. She can tell by the worried look in their eyes that she is sometimes too blank and monotonous, at other times she sounds accidentally chipper.

She can hear them in the kitchen, washing the breakfast dishes right now. They flit between safe topics: schools are not what they used to be and, for that matter, neither are children. ("Hormones, my foot!" Nausori Aunty scoffs. "I said to my daughter, what that teenager needs is a twisted ear.")

Their well-intentioned chatter washes over Rishika. It's the little things her thoughts are laboring over, the little facts that churn in her head. Akesh said that the house was ransacked, everything rifled through, everything turned over. He said that towels were emptied from the bathroom cupboards, bookshelves cleaned out, clothes strewn from the wardrobes.

She has of course already checked, but she feels the compulsion to get up from the sofa now and walk back down the hallway to her bedroom. She wants to make doubly sure that she is not imagining it.

Lakshmi gave her the jewelery box as a present when she came back from a trip to the United States. The box was conspicuously expensive-looking – gold painted, encrusted with multicolored diamantes. It had lots of useful compartments.

She opens the lid again, already knowing what she is going to see. Her twenty-four-carat gold necklace and earrings still sit there limply, waiting to be worn, just like they always do, sitting right next to the three *mohur* gold coins she inherited from her mother.

It reaffirms what she was already thinking.

This was no opportunistic petty thief. This was no burglary-gone-wrong.

Someone wanted him killed. Maybe they ransacked the place to make it look like a burglary.

She mentioned this possibility to Akesh earlier, but he brushed it aside. He says the thieves just got spooked and ran.

And yet it doesn't make sense. No thief would ransack everything and leave the gold jewelery behind.

But who would want to kill Vijay?

HANNAH RELAXES when she sees Peniasi appear at the café door, immediately defusing the tension.

"Fiji Time, eh?" he puffs apologetically, and Ethan gets up to order his friend a coffee.

They all lean in toward each other and speak in quiet, confidential whispers about the case.

Ethan made a phone call this morning to his supervisor at legal aid. "It's not looking good," he says flatly. He explains there is a long backlog of cases in the courts and legal aid staff are struggling to keep up. Best case scenario, the lawyers are handed the brief just before the hearing and try to hurriedly take instructions from the client minutes before they appear before the magistrate. But because of the cyclone, the office won't be open for another week. Isikeli's bail hearing is likely to be postponed, or it will happen without a legal aid lawyer. That sometimes happens.

"Oh, God," says Hannah, rubbing her eyelids, trying to take all of this in. She dreads having to tell this to Bu.

"But there is an avenue we could take," Ethan says slowly. He did ask his supervisor whether he could represent Isikeli, given he is a friend of a friend. His supervisor said he could.

"So, we could give that a try," he finishes.

"That sounds good," says Hannah, her mood lifting slightly.

Peni adds that he used his media status to make inquiries. The victim was apparently a government driver. Autopsy results have not yet been released. Peniasi could not ascertain what evidence they have against Isikeli.

Ethan nods, writing notes on his yellow lined pad. "If I'm representing him, the police'll have to hand over any evidence they have against him to me." He seems to be talking more to himself than anything else. Peniasi looks at Hannah over Ethan's head and mouths, "So profesh!"

She bites her lip, repressing a smile. Ethan finishes writing his last sentence and then gulps the last of his coffee. "Here goes nothing," he declares.

On the short walk to the police station, Hannah catches up so that she is walking alongside him.

"Hey, thanks for doing this Eth."

He catches her eye. For a split second it feels like their old connection is back, but then he looks away. "Don't thank me yet. Let's see how it goes."

A LOUD knock at the door of the confined room startles Isikeli. It is the detective again. Isikeli stops breathing for a moment, steeling himself against the violence he knows is coming.

"Morning!" the detective says, sounding oddly cheerful. "I have your lawyer here with me."

Isikeli squints his eyes in confusion.

"Your solicitor has arrived to represent you," the man says. He slowly opens the door wider to reveal a *Kai Valagi* man with a briefcase. Even through his haze of pain, Isikeli can see that the man is wearing a *sulu*, his skinny white legs poking out underneath.

"Ethan Sommers, legal aid," says the man, holding out his hand to Isikeli. The lawyer winces slightly when he gets a closer look at Isikeli's face. It feels swollen and tight, and it hurts to blink.

Behind them, the detective seems to grab the clipboard. He closes it shut, hiding it by his side.

The lawyer smiles at the police officer. "I would like to speak to my client alone, please."

"*Io, io*, of course." Detective Seki begins to walk out of the room. Just before the door pulls shut, he glances back at Isikeli with an almost imperceptible wink.

They are left alone. The lawyer puts down his briefcase next to the table and softens his voice. "Looks like you've had a rough night, Isikeli. Did they do that to you? Have they been hitting you, mate?" Isikeli wonders whether this is a ploy, whether this man is, in fact, one of the police.

"I work at legal aid. I think you might know my friend, Hannah? She asked me to meet with you."

It takes a moment for Isikeli to place her. Hannah … the Australian girl, the researcher. *She's helping me?* Isikeli looks down at his feet.

"I'm going to represent you, Isikeli. I'm on your side."

The lawyer brings out a yellow pad and begins to look through some handwriting on the page. "So Isikeli, they've charged you with manslaughter. That means they are saying you killed a man accidentally when you were doing something unlawful."

Isikeli cannot bring his eyes to look at the lawyer.

"And ... I've spoken to the police, and it sounds like they've got evidence that seems to place you at the scene. Or near it at least."

Isikeli remains silent.

"Now, I'm not sure if you did this, or you didn't. But either way, I need to build a defense for you. Okay?"

Isikeli keeps his eyes on the table.

The lawyer stays quiet for a moment, and then says strongly, "I need you tell me why your hat was on Chamberlain Street."

Finally, that question feels answerable. Isikeli looks up, composes himself, and slowly begins to speak.

"SO HE just ... robbed the wrong place at the wrong time?" Peniasi asks, pouring three glasses from a jug of sangria.

Ethan nods. "That's what he says. He reckons he just used a long pole-type-thing to fish out a backpack through the window – I mean you've gotta admire the kid's ingenuity – and then he ran away. The hat fell off when he was climbing back over the fence. He reckons he never saw the Indo-Fijian guy."

Hannah watches as a pink-orange rind plops into the glass of maroon liquid. Peniasi slides one glass sideways to her and the other across to Ethan. She takes a sip and savors the sweet tang, experiencing a little shiver as the alcohol enters her body. It is slightly worrying how much she is enjoying this drink. She definitely needs to detox whenever this craziness is over.

"Do you think he's telling the truth?" she asks. "That it was just some crappy coincidence?"

"It's hard to say. It's *possible*, I guess. Technically it's not a lawyer's job to believe their client or not. I just have to plead his case in the best way I can."

They all take another sip.

"I *want* to believe the guy," Ethan adds, swirling his drink and staring down at the glass. Peniasi nods in agreement.

"I know, me too," Hannah adds.

Ethan catches her eye then. She can see little gray specks in his eyes that she hasn't noticed before. He looks away, and downs the rest of his drink, quickly pouring himself another.

There is a pause. Then Ethan says, "You should have seen his face. He's been roughed up really badly."

Peniasi raises his eyebrows. "*Isa.* Happens a lot."

"Well, it's fucked up."

"*Io.*"

A waiter arrives with a tray of hot tacos, and the room fills with the fresh piquancy of coriander and chili.

Ethan grabs a taco. "Ow!" He drops it, allowing it to cool, and keeps talking. "They only have circumstantial evidence. His hat was actually outside the fence – it wasn't even at the scene. It's an outrage that they got an arrest warrant for that."

Peniasi shakes his head. "Everyone wants to close this case quickly. It's easy to pin it on him." He winks. "They didn't expect him to have such a hotshot lawyer."

Peniasi and Hannah smile at each other. Ethan ignores the compliment, looking down at his taco.

A question occurs to Hannah. "He can get bail, right?"

"The bail hearing hasn't been scheduled yet. We'll try, but they don't usually grant bail in cases like this."

"But ... doesn't everyone have a right to bail?"

"Not when it's a violent crime. The presumption of bail gets reversed."

Hannah can hear a shrill tone creeping into her voice. "But what happens if he can't? What about his grandma?"

Ethan looks at her and shrugs. "He'll be detained until the trial. Could be months. Could be years."

Peniasi shakes his head sadly. "Who knows what they'll do to him in there."

Monday

HANNAH IS awoken from a deep, dreamless sleep to the sound of her phone ringing. She answers groggily, expecting her parents.

"Hannah, it's Ethan."

She wakes up fully now, sitting up, leaning against her pillow. "Hey Ethan." It still feels strange to be calling him by his full name, but that seems to be how it is now, as though their friendship has slid backwards.

"Sorry to wake you," he says.

"That's okay! No, it's absolutely fine."

"I've been reading up on ... stuff, and I've thought of something," he says. He tells her to meet him at the police station later.

Over breakfast, she places a call through to Bu via her granddaughter's phone to update her, albeit without much news to share.

"*Vinaka*, Ana," the woman says quietly. When Hannah hangs up, a Fijian word oddly comes to mind – *kavoro*. Isikeli's grandmother sounds shattered.

Later, Hannah sits on the wooden bench at the police station with Peniasi sitting beside her. He muses about the uncharacteristic silence of the legal precinct; he's been here before for big cases, when the place was swarming with media and angry family members. Usually a high-profile murder would invite such a reaction, but everything seems to be on hold after the cyclone.

The security guards sit at the door, scrolling through their phones and showing each other their screens. From their faces, it looks like they are sharing cyclone footage.

If Hannah understood Ethan correctly, this is his thinking: he knows the police don't want to let Isikeli out on bail. None of the usual arguments will work. So Ethan is going to have to try something that, in his words, "might be more persuasive." He'll threaten that he can prove that Isikeli's injuries were sustained in custody. He read up all night about precedent regarding police brutality and anti-torture laws.

When he first explained it all this morning, it sounded possible to Hannah, brilliant even. "Io," Peniasi kept saying. And yet, just before Ethan disappeared through the doors with the security guard, he looked back at Hannah with a look of apprehension. Now he has been gone for over two hours and Hannah is feeling a rising sense of panic.

Sounds from outside the police station suddenly interrupt her thoughts. The security guards look up from their phones. Hannah follows Peniasi's gaze outside the window. There, an elderly iTaukei woman in a wheelchair is being pushed up the pathway. The tires of the wheelchair are flat and rolling begrudgingly, the young man behind it angled at forty-five degrees in order to push it along. Hannah recognizes the woman immediately. "That's Bu!" she says and walks quickly out to greet them. Bu holds Hannah's hand in both of hers for quite some time, which makes Hannah feel emotional.

The security guards help lift Bu up the two steps to the police station. Hannah introduces Bu to Peniasi. A look of surprise appears in her eyes when she notices his *qauri* appearance, but it quickly disappears. She asks him where he is from, and they have a brief chat in Fijian. Then they have nothing to do but wait, and the foyer descends back into silence.

Bu hangs her head and Hannah can see her lips moving in prayer.

Eventually, the sound of the reception phone ringing makes them all startle; the quaint sound of a landline that one hardly hears anymore: *brrring brrring … brrring brrring.*

The receptionist answers. "*Io … io … donu.*" She says something to the security guards in Fijian, and they both jump into action, one standing to attention at the front door while the other walks across the foyer toward the locked door. He keys in a pincode and walks through it, pulling the door closed behind him.

Hannah looks at Peni questioningly. Bu sits up.

Finally the inner station door opens. It is the security guard again. He stands at the door, holding it open. Ethan appears, manila folder under one arm and briefcase in the other hand. Hannah stands up and tries to read his face.

There is a collective gasp, and now she sees Isikeli appear behind Ethan, walking gingerly. His shirt is clinging to him, damp with sweat, his left eye black and swollen.

Isikeli walks straight past Hannah to his grandmother, head bowed. Hannah glances at Bu, expecting her face to be crumpled in deep emotion at the sight of her grandson. Instead, it is surprisingly stoic – even fierce. "*Io!*" she says loudly and the old woman reels off a stream of loud, angry words in Fijian. Isikeli keeps his eyes trained on the wooden floorboards.

Hannah looks away, trying to give them privacy.

Bu's tirade stops. The room is perfectly silent, except for the ceiling fan blowing some papers on the receptionist's desk. All of a sudden, Bu pulls Isikeli down toward her, resting her forehead on his and uttering softer words as tears stream down her face. Isikeli's shoulders begin to convulse.

Tears prickle behind Hannah's eyes. She shoots a sidelong glance at Ethan, his eyes also glistening. He looks down and busies himself reading his notes.

Eventually, the other teenager puts out his hand toward Isikeli.

The two young men share a gentle sliding handshake. Isikeli gives him a sad smile. "*Set*, Epi."

THE *KAI VALAGI* lawyer stands on the steps of the police station with everyone gathered around him, as though the coach of a motley team. The lawyer keeps his voice low as he explains how he negotiated Isikeli's bail. Exhausted and in pain, Isikeli flops on the steps, his head in his hands.

"But we're not out of the woods by any means, mate," the lawyer continues, looking down at Isikeli, then sitting down next to him on the steps. He talks to him slowly, in a patient voice – something about the legal process, the conditions of bail, the consequences if he breaches them.

But Isikeli is not listening, thinking instead of what Epeli whispered earlier. Apparently before the police arrested Isikeli, they had been asking around the settlement, and someone had identified the hat as his. Thankfully the police don't seem to know that Seru was with him that night.

Isikeli feels like a weathered piece of driftwood. For two days, intense, unfamiliar feelings have pulsed through him one after the other: fear, shame, betrayal, relief. It has left him utterly drained. He nods at the lawyer's words, but they wash past him.

"Okay?" the lawyer says finally. "Anything you didn't understand?"

Isikeli raises his eyebrows.

"Great." He pats him on the back. "We're gonna fight this."

Bu hasn't spoken all this time. She has been sitting quietly in her wheelchair next to the stairs, listening to the lawyer speak, her face drawn and sad.

"That poor woman," she says now, and everyone looks a bit confused, trying to work out who she's referring to.

Isikeli knows she is talking about the man's wife, his widow. He hasn't really thought about her. All he knows of her is the silhouette that he saw on that first night when he was casing the Chamberlain Street joint with Seru. He knows she will be wearing white now, immersed in Hindu grieving customs.

Bu is staring at Isikeli. "You're going to give that bag back to her."

He feels a wrench in his stomach. He can't possibly face that woman.

The lawyer coughs uncomfortably. "Sorry, Mrs Tiko, you can't do that. It's highly inappropriate for the accused to make contact with the victim's family. It breaches the conditions of bail."

Isikeli takes a slow breath of relief.

But Bu raises her chin in matriarchal defiance. "We have to. We'll do *matanigasau*. Say sorry. It's the Fijian way, eh?" She speaks louder now, reinforced by the authority of a thousand-year-old tradition.

The lawyer looks taken aback.

"You'll come, too," Bu says to him, then looks at Hannah and the *qauri*, including them in the command. "We'll go tomorrow."

They all look wide-eyed and submissive, like students in a principal's office. The lawyer opens his mouth, about to say something, and then shuts it again.

In other circumstances, Isikeli might have smiled. *No one argues with Bu.*

HANNAH FEELS victorious as the three of them walk toward the Old Victoria Hotel, after a taxi took the others back to the settlement. Even Ethan is smiling now. "I can't believe we did that, Han," he says. She likes the way he said "we" and feels a rush of relief that he is using her nickname again. "It was amazing," she said. "I can't believe your plan worked."

"Well, I kinda lied that I had a direct line to the attorney general and would be meeting with him later today about the case," says Ethan.

Hannah looks at him wide-eyed, impressed and surprised.

He shrugs wryly. "Being white helps. They don't want trouble from the embassies."

It's lunch time when they reach the hotel, the sky hazy in the midday heat. A speedboat cuts through the water as it heads out to sea, splitting it apart like a zip. At the table beside them sits a family with Australian accents who, by the looks of their sun-tinged faces and the thin braids tightly woven into the little girl's hair, are on a day trip from one of the resorts.

They sit down and stare wordlessly out at the glassy harbor, lost in their own thoughts about the morning's events.

"I'm worried for him," Peniasi announces suddenly. He takes a look around them and lowers his voice. "The police have been humiliated now, eh? Kid needs to watch his back. People have been killed for less."

Ethan places his glass back on the table, smile dissipating. He nods slowly, staring out at the harbor. He seems about to ask another question, but a waitress arrives with the bowl of chips they just ordered. They wait for her to leave.

"Peni, we can't do this thing tomorrow," Ethan states. "This thing that Bu's talking about."

"*Matanigasau*," Peniasi says.

"Yeah, that. What is it exactly?"

"It's when ... how to say ... it's the Fijian ceremony for asking for forgiveness. The people bring an offering. Usually *waka* – *yaqona* root – or sometimes *tabua*."

Hannah turns to Peniasi. "Do we bring that?"

"*Sega*, no, they'll bring that. They're the ones saying sorry, eh? There's lots of speeches and clapping. And then the two groups drink *yaqona* together. As a symbolic act of acceptance."

"So ... why does she want *us* to go?" Hannah asks.

"We're not going," Ethan insists.

Peni shrugs. "They'll go with or without us. I think it's better if we are there."

"Isn't this bad timing?" Hannah continues. "The poor woman is, like, grieving her husband. She doesn't want *us* rocking up, surely?"

"I'm more worried about him violating his bail conditions," Ethan urges. "If she makes a fuss, he'll go to prison. Not to mention me breaching the lawyer's code of ethics. Probably lose my license."

Peniasi raises his eyebrows. "She'll get it. It's the Fijian way, eh?"

That familiar refrain. The Fijian way.

"Right," Ethan says uncomfortably.

Tuesday

IT IS the fifth day of mourning and the spare mattresses have been rolled up, the bedding folded and returned to the linen cupboard. Alone again for the first time in days, Rishika sits at the kitchen table. They'll be back soon, but for now the weight of her relatives' opinions is lifted, temporarily relieving her of the burden of having to look like a woman grieving properly.

When the gecko chirps, she looks up. "Why *do* cyclones have names?" she asks the dog. Everyone's still talking about the cyclone; she remembers her awkward interaction with the neighbor this morning. A few moments later, with the dog following at her heels, she makes her way to the dusty computer in the study. She awakens the sleeping screen and stares at the keyboard, words momentarily escaping her. She used to love words. She stares at the letters until they begin to crystallize again. She taps it out slowly, staccato. *Why … do … cyclones … have … names?*

She learns about a Queensland meteorologist who began to name cyclones in the late 1800s. He used names from Greek and Roman mythology: Cyclone Zeus, Cyclone Venus, Cyclone Aphrodite.

Rishika liked these majestic names. She could understand destruction if it were called something that commanded fear and
respect. But when those names were all used up, the man began
to call storms after his least favorite politicians as a personal joke,
a funny little legacy. Now there is a long list of names reserved for
cyclones in each region, waiting in the wings to reap destruction.
Each new storm gets dubbed the name at the top. Rishika scrolls
through the cyclones past – Cyclone Yasa, Cyclone Zazu, Cyclone
Ana, Cyclone Cody. Her name isn't on there of course. There has
never been a Cyclone Rishika, a Cyclone Subramanyam, or a
Cyclone Shakuntla. Rishika can't decide whether to be offended
by this or not; whether she would actually enjoy meteorological
fame. One thing is for certain: if this ever changes, there will be a
lot more mispronunciations in the weather bulletins.

The words swim before her and she wants to stop thinking
now. She considers calling Lakshmi, who is always good to not-
think with. Maybe they can download a movie together. But
Lakshmi is treading on eggshells around her and will probably
think she has gone mad.

Back in the loungeroom, she plops onto the couch. Solomon
lies down on the floor in front of her, his fur tickling at her feet.
She pats the vinyl beside her, gesturing for him to jump up. He
looks at her incredulously.

"It's okay," she says. "He's not here anymore. Come on!"

He cocks his head.

"Up! Silly dog."

He puts one paw on the sofa.

She gets down on the floor so that she is level with him and
lifts his heavy, unwieldy limbs onto the sofa. He yelps in arthritic
discomfort. When he is eventually standing on the seat, the dog
walks around in a tight circle twice, and then once in the opposite
direction. Finally, he flops down in his carefully chosen position.

They sit there together while the loungeroom clock continues its relentless march toward tomorrow. Minutes pass. Perhaps hours.

Suddenly Solomon barks loudly. The dog jumps off the sofa – forgetting his elderly pains for a moment – and ambles toward the door. He barks again.

Now Rishika hears it too. A tinkling, like a butter knife against a champagne glass. *The gate. Someone is rattling the gate.* Her breath quickens. Maybe it is Akesh coming back. He was the last to leave this morning. He gave her a hug – just a harmless, comforting hug from a cousin-in-law – which lasted slightly longer than it should have. When he pulled away, he seemed about to say something, but obviously decided against it.

Heart racing, she peers out the window. It isn't Akesh. There, outside her gate, stand six people who she has never seen before. It is a funny-looking lineup of two Europeans and four iTaukei, including an elderly woman in a wheelchair. They are all smartly dressed and look slightly nervous.

Jehovah's Witnesses!

She could pretend she is not here, like Vijay used to. But there is something about them that compels her to open the door. She is curious. Besides, she has literally nothing else in the world to be doing right now. She might even be up for reading their magazine.

She holds Solomon's collar as she opens the door, but then lets him go; he is too old to run and lunge at them. She stands on the balcony and calls, "Hello? *Bula*?"

They call a chorus of greetings to her. The old woman calls, "*Bula vinaka, Marama.* We come inside the gate, eh?"

Rishika hesitates only briefly, and then nods. She grabs the keys from the hook and walks down the stairs, talking soothingly to Solomon, reassuring him that they are friendly. At least she hopes they are. Perhaps this is their missionary strategy. Widows are probably prime candidates for conversion; adrift and searching for meaning. The visitors probably think it's their lucky day; they've hit the jackpot. She would hate to disappoint them.

As she moves toward the gate, she analyzes them for more details. The two white people and the *qauri* hang back, with small, uncomfortable smiles pasted on their faces. The tall iTaukei teenager is standing slightly in front of everyone else, with a purple, swollen eye. The older woman in the wheelchair holds her hand on the boy's lower back, propping him up, thrusting him forward. He is holding something in front of him with both hands. As Rishika gets closer, she sees that it is a package wrapped in newspaper. It looks like an offering?

The elderly woman speaks up by way of explanation. "We do *matanigasau*, eh?"

So they are not Jehovah's Witnesses. Rishika has grown up with Fijian ceremonies, formal openings and receptions at school and in her village. She can't remember what *matanigasau* means exactly, but the word is familiar. She knows enough about iTaukei culture to know that it will only be revealed in time, after the formalities. The somber faces of this strange multi-racial group tells her this is important. She hopes she doesn't have to drink kava, though. She hates kava; it tastes like mud, and it is a boring activity men waste too many hours on. She gestures for the people to follow her up the stairs.

The tall boy carries the package with him. Oddly, Solomon walks beside him, wagging his tail, as though they know each other. The other iTaukei teenager and the young white man lift the elderly woman in the wheelchair up the stairs and then place the chair down carefully on the balcony. In silence, everyone bends to take off their shoes. They stand awkwardly in the loungeroom while Rishika goes to the laundry to pull down the woven mat that Vijay always kept for kava sessions. Her aunties clearly hadn't found it in their cleaning frenzy.

The pretty *qauri* with the flower in his ear takes the mat from Rishika with a smile and rolls it out. The teenagers lift the old woman out of her wheelchair so she can sit on the mat. She re-adjusts her *sulu* so that it covers her one leg stretched out before her. One of the boys pulls up a chair, gesturing for Rishika to sit down, which she does, obligingly. One by one, everyone else sits down on the mat in front of her in surreal silence.

The old woman coughs now, glaring at the tall teenager. She seems bossy with him, in a way that suggests they are related. A grandson, maybe, or a great-nephew.

The boy unwraps the newspaper to reveal a *tabua*. He kneels in front of Rishika, holding the ivory-colored whale's tooth in both hands.

"Thank you for accepting us into your home today," the boy says. His voice comes out weakly at first.

"*Ei, dina,*" says the other teenager, clapping formally.

The boy speaks in Fijian and every once in a while breaks into English.

"My name is Isikeli. This is my grandmother Bu Lia, my cous-in-brother Epeli, and our friends Mr Peniasi, Miss Hannah, and Mr Ethan."

The girl called Hannah half-waves awkwardly, and then drops her hand.

Rishika finds herself bobbing her head, defaulting to her own culture's gesture of welcome. She has a brief stab of empathy for her great-great-grandfather, Arjun. How strange it must have been when he met the iTaukei villagers for the first time in the late 1800s, not even sharing a word between them.

"We offer our deepest sympathies for the loss of your hus-band," Isikeli continues.

"*Ei, dina*," says Epeli while clapping.

"*Vinaka*," Rishika says. They seem so young to her, as though they are play-acting their fathers' roles, and yet they have a certain authority about them.

"May peace be with him in the afterlife," the teenager says, the phrase rolling off his tongue as though he has heard it many times before.

"*Emeni*," Bu Lia and Epeli chime.

"*Vinaka*," Rishika mutters again, wondering how long this may go on for. *Who are you?* she feels like asking.

"We bestow this *tabua* on you to ask for your forgiveness." Finally, at this point in his speech, he falters. "I was here, last week."

Rishika squints at him, unsure what he means.

"In your compound. On Wednesday night."

Rishika begins breathing quickly now. *That was the night my husband was killed.*

"I took something that was yours. Through the window. Now I give it back."

The boys speak in Fijian and then clap their hands. He gives the *tabua* to Rishika. He stands up now and goes to the wheelchair, bending down to retrieve a black bag from a makeshift pocket at the back of the chair. She can see even from a distance that his hands are shaking. "*Tulou, tulou*," he says as he walks into the circle, bowing in respect as he hands it to Rishika. He retreats backwards and kneels in front of Rishika a few meters away, his head bowed. Slowly, Rishika stares at the bag, wide-eyed, recognizing it immediately. *Vijay's backpack.* Her hands begin to shake involuntarily. She zips open the main pocket to see some papers in there and a stainless steel lunchbox, with all its compartments that she used to fill with curry and roti. Solomon comes up behind her and nudges her arm with his nose, trying to get closer to the bag. It must still smell of Vijay. Or, more likely, curry. She zips it up again.

The boy is talking again, faster now. "I did not see your husband that night." He goes on to explain that he used a pole to get the bag through the window. "Please believe me. I did not go in the house. I did not touch him. I promise. I would never ..." He lets that sentence slip away incomplete. "I am sorry for stealing from you."

The moment is already so strange that Rishika simply stares at the boy, who is looking respectfully at the ground. She finds herself cocking her head, like Solomon. The other people in the circle remain deadly quiet. She can sense their discomfort.

Moments pass while the intense silence continues. The loungeroom clock continues ticking with no regard for what is happening below it. As a matter of habit, Rishika strokes Solomon absentmindedly, all the while continuing to stare at the boy, trying to process the new information. Incomplete snatches of thought flash across her mind. *Vijay finding the pole outside the window when the first break-in happened.*

Solomon's tail wagging when Isikeli arrived today. The dog remembers him – fondly.

And somehow, at the end of her thought process, she emerges with absolute certainty that he is telling the truth. She doesn't believe it was this boy who ransacked her house. She doesn't believe it was this boy who killed her husband. Gradually, her surroundings come back into focus.

"Thank you for bringing the bag back to me," she says.

He nods.

"And ..." she feels like she should add something, "... you are forgiven."

Very quietly, his voice breaks. "*Vinaka, marama.*"

Everyone in the circle seems to exhale in relief – chests rise and fall in tandem.

Rishika has no idea what to do now.

"Would anyone like a cup of tea?"

RISHIKA IS, quite possibly, the most beautiful woman Hannah has ever seen. Hannah's eyes follow her across the room as she walks into the kitchen, the dog at her heels. Her sari hugs her slim figure, the ivory-white folds of material giving her coffee-brown skin an ethereal glow. The heavy-looking traditional dress is off-set by a fashionably short hair cut, which makes it impossible to tell how old she is.

It is hard to believe she was so recently widowed. Her husband was *murdered*, and yet she has a sort of quiet, graceful strength. If anything like that ever happened to Hannah, she feels certain she would be a blubbering, red-faced mess.

The hiss of the kettle and the tinkling of teacups can be heard in the kitchen. Peniasi gets up to help Rishika and soon returns holding a tray of cups full of spicy tea, the smell of cinnamon and cloves pleasantly filling the loungeroom. Rishika follows him with a tupperware container of white and luridly colored Indian sweets, which she places on the mat. "My aunty made these," she says. "Please help yourself." She has impeccable English and only a subtle accent. Hannah wonders whether she has lived overseas.

Peniasi hands out a teacup to everyone and Hannah bites into a bright pink sweet. "Mmmm," she says politely. She actually finds these sweets too sweet.

While they eat, Bu tells Rishika where they are from. Rishika mentions the name of her former garden boy who lived in Para-dise Estate. Bu nods and says she knows the man. He used to live just down from Bu's house.

"Huh. Small world," says Ethan.

Everyone retreats back into silence, sipping and munching.

Isikeli hands Bu a little cube of *barfi*. Hannah tries to forget her professional knowledge of what that sugar will do to her diabetic body. *Let the poor lady enjoy the sweet.*

"Milk powder," Bu says to Rishika after her first bite. "And ... cardamom, eh?"

"Yes, that's right."

"*Maleka*," Bu says appreciatively, taking another bite.

"Bu is the best at making *barfi*," Isikeli announces proudly.

"*Sega*." Bu shakes her head bashfully.

"*Io*," Isikeli says forcefully. "She made it for the Reddy family. Twenty years, eh, Bu?"

Rishika's eyes widen in recognition. "Oh, Mahendra Reddy? Reddy Shipping?"

"*Io*."

Rishika's head wobbles slightly and she smiles. "My *barfi* always goes soggy. Maybe you can teach me."

Bu chuckles. "It's the mix, eh?"

No one talks again for a while. The gecko chirps in the kitchen. Hannah is resisting her instinct to fill the gaps with small talk, so she simply sits there. She is starting to feel more comfortable amidst Fijian silence these days. She steals a look at Ethan drinking his tea.

Rishika places her teacup onto a saucer, decisively it seems, and looks up. "I thought maybe they came for the bag," she says, to no one in particular.

Ethan looks at her, leaning his chin forward. "Sorry, who's 'they'?"

"The person who killed Vijay."

It is the first time Hannah has heard Rishika say her husband's name. It seems sadder now that he has a name. She wonders how the two of them met. Was it an arranged marriage? Did they fall in love? He must have felt so lucky to get this woman.

Ethan is still asking questions. "What made you think they were looking for something?" he asks. Hannah wonders whether he is being too pushy, pressing her for information. But Rishika seems to want to talk. She tells them about her jewelery box being untouched, even though it was sitting in full view. "I just think that if a thief went to the trouble of ransacking the house, they would specifically have been looking for jewelery."

The room descends into silence again. Hannah can tell that Ethan is itching to keep going with the questions.

Finally he says, "Any idea what they would be looking for?"

She shrugs. "He's the driver for the ministers. I thought maybe he brought something home, something incriminating, or … it doesn't matter now anyway."

Ethan nods. He opens his mouth and then closes it again, clearly deciding to leave it at that.

When everyone finishes their tea, Hannah and Peniasi collect the cups and stack them in the dishwasher. They all say an awkward goodbye to Rishika, unable to find the right words to wish her well. On the way out, Ethan gives her his business card, almost apologetically, explaining that it is just in case she ever wants to talk about the case. Then they exit in a strange single file procession out the door.

RISHIKA CLOSES the door on the bizarre group of guests and immediately feels a desperate sense of loneliness. She enjoyed doing something social again, something that distracted her from her thoughts.

She stares now at Vijay's bag, still sitting on the mat. It looks strangely displaced, away from his back. She used to see him wearing it so often. She picks the bag up and takes it with her to sit on the chair on the balcony.

She unzips the second pocket. There's an instruction manual and a *Fiji Herald* newspaper, dated last week. The newspaper is folded, unsurprisingly, at the crossword page. Vijay was the only person she knew that did the crossword. It looks like Vijay completed half the puzzle. It was one of the things he always did while he waited in the car for his passengers. He was never very good at them. In the early days, he used to ask her the words that eluded him. Sometimes it was the first thing he said when he got home from work, placing his backpack on the table, pulling out his newspaper and turning to her: "Okay Rish, 'In good time,' eight letters, fourth letter is a C," he'd say. She'd narrow her eyes for a minute and then point at him excitedly. "Punctual!" He'd break into a smile and fill in the squares. "Brilliant. Of course it is."

She stares now at his scribbled writing, focusing mostly on the empty spaces. The words he didn't get, the words he didn't come home and ask her about. She knows, objectively, that this is very sad, and yet she feels as empty as the crossword, a vast nothingness inside her.

Instead, she looks through a few pages of the newspaper. It is a strangely recent time capsule – only seven days old – and yet it describes a world that is almost unfamiliar to her.

She puts the newspaper down and picks up the instruction manual. It's for that silly dashcam. Vijay bought it because he was angry at his boss, an officious man named Mr Lal. Mr Lal once docked Vijay's pay because of a small dent in the bumper, which Vijay swore happened when the car was parked overnight. Vijay thought this was outrageous, so he bought his own dashcam to install in the car so he would not be held liable for further damages. He did not trust Mr Lal.

Of course, Mr Lal called two days ago to express his sympathies to Rishika. He said he would dearly miss Vijay, which Vijay would have found hilarious.

She flicks through the booklet, the instructions written in English, Chinese, and something that looked like Russian. It is only then that a thought flashes across her mind. What if that dashcam witnessed something? Something about Vijay's last days, a reason why someone would want to kill him? Maybe he saw or heard something.

The footage, she reasons, would still be on the camera, sitting in Vijay's work car. Mr Lal did say that Rishika could call him if she needed anything.

Well, she does need something.

She scrolls back through the recent calls on her phone and tries his number, but it rings out. She tries again immediately, with the same result.

"Okay, Solomon," she says. The dog's ears prick at his name. "Looks like I've got to go down there."

And it feels good to have something to do.

BU'S HOUSE still smells musty from the flooding, even though they've done their best to dry everything in the sun.

Isikeli watches his sister fuss around the bench while Bu calls out recipe instructions from the mat. This morning, Mere came home with bags full of grocery shopping. It would have cost all of her paycheck. She is roasting a chicken now, the big fat bird with a lemon up its bottom – as instructed by Bu – sitting in a flimsy aluminum tray. Mere pushes it into the toaster oven, barely fitting in.

Epeli is lying next to Isikeli on the mat, his eyes closed, having a nap it seems. He came back here after the *matanigasau* and stayed when he heard Mere was cooking a roast. On the other side of him, Eta is wriggling with excitement. Her mother has allowed her to take photos with her phone, which the little girl is normally banned from using. She snaps a dozen shots a minute, capturing everyone in the room from different angles. She cackles now and holds up the phone to Isikeli, brandishing a photograph she just took of him. Her fingers have covered part of the image, but he can see his face, the bruising over his eye, the yellowy tinge around his nose. Snatches of his time at the police station jolt through him.

He feels a moving lump of dread in his chest. He is out of jail for now, but he knows how these stories usually end for people like him. Seru is on his way to the Yasawas for a family funeral and won't be back for a few weeks. When he spoke to Seru this morning, Isikeli insisted he go; it is wise that his friend stays out of town for a while at least.

Mere keeps looking over at him, saying things like, "Can I get you anything, Keli? Cup of tea? Glass of water?" He wishes she would stop acting so nice.

AN OLD Toyota Crown does a u-turn and pulls in at the curb alongside Rishika. The driver is a softly spoken, bearded man with a skullcap. He pretends not to notice that she is dressed in the color of mourning.

"Where to, my dear?" he says. She gives him the address of the government depot. He bobs his head agreeably and begins to wind the car into the city center. Two fluffy dice and an air freshener in the shape of a Hi-5 swing from his rearview mirror.

Rishika watches the red numbers on his meter clocking up every kilometer. She feels for her purse, grateful to find it in the usual spot in her handbag. She hasn't thought about the money side of life without Vijay yet. Vijay always handled their finances. Not in a controlling way, but because he knew she couldn't be bothered. They always shared access to their bank account, which Rishika knew was slightly unusual. Unlike Lakshmi, for example, who receives a small allowance from Sachin. Every time Lakshmi wants to buy something extra, Sachin has to give her the money. With Vijay, their money was always shared, a joint thing, a non-issue. Now that she thinks about it, Rishika should probably check that account. Most likely, she will have to fill in many forms. She wonders if she will even remember the pin number.

Banking. Another aspect of widowhood that is, in fact, very boring.

As the recovering streets of Suva fly past her window, she wonders what she will see on that dashcam. Even if it doesn't reveal anything about Vijay's death, it is a little slice of his work life, a little window into the world she lost him to. It was not just his morose silence over the last few months. Even before that, for several years at least, he was in a rut. Working, kava, soccer, home, working, kava, soccer, home. She asked him a thousand times, "How was your day?" but he always gave her some glib answer, the kind you give a neighbor or an aunty. What she really wanted was to discuss the little moments of his day, like they used to. She didn't care how famous or powerful his passengers were. She just wanted to know the little things – who was polite and who wasn't? Did any of the ministers sing badly to songs on the radio? Did they swear or make inappropriate jokes as soon as they stepped out of the public eye? But Vijay simply stopped volunteering that information, and Rishika stopped knowing how to open him up. The camera will, at least, give her a glimpse into his world.

The taxi pulls into the street. Thin coconut palms lean over the fence of the depot, casting long shadows over the cars in the late afternoon sun. The fleet of four-wheel drives with tinted windows and government number plates are parked in parallel on the bitumen, standing to attention with militaristic precision.

"Happy to wait, my dear," the taxi driver says to Rishika, and pulls out a newspaper from the glovebox. Rishika steps out of the taxi and walks toward the small demountable office block at the southern end of the depot, up the wooden steps to the glass sliding door. The receptionist looks up from her book of accounts, her face contorting when she recognizes Rishika. She races around her desk, and holds Rishika in her arms, sobbing. Rishika pats her back and patiently waits for the sobbing to subside. Eventually, she pries the woman off, giving her one final pat.

"He was so kind," the woman intones, wiping her nose with a tissue.

People always say generic things about the dead. They are "nice." They are "kind." They are "good." Rishika wishes they would say something a bit more specific. (Although, to be fair, Vijay actually *was* quite kind. He would have treated the receptionist with exactly the same dignity as he did the prime minister. His humility was one of the things Rishika loved about him.)

"Thank you," she says. "Is Mr Lal here? I just want to get something from Vijay's car."

"*Gee ha*, that should be fine. He just stepped out for a moment, but he should be back soon. Take a seat."

Rishika sits down on the plastic chair and stares outside the glass doors. The receptionist keeps sniffling and looking over at her. Rishika is relieved when she sees Mr Lal's sedan finally approaching from a distance, parking just down from the office block. He steps out and adjusts his thin comb-over, his hair unnaturally jet black for a man in his sixties.

Even in the early days, Vijay never liked Mr Lal. He called him "a petty little bureaucrat with a superiority complex." Just last year Rishika went with Vijay to a Christmas party at Mr Lal's house, and the man spent the whole time making subtly condescending jokes about his wife.

He walks through the door now and looks her white attire up and down with surprise, hiding it quickly.

"Mrs Prakash," he says, bobbing his head.

"Mr Lal," she replies.

He blinks. "Sorry again for your loss."

"Thank you, Mr Lal."

He looks at her blankly, waiting for an explanation.

"Can I please get Vijay's camera from his car, you know the dashboard camera?" she asks.

Mr Lal pauses for a moment and then replies, "There was nothing in the car."

"But ..."

He walks across the room toward the reception desk. "It has been thoroughly cleaned."

"*Acha*. It was just that ..."

"We have a policy. Unauthorized persons cannot enter the depot. But don't worry. There was nothing there. A couple of empty bottles of water. That's it." He throws his keys onto the desk and then takes a receipt out of his pocket, impaling it violently on a spike.

Rishika tries again. "I only wanted to get his camera?"

He looks up at her. "There wasn't one. None of our cars have one."

"Oh. But he installed one himself, it was his."

Mr Lal chuckles, bobbing his head again. "Well, he must have taken it out. There's nothing in the car."

Rishika takes a look at the receptionist, but she looks away, shuffling through papers. Rishika makes a small step toward the door that leads to the depot, subtly craning to see the cars through the window. Mr Lal makes a small step in the same direction, obstructing her vision.

It is futile. She feels her first little twinge of wishing she could tell Vijay something. *You were right! He's so annoying!*

With all of her resolve, she forces herself to smile. "*Acha*, my mistake. Thank you, Mr Lal."

Mr Lal's smile widens. "Thank you, Mrs Prakash. Call if you need anything, *acha*?"

She turns away, gritting her teeth.

And the thought comes clearly. *The man is lying.*

HANNAH'S VOLUNTEER friends want to take advantage of their remaining free days before everyone goes back to work after the cyclone. Most of the swimming pools in Suva are still full of debris and – according to German Jana – going green with algae. So Aaron has organized an afternoon trip to the resort in Lami, where the pool is reportedly in action and you can swim there if you can pass for a guest.

At first, Hannah doesn't want to go with them. It feels strange to do trivial things after the profound events of the last couple of days. Besides, Jean will be going, and she finds him increasingly repellent. German Jana will also be there, telling boring anecdotes.

And yet. She is also sweaty and uncomfortable and desperately craves the relief of a swim. Jess also said that Ethan is going. Hannah has a glimmer of hope that she might spend the time with him in a whispered conversation about Isikeli's case. With that thought, she steps into a taxi alongside Jess and Pip, laden with crocheted bags of towels and sunscreen and half-read novels.

Her skin sticks to the vinyl seat of the taxi. Jess talks about a project that her organization, GoGirl, is trying to get funded, an all-female youth theater production that they want to take on a tour of the villages.

Pip shakes her head. "No one's funding gender anymore. It would be better if you made it about climate change."

Jess looks dejected.

"I can imagine it," Hannah says. "*Rising Sea Levels – The Musical.*" She is being sarcastic, of course, but Jess has an inspired look that suggests she is thinking seriously about it.

When they arrive at the hotel, they peel their skin off the seats and try to stride confidently through reception to give the impression that they are, in fact, guests. None of the staff bat an eyelid.

Some of their friends are already at the pool. Ethan, however, is notably absent. Hannah whips off her clothes and dives in, feeling instant relief at the cool water rushing over her. She swims down to the tiled bottom of the pool.

Away from the muffled sounds of the world above, she dwells on her conversation with Pip earlier over lunch. Hannah was buzzing after the *matanigasau* ceremony and wanted to share it with someone. She started from the beginning: how she met Isikeli, how she found out about his arrest, how Hannah got Ethan involved, the boy's release on bail, and finally, the apology.

"I can't believe they let him out," Pip said after Hannah finished the whole story. She licked the back of her spoon. "Who paid for his bail?"

At the time, this response irked Hannah. But she actually didn't know the answer to that question; it hadn't occurred to her. As she swims back up to the surface now, she begins to think about it. Who *did* pay for his bail? She wonders whether Ethan might have paid for it without telling anyone. That is – she has come to realize – the kind of thing he would do.

After swimming another lap, she stands up in the shallow end, taking a deep breath. When she looks up, she sees that Ethan has arrived. He is sitting down on a banana lounge, bare-chested, in boardshorts and a cap, engrossed in the *Fiji Herald*. His arms are spread widely to hold the broadsheet newspaper.

Hannah casually splashes over so that she is directly below him, leaning both elbows on the edge of the pool. He has a white streak of sunscreen still visible on the skin of his upper arm. She is so close that she can read a couple of the headlines on his newspaper. China is stepping in with Dorothy aid, and Australia is urging Fiji to be cautious. Parliament will be back next week and finally voting on the Soft Drink Bill. The copyright hearing is on hiatus until the courts start sitting again.

"Hey," she says.

He bends the corner of the newspaper and peers over at her. "Oh, hey Han," he says.

She grins goofily. She cannot for the life of her think of anything to say. "Bit of a different vibe to this morning, huh?" she lands on.

"Yep," he says. There is an awkward pause. He eventually half-smiles and goes back to reading. Slightly disappointed, she slinks back into the water.

She pushes off the edge of the pool with her feet and glides on the surface, doing another couple of laps. Under water, she does a half-yelp, a muted little scream. It seems – she now admits to herself – that her feelings about Ethan have flipped over; about-turned. And yet she doesn't know what to do about it. She doesn't know if he still feels how he did the other night. Perhaps he regrets ever saying anything. Perhaps he has realized that she is actually very naïve and a little bit self-absorbed, which she has been reflecting on lately.

When she re-emerges, she catches a movement in the corner of her eye. Ethan's newspaper moves swiftly back into place. She can't be sure, but she *thinks* his eyes just danced away from her. The thought that he might be watching her while she swims makes her stomach do a little cartwheel. She slips back under the water and glides away again, more aware, now, of how her bathers are clinging to her body.

RISHIKA STEPS through the door of the government depot onto the sidewalk, sliding the door closed on Mr Lal and the receptionist. She imagines what it would feel like to slam the door shut. She wonders if it would come off its rails, if the glass would shatter, and how satisfying that would feel. Walking back to the taxi, she passes Mr Lal's car, parked beside the road. Rishika imagines what it would feel like to scratch the sedan with a twenty-cent coin. Perhaps, if she were Wendy, she would make a long ugly mark that would extend from the petrol cap to the sideview mirror, significantly devaluing the price of the car.

She stops. Through the car window she can see something to the left of the steering wheel. *That*, she thinks, *is a dashcam*. She stares at the little camera, feeling rage bubble up inside. "That's *Vijay's* dashcam," she mutters aloud. At least, it looks like it – the same silver color, the same little logo. *The weasel stole Vijay's dash-cam.* She looks either side of her on the sidewalk to ensure no one is looking. Emboldened by indignation, she tries lifting the car door handle. It immediately snaps back, locked.

She keeps walking toward the taxi and slips into the backseat. It is not clear whether the taxi driver saw what she just did. In the rearview mirror, his eyes remain consummately unreadable, and he casually places the newspaper back into the glovebox.

"Back to Chamberlain Street now, my dear?" he prompts her gently.

"*Gee haan*," she says sadly. "Thank you."

He nods and begins weaving through the city traffic.

The sun beams through the windscreen, heating up the car. Rishika's sari feels prickly and suffocating against her skin. She doesn't want to go home to her silent house, empty of souls except for Solomon. That dog, she thinks sadly, is the only thing keeping her sane right now. The taxi slows down to a stop at a traffic light. She makes a flash decision, one that surprises even her. "Wait, Uncle. Can you take me to Paradise Estate please?"

For the first time, the driver's eyebrows lift, ever so subtly. "The squatter settlement?"

"*Gee haan*." She avoids eye contact with him.

He thrusts the gearshift into position. "The SupaValu end?"

"Please."

He nods and the car lurches forward.

RUNNING WATER gurgles out of taps in the settlement for the first time since the cyclone. Bu says it's not safe to drink, but it means Isikeli can finally have a shower – the first one in days.

The dribble of cold, brown water on his back soothes the aches and pains in his body. The lump of dread is still there in his chest, but he can slowly feel himself regaining strength, no doubt helped by Mere's roast chicken.

He dries himself, slipping his shorts back on and flinging his towel over his shoulder. He walks back through the settlement, avoiding the puddles still left from the flooding. The light is fading now. He can see Mrs Karawalevu over there, taking in the washing before the spirits come. He pretends he doesn't see her. He doesn't want to see if there has been a change in her eyes. He doesn't want to know if she has already decided he is guilty. He knows that everyone is watching him closely.

When he opens the door to Bu's house, he does a double take. The *Kai Idia* woman is sitting right there on the mat beside his grandmother and cousin-brother. Rishika looks up and gives him a rueful smile. She explains that she remembered where her old garden boy used to live, having dropped him off there once or twice, so she made her way back and asked someone where Bu's house was.

"Everyone knows Bu Lia around here," Epeli grins proudly.

Mere walks in the room carrying Bu's special china tea set, pouring a drink for the guest. She must have boiled bottled water. She lays down a plate of biscuits, and they all sip their tea in silence.

Eventually, Rishika starts to explain why she is here. It is a story about an instruction manual, a camera, and a visit to a government depot. "I'm certain that it's my husband's dashcam in his boss's car," she finishes.

"*Oilei*," says Bu, although Isikeli's grandmother also looks a bit confused.

Isikeli can't quite put his finger on it, but the *Kai Idia* woman looks different than she did this morning. There's a fire in her eyes now.

"It's just the sort of thing he would do," she continues resentfully, "to take Vijay's camera for himself." She laughs, but there is no humor in her eyes. "And I can't stop thinking about it. That camera captured Vijay in his last few days. It might show us something about why he died. And if it does, it will prove your innocence, Isikeli."

Isikeli nods, avoiding eye contact. He isn't sure what she wants.

"I know where Mr Lal lives," Rishika announces suddenly. "I've been there before."

Bu raises her eyebrows.

"For a Christmas party," Rishika clarifies, unnecessarily.

Bu raises her eyebrows again. "For a Christmas party, eh?"

Rishika nods and wipes away some invisible crumbs on her sari. "I was thinking it would be pretty easy to just, you know, *get* it." She looks up at them, affecting a casual tone, her head bobbing slightly. "You know? Just go to his house, open his car, and get the memory card from the dashcam."

Isikeli's hand stops with a biscuit halfway to his mouth. He glances quickly at Epeli, but his cousin-brother is eating his biscuit with surprisingly loud crunching.

Bu gently places her cup back on the saucer. "Like a burglary?"

"Well yes, *sort of*, but not *really*. It's mine, technically, so I would just be … taking it back." Her eyes are particularly shiny now – dangerously so. "And I know someone who might be able to pull it off."

She is looking straight at him. Isikeli's heart begins to speed up. She uses a Fijian word. "*Kerekere*, Isikeli, can you help me?"

Isikeli casts a fearful look at his grandmother.

Yet Bu simply raises her eyebrows.

Her meaning is crystal clear.

IT IS a shortcut he has taken a thousand times, across the darkened oval of the primary school and into the small valley, along the skinny dirt path that winds its way through the long grass.

Adrenaline is coursing through Iskeli's veins, spurring him on,
drowning out the ache of his body. He looks over at Epeli jogging
along beside him. Even in the moonlight, his cousin-brother's
fear is visible, and Isikeli wonders whether it was a mistake to
bring him.

The boys emerge out of the shrubbery at the bottom of Elgar
Street. Mr Lal, Rishika explained, lives at number 22. They sit in
a stormwater drain under the dark shadows of a tree, watching
the house from a safe distance. It is a plain, two-storey house in
a row of similar houses. Mr Lal's sedan is parked at the bottom
of a sloped driveway, in an open carport attached to the bottom
storey. The lights are out – Mr Lal and his family must be sleeping. A high barbed wire fence circles the compound. Isikeli has
climbed countless barbed wire fences, so this is not going to be
a problem. More problematic, however, are the two rottweiler
mongrels sleeping just inside the fence.

He gestures to Epeli to wait there. He strolls along the sidewalk
on the other side of the road. The dogs wake up as soon as they
hear the scuff of feet against the concrete, and leap to their full
muscly height. They run to the corner of the fence and bark viciously, following him with their eyes. Like most dogs, they have
a sixth sense for strangers with dubious intentions, and like most
dogs in this suburb, they have absorbed their owners' particular
suspicion of young iTaukei men. Isikeli will, he thinks regretta-
bly, be reinforcing this stereotype tonight.

The rottweilers start a street-wide cacophony. In the compound to the left of Mr Lal's, a puppy bounds to a fence and
yelps, jumping on its two back legs with furious enthusiasm. In
the next house over, a tall German shepherd–cross barks deeply.
But in the property on the other side of Mr Lal's, there is no activity: no dogs have come to the fence, there are no cars in the
driveway, and there are no lights on. It seems empty, abandoned.

Isikeli doubles back around and comes back to squat next to Epeli in the drain, waiting for the commotion to die down. The puppy soon gets bored and retreats to its post under the verandah. The German shepherd quietens down. Mr Lal's rottweilers eventually stop barking – believing the threat to have passed for now – and flop back down to sleep, albeit leaving one eye open.

After a short while, Isikeli whispers to Epeli and the boys part ways. Isikeli remains in the drain while Epeli pads to the abandoned house adjacent to Mr Lal's, scaling the fence and landing deftly on the lawn. At the sound of the quiet thud, the two rottweilers' ears prick up. They run to the fence between the two houses, barking at Epeli's dark silhouette sprinting toward the mango tree at the back of the property. The dogs follow him, separated only by a thin barbed wire fence, barking and yelping. Isikeli can see his cousin-brother expertly shimmy up the trunk, just like he has a thousand times. This time, however, he climbs onto a low-hanging branch that leans over into Mr Lal's property. He stays there nestled in the leaves. The dogs stand below him, barking vigorously at the mango tree.

With all the attention at the back of the property, Isikeli makes his move. He jumps Mr Lal's gate and runs toward the carport, stopping only to scoop up a large rock from the garden. He ducks behind the car so that people will not be able to see him from neighboring balconies. Isikeli makes a brief apology to *Turaga Jisu*, then holds up his hand and smashes the front passenger window with the rock. It is hardly audible over the barking, but he winces at the sound nonetheless. Knowing he only has seconds, he quickly stands up, reaches into the car window, and disables the lock on the door, opening it. He slinks into the passenger seat, ignoring the sharp shards of glass underneath him. He works quickly to remove the memory card from the dashcam like Rishika demonstrated. Miraculously, it slips out easily. He steps out. Thongs crunching on broken glass, he runs as fast as he can toward the fence, jumping over it with a grunt and onto the sidewalk. He gives a piercing whistle to Epeli. He can see Epeli's silhouette dismount the tree and sprint through the property.

All of a sudden, the house that Isikeli thought was abandoned lights up, and two male figures spill onto the balcony, leaning over the railing. They see Epeli running through the compound below them and shout frantically. In rapidfire succession, they hurl one potted plant after another through the air toward Epeli's head. Each one seems to miss him by the narrowest of margins, shattering on the concrete driveway. All down the street, lights flick on and neighbors can be seen emerging from their houses. Epeli artfully scales the fence and bounds onto the bitumen. Together, the cousin-brothers sprint down the street to the distant cries of *"Butako!"* and a stream of Hindustani swear words.

They run as fast as they can through the valley. Just before they reach the open space of the oval, Isikeli gestures that they should stop to catch their breath. Epeli holds onto a tree while he bends over, his chest heaving.

Isikeli withdraws the data card from his pocket and holds it up for Epeli to see. Epeli nods. "Probably nothing on there," Isikeli says, and Epeli lets out a stifled giggle, the white of his teeth gleaming in the moonlight.

Isikeli feels a rush of affection for him. Pious, prudent Epeli has just pulled off a heist, and he did it for no other reason than to help Isikeli. No one can climb a tree like Epeli can; no one can scale a fence with such skill and speed. Isikeli makes a quiet resolution not to tease him anymore. They make a good team, Keli and Epi. They're cousin-brothers.

In the distance, they hear the wail of a police siren getting louder.

Isikeli looks urgently at Epeli. "Run now."

Wednesday

RISHIKA LIES awake on her side of the expansive queen-size bed, the ceiling fan whirring above her. She slips fitfully in and out of sleep, throwing the sheet off and then clawing it back when she feels cold. She dreams that she is rifling through the stack of photos she keeps in the shoebox in the bookcase: Vijay and Akesh looking serious after a soccer game, with matching, muddy socks; a young beaming Vijay with his arm around Rishika, splotches of brightly colored powder all over them after a *holi* celebration; Vijay reading as a child, quiet and conscientious. In the dream, Rishika realizes the photos are out of order. She starts trying to sort them – one after the other – but they keep getting muddled and remuddled. "*This* is why he died," her mother-in-law spits at her.

She wakes to the sound of Solomon barking urgently. She calls for him to stop. When he does, she hears a knocking at the door. The alarm clock says it is two in the morning. There is knocking *at the door*. That means that someone is inside the compound. Barely able to breathe, she pads out of the bedroom and walks toward the front of the house, heart thudding in her ears.

Peering through the glass, she feels a rush of relief. On her doorstep are Isikeli and the other boy, Epeli.

Of course they climbed the fence. That's their thing.

"Sorry to wake you, *marama*," Isikeli whispers when she opens the door. He bends down to give the dog a pat, who wags his tail appreciatively.

"It's okay," she says. She waits for him to speak.

Isikeli holds something up for her to see.

She gasps. "Already?!"

"*Io*." He gives a small smile.

"Wow," she says. Words feel insufficient. "Thank you."

He drops the card in the palm of her hand.

"*Sega ni dua na lega*," he says – no worries. Almost as soon as they arrive the boys are retreating again. She watches them climb the fence effortlessly and jog up the street. Then they are gone, as though they were part of her dream.

She looks at the little card in her hand, with its glinting metal chip.

There is no way she will be able to sleep now. She goes to the study and starts up the computer. When the screen lights up the darkened room, she plugs the chip in and navigates to the folder. The folder reveals more folders which reveal more folders, like Russian babushka dolls.

Suddenly, there, in front of her, is a list of files in date order. Each seems to last for exactly thirty minutes. The latest files are dated the day Vijay died, so it looks like Mr Lal has not even used it. He probably doesn't know how, happy with it sitting on his dashboard as a status symbol. She clicks on one folder and accesses a random piece of footage. It appears as a split screen. The scene on the left is a view of the road in front of the car and the scene on the right is from the camera angled inside toward the driver and passengers. There's audio too, she realizes, turning up the volume.

In the backseat of the car, a man who looks vaguely familiar to Rishika – one of the ministers, perhaps – is talking to a young woman who is probably his personal assistant. He is making some dull observation about the difference between his new iPhone and his previous one. But Rishika is not interested in them. She is looking at Vijay in the foreground, his arm casually draped across the steering wheel, his hand absentmindedly pushing his fringe back. She watches him drive like that – turning left, turning right, indicator on, indicator off. The road ahead of him is reflected in his eyes. It is strangely mesmerizing to watch him. That is exactly how she remembers him in those last few months. Handsome. Professional. Distracted.

Rishika's head jerks up from where it has been lying in the crook of her arm, the room now flooded in daylight. Her arm is sticky and wet; she must have fallen asleep. The clock on the computer says it is 8:30 in the morning. The *pundit* will be coming in a few hours for the sixth day prayer and the reading of the *Bhagavad Gita*, along with all of her relatives. On the computer screen, Vijay is driving with someone else in the backseat. Again, Rishika vaguely recognizes the passenger, but cannot think of his name.

She pauses the video. It will take her many hours to watch the rest of the footage, even if she does nothing else in her day. She doesn't have the energy for this. Her bones feel tired. And yet she is not ready to give up on it yet. On Vijay. On why he died. On Isikeli.

ETHAN IS distracted when he opens the door of his apartment to Hannah. "Hey," he says, "come in," and goes back to bending over behind the television where he is attempting to connect a cable from his laptop to the television.

It is only the second time that Hannah has been to Ethan's apartment. The first was for a party way back when she first arrived in Suva. She marvels at how different she was then. How differently she felt about Ethan. He was just some guy with an inappropriate sense of humor. Now she relishes the little details of his home, seeking insights into the kind of person he is.

His place is sparsely furnished in the classic bachelor palette of black, silver, and various shades of wood. The walls are bereft of artwork or photos. A largely empty bookshelf contains a small selection of books – an eclectic mix of legal textbooks, Jack Kerouac, Jonathan Franzen, and an autobiography of Dolly Parton. She looks over at Ethan kneeling next to his laptop, which doesn't seem to be connecting properly.

"Dolly Parton fan, are we?"

"Don't laugh," he says. "*Jolene* is one of the best songs ever written."

She smirks and keeps browsing.

The doorbell rings and Hannah goes to let Peniasi in.

Ethan finally gets the television to light up with a mirror image of his laptop screen. His desktop photo is a picture of an unmistakably Australian beach, with its long yellow sand dune and windswept shrubs. Hannah wonders if it is Merimbula, Ethan's hometown, but it doesn't seem like the best time to ask.

Peniasi asks Ethan to tell him in more detail about the events of the morning. "So it was pretty weird," Ethan says. Apparently Rishika had used his business card to contact him, asking him to come to her house immediately. She handed over a memory card and said it was dashcam footage from her husband's work car, which might contain something interesting, or something to absolve Isikeli – or it might not. She then ushered him away.

"She was a little manic. She looked different," Ethan finishes.

"How so?" Hannah asks.

"I don't know. Just … different."

The three of them settle in to examine the footage together. Peniasi sits on the floor and grabs a pen and paper. Hannah makes herself comfortable on the sofa. Ethan taps the mouse and scrolls his way through the data files.

"Whoa," he says.

Peni widens his eyes.

"What?" asks Hannah.

"That's a lot of footage. That's going to take a couple of days to wade through."

"*Io*," says Peniasi.

They stare at the screen, slightly overwhelmed, trying to determine how best to proceed.

"We could fast forward through the bits when nothing's going on," Peniasi says, "and then slow it down if anything interesting happens?"

"Guess that makes sense," Ethan says. He scrolls through all the files. "Shall we start with the more recent stuff and work backwards?"

Hannah and Peniasi nod uncertainly.

They pull up the first video and see the split screen in front of them. The driver is in the foreground of the car shot. Hannah grimaces when she remembers that he is, in fact, dead.

Peniasi suggests that Hannah focuses on the road image while he and Ethan focus on the people in the car. He will keep a list because he is most likely to know who the passengers are.

Ethan is just about to let it play.

"Wait, sorry, what are we looking for exactly?" Hannah asks.

Peniasi shrugs. "Anything unusual, eh?"

They all know how ridiculous this is. It is like a needle in a hay-stack and no one quite knows what the needle is going to look like, or if there is a needle at all.

Ethan sets the footage in motion.

After three hours of footage, Hannah's eyesight is beginning to go blurry. She can't get comfortable anymore. Sometimes she stands, leaning against the sofa; sometimes she sits on the chair, knees against her chest; sometimes she stretches her limbs in vague yoga poses, all the while watching the television. She tries to stay focused on the road stretching in front of Vijay's vehicle, slowing to a stop at traffic lights, and then speeding up again as other cars whiz past. Ethan somehow manages to sit still on the sofa, his eyes fixed on the screen. She is hyper aware of his leg resting just millimeters away from hers and yet never quite touching.

Hannah makes the banal observation that Vijay is a cautious driver, always keeping a safe distance between him and the car in front. She means it as a compliment to him, but as soon as it's out of her mouth, it sounds silly and irrelevant.

Peniasi has an impressive knowledge of the people that come and go in the car. He is keeping notes of names and locations. The ministers sit in the backseat, scrolling through their tablets, making calls, or being briefed by personal assistants, barely paying atten-tion to Vijay. Sometimes they bring other people with them on their way to or from meetings – businesspeople, foreign diplomats, and others. It is, Peniasi says, a veritable who's who of Fijian dignitaries.

Whoever his passengers, Vijay always looks straight ahead, discreet and expressionless, allowing them to go about their business undisturbed.

On this particular afternoon in the video, he was chauffeuring the minister for defense. At one point, the minister was sitting in the back seat of the car with a senior military official.

"This is interesting," remarks Peniasi, a note of urgency in his voice.

Perhaps it will be a whispered conversation about a coup, proof that the rumors are true? But the two men only speak about mundane administrative matters.

The last passenger that day was the prime minister. He is the only one who sits in the front passenger seat and engages Vijay in conversation. Peniasi perches himself on the edge of the couch, muttering that the prime minister might divulge something of political interest. But the prime minister is only venting about the challenges of raising two headstrong teenage daughters.

They keep watching. Another clip shows Vijay driving the minister for agriculture and fisheries, according to Peniasi. All of a sudden Hannah says, "Wait, pause it there for a second?" On the left side of the screen, she has seen the car pull into an unfamiliar car park. Something about the scene seems strange, clandestine.

"Ok, play," Hannah commands.

Ethan plays the footage. They can see the minister get out of the car and walk out of view. Vijay's hand taps against the steering wheel while he waits, the car idling. Hannah thinks he looks nervous.

The agricultural minister reappears in the camera's field about fifteen minutes later. "What's he got in his hands?" Hannah shouts excitedly. "He's holding something!" They all lean forward, on the edge of their seats. He is carrying something carefully – with respect. Dramatic possibilities run through Hannah's mind. A bribe? A wad of cash? A gun?

The minister slides into the backseat and closes the door, opening a small box. Slowly, he pulls out a greasy chip, followed closely by a chicken leg.

"Shit. Takeaway. Sorry," Hannah says. On the screen, the minister licks salt off one of his fingers, as though taunting her.

"Scandal," Peniasi laughs. "I can see the headlines already."

Ethan joins in. "Hashtag chipgate."

Hannah slaps Ethan's knee. He nudges her leg back with his own, and then leaves it there, lingering against hers for a moment. Then he moves his leg away again and she can't tell whether he meant to do it or not. She can feel his closeness tickling against her skin.

He presses play, and they continue to watch the seemingly endless road in front of them.

ISIKELI'S SISTER seems to be playing a game, where she pretends that everything is going to be okay. He can see that she desperately needs him to play along too.

Bu keeps praying over and over, late into the night. Last night he heard her whispering "*taba*" – photo – to the Lord, presumably asking that the footage will prove his innocence. In his own conversations with *Turaga Jisu*, Isikeli has asked for another chance. Is this trial all part of His plan? Perhaps it is a test he needs to pass. Maybe if he just keeps his head down and works hard and looks after his family. Mere is right. Maybe it will all turn out okay.

He reluctantly decides to meet his friends at the coconut stand – they need money – and Eta begs to come too. The boys always like it when she comes. She makes them laugh, and they sell more coconuts when she's there, so he agrees with a sigh. They begin to walk hand in hand out of the settlement and onto the sidewalk, her thongs slapping loudly against the concrete.

For a moment, it is easy to forget everything, out here. The sun is bearing down on his face, and Eta's chatter bubbles smoothly beside him. They pass a roadside stall, where two women are marinating slabs of meat to sell at their makeshift barbecue tonight.

All of a sudden Eta turns around, her chatter turning into an excited shout. "*Na polisi!*" she screams. Isikeli's head whips around and the lump of dread in his chest turns over. Sure enough, a white and blue police car is crawling deliberately slowly behind them, tinted windows reflecting the palm trees above. Isikeli's hand tightens. At first he thinks it is the girl's hand clenching his in fear, but he soon realizes it is him clutching at hers. She tries to wriggle free, but he walks on, pulling her forward. He is trying to get enough breath into his lungs, but his throat is constricted, closing up. The police car continues to follow them, a slow shadow.

Isikeli begins to jog, speeding up to a canter, dragging Eta. Behind them, the crunch of gravel under wheels has never sounded so ominous.

The police car then revs aggressively and screeches away down the street.

When the taillights disappear around the street corner, Isikeli stops on the sidewalk, chest heaving and knees weak.

He forces himself to smile at his niece.

"*Isa*, what a silly loud car!"

"*Io.*" She smiles, her hand finally wriggling out of his.

Thursday

IT IS still the same old passengers, the same old roads, the same old unremarkable driving. Hannah is beginning to lose concentration after a day and a half of staring at a screen. They looked at the footage until the early hours of the morning and then reconvened a few hours ago, weary-eyed.

The search seems desperate and fruitless.

As the afternoon sun begins to fade, they watch yet another unremarkable clip of footage. Nothing out of the ordinary. Ethan pauses it, sighs, and stretches his back, elbows pointed out like wings. He stands up, asking if anyone else would like a glass of water, then laughs at Hannah. "Han, you just raised your eyebrows. Like a Fijian."

"Did I?" she asks, shocked and flattered. "Yay!"

"So … *do* you want one?"

"Oh! Sorry. Yes."

He returns with three glasses of water and places them on the table in front of them.

Peniasi's gaze is fixed on the computer screen. Suddenly his head whips up. He takes control of the computer and scrutinizes the files.

"Look at this," he says.

"What?" Ethan and Hannah say in tandem.

"I should have noticed this before. This one at the bottom has a different file name. See? Instead of just being a number, it has 'VP_edit' at the end. He specifically saved this."

Ethan's eyes widen and he rejoins them on the couch. "Play it," he says, his voice lowered with anticipation now.

The footage starts abruptly, as they all do, with Vijay driving and someone in the backseat.

"*Qori!*" Peniasi says suddenly.

"What?" Hannah says.

"It's your friend."

She looks closely and realizes it's Hinal Singh, the health minister.

A ringtone sounds out, and the minister answers a phone call. "*Haan*, Singh."

He looks out the window of the car contemplatively.

"*Thik hai*," the health minister soothes into the phone.

He continues listening to the person on the other end, beginning to look increasingly agitated. He lowers his voice, which becomes barely audible over the noise of the car. After playing the footage a few times, they decipher his words: "We still have a few days. I'll convince them, like I told you."

Singh continues to listen, bobbing his head. "What? Right now?" He talks slightly louder now but his tone soon softens again. There is a pause. "Okay, okay. I'm on my way."

Singh looks at his phone as he hangs up. He leans forward to Vijay and commands him to take them to the Na Cakau Apartments.

"Pause it there," barks Peniasi. "Who was on the phone? Convince who?"

"Beats me," says Ethan.

"Let's see what happens," Peniasi says, and Ethan presses play.

The footage shows the government car pulling up to an exclusive apartment block. At the security gate, Singh gets out. Vijay turns the car around such that the entrance to the apartments is behind him. He sits and waits, noticeably looking in the rear-view mirror. Although the outside footage from that distance is grainy, Hannah can see Singh waiting at the main door of the complex. After a minute, a white man wearing a Bula shirt and three-quarter length pants fixes his gaze on Vijay through the window while continuing to walk past the car toward the gate of the apartment block.

"Rewind it," Peniasi says.

Ethan rewinds it.

"Just there," Peniasi exclaims, pausing on the man.

"Do you know him?" Hannah asks.

"Never seen him before," Peniasi concedes.

"Vijay knows him, don't you reckon?" Ethan asks. "You can see from his reaction."

"Mm-mm. The man also knows Vijay," Peniasi adds. "Keep playing it, see what happens." Peniasi looks energized.

The white man approaches Singh and they enter the apartment block. Nothing happens for about ten minutes until Singh can be seen leaving the building and entering the car again. He commands Vijay to take him back to the office. The footage proceeds for another few minutes and then ends as abruptly as it started.

The three of them look at each other.

Ethan sits back on the couch. "So what do you reckon, Peni?"

Peniasi looks at the others. "Well, Vijay specifically saved this footage. He didn't want to lose it."

"Who's the white guy?" Hannah contemplates. "We could find out who lives in those apartments?"

Ethan looks skeptical. "Those apartments will be full of white guys. Most of them will wear three-quarter length trousers. It's 'Island Casual.'"

Peniasi is deep in thought.

"We still have a few days. I'll convince them ..." Peniasi repeats slowly.

Ethan presses his lips together and shakes his head. "We have to think. Some kinda corruption?"

"It's definitely dodgy," Hannah said.

Peniasi takes control of the laptop and navigates to see the properties of the file. It was created about two weeks ago and edited that same evening.

Suddenly, Peniasi's eyes widen. "You know what's going to a vote in parliament next week?"

Hannah stares at him, blinking. Then she sits up. "The Soft Drink Bill!"

"Exactly." Peniasi looks at his friends. "I think our friend the health minister was up to something, and Vijay knew about it."

❈

THE PUNDIT is staring straight into Rishika's eyes, his wooden-beaded necklace looped around his neck. He is midway through a verse of the *Baghavad Gita* and she nods dutifully, trying to arrange her face with appropriate gravity. Her relatives surround her, listening closely to the profound spiritual lessons in the ancient text.

With impeccably bad timing, she feels a vibration on her thigh. Her phone is buzzing in the pocket of her *salwar kemeez*. The sound is surprisingly loud, urgent seeming.

bvvvvvvvvvvvvvv

Around the circle, she can feel people's eyes searching for where the sound is coming from; Akesh to her right, Samriti to her left.

bvvvvvvvvvvvvvv

Horrified, Rishika tries to look innocent. She hopes that the caller will give up soon, but the ringing is incessant.

bvvvvvvvvvvvvvv

Even the *pundit* stops mid-sentence about the journey that will be taken by Vijay's soul, distracted by this earthly sound.

Eventually, Rishika looks down discreetly and removes the phone from her pocket enough to see the display – it's the Australian lawyer. When she looks up, Samriti is flashing her a look of disgust. Rishika coughs. "Would you excuse me for a second?" she says to the circle. She considers saying something to make it better, but nothing comes to mind. What could she say that they would approve of?

She sits on the toilet lid and swipes to answer the call. She hears a female voice. It's the girl, Hannah. They have found something, and they need Rishika's help.

After the musicians have played their *bhajan* and the grieving family members have left, a taxi soon arrives at Rishika's gate and the three young people emerge. Even from a distance, their excitement is palpable. Rishika unlocks the gate in the darkness and invites the guests in, offering them a cup of tea. They all decline the offer, anxious to get started. Ethan begins to explain what they have found. He is agitated, stumbling over his words, and ends up saying, "Probably best if you just watch it."

They huddle around Ethan's laptop at the kitchen table.

Rishika is exhausted and emotionally drained. She did not sleep well again, and the house has been a revolving door of guests all day. She musters up the energy to focus on what she is about to see.

Ethan double-clicks on the file. They all watch in silence.

When the footage finishes, the three of them fix their gaze on Rishika.

"That's it, eh?" Peniasi says excitedly. "The health minister, you recognized him didn't you? It's most likely something to do with the Soft Drink Bill."

Rishika nods uncertainly.

Peniasi continues, "Sounds like he's trying to secure votes against it. There's probably a kickback of some sort. But we need to know who that white guy is." Peniasi interrogates her face for her reaction. She blinks at him.

"Do you know that guy?" Ethan asks. "Did Vijay have anything to do with him?"

Rishika's mind is spinning. The white man did look slightly familiar, but then they all look similar to her. She tries to wrap her head around the information she has just received. "So ... you think the minister for health has made some kind of deal?" she asks uncertainly.

"*Io*," says Peniasi. "It sounds like it. To convince his colleagues to vote against the bill."

"Han, explain the bill," Ethan says.

"Right." The girl takes a deep breath. She looks eager, proud to be able to share her professional knowledge. "Basically, the Soft Drink Bill is supposed to ban front-of-bottle branding. It's ..."

"Can we watch it again please?" Rishika interrupts. This time when Ethan plays it back, Rishika concentrates solely on Vijay's face in the foreground. His eyes remain fixed on the road for the first part, his expression blank as always. When he is parked at the apartment block, there is a moment she thinks she sees something – anger, or indignation – flash momentarily in her husband's eyes, but it soon disappears. She might have imagined it.

"If it's what we think it is, we're talking serious corruption," Ethan continues. "Did Vijay speak to you about this at all?"

Rishika is feeling a wash of renewed disappointment in her husband. If he knew what was happening, why didn't he turn around and confront Singh at that point? Why didn't he come home that night and tell her about this sinister meddling he witnessed? They could have been outraged together. It was the kind of thing they used to talk about all the time when they were first married – the injustices of the world, the exploitation of Fiji's poorest. She could have researched whistle-blower protection laws and supported him in speaking out.

But no. He didn't mention anything to her.

The others are staring at her, and she wonders whether she was supposed to respond to something.

"Did Vijay say anything about this? Do you have any idea what might have happened?" Peniasi is saying.

Rishika has a vague recollection of reading about the Soft Drink Bill but had never spoken about it with Vijay. The more she looks at her husband's blank face on the screen, the more she remembers his unfailing commitment to discretion. He was always perfectly loyal to his ministers. Her last little hope that he might have done something surprising – something with conviction – starts to dissipate. She had wanted to see an argument or an altercation – Vijay sticking his neck out for something he believed in. But no, he just sat there quietly while these men seemingly conspired against his nation.

She becomes vaguely aware that the others are getting restless, subtly gesturing to each other.

"Rishika?" Hannah's soft voice breaks Rishika's trance.

She looks up, remembering her manners. "Sorry, yes. The man looks a little bit familiar, but I don't know. Vijay didn't tell me anything. He never told me anything." Her voice trails off and she begins to stare out the window, looking at nothing in particular. She can't seem to move her gaze – it is easiest to keep her eyes there, the path of least resistance.

"No worries," Hannah says softly. "It's late. We can talk again later."

They leave her a copy of the file on a thumb drive and make their own way out.

Friday

IT IS only ten o'clock in the morning, yet the heat is stifling. On the balcony, Solomon is panting, droplets of saliva falling from his tongue onto the concrete floor. Rishika moves the bowl of water so that it is directly beneath him, and he laps it up gratefully.

She slept better last night, which has given her thoughts a crispness that she hasn't felt for days. She is still wearing her white *salwar kemeez*, the same one she wore yesterday and the day before that and the day before that. It is no longer as white as it used to be; the pretty embroidered material has stains on it from sitting on various unmopped floors around her house. Whoever decided white should be the color of mourning? Surely death is always going to be a bit messy. She looks down, folding the dirty pieces of material under the cleaner pieces – wondering if she can get away with it. Yet she knows it won't get past the watchful eyes of her aunties who will be arriving before long. They will probably stand over her, supervising her as she gets changed, if not physically undressing her.

The sight of the embroidery reminds her of the sari she wore to Lakshmi and Sachin's Diwali party last year. That Australian woman was there, blond and freckle-faced, eager to fit in, uncomfortable showing her midriff under her sari. What was her name again? Kylie? Kelly? Carly! It was Carly. The fact that Rishika remembers gives her a small sense of pride. She can't be going mad if she can still remember names! The woman's husband was there, too, a loud and jokey man, overly familiar, in the way that Australian men often are. What was *his* name?

Realization dawns on Rishika, slowly at first, and then in a sudden flood. That's him. The white man in the footage, meeting with the health minister. *That's* why he looked familiar. He was at the Diwali party because, she remembers, he was a client of Sachin's. Sachin was trying to impress him with his expensive whiskey.

Basinger. Sachin called him Basinger. The name stuck with Rishika because it sounded like a movie star. Rishika loads up the video on the computer in the study and watches it again. It's definitely him.

Her thoughts reel. This new insight means that a few months before Vijay drove the minister to see Basinger, they were at a party together. She sits back against the chair. Did Vijay talk to the Australian that night? Maybe they did. And maybe that's important.

"Solomon," she says, and the dog pricks his ears. "We need to talk to Sachin."

Lakshmi kicks away the knitted puppy-shaped doorstopper and looks Rishika up and down, unsubtly taking in her disheveled hair and dirty *salwar kemeez*. Her expression is of pity and horror, the kind one reserves for a loved one who is becoming unhinged.

"Everything okay, *Rish?*" she asks uncertainly.

"*Thik hai*," Rishika says blandly.

"Come sit down. I'll make you a cup of tea."

"*Nahi*. I've actually come to speak to Sachin."

Before Lakshmi has a chance to answer, Arveen runs up the hallway holding a Lego helicopter. "Aunty!" he cries, ready to lunge. Lakshmi holds him back with a forced smile. "Leave Aunty," she says, holding his hand as they lead the way down the hallway. To Rishika, she says, "He's in his study."

They open the door of the study to find Sachin, a fountain pen in his hand and an empty pad of paper in front of him.

Rishika half-smiles. "*Kaise*, Sachin."

He flashes a look of confusion at his wife before turning back to Rishika. "*Right hai.*"

Lakshmi retreats slowly. "I'll make some tea," she says, seemingly closing the door behind her. And yet Rishika notices the door remains slightly ajar. Lakshmi will listen from around the corner, and Rishika can't blame her. An age-old tactic passed down through generations of women sidelined from discussions of importance.

Rishika has hardly ever been in this study. The Suva City Council Business Calendar hangs on the wall behind the desk, still open to last month's page. A cardboard photoframe encrusted in shells sits on the desk, encasing a family photograph taken when Lakshmi was heavily pregnant with Karishma. The three boys are wearing matching safari suits and the image has been Photoshopped to make everyone's teeth whiter.

She realizes that Sachin is staring at her, waiting for her to speak, tapping his pen against the notepad. She takes a deep breath. It feels so unnatural to be talking to Sachin about business.

"I have been investigating the circumstances surrounding Vijay's death," she says, surprised at the confident sound of her own voice.

"What?" he says.

"I've been trying to piece together what happened to him."

"*Haan*. The burglary," Sachin says. *Tap tap tap tap tap.*

"Well, the thing is, it wasn't."

He stops tapping. "What do you mean, it wasn't?"

"It wasn't a burglary."

Sachin's eyes soften, mirroring the look of concern Lakshmi gave her earlier. "Rishika, how about you go and have some tea with Lakshmi, *acha*? You're not thinking clearly right now."

"Actually, Sachin, I've rarely had more clarity." As soon as she says it, she knows it to be true. She feels acutely aware of her surroundings – able to take in more details than usual, able to react in a split second.

Her voice too has changed. It is lower and more measured. "Vijay drove the health minister to meet with Basinger."

Sachin blinks in confusion. "How … why would … Vijay told you that?" He stumbles over his words. She can understand his confusion. This is probably a lot to take in. She continues; it's better to tell him everything she knows immediately, like ripping off a Band-Aid.

"Basinger was at your Diwali party last year, *haana*? Well, it turns out he was lobbying the health minister to get a 'no' vote on the Soft Drink Bill. Vijay knew about it." She looks at him, interrogating his reaction. If he doesn't believe her, she will have to show him the footage.

Sachin sits, stunned.

"So, I'm wondering, could Vijay have confronted Basinger later on when he knew of the corruption?"

Sachin is looking at her with his mouth half open.

His eyes blink again, and she starts to feel a little inkling of hope.

And yet, now that she looks closer, all the color seems to have drained from his face. In front of her eyes, he has turned a very pale shade of gray. He looks ill, as though he might be about to vomit.

"Are you okay?" she asks.

When he speaks finally, his voice comes out quietly, almost a whisper. "I knew, as soon as I heard," he says cryptically.

"What?"

"I knew it wasn't a burglary."

Rishika's vision darkens around the edges, homing in on nothing but Sachin's eyes. "What are you talking about?"

"I never meant to get him in trouble!" His face collapses, and all of a sudden he is sobbing quietly.

Rishika stares at him. *What have you done, Sachin?*

The story starts as a dribble, literally. Sachin is a mess. He says Vijay came to his house late one night, on the same day that he drove the health minister. "I had never seen him so angry," Sachin says. "He was spitting, you know? Something about the prime minister trying to help people and his good work being 'jeopardized by greed'; they were the words he used."

Rishika feels the hairs on her skin like a million little shards of glass.

Sachin keeps pouring out the events. Vijay knew Sachin and Basinger worked together, because the Jogia Group does all the distribution in the Pacific for Basinger's company, Island Cola. When Vijay first learned about the deal between Basinger and Singh, he came to Sachin first, to give his friend the opportunity to rectify the situation, before he escalated it. He told Sachin to stop the corruption and allow the bill to pass, or he'd go straight to the prime minister. Sachin poured Vijay some whiskey and promised to sort it out.

Now Sachin begins to sob again. "But I didn't ... I couldn't. Vijay thought I had influence, but I don't. I don't have any power," he says. "They didn't listen to me." He opens his drawer and pulls out a bottle of whiskey and a glass. The bottle shakes in his hand as he pours a glass for himself and takes a gulp. "I genuinely wanted to fix it. I didn't think it was right for Basinger to be meddling either. But you have to understand. This Bill was going to mean a huge loss in our market. People would stop buying Island Cola. And then the other Pacific countries would follow. Our stock value would plummet, *janta*?"

He gulps more whiskey. Last Wednesday evening, Sachin says, he organized a meeting with Jogia and Basinger in one of those private rooms at the top of the Military Club.

Of course it was there, thinks Rishika, the old smoky gentleman's lounge with the sports TVs in the corners. Women have only recently been given the right to enter. Few exercised the right, seemingly content to pass up the ogling and innuendo.

Sachin continues, "I told them, people are starting to talk. Word is getting around about Island Cola trying to influence the ministers. I thought that maybe I could convince them to let the bill pass and go about their marketing in another way. Even branch out into other products. I was not expecting their reaction."

Rishika keeps staring at him.

"They got very angry," he says. His voice is piteously small, like a little boy being reprimanded. "He was right in my face. Shouting."

"*Who* was?"

"Basinger. He kept saying, 'No one knows about this! Who's talking about it?' F'ing this and f'ing that. I tried not to tell them about Vijay. I tried, I promise."

Rishika leans in, then, and Sachin flinches slightly. "I just mentioned it was a friend!" he says. "I didn't betray who it was. I swear! But Basinger worked it out by himself. He went all red, and he got this look of recognition. He said, 'I knew he looked familiar. Little prick.' Then he cursed the health minister for not being more careful."

Tears are streaming down Sachin's face now, silver trails down his pale cheeks. "I should have said something. I should have warned him." He looks in Rishika's eyes, pleading for her to understand. "But if Jogia found out I would lose my job."

He looks down at his desk. "When I heard about the break-in the next day, I knew what must have happened." Sachin lets out one last sob, then sniffs, wiping his nose with his sleeve. When he looks up, he looks lighter somehow, relieved at having purged his secret.

Rishika stares at him, amazed at his insensitivity. "So Basinger killed Vijay? To silence him?"

"*Nahi!*" Sachin looks horrified. "No, no, no, no. It was all a terrible accident. Basinger is a family man. He would never … he didn't kill him. Basinger just wanted him roughed up a little; scared. He called someone who called someone who called someone, *janta*? But they messed it up. Idiots beat him up too much. Ex military guys, I think. He hit his head on the table. Dead, just like that. They panicked. Made it look like a burglary and ran."

Rishika hears whispers outside the study door; Lakshmi imploring the children to be quiet. Sachin doesn't seem to notice and plows on with his story.

"Believe me, Basinger feels terrible. He looked so stressed when I saw him a couple of days later. All those police swarming around your house. Although the cyclone was good timing, obviously."

Good timing. She can't believe his callous turn of phrase.

"We'll never be able to prove it was him," he continues, as though he is on Rishika's team. "The police think it's a burglary.

Apparently they've got some squatter boy. Frankly Rishika, it's probably best we don't push it."

Rishika wants to run as fast as she can, down the hallway and down the street. And yet there is just one thing she needs to understand first.

"What do you mean they can't prove it?" she asks.

"No one knows. You can't tell anyone Rishika," he pleads.

He clearly doesn't know Vijay had footage of the meeting.

So, Vijay did keep one card close to his chest. She watches Sachin shuffle in his seat in front of her.

"It's okay," Rishika reassures him.

He nods solemnly at her, careful to hide his relief.

Rishika gets up from her seat. He stands up too. She walks straight out of Sachin's office, ignoring his voice behind her. She passes Lakshmi just outside the door. Her cousin is pretending to fold a basket of washing, but Rishika knows her too well; her face is tense, lips pressed together. Lakshmi says something to Rishika, but Rishika keeps walking, down the hallway and out the door. She lets herself out of the gate and onto the sweltering bitumen.

THE CUBICLES of FijiHealth are deserted. No one will be back at work until Monday. Hannah walks down the unlit corridor, past the small workspaces of her absent colleagues. Family pictures are pinned to the walls of their cubicles – big, laughing extended families. Bible passages typed in decorative fonts are sticky taped to their computers. When she gets to her own cubicle, she is struck by how colorless it is. She has pinned one faded Polaroid on the wall. It's of her, Jess, and German Jana, arms thrown tipsily around each other's shoulders during one of their resort getaways. She cringes, suddenly aware of the contrast. For a reason that isn't entirely clear to her, she unpins the photo and places it face down on her desk.

She continues down the hallway. The only light in the place is emanating from under Dr Sireli's door. Ethan and Peniasi agreed that Dr Sireli is one person they can trust. It made more sense for Hannah to meet with him alone, so they are waiting for her in a café down the road.

She knocks softly and her boss welcomes her in, expecting her after their detailed phone call earlier.

She hands over the thumb drive with the footage. He holds it and remains silent for a long time. "I suspected there was a roadblock. There were always people fighting the idea. Things didn't add up."

Hannah nods.

"Now we know a bit more," he adds.

She smiles at him weakly. Unsure what to say next, she says a quiet goodbye and pulls the door softly behind her.

RISHIKA EXPECTS to feel numb. That seems to be how her body responds these days. She even wonders whether she might feel a perverse elation at having uncovered the truth, as though having finally submitted an essay.

And yet, she feels none of those things.

Instead, she feels a distant pain beginning to spread through her body, slowly filling each capillary, stretching to the edge of each limb.

For the first ten years of her marriage, she and Vijay were best friends. There were, of course, the usual arguments and moody misunderstandings, but they always made up. Even after their first and second miscarriages they shared each other's pain through hugs and tears and black humor, their annoyance at prying aunties, their irritation at the tone-deaf smugness of their fertile cousins. It was not until the third and fourth miscarriages that they began to hide their pain from each other and deal with it in separate, clashing ways. Over time, they just drifted apart, even while they shared the same house and the same bed.

When Lewanivanua first got elected, Vijay had a spring in his step for the first time in years. He even came home and spun Rishika around in a rare show of his old kind of affection. He genuinely believed Lewanivanua was the man to take the country forward.

It didn't take long for Vijay's misery to reappear. In the last few months of his life he was desperately, miserably flat.

And now, Rishika finally understands why.

He was overhearing conversations. Witnessing clandestine meetings. Some of the ministers were turning against the prime minister for their own self-interest. Vijay must have felt so disillusioned. He must have felt so crippled by indecision, so torn, when discretion was so central to his professional identity. How stifled he must have felt, driving people he abhorred, held down by secret knowledge and carrying the weight of the nation on his shoulders.

It still hurts that he didn't open up to her. But it helps to know that Vijay *did* speak up. He never did lose that fight for justice that she used to love in him.

In fact, he gave his life for it.

PART III

Monday

THE BRAWNY security guard smiles in recognition as he opens the heavy door for Hannah. She is met with that old familiar smell of stale beer and cheap cologne. Her friends are sitting at the back of O'Hannigan's on tall bar stools, clinking their glasses together. Most of them are there: German Jana, the Daves, Michelle, Aaron, Jess, and Pip. After not seeing them for a few days, Hannah's irritation with them has lessened, and she feels genuinely pleased to see them.

Jess sees her from across the crowded room and waves. Pip stops arguing with World Bank Dave and rushes around the table to embrace her in a long, tipsy hug. Aaron says, "Hannah! I feel like I haven't seen you in ages! Where have you been?"

It's a good question.

Last Friday afternoon, Rishika told them the whole grisly story in her loungeroom. She did not cry, nor was she the gracefully aloof woman that Hannah had first met. She seemed *angrier*. When she finished, she told them that they were welcome to pursue Basinger and Jogia in any way they wanted, with one condition: she did not want Sachin getting into any trouble, for Lakshmi and the children's sake. "No more lives should be ruined by this," she said firmly.

That was when it was decided that Hannah would confide in Dr Sireli, and they presumed he would communicate directly with the prime minister. Peniasi would expose the entire story on his blog.

By Saturday evening, the rumor was that Basinger was in hiding at the Australian embassy. He and his family were rushed to Nadi and flown out of the country by Sunday afternoon.

On Sunday morning, the *Fiji Herald* printed the front page headline ISLAND COLA TO SHUT PLANT IF BILL PASSES: 500 JOBS IN PERIL. It was public relations damage control; a last-ditch dirty tactic by the corporation to blackmail the public into opposing the bill. Sure enough, in the next day's newspaper, all of the letters to the editor were filled with fear about job cuts and anger that "bureaucratic red tape" is going to scare off "our international friends." The Sunday edition also reported that the health minister had resigned, citing "a desire to spend more time with family."

Dr Sireli is hopeful that the bill will be passed, but it is far from certain. Lewanivanua's position still seems precarious.

While her friends mingle around the bar, Hannah takes a long sip of her white wine and shivers. It is actually exhausting taking politics personally. She has been feeling things more profoundly these last few days. Tears well easily in her eyes. She finds small things – things that once used to pass her by – deeply meaningful. Last night, when she went out for dinner with Jess and Pip, just after the steaming tandoori chicken pizza arrived at their table, she blurted, "Wait, can we say thanks first?"

Pip raised a skeptical eyebrow.

Hannah backtracked. "I mean, not *Grace* or anything, but just *thanks*, to the universe or something. I just think we're pretty lucky to have all of this."

Jess laughed at her affectionately, Pip closed her eyes and clasped her hands together in mock piety, and Hannah made a short awkward speech in the middle of the pizza joint.

Rishika is often on Hannah's mind. She knows Rishika cremated her husband on the weekend. Apparently, she will be having the twelfth day ritual tomorrow. In the few short days Hannah has known her, she has come to like Rishika's quirky sense of humor and the weird facts she comes out with sometimes.

"You have a lot of rabbits in Australia, *haana*?" she randomly asked last Friday.

"Er, yeah. I guess we do." Hannah smiled.

"And they introduced a disease to kill them, didn't they?"

Hannah stretched her memory back. "Yeah, that's right. Mixama-something-or-other."

"And they put up a big fence, to keep them out?"

"Ha! True. The rabbit-proof fence."

Rishika nodded sagely. "Men and their fences," she said, cryptically.

Hannah might even call in and visit Rishika from time to time. It feels possible that they could become friends.

Jess jumps in front of Hannah now and tries to convince her to dance. Hannah twists out of her grasp, preferring just to watch instead. She is also – if she is being honest – reluctant to leave her stool. It has a perfect vantage point to see anyone arriving at the door.

Between songs, the Dutch medical intern takes a seat next to her. Hannah looks at him and suddenly wonders why she never just asked him before. "I'm so sorry, this is way overdue, but I never did catch your name. And then it got weird, and beyond the point of no return. I'm Hannah, and you are ...?"

"Andrew," he says, smiling breathlessly, thankfully unoffended.

"Huh. Andrew. Cool." Less Dutch than she remembered. She commits it to her memory. He soon returns to the dance floor.

The volunteers are bobbing up and down in a misshapen circle, joined by a large group of students from the university. They all cheer in unison when the Shaggy song "It Wasn't Me" comes on.

While she is laughing at her friends shouting out the lyrics, she hears a familiar voice.

"Hey, Han." Her stomach flips. Ethan must have come in unnoticed when she was talking to Andrew. He sits down next to her with a glass of red wine. "Long time no see." His eyes twinkle.

He is joking, but it does feel like that to Hannah. She didn't see him over the weekend, which, after the intensity of last week, left her with an ache of uncertainty. She kept her phone beside her at all times. Sometimes she checked for messages from him – on Facebook and email and Instagram – and then double-checked, just in case she had missed something. She even started to call him once, but couldn't think of the right thing to say.

They sit shoulder to shoulder now, watching their friends on the dance floor. His hand lies on the table next to hers, her little finger tingling with the closeness of his.

"Peniasi has nearly finished his article," he says. He explains that, in Peni's investigations so far, it turns out that the Soft Drink Bill is just the tip of the iceberg. Sugar, it seems, is the new tobacco. Fiji is again being bullied by big business, and Pacific islanders are dying young because of it. Hannah shakes her head, unsure of what else to say.

Hannah tells Ethan about her coffee with Dr Sireli this morning. She asked her boss for permission to change the focus of her research project. She has realized how patronizing her initial approach was, to ask why Fijians don't take more responsibility for their own health. Now she is going to focus her research on food sovereignty, working alongside local communities and advocates who are increasingly aware of how politics and corporations shape what they eat. Dr Sireli is receptive to the idea. In fact, Hannah has a funny feeling that he's been gently guiding her toward this conclusion all along.

"Your boss sounds so cool," Ethan says, the dance floor lights reflecting in his eyes.

With another gulp of her drink, Hannah feels emboldened, and slightly drunk. She places her glass on the table with slightly too much force. It tips over, and she bustles to correct it. "Sorry." *Don't chicken out now, Hannah Wilson.* "Eth, can I talk to you about something?"

"Sure," he nods, taking a sip of his wine.

"You know that conversation we had at the Hibiscus Inn, where you said you, um, liked me? And I was kind of, um, dismissive?"

He puts his wine down, his lips curling at the edges. "Doesn't ring a bell."

"Haha. Well. You probably feel differently now, but," she keeps her eyes firmly on the dance floor, "I just wanted to say that I got that really wrong. Turns out I like you, too. More than I knew."

He doesn't say anything for a second, and then two.

"So much that it kind of hurts," she adds. Petrified, she finally lifts her gaze to his and there, his gray eyes are waiting for hers.

"I feel completely the same, Han," he says.

"Do you?"

"*God* yes. Are you kidding me? This last week has been hell for me."

She bites her lip. He stares at her with those shining, stormy eyes, and the other people in the bar disappear. His little finger touches hers finally, a tiny point of contact sending a jolt of warmth through her. He leans in toward her, smelling faintly of woodsmoke, a sexy, earthy smell. And finally, he kisses her, red wine lingering on his lips. Hannah melts with how right it all feels, the pleasant yearning settling in at the very base of her spine.

ON THE other side of Suva, Isikeli walks alone along the darkened sidewalk. With each footstep he takes, another brown toad hops away lazily. He turns into the street where all the expats live, winding his way between the *Kai Valagi* estates. From what he can see through the wrought-iron gates – beyond the small huts where nightwatchmen are scrolling through their phones – the houses are unlit, their occupants out for the evening. He imagines their houses to be full of expensive stuff – wall-sized flatscreen TVs and other shiny things.

The lawyer, Ethan, came around to the settlement this morning. He sat down on the mat to tell him and Bu about the investigation. Apparently the *Kai Idia* was killed by some thugs who were hired by an Australian man.

"*Oilei!*" Bu kept saying.

Ethan also spoke directly to Isikeli. "But we should also talk about you, mate."

He said the police have evidence that places Isikeli at the scene. Ethan advised him to plead guilty to petty theft. It is a minor offense and his first, so he will most likely get a good behavior bond. As long as he behaves, Ethan said, this is a good option.

Good behavior, Isikeli thinks now. *Whatever they mean by that.*

He keeps walking, sizing up the accessibility of each gated house. Which ones have CCTV, which ones have climbable fences. He can hear the snuffle of dogs poking their noses under fences at him. A sign says "Beware: Vicious Guard Dog," and Isikeli smiles to himself. The dogs in this area are bred to be family pets – they are pampered labradors, cocker-spoodles, and rescued, reformed street dogs – all so loved that they can hardly raise a snarl.

He keeps walking until he finally rounds the corner and reaches the top of the hill where he can see down to his destination. Overhead lights drown the field in an amber glow. In the corner of the oval farthest away from Isikeli, a motley circle of boys are jumping up and down, knees touching their chests, warming up.

Isikeli feels a rush of energy bolt through his body and he begins to sprint toward his rugby team.

Tuesday

RISHIKA IS thinking about sugar, the way it has sprinkled down through history. It has made people rich and propped up empires, like diamonds and cotton and gold. It has enslaved Indians on foreign shores and forged ethnic conflict between them and their hosts. Distilled into rum, it has eaten away at people's livers, their personalities, their relationships. Dissolved into drinks it has spread diseases, meddling with pancreases and kidneys. Her husband is not the first person to die at the hands of sugar merchants, and he certainly won't be the last.

Around her, family and neighbors are placing plates full of flowers on a large white cloth alongside Vijay's favorite vegetarian dishes: kadoo curry, bindi curry, and a stack of roti. To help his soul reach the world of the ancestors on the twelfth day of mourning, rice balls, signifying the circular nature of life, have been molded and placed on a banana leaf, just as they have each of the last eleven days. A photo of her husband looking young and vibrant, taken about ten years ago, is adorned with a string of flowers, leaning against the wall as if looking over the offerings.

Rishika watches her aunties frantically prepare for the guests behind the scenes while the *pundit* chants his mantras in a perfectly
choreographed ritual, and she feels a renewed rush of affection
for them all.

Solomon has been banished to the corner of the garden near
the fence, away from the spread of food. He keeps inching closer
and has already been shouted at several times by Nadi Uncle,
who wanted to chain him up but Rishika refused. Now the dog
is looking at Rishika pleadingly. She shrugs apologetically. *Sorry
little one. We have to behave today.*

She sits now on the mat with her head bowed. She finds
strength in her unfaltering traditions, ancient customs that have
survived conquering armies and administrations. She can take
that all in now.

Akesh sits near her, his head newly bald; he and Vijay's brothers shaved their heads on the tenth day of mourning. She takes
a discreet look at Akesh's profile, his chiseled jaw now more dis-
tinguished without hair. It suits him. Earlier this morning, she
was standing in the hallway when Akesh walked in behind her.
They were alone – the aunties were setting up the food outside
while the uncles unstacked the chairs. She didn't look away this
time when Akesh looked at her; instead she stared straight back
into his brown eyes for what seemed like a very long time. Mutual understanding passed between them, and they both smiled
sadly.

"In another world, Rishika ..." he trailed off.

"I know," she said. Nadi Aunty interrupted them at that point,
shuffling past them to get to the kitchen.

And now, he is sitting over there. Something has settled between them. His presence no longer gives her a quiver, but rather
a kind of strength. He will always be her friend, and he will always understand her pain, probably better than anyone else.

Years ago, she and Vijay used to drive to the sea wall after these kinds of family events. They would sit together, his arm around her, listening to the waves lapping against the concrete wall, debriefing about their eccentric families. She used to love these conversations, the deep comfort of being understood.

"How annoying was my mother today?" he would say.

"Yes! So annoying. She couldn't stop talking about that wedding."

"I know. I couldn't care less about that minor celebrity she sat next to. What was his name? I can't even remember."

Sitting on that sea wall, time and time again, they returned to the topic of emigration. It seemed a natural segue as they looked at the container ships sailing out toward the horizon. Over the years, so many friends and family had moved overseas, taking job opportunities and visas when they arose. Rishika's brother was in San Francisco; Akesh spent several years in Sydney; most of Rishika's university friends were scattered throughout the West. Accountants, lawyers, dentists, software engineers. They all seemed to be doing well with their incomes and property portfolios and private schools for their children. Rishika and Vijay considered following them, of course – it would be nice to travel, to have more money, to have less unannounced visits from the in-laws. But something stopped them. They both shared a deep commitment to this place. Even during the hard times – the military coups, the cyclones, and, on a personal note, the relentless miscarriages – they both had faith that Fiji was going to be okay, and so were they. Like Rishika, Vijay loved this country and its endearing mix of people.

And that's why it's very sad, Rishika thinks now as she looks around the crowd slowly seating themselves around the mat, *that not one of his iTaukei friends has shown up to his funeral.* She had invited some of his colleagues, his old high school friends, and some of those guys he used to play soccer with. Even Bu and Isikeli knew it was the twelfth day today. Yet she has only seen Indo-Fijians in their white robes, milling around in somber anticipation while they wait for the *pundit* to start. The only exceptions were Hannah and Ethan, both looking sweet in their collared white shirts and light-colored pants. They waved hello to her earlier and are now lingering at the back of the group with somber faces. Rishika noticed them whispering to each other in that intimate dance of new lovers. She feels a spark of happiness for them.

The *pundit* continues his mantras. With her eyes closed, Rishika has blocked out the human sounds around her – the ruffle of clothes, the readjusting of seating arrangements to include some guests arriving late into the circle. She finally understands the healing power of the *pundit*'s words, letting their poetic cadence wash over her.

The prayer is a long one, and Rishika loses track of time.

When the *pundit* finally finishes, she opens her eyes, momentarily blinded by the brightness of the sun.

It is then that she hears the voices launching into a soaring hymn behind her, unmistakably iTaukei voices. As her vision gradually returns, Vijay's colleagues come into focus, alongside Isikeli and Bu in her wheelchair, her leg wrapped in a blanket. They sing generously, eyes closed in reverence, harmonies layered one on top of another. Rishika and her relatives listen, deeply touched. Vijay's compatriots *did* come; they were just on Fiji Time.

When the singing stops, everyone takes a collective breath. Rishika's aunties spring into action, unwrapping food and passing around curries. Nausori Aunty squeals, declaring that half of the roti went missing during the prayer. Nadi Aunty says it is proof that Vijay's soul has been here – he always did love her roti – but

Rishika can see Solomon sitting guiltily in the corner, deliberately avoiding eye contact with her.

Midway through the meal, everyone's eyes are drawn to a commotion further up Chamberlain Street. Two police cars are approaching slowly, escorting a black four-wheel drive. The cars come to a stop directly outside her gate. It takes Rishika a while to realize what is happening, and she momentarily holds her breath. Sure enough, the prime minister emerges from the front seat, security guards quick to rush to his side. Her uncles scramble to welcome him.

They usher him through the gate and sit him and the security guards down in front of large plates of food thrust upon them by Nadi Aunty. All eyes are on the prime minister as he eats, paying compliments for the delicious spread. He makes small talk with the uncles. When he finishes his plate, he leaves the guards to continue the conversation and shuffles across the mat to sit cross-legged beside Rishika. He lowers his voice to speak privately to her.

"I'm going to miss him, eh? Vijay was a good man. A friend."

Rishika swallows. "Thank you, Uncle."

"He talked about you," the prime minister continues. "All the time. You were writing a history, eh? Of the *girmitiyas*?"

Her breath catches in her throat. She looks down at her feet, hiding her surprise. Vijay *was* listening.

"I would like to read it," Lewanivanua says. "Can you send it to me?"

She nods.

"*Vinaka*." Then he chuckles. "He used to say you were the smartest person he knew."

When she does not respond, he pats her on the back with warm sympathy, and stands up to leave, his security detail shadowing him closely. They graciously thank their hosts and then walk back through the gate. The sleek convoy leaves, one car after another, purring back up Chamberlain Street.

She wishes she could take Vijay to the seawall and tell him about it. She would make him laugh at her descriptions of all the different people she has met over the last few days. She knows he would be moved. And then she would say sorry, and that she loves him. And he would say sorry, and that he has missed her, and that things were going to be okay.

It is then, and only then, that Rishika Prakash begins to cry, finally giving way to deep, wrenching sobs. The old dog ambles quickly to her side, nudging her arm with his nose.

THE END

Reading *Sugar*

A Supplementary Chapter

We chose the form of the ethnographic novel to portray the dazzling contradictions of modern-day life in Suva. At its heart, *Sugar* is about the historically entrenched inequalities that continue to shape everyday life in Fiji and across the Global South. By exploring twenty-seven days in the life of three characters who are very differently placed within this system, we seek to evoke a deeper understanding of the banal and often unconscious ways in which people respond to and reproduce inequality. We hope this will encourage readers to apply the same anthropological analysis to their own lives, and in doing so spark new and imaginative ways of thinking and acting.

In this supplementary chapter, we outline how *Sugar* draws upon and relates to ethnography, our positionality as authors, the possibility and limitations of ethnographic fiction, and the key threads of critical theory embedded in the book. It is designed to provide guidance to instructors and students on how to read the book from an ethnographic perspective and concludes with a series of questions to inspire classroom discussion.

References are provided throughout to direct readers to further helpful resources. **Warning – this chapter contains plot spoilers** and is designed to be read after the story. Before we begin, it is useful to contextualize the tensions alluded to throughout the story.

Reading Race and Class in Fiji

With a population of just under a million people, Fiji is an archipelago of over 330 islands, although only 110 of these are inhabited. Fiji was ceded to the British colonial administration in 1874 by Ratu Seru Cakobau, the then chief of Fiji. The official narrative is that Cakobau represented the interests of all Fijians, who in turn were grateful to be disavowed of their "savage" lifestyles and placed under British "protection." This discourse erases the unequal power dynamics, domestic struggles, and coercion that led to such an arrangement and elides the colonial dispossession, violence, and resistance that ensued (Kaplan & Kelly, 1994). Around the same time, the mobilization of Christian missionaries throughout the Pacific led to a widespread uptake of Christianity amongst Indigenous Fijians (or *iTaukei*, which literally means "owner [of the land]"). The church remains a crucial – if politically contested and multidenominational – pillar of Fijian statehood today (Tomlinson, 2009; Ryle, 2005).

During the colonial period, oppressive policies confined most iTaukei to their villages and required them to maintain "traditional" lifestyles. At times, colonial administrators shaped and constrained which aspects of iTaukei culture were reified as "tradition" and which were ignored or adjusted, disrupting the social order (Nayacakalou, 1978; Tanner, 2007). The chiefly system was restructured to be hereditary in the new regime, creating a new class structure in which chiefly families had access to more opportunities than commoners, including education and employment. Moreover, new categories constructed Fijians as being either "civilized" or "uncivilized"; "loyal" or "disloyal"; "good Christians" or "heathens" (Ravuvu, 1988). All of these processes entrenched cycles of privilege and disadvantage within and between iTaukei communities that would continue long into the future.

Like Rishika's great-grandfather in the book, thousands of Indians were coercively recruited by the British colonial administration in the late 1800s and early 1900s to work on sugarcane plantations in Fiji, just as they were throughout colonies in Africa and the Caribbean. While some Indo-Fijian laborers eventually paid their way home, others stayed, many ultimately securing land leases to continue sugar farming independently (Lal, 2012). Indo-Fijians are unique amongst the indentured diaspora for having maintained a form of Hindi, albeit one that is a combination of languages from India and English. Historically entrenched class tensions continue to exist between the *girmityas*, who tended to hail from the southern parts of India, and the more privileged descendants of economic migrants, who were usually from the Gujerat and Punjab regions (Jayawardena, 1980). Despite many Fijians of Indian descent not having physically been to India during their lifetimes, they, like many diasporic communities, maintain an (often romanticized) image of the "motherland" and an ongoing connection with Indian fashion, music, and popular culture (Miller, 2008). There is, nonetheless, a fraught but powerful patriotism amongst many Indo-Fijians for their adopted island home (Trnka, 2005).

Granted independence in 1970, Fiji today has a population made up of approximately 57 per cent iTaukei and 38 per cent Indo-Fijians, although these statistics belie the fact that for much of the twentieth century Indo-Fijians outnumbered iTaukei. Eth-nonationalist tensions between the two groups have sometimes erupted into violent conflicts, especially after the military coup of 1987 and the nationalist overthrow of the Indian-led government in 2000. Despite the salience of geopolitical and corporate motivating factors for these coups (Akram-Lodhi, 1996; Emde, 2005), explanations tend to focus on Indigenous land rights, Indo-Fijian dominance in the business sector, preferential representation of iTaukei in the national parliament, and a racialized voting system. These factors have led to the marginalization of the Indo-Fijian community and mass migration, particularly after the periods of political unrest (Lal, 2008; Trnka, 2005, 2008). Despite government rhetoric and metrics about multiculturalism, unresolved tensions between iTaukei and Indo-Fijians have remained muted but ever present. In this story, brief flashbacks into Isikeli's childhood, alongside Rishika's research into her family history, are intended to trace the colonial forces that have set the conditions for these tensions to fester.

Inequality is glitteringly obvious in Fiji. Although poverty statistics are politically contested, between 24 and 30 per cent of Fiji's population live in official poverty while a further 30 per cent live precariously and are categorized as "near poor" (fBoS, 2021), a situation that has only worsened during the economic downturn of COVID-19. Certainly, some iTaukei who may be considered poor in monetary terms nonetheless maintain their well-being due to ongoing connections to customary land, subsistence agriculture, and strong extended family networks (Scheyvens et al., 2021). However, many leave these safety nets in rural communities to seek some of the limited formal economic opportunities in the cities. Fiji is one of the most urbanized countries in the Pacific, with more than half of the population now living in urban or peri-urban spaces. This has led to a rise of informal settlements and the kind of cramped conditions in which Isikeli and his grandmother live, along with many iTaukei and Indo-Fijians who have migrated to urban centers. These settlements often have poor access to water and hygiene, limited healthy food options, and high rates of nutrition-related non-communicable diseases (Phillips & Keen, 2016). Disproportionate amounts of household income tend to be spent on mobile phone data, as people seek to keep up with the rapidly accelerating digital economy. The popularity of social media sites like Facebook amongst urban Fijians reflects an opportunity for younger people to escape hierarchical kin relations (albeit while often reproducing them). Social media can be a vehicle for keeping in touch with kin who have migrated overseas and a way to aspire toward migration (Brison, 2017). This aspirational use of mobile phones is aggressively capitalized upon by multinational telecommunications companies in the Pacific, represented by Pac-Fone in the book (Horst, 2018). Crucially, just as there are many poor Indo-Fijians who live in equally harsh conditions to Isikeli, there are also elite iTaukei who live in gated communities alongside expats like Hannah. In other words, while class inequality sometimes coheres along racial lines in Fiji, it doesn't always.

Meanwhile, Fiji is marketed to international tourists as a tropical island "paradise" and Fijians as friendly, smiling hosts (Kanemasu, 2013; Phillips, Taylor, et al., 2021). Hundreds of thousands of tourists arrive at the resorts each year, especially from Australia and New Zealand. Relaxing by the poolside, they are served cocktails and have their children cared for by locals, many of whom, like Isikeli's mother in this novel, have left their own families to seek (usually low-paid) employment opportunities. This is not to mention the "Blue Lane Program," a haven on the mainland coast for superyacht owners, or the celebrities who own private Fijian islands. Such disparity in wealth and opportunity, and the marginalization of locals over foreigners, leads to what some have called in other developing contexts a "tourism apartheid" (Mazzei, 2012).

In Suva, there is a different class of privileged foreigner represented in this story by Hannah: expatriates volunteering professional expertise to local organizations or employed at various multilateral organizations. On their international salaries or stipends, this cadre of expatriates frequent the higher-end cafés, restaurants, and bars and drive up the price of rent in Suva. Many of these *voluntourists* are well-meaning individuals with an interest in social justice and a desire to help people, albeit in ways that will "look good on their CV." Yet scholars have found that many are also "ignorant of the underlying power and privilege issues inherent in voluntourism" (McLennan, 2014). Some argue that the system ends up doing more harm than good by further "entrenching paternalism and inequitable relationships" (McLennan, 2014). Critical voices have called for foreign development practitioners to yield some of their power (Tawake et al., 2021), leaving space for development to be more locally led and decolonized (Meki & Tarai, 2023).

One of the logics that perpetuates inequalities is the discourse that Fijians are happy and willing to take any kind of employment irrespective of the style of work or however low the income (Scheyvens, 2007). With minimum wage currently sitting at $3.34 FJD/$1.50 USD an hour, this "cheap labor" discourse incentivizes multinational businesses to invest in Fiji as operating costs are kept low. As alluded to in the book, this typecasting of Fijians as cheap and willing workers limits their opportunities both domestically and on a global stage, with increasing numbers of Fijians recruited for and exploited in seasonal agricultural and abattoir work in Australia and New Zealand (Stead & Davies, 2021) and treated as as "expendable bodies" in international military campaigns (Bolatagici, 2011).

In this book, we have sought to juxtapose these social worlds through the characters of Isikeli, Rishika, and Hannah. Placing them alongside each other makes the contrast between their daily lives more obvious. By focusing on each character's everyday experiences, families, romantic lives, hopes, and fears, we have sought to make each just as relatable, endearing, and flawed as the other. Through this in-depth and humane portrayal, as in all good ethnography, we have sought to make the familiar strange and the strange familiar.

Reading Ethnographic Fiction

Methods and Positionality

Sugar is grounded in ethnographic research. Ethnography is a field of study in which the researcher gains an in-depth understanding of social and cultural life through long-term, hands-on learning. Using methods such as participant observation and interviews, ethnographers are able to convey rich and detailed knowledge of peoples' lives and what is meaningful to them (Madden, 2017).

Tarryn has conducted ethnographic research alongside iTaukei and Indo-Fijian communities since 2011. Raised on unceded Noongar country in Western Australia, Tarryn graduated from her PhD in medical anthropology in 2010, and in 2016 took up a visiting research fellowship at the University of the South Pacific in Suva. With ethics approval from Fijian and Australian universities, and with a particular focus on diabetes and nutritional justice, she has held many interviews with community members and healthcare practitioners on the northeastern island of Ovalau; in the informal settlements between Suva and Nausori; and with health and nutrition policy-makers in Suva. She has spent months hanging out in villages, in and around hospitals, and on nurse outreach visits to informal settlements. Collaborating with iTaukei, Indo-Fijian, and

Australian colleagues, this research has led to an in-depth appreciation of the historical, politico-economic, and sociocultural drivers of poor nutrition in Fiji (Phillips, Ravuvu, et al., 2021; Phillips & Narayan, 2017; Phillips, 2020). This book has been built around these conversations, observations, and experiences.

Sugar also benefits from Edward's lived experience. Born and raised in Suva, Edward's grandparents were Indian indentured laborers. Over time he has come to reflect upon the ongoing impacts of intergenerational trauma brought about by this family history of dislocation. Like many Indo-Fijian parents who accrued privilege in the 1970s, Edward's parents left him as a baby in the care of an Indigenous Fijian nanny, whom Edward came to refer to as *Na* (Mum) and with whom he remains close today. Spending much of his early childhood with her and her village, Edward's first language was Fijian, followed by Fijian Hindi and English. Edward's family eventually migrated to Australia, although he has continued to return regularly and lived there with Tarryn and their three children from 2016 to 2018. Edward has worked for a Fijian NGO advocating for the poor, is currently an advisor to the Fijian Labour Party, and regularly writes for the *Fiji Times* and *Fiji Sun*. More recently embarking on a PhD in development economics, Edward's intimate understanding of race and class politics in Fiji underpins the portrayal of daily life in this book.

Thus, as authors, we both have distinct relationships to Fiji and bring various insider (emic) and outsider (etic) perspectives to this project. These positionalities inevitably shape the way we have represented Fiji in *Sugar*. Crucially, however, our perspectives are also situated in dynamics of power and privilege. Through the writing process, we have imagined and written about different characters, some of whose experiences (such as those of poverty, Indigeneity, and queerness) are less familiar to us than others. It is a valid question to ask why, or even whether, as outsiders, we have the right to tell the story of these communities. This is an ethical dilemma faced by many ethnographers: giving voice to the marginalized "other" always carries with it politics of representation. While we agonized over this dilemma at times, we also did not want to perpetuate the ways in which these groups are often absent or silenced, and we wanted to give equal justice to them in the story. We feel that the value of ethnographic fiction lies in its ability to prompt one to imagine what it is like to live in someone else's shoes. Like Sparkes (1997, p. 38), we argue that ethnographic fiction can foster critical reflection by encouraging readers to "live outside of themselves, perceiving, experiencing, and understanding what has previously been neglected."

While we have sought to stay true to the essence of Fiji's history and social life, writing ethnographic fiction has enabled us to take some creative liberties to tell a more impactful story. Isikeli, Hannah, and Rishika are not real people, nor are the other characters in this book, barring some key identifiable historical figures. Where "genre-normative ethnography" (McGranahan, 2020) requires the researcher to rigidly adhere to fieldnotes and interview transcripts, ethnographic fiction writers are more empowered to rearrange facts, events, and identities. While this imaginative element removes the usual scientific standards of trustworthiness and validity against which ethnography is usually judged, it can "draw the reader into the story in a way that enables deeper understandings of individuals, organisations, or the events themselves" (Tierney, 1993).

Our book is strategically set in a parallel contemporary Fiji – during a fictional Cyclone Dorothy – with a different government, a different prime minister, and a different minister for health. The reasons for changing these details in *Sugar* are twofold. First, we were fictionalizing a murder, and thus needed to avoid causing reputational damage by linking real people to fictional events. Second, social problems in Fiji are often blamed solely on poor local governance, corruption, and domestic racial tensions. While these elements are obviously critical, such a localized focus veils the ongoing legacy of colonization and the pervasive influence of transnational corporate interests. Despite Fiji's "independence," international vested interests continue to wield significant power over local politics in many ways, including through neoliberal economic reforms and conditional aid (Ravuvu & Thornton, 2016) and trade negotiations (Gewertz & Errington, 2010). The more powerful international players in Fiji have traditionally been Australia, New Zealand, and the United States, although Fiji has increased its ties to China since 2006 (Yang, 2011). In order to convey the sometimes insidious nature of these geopolitical influences, we created a fictional prime minister who was continually thwarted in his efforts to protect Fiji's sovereignty.

The Possibilities and Limitations of Ethnographic Fiction

Presenting ethnography through fiction, we argue, can be an act of inclusion. Academic scholarship is an elite register of writing that is often less accessible and engaging to those outside the academy and intimidating to undergraduate students, especially those for whom English is a second language or those who are the first in their family to attend university. This limits the reach, accessibility, and power of anthropological ideas. We hope that by stripping away the disciplinary jargon and avoiding academic conventions such as literature reviews, methodology sections, and in-text references we could simply tell a story that would be a more welcoming and inclusive introduction to critical social theory.

We also wanted to foster a love of reading amongst students. We have noticed that when students are compulsorily required to read non-fiction texts in a university setting, they often seem intimidated by the notion that there is a correct way to read and write about the work and that their interpretation may be judged. Such self-consciousness creates an inevitable distance between them and the text, which can make it less enjoyable and inhibit the powerful feeling of being immersed in a story. In writing this book, we wanted readers to be transported to a different time and place and to come to love or be frustrated by the characters, a resonance that would allow them to approach theory from a different angle.

Like all fiction, *Sugar* is likely to resonate with readers in varied ways, depending on their own relationship with the story. Where a traditional scholarly article tells the reader how to interpret the ethnographic data and why it is important, ethnographic fiction "has the potential to provoke multiple interpretations and responses from readers" (Sparkes, 1997). Some readers may identify most closely with the Australian volunteer Hannah, and thus similarly experience her gradual recognition of her own white privilege. Others with parallel experiences of inequality to Isikeli may resonate more with his struggles and his dreams of upward social mobility through sport, which is commonly seen as a "way out" for disenfranchised men across the Global South (Besnier, 2012). Those from migrant backgrounds may see themselves or their families in Rishika and her family's complicated identity politics and quest for belonging (Trnka, 2005). Other readers might be interested in the experiences of the *qauri* journalist and activist, Peniasi, and the navigation of masculinities in postcolonial Fiji (Presterudstuen, 2014; 2017). Classroom discussion is likely to be enlivened when students compare and contrast their self-referential interpretations, learning from what others took away from the story.

The most potent power of ethnographic fiction is that it can be a "tool for critical pedagogy" (Sparkes, 1997), helping to inspire in students an outrage about social injustices in the world around them. The idea for this story was sparked when our house was burgled one night in Suva in 2017, just after our youngest son was born. A makeshift pole was used to fish a backpack containing our passports through an open window and security grill. Hours after contacting the police and the embassy, we received a phone call to notify us that both the bag and passports had been found abandoned nearby, clearly having been a disappointment to the opportunistic thieves. We learned a lot from this experience. Almost everyone we spoke to – Indo-Fijians, expats, and iTaukei alike – assumed the culprits were young iTaukei men from the nearby informal settlement. Some told us it was "probably the coconut boys," the young men who sold coconuts by the roadside nearby. These were the "usual suspects," blamed whenever there was crime, violence, vandalism, or social disorder. This profiling that positioned poor, young Indigenous men as the most likely cause of any social problems that arose seemed to function as "common sense" and aligned with a broader national discourse in which iTaukei men are often stereotyped as being less hardworking than their Indo-Fijian counterparts and thus a burden on the economy (Presterudstuen, 2014). Meanwhile, in both of our lines of work we were increasingly aware of broader structural injustices, such as the ways in which corporations were knowingly marketing and selling deadly products to consumers, and how local governments were seemingly powerless to stop them. By contrast to the petty crime described above, these sources of widespread social harm were normalized as "development" and hardly ever questioned. We wanted to write a story that made people feel as angry about this double standard as we did.

In seeking to unravel the complexity of racialized assumptions of criminality, we have cast Isikeli as engaging in petty theft to make a living. This element of the book aligns with Vakaoti's (2018) moving work on street-frequenting young people in Suva, for whom frequenting the streets is "both an outcome and a process available to them" in response to "structural inequalities, spatial control, and moral expectations." It is critical, however, that this plotline about Isikeli not be misread as reinforcing the problematic stereotypes of "criminal Indigenous men" in contrast to "hardworking and victimized Indo-Fijians" and "knowledgeable and powerful white saviors." We purposely drew the complex characters of Isikeli, Rishika, and Hannah to highlight the history and circumstances behind such moralizing assumptions and eventually reveal their inaccuracy. Moreover, we have cast a host of heroic and villainous peripheral characters from different backgrounds to prevent any oversimplified conclusions about race, and we encourage a critical look at notions of white saviorism.

Reading the Murder(s): Necropolitics in Oceania

The death of Vijay operates at three levels in this book. First, a murder mystery is a device through which to make the story more compelling – a page-turner of sorts – and thus capture and maintain readers' interest. At a deeper level, the dramatic nature of the murder enables a particular kind of interaction between Isikeli, Hannah, and Rishika that may not have happened otherwise. Ethnographic fiction allows writers to "flagrantly put real [kinds of] people into imaginary situations to get to the heart of the matter" (McGranahan, 2020). One of the themes we explore at the start of the book is the way in which inequality and racism are perpetuated when people live parallel lives, rarely gaining meaningful insight into or truly comprehending the lives of the "other." A dramatic event like a murder, however, has the capacity to jolt people out of the familiar and the commonplace. Being entangled in the murder forces Isikeli, Rishika, and Hannah to work together, which in turn enables us to imagine ordinary people in extraordinary circumstances. The characters' forced cooperation during the murder investigation reveals the messiness of everyday multiculturalism – moments of awkwardness and anxiety, nuances lost in translation and misunderstandings, alongside the characters' growing empathy for each other and self-reflexivity over time.

At a third level, while the murder of Vijay is the most attention-grabbing death in the story (and immediately blamed on Isikeli), there are many more normalized forms of premature death facing iTaukei and Indo-Fijians explored in the book. The low life expectancy in Fiji (currently sixty-nine years) is a result of tragically high rates of workplace accidents (Isikeli's father), alcoholism (Rishika's great-grandfather), police brutality (Isikeli), and non-communicable diseases (Bu, along with Hannah's other research participants). While murder tangibly offends the political and social order for all socioeconomic groups and is therefore taken seriously, these more subtle, insidious, and state-sanctioned forms of social harm are generally experienced only by marginalized groups and thus easily ignored.

This aspect of the story unveils the *necropolitics* of Fiji, or the ways in which social and political power is wielded to extend and improve the lives of the privileged while reducing the life chances of many across the Global South (Mbembe, 2001). In particular, we seek to highlight how the lives of racially marginalized groups are routinely cheapened and treated as expendable, meaning loss becomes a normalized part of life for them (Mbembe, 2001). (Unlike Mbembe, however, we do not wish to characterize the lives of those living in extreme poverty as "living death." Rather, we wanted to show through Isikeli and the "Paradise Estate" settlement community how people nonetheless live meaningful lives despite these conditions: their dignity, strength, work ethic, creativity, resourcefulness, sense of humor, loving relationships with kin, and deep spiritual connectedness.)

Underpinning such necropolitics are two interrelated concepts implicitly explored in this book: structural violence and neoliberalism. Popularized by Paul Farmer (2004), structural violence is a tool to understand what happens when neglect is built into wider political and economic systems. Although often more insidious and hidden than outright physical brutality, the harms that result from inequality and poverty are just as violent and lethal. Our book joins recent scholarly engagements that have pointed out the failure of neoliberal institutions to improve the living conditions brought about by advanced capitalism (Keshavjee, 2014; Povinelli, 2011). International development institutions such as the World Bank and the International Monetary Fund have achieved little in addressing global inequalities, and in some cases have exacerbated them (Appadurai & Alexander, 2019). Going further, these institutions have pushed neoliberal policies onto developing economies, including the privatization of public goods and services, the devaluation of currencies, and the deregulation of markets (Phillips, Ravuvu, et al., 2021; Povinelli, 2011). While these processes are designed to incentivize and increase profits for businesses of the Global North and local elites, they have harmed and abandoned many poorer communities. Moreover, the widening gap between rich and poor has been justified and reinforced by the neoliberal rhetoric of "individual responsibility," which casts those who are poor, unemployed, or ill as blameworthy for making "bad choices" and burdening the economy, and thus less deserving of state assistance (Wacquant, 2009). This discourse is convenient for multinational corporations as it absolves them – and the systems they perpetuate – of responsibility.

The central case study through which this is explored in the book is the crisis of type two diabetes currently facing the Pacific region, and more broadly communities across the Global South (Gálvez, Carney, & Yates-Doerr, 2020; SturtzSreetharan et al., 2021). (In Fiji, while Indo-Fijians suffer from equally high rates of diabetes as their iTaukei counterparts, iTaukei are more likely to suffer from complications due to undiagnosed, uncontrolled, or untreated diabetes [Kumar et al., 2014]. There is a complex web of reasons for this disparity, including a historically entrenched distrust of biomedicine in iTaukei culture, alongside strong ethnomedical and faith-healing traditions, spiritual explanatory models for disease, and poor access to health services and effective medicines, especially in more remote areas [Phillips, 2020].) Public health discourses typically frame the problem of diabetes as one of "poor lifestyle choices," an ideology to which the Australian character Hannah initially subscribes. However, over time Hannah (and hopefully the reader) is led to understand the colonial histories, ongoing racial inequalities, and neoliberal structures that uphold global food and economic systems, which set the conditions for who develops diabetes, who is likely to suffer from extreme complications, and, ultimately, who will die prematurely (Gálvez et al., 2020; Mendenhall, 2019).

To explore this dynamic further, we harnessed our creative license to imagine Prime Minister Lewanavanua endorsing a world-first initiative to plain-package soft drinks. This is a hypothetical situation because, although research suggests such a policy initiative would be effective (Bollard et al., 2016), it has not yet been implemented in Fiji or anywhere else in the world. The fictional corporate beverage giant in the novel, Island Cola, sabotages the progressive policy, relentlessly pursuing profits without any genuine empathy for the Fijians who consume their harmful products. This element of the story, although dramatized, is far from fanciful. Multinational food and drink manufacturers can be as aggressive as tobacco companies when it comes to influencing local marketing and importation policies (Foster, 2008; Phillips, Ravuvu, et al., 2021; Phillips, 2020), all of which tends to have the biggest impact on the diets of the urban poor (Gewertz & Errington, 2010). Iconic beverage brands are estimating they will lose billions of dollars if plain-packaging is mandated, and they are "vehemently opposing" the potential legislation (Bourke, 2017).

Reading with the Anthropology of Food

To highlight the more subtle ways in which such inequalities play out, we pay particular attention to everyday eating and drinking in this story. The anthropology of food is a branch of study that examines broader societal processes through the way humans prepare and consume food and beverages (De Garine, 2022; Mintz, 1997; Wentworth, 2016). Food studies reveal how cultures imbue meaning in consumption rituals, the politico-economic forces that shape people's nutritional choices, and the ways in which social change is reflected in, and brought about by, dietary transformation. In this book, we seek to capture the difference between the smell of fresh food versus that of highly processed foods, the choosy taste of the privileged versus the resigned taste of the poor, and the feeling of hunger versus that of plentifulness. The story also touches on the culturally sanctioned and sometimes unhealthy reliance on drink in both iTaukei culture (kava) and expatriate and Indo-Fijian communities (alcohol).

There is a rich history of ethnographies that trace the social life of edible commodities such as mushrooms (Tsing, 2015) and

two-minute noodles (Errington et al., 2012). These studies unveil how food commodities can be suffused with power, symbol-
ism, and status, shaping not just diets but also human migration
and global politics. In this book, sugar is the central symbol. The
three protagonists' lives are entangled with sugar in very different ways: Hannah is privileged enough to be a traveling volunteer who dabbles in diet-related research; Rishika is investigating
the traumatic family history of sugar slavery that still echoes in
her life; and Isikeli is the main carer for his grandmother, whose
leg has been amputated due to complications resulting from type
two diabetes. This sugary assemblage provides a lens through
which to examine the way broader processes of colonization and
transnational capitalism become embodied.

We hope that *Sugar* renders the concepts outlined above more
intriguing and more accessible to students. The book is intended
to take readers on a journey with the characters, who in turn become increasingly aware of the (unequal) impact of these forces
on their lives.

Questions for Discussion

The questions below are designed to be thought about individu-
ally before sharing and comparing with others' answers.

Self-reflection: What are your personal emotional reactions to
this story? Which specific scenes or statements affected you? Of
the characters Hannah, Isikeli, and Rishika, who resonated with
you most? Why was that, and did their relatability change for
you throughout the narrative?

Anthropology of food: Reading the book with a particular focus on eating and drinking illuminates the very different social

worlds and embodied experiences of Isikeli, Hannah, and Rishika. Compare and contrast, for example, the scene in which
Isikeli remembers a feast on his father's island (p. 31) relative to
the time he goes grocery shopping with his niece (p. 107). Juxtapose this with the volunteers dining at restaurants (p. 95; p. 144)
or Rishika cooking *pilau* (p. 139). What can we learn from this
comparison? What does it tell us about how inequality might
feel, smell, and taste? How does a focus on embodiment make
you reflect on your own life and position in the world?

Cross-cultural encounters: One narrative thread within this book
is the theme of awkwardness, or the discomfort that can ensue
when people from vastly different backgrounds must navigate
cultural difference to live or work together. Which encounters feel
awkward to you in the book? Examine, for example, Hannah's
uneasiness in her workplace meetings (p. 41) and during interviews (p. 75), or the discomfort for everyone during the *matanigasau*, the sorry ceremony (p. 258). What makes these cross-cultural
encounters awkward? Do you have any similar, relatable experiences of such discomfort? Is the awkwardness always negative,
or can it be productive? What role might awkwardness play in the
ethnographic encounter between researchers and participants?

Necropolitics: Compile a list of all the ways in which the lives of
iTaukei and Indo-Fijian characters are precarious in the story, both
historically and in the present day. To help you do so, conduct a close
reading of Rishika's description of her great-grandfather's life (p. 50;
p. 87) and Bu's oral history (p. 156). How can the conceptual tools
of *necropolitics*, *structural violence*, and *neoliberalism* help us to explain
why both iTaukei and Indo-Fijians have a low life expectancy?

Voluntourism: At the start of this story, Hannah represents a typical voluntourist, wanting to help people while being naïve to

her privilege and whiteness. What does Hannah learn by the end of the novel? Which moments prompt these changes? In answering this question, you may want to reflect on Hannah's moments of insight during the cyclone (p. 187; p. 189; p. 195) or the way her feelings changed about Christianity between the start of the book (p. 39) and the end (p. 312). How do Hannah's experiences align with or contradict the broader literature on voluntourism?

Globalizing the local, localizing the global: The story of the sugar industry in Fiji resonates with stories of exploitation around the world, just as poverty and volunteerism often share similarities globally. So, while ethnicity matters a great deal for social dynamics in Fiji and elsewhere, it is important not to get fixated on characters' ethnicities as emblematic of their moral status. What if we shuffled the characters of Isikeli, Hannah, and Rishika to instead imagine an expatriate Fijian doctor or nurse working in a poverty-stricken white community in Australia or the United States? How might the power dynamics shift? In what ways might such inequalities be reproduced in a different setting?

Commodity ethnography: The three protagonists' lives are entangled with sugar in very different ways throughout this book. In what ways does sugar provide a lens to have a closer look at race and class politics in Fiji and globally? Can you think of other single commodities that might have a similar analytic potential? Which objects have shaped your family's history or your community?

Ethnographic fiction: In ethnographic fiction like this novel, the authors take creative liberties with facts, events, and identities. What are some of the ethical concerns of bending reality in this way? How does this shape your response to the work as

compared to reading non-fiction? How does it change your orientation toward the place and characters? To what extent has it
motivated you to think and act differently?

References

Akram-Lodhi, A.H. (1996). Structural adjustment in Fiji under the interim
government, 1987–1992. *The Contemporary Pacific, 8*(2), 259–290.

Appadurai, A., & Alexander, N. (2019). *Failure*. Wiley.

Besnier, N. (2012). The athlete's body and the global condition: Tongan rugby
players in Japan. *American Ethnologist, 39*(3), 491–510. https://doi.org
/10.1111/j.1548-1425.2012.01377.x

Bolatagici, T. (2011). Export quality: Representing Fijian bodies and the
economy of war. *Asia Pacific Viewpoint, 52*(1), 5–16. https://doi.org
/10.1111/j.1467-8373.2011.01438.x

Bollard, T., Maubach, N., Walker, N., & Mhurchu, C.N. (2016). Effects of plain
packaging, warning labels, and taxes on young people's predicted sugar-
sweetened beverage preferences: An experimental study. *International
Journal of Behavioral Nutrition and Physical Activity, 13*(1), 95. https://doi.org
/10.1186/s12966-016-0421-7

Bourke, L. (2017, December 7). The cost of extending plain packaging to
alcohol, soft drinks and junk food. *Sydney Morning Herald*. Retrieved from
https://www.smh.com.au/politics/federal/the-cost-of-extending-plain
-packaging-to-alcohol-soft-drinks-and-junk-food-20171206-gzzhck.html

Brison, K.J. (2017). Facebook and urban kinship in Suva, Fiji. *Journal de la
Société des Océanistes, 144*(145), 209–220. https://doi.org/10.4000/jso.7707

de Garine, I. (Ed.). (2022). *Drinking: Anthropological approaches*. Berghahn Books.

Emde, S. (2005). Feared rumours and rumours of fear: The politicisation of
ethnicity during the Fiji coup in May 2000. *Oceania, 75*(4), 387–402. https://
doi.org/10.1002/j.1834-4461.2005.tb02898.x

Errington, F., Fujikura, T., and Gewertz, D. (2012). Instant noodles as
an antifriction device: Making the BOP with PPP in PNG. *American
Anthropologist, 114*(1), 19–31. https://doi.org/10.1111/j.1548-1433.2011.01394.x

Farmer, P. (2004). An anthropology of structural violence. *Current
Anthropology, 45*(3), 305–325. https://doi.org/10.1086/382250

Fijian Bureau of Statistics (fBoS). (2021). 2019–2020 household income and
expenditure survey, main report. Retrieved from https://www.statsfiji.gov
.fj/images/documents/HIES_2019-20/2019-20_HIES_Main_Report.pdf

Foster R. (2008). *Coca-globalization: Following soft drinks from New York to New Guinea*. Springer.

Gálvez, A., Carney, M., and Yates-Doerr, E. (2020). Chronic disaster: Reimagining noncommunicable chronic disease. *American Anthropologist, 122*(3), 639–640. https://doi.org/10.1111/aman.13437

Gewertz, D., & Errington, F. (2010). *Cheap meat: Flap food nations in the Pacific*. University of California Press.

Horst, H.A. (2018). Creating consumer-citizens: Competition, tradition and the moral order of the mobile telecommunications industry in Fiji. In R. Forster and H. Horst (Eds.), *The Moral Economy of Mobile Phones* (pp. 73–92). ANU Press.

Jayawardena, C. (1980). Culture and ethnicity in Guyana and Fiji. *Man, 15*(3), 430–450. https://doi.org/10.2307/2801343

Kanemasu, Y. (2013). A national pride or a colonial construct? Touristic representation and the politics of Fijian identity construction. *Social Identities, 19*(1), 71–89. https://doi.org/10.1080/13504630.2012.753345

Kaplan, M., & Kelly, J.D. (1994). Rethinking resistance: Dialogics of "disaffection" in colonial Fiji. *American Ethnologist, 21*(1), 123–151.

Keshavjee, S. (2014). *Blind spot: How neoliberalism infiltrated global health*. University of California Press.

Kumar, K., Snowdon, W., Ram, S., Khan, S., Cornelius, M., Tukana, I., & Reid, S. (2014). Descriptive analysis of diabetes-related amputations at the Colonial War Memorial Hospital, Fiji, 2010–2012. *Public Health Action, 4*(3), 155–158. https://doi.org/10.5588/pha.14.0026

Lal, B. (2008). Fijicoup.com. In B. Lal and M. Pretes (Eds.), *Coup: Reflections on the political crisis in Fiji* (pp. 1–7). ANU Press.

Lal, B. (2012). *Chalo Jahaji: On a journey through indenture in Fiji*. ANU Press.

Madden, R. (2017). *Being ethnographic: A guide to the theory and practice of ethnography*. Sage.

Mazzei, J. (2012). Negotiating domestic socialism with global capitalism: So-called tourist apartheid in Cuba. *Communist and Post-Communist Studies, 45*(1–2), 91–103. https://doi.org/10.1016/j.postcomstud.2012.02.003

Mbembe, A. (2001). *On the postcolony*. University of California Press.

McGranahan, C. (Ed.). (2020). *Writing anthropology: Essays on craft and commitment*. Duke University Press.

McLennan, S. (2014). Medical voluntourism in Honduras: "Helping" the poor? *Progress in Development Studies, 14*(2), 163–179. https://doi.org/10.1177/1464993413517789

Meki, T., and Tarai, J. (2023). How can aid be decolonised and localised in the Pacific? Yielding and wielding power. *Development Policy Review*, p.e12732.

Mendenhall, E. (2019). *Rethinking diabetes: Entanglements with trauma, poverty, and HIV*. Cornell University Press.

Miller, K.C. (2008). *A community of sentiment: Indo-Fijian music and identity discourse in Fiji and its diaspora*. University of California Press.

Mintz, S.W. (1997). *Tasting food, tasting freedom: Excursions into eating, power, and the past*. Beacon Press.

Nayacakalou, R.R. (1978). *Tradition and change in the Fijian village*. University of the South Pacific Institute of Pacific Studies.

Phillips, T. (2020). The everyday politics of risk: Managing diabetes in Fiji. *Medical Anthropology: Cross Cultural Studies in Health and Illness, 39*(8), 735–750. https://doi.org/10.1080/01459740.2020.1717489

Phillips, T., & Keen, M. (2016). Sharing the city: Urban growth and governance in Suva, Fiji. *State Society and Governance in Melanesia Discussion Paper Series, 6*. https://openresearch-repository.anu.edu.au/bitstream/1885/140087/1/dp_2016_6_phillips_and_keen.pdf

Phillips, T., & Narayan, A. (2017). The healthcare challenges posed by rapid urbanisation in the Pacific: The view from Fiji. *Development Bulletin: Servicing the Cities, 78*, 79. https://nauru-data.sprep.org/system/files/Development%2520Bulletin%252078%2520Web%2520Version.pdf#page=86

Phillips, T., Ravuvu, A., McMichael, C., Thow, A.M., Browne, J., Waqa, G., Tutuo, J., & Gleeson, D. (2021). Nutrition policy-making in Fiji: Working in and around neoliberalisation in the global south. *Critical Public Health, 31*(3), 316–326. https://doi.org/10.1080/09581596.2019.1680805

Phillips, T., Taylor, J., Narain, E., & Chandler, P. (2021). Selling authentic happiness: Indigenous wellbeing and romanticised inequality in tourism advertising. *Annals of Tourism Research, 87*, 103115. https://doi.org/10.1016/j.annals.2020.103115

Povinelli, E.A. (2011). *Economies of abandonment: Social belonging and endurance in late liberalism*. Duke University Press.

Presterudstuen, G.H. (2014). Masculinity in the marketplace: Geographies of post-colonial gender work in modern Fiji. In A. Gorman-Murray & P. Hopkins (Eds.), *Masculinities and place* (pp. 401–414). Routledge.

Presterudstuen, G.H. (2017). Entering the living room: Sex, space and power in a cross-cultural and non-heteronormative context. In A. Gorman-Murray & M. Cook (Eds.), *Queering the Interior* (p. 26). Routledge.

Ravuvu, A. (1988). *Development or dependence: The pattern of change in a Fijian village*. University of the South Pacific Institute of Pacific Studies.

Ravuvu, A., and Thornton, A. (2016). Beyond aid distribution: Aid effectiveness, neoliberal and neostructural reforms in Pacific Island countries. In V. Jakupec & M. Kelly (Eds.), *Assessing the impact of foreign aid: Value for money and aid for trade* (pp. 79–93). Academic Press.

Ryle, J. (2005). Roots of land and church: The Christian state debate in Fiji. *International Journal for the Study of the Christian Church, 5*(1), 58–78. https://doi.org/10.1080/14742250500078071

Scheyvens, R.A. (2007). Exploring the tourism-poverty nexus. *Current Issues in Tourism*, *10*(2–3), 231–254.

Scheyvens, R.A., Movono, A., & Auckram, S. (2021). Pacific peoples and the pandemic: Exploring multiple well-beings of people in tourism-dependent communities. *Journal of Sustainable Tourism*, *31*(1), 1–20. https://doi.org/10.1080/09669582.2021.1970757

Sparkes, A.C. (1997). Ethnographic fiction and representing the absent other. *Sport, Education and Society*, *2*(1), 25–40. https://doi.org/10.1080/1357332970020102

Stead, V., & Davies, L. (2021). Unfree labour and Australia's obscured Pacific histories: Towards a new genealogy of modern slavery. *Journal of Australian Studies*, *45*(3), 400–416.

SturtzSreetharan, C., Brewis, A., Hardin, J., Trainer, S., & Wutich, A. (2021). *Fat in four cultures: A global ethnography of weight*. University of Toronto Press.

Tanner, A. (2007). On understanding too quickly: Colonial and postcolonial misrepresentation of indigenous Fijian land tenure. *Human Organization*, *66*(1), 69–77. https://doi.org/10.17730/humo.66.1.9100j416430k745k

Tawake, P., Rokotuibau, M., Kalpokas-Doan, J., Illingworth, A.M., Gibert, A., & Smith, Y. (2021). Decolonisation and locally led development. Retrieved from Melbourne, Australia: https://acfid.asn.au/wp-content/uploads/2022/08/ACFID-Decolonisationand-Locally-Led-Development-Discussion-Paper.pdf

Tierney, W. (1993). The cedar closet. *International Journal of Qualitative Studies in Education*, *6*(4), 303–314. https://doi.org/10.1080/0951839930060403

Tomlinson, M.A. (2009). *In God's image: The metaculture of Fijian Christianity*. University of California Press.

Trnka, S. (2005). Land, life and labour: Indo-Fijian claims to citizenship in a changing Fiji. *Oceania*, *75*(4), 354–367. https://doi.org/10.1002/j.1834-4461.2005.tb02896.x

Trnka, S. (2008). *State of suffering: Political violence and community survival in Fiji*. Cornell University Press.

Tsing, A.L. (2015). *The mushroom at the end of the world*. Princeton University Press.

Vakaoti, P. (2018). *Street-frequenting young people in Fiji: Theory and practice*. Springer.

Wacquant, L. (2009). *Punishing the poor*. Duke University Press.

Wentworth, C. (2016). Public eating, private pain: Children, feasting, and food security in Vanuatu. *Food and Foodways*, *24*(3–4), 136–152. https://doi.org/10.1080/07409710.2016.1210888

Yang, J. (2011). China in Fiji: Displacing traditional players? *Australian Journal of International Affairs*, *65*(3), 305–321. https://doi.org/10.1080/10357718.2011.563778

Acknowledgments

Sugar took over five years to come to fruition and would not have been possible without the help of many friends, family, and colleagues in both Fiji and Australia. We extend our deepest gratitude to those who have offered advice and suggestions along the way, especially to those who read various draft forms of the book, including Mark Phillips, Susie Williams, Asha Lakhan, Tara Dias, Lise Cooper, Louise Olsen, Joanna Moore, Catie Gressier, Catherine Trundle, and Poh Lin Lee. Heartfelt thanks to the amazingly committed Philippa Chandler, who read it several times and was a supporter from day one. We sincerely appreciated the three anonymous reviewers, whose incisive insights about Fijian life made the book better. We have also greatly appreciated the editorial guidance and support of John Barker, Carli Hansen, Leanne Rancourt, and Janice Evans at University of Toronto Press.

As always, we could not have written this book without an incredibly supportive community around us. Colleagues at La Trobe have been a wonderful sounding board, especially Jack Taylor, Natalie Araújo, and Yeshe Smith, as have colleagues in

Fiji, Mahendra Chaudhry, Jacqueline Ryle, and the late Father Kevin Barr. We have benefited from incredible care and friendship in Fiji, especially from Ruci and Sam Steiner, Ana and Sireli Cakacaka, everyone at Nakuvukakuvu, and the "Downstairs Narayans." Around the world we are surrounded by incredible friends: too many to name here, but special mention to the Miller family, the "Fairfield fathers," our soccer mates, Kim Woo, Simon Martin, Mark Fox, Briar Stevens, and Raili Simojoki. The unwavering support from Diana and Chris Phillips, along with Simon, Mark, Sara, Satya, Lila, Daya, Phul, Vidhya, Asha, Khemindra, and Yohann and their families, is always felt and appreciated. Thank you always to our children, Raajni, Navin, and Ajay, who help to place everything in perspective and make us laugh on a daily basis.

This story has been enriched by conversations with many research participants who have generously shared their time, experience, and knowledge over the years, for which we thank them sincerely. Special thanks to Adi Ranadi Gukibau and Unaisi Navusolo-Adamowicz for their assistance with the glossary, and to Simone Craig and Steven Tudor for insightful conversations about aspects of the book. We are also deeply appreciative of Katinka Samuel for her help in thinking through design ideas.

Finally, this book is dedicated to Karalaini Veiluvaki, or Bubu Kara. Without the love, care, laughter, baby-holding, advice, incisive social observations, and incredible food that you have nurtured us with over the years, none of this would have been possible. You are forever in our hearts, along with your unrivaled cinnamon buns.

Glossary

Fijian

Pronunciation Guide

Vowels
a is pronounced like the **a** in "rather"
e is pronounced like the **ai** in "wait"
i is pronounced like the **ee** in "feet"
o is pronounced like the **oa** in "float"
u is pronounced like the **oo** in "boot"

Consonants
b is often pronounced **mb** ("Bure" is pronounced "*m*Bure")
c is pronounced **th** ("Cakobau" is pronounced "*Th*ako*m*bau")
d is pronounced **nd** ("Nadi" is pronounced "Na*nd*i")
g is pronounced as a soft **ng** as in "singer" ("Sigatoka" is pronounced "Si*ng*atoka")
j is pronounced **ch** ("Jone" is pronounced "*Ch*on*ei*")
q is pronounced as a hard **ng** as in "stronger" ("leqa" is pronounced "le*ng*a")

Terms

bilibili – a bamboo raft
bubu – grandma
bula – hello
dina – true, sincere
donu – that's right / I agree
ei, dina – call of agreement during ceremony
Emeni – Amen
iko lako i vei? – where are you going? Similar to "how are you?" in English
io – yes
isa – expression of regret or yearning, in terms of being empathetic/ sympathetic
italatala – Christian priest / pastor
kai colo – person from the interior [derogatory meaning: unsophisticated]
Kai Idia – person of Indian descent
Kai Loma – half-caste, part Fijian person
Kai Valagi – visitor, usually referring to white people or foreigners
kakoda – savory traditional dish of fish cured in lemon juice and coconut
kalavata – matching outfits made out of tropical floral material worn by family members
kalou vu – ancestral spirit, founder ancestor to which members of a clan trace their common descent
lali – Fijian percussion instrument
lamu – scaredy-cat
lewa (slang for *yalewa*) – girl
lialia – crazy
loloma – love (platonic)
magai / magaitinamu – vulgar language, usually uttered when someone is angry or shocked
maleka – delicious
mana – spiritual or special powers to perform an act
masu mada – let's pray
matanigasau – a "sorry" ceremony performed or presented to try to amend broken relationships
mateni – drunk
mate ni suka – diabetes; literally, the sugar sickness
moce – goodbye

moli – lemon

momo – Uncle

na cava? – what?

o cei na yacamu? – what is your name?

oilei – oh my goodness!

palusami – savory traditional dish made of corned beef with taro leaves and coconut milk, wrapped in banana leaves

qauri – a Fijian identity category that can be loosely translated as gay / transgender / queer

qori – here you are / there you go / take that! / serves them right

rairai vinaka – looking great

Ratu – chief

sega – no

sega na leqa (informal) / *sega dua na leqa* (polite) – no problems / no worries

set – all good / all sorted

so (short form of *oso*) – expression of annoyance meaning, "Really?!" or "Come on!"

soli – fundraising event

sulu – sarong worn by men or women / formal business skirt worn by men

tabu – sacred, holy, unapproachable

tabua – cleaned sperm whale's tooth, considered highly valuable and often exchanged as a ceremonial gift

talevu – cousin-brother

tavale – cross-cousin (the son or daughter of a father's sister or a mother's brother)

Toso Viti – Go Fiji!

tulou, tulou, tulou – excuse me, while walking past someone or invading someone's space

Turaga Jisu – Lord Jesus

vinaka – good / thank you

vinaka vakalevu – thank you very much

vuniwai – traditional Fijian healer (also used to refer to Western doctors)

waka – the root of a plant

yadra – good morning

yaqona – kava: a drink made with the root of the *Piper methysticum* plant, with sedative, anesthetic, and euphoriant properties; used ceremonially in traditional events and at social gatherings across the Pacific

Fijian Hindi

Terms

acha – okay
Babbi – common nickname for a female
bahut – very
beti – term of endearment from an elder to a younger person
Bhagavad Gita – Hindu text
bhajan – a devotional song
butako – thief (from Fijian word meaning "to steal")
chana dal – chickpea curry
dekho – watch this
girmit – indentured labor agreement
girmitya – indentured laborer
gora (m) / gori (f) – white person (derogatory)
haan – yes
haana? – don't you think? / is that right?
halwa – semolina-based dessert
jaati-log – natives (slightly derogatory)
janta? – don't you know?
kaise – how are you? [*Aap kaise* (formal) / *Tum kaise* (informal)]
karma – the sum of one's actions in this and earlier lives, which
    decides one's fate in future lives
khao – eat
lakri – sweet pastry sticks
masala – spice mixture
mehendi – henna (temporary) tattoo worn by brides
nahi – no
pilau – spicy rice dish
pooja – devotional prayer or ritual in spiritual celebration
pundit – Hindu priest
right hai – I'm fine, I'm good
roti – flat bread eaten with curry
sardar – Indian boss on sugarcane plantations
tabla – Indian drum

TC▸ TEACHING CULTURE
Ethnographies for the Classroom

Editor: John Barker, University of British Columbia

This series is an essential resource for instructors searching for ethnographic case studies that are contemporary, engaging, provocative, and created specifically with undergraduate students in mind. Written with clarity and personal warmth, books in the series introduce students to the core methods and orienting frameworks of ethnographic research and provide a compelling entry point to some of the most urgent issues faced by people around the globe today.

Recent Books in the Series

Bloom Spaces: Reproduction and Tourism on the Caribbean Coast of Costa Rica by Susan Frohlick (2024)

Under Pressure: Diamond Mining and Everyday Life in Northern Canada by Lindsay A. Bell (2023)

Fat in Four Cultures: A Global Ethnography of Weight by Cindi SturtzSreetharan, Alexandra Brewis, Jessica Hardin, Sarah Trainer, and Amber Wutich (2021)

Esperanza Speaks: Confronting a Century of Global Change in Rural Panama by Gloria Rudolf (2021)

The Living Inca Town: Tourist Encounters in the Peruvian Andes by Karoline Guelke (2021)

Collective Care: Indigenous Motherhood, Family, and HIV/AIDS by Pamela J. Downe (2021)

I Was Never Alone, or Oporniki: An Ethnographic Play on Disability in Russia by Cassandra Hartblay (2020)

Millennial Movements: Positive Social Change in Urban Costa Rica by Karen Stocker (2020)

From Water to Wine: Becoming Middle Class in Angola by Jess Auerbach (2020)

Deeply Rooted in the Present: Heritage, Memory, and Identity in Brazilian Quilombos by Mary Lorena Kenny (2018)

Long Night at the Vepsian Museum: The Forest Folk of Northern Russia and the Struggle for Cultural Survival by Veronica Davidov (2017)

Truth and Indignation: Canada's Truth and Reconciliation Commission on Indian Residential Schools, second edition, by Ronald Niezen (2017)

Merchants in the City of Art: Work, Identity, and Change in a Florentine Neighborhood by Anne Schiller (2016)

Ancestral Lines: The Maisin of Papua New Guinea and the Fate of the Rainforest, second edition, by John Barker (2016)

Love Stories: Language, Private Love, and Public Romance in Georgia by Paul Manning (2015)

Printed and bound by CPI Group (UK) Ltd, Croydon, CR0 4YY

02/02/2025

14636481-0001